Pitchfork Murders

Wild Onion Saga

By Thomas Reimer

Design of covers by Amy Reimer

Front cover: Photo of antique pitchfork by Thomas Reimer. The pitchfork is owned by Lois Goff. It once belonged to her grandfather.

Inside back cover: Photo of the author by his son, Scott Reimer

Back cover: Photo of prairie by Thomas Reimer

Library of Congress Control Number: 2012916807

This book is a work of fiction. Any resemblance to actual events or persons, living or dead, is entirely coincidental.

"Pitchfork Murders," by Thomas Reimer. ISBN 978-1-62137-133-5 (softcover), 978-1-62137-134-2 (eBook)

Manufactured in the United States of America.

Also by Thomas Reimer

Fiction

Death of the King

Wild Onion Saga

> *Wild Onion*

> *Pitchfork Murders*

Non-Fiction

The Luecks – Posen to Princeton

The Albrechts & Reimers – Mecklenburg to Michigan

The Baruths & Janssens – Germany to Chicago

My Journey Through the Past

To our daughter Amy

Prologue

The story of Seamus O'Shea and Axel Konrad began in *Wild Onion*, published in 2011. Axel was sixteen years of age and Seamus, fourteen, when they met on the docks of New York. Both arrived in America on July 2, 1831. Axel had fled from Germany, Seamus, from Ireland. Thrown together under difficult circumstances, they overcame differences in their languages, personalities and appearances to learn to rely upon one another.

After a year in New York, they rebelled against the constraints of poverty and prejudice and headed west. Their goal, to follow the Lewis and Clark trail to Oregon. They never made it. By the time they arrived in the small settlement known as Chicago, the hardships of travel and an Indian attack in the Michigan Territory convinced them to go no further.

Each, in his own way, settled down. They made friends, found employment and called Chicago home.

Pitchfork Murders is the first of what I hope will be a series of sequels following the lives of Axel and Seamus and their descendants through the decades of Chicago's history.

Part One

Ancestors

Chapter One

"I am with child, Axel!" Getting no response from her husband, Lina spoke louder. "Did you hear me? I am with child." I was so absorbed writing, I was unaware of Lina talking to me. "I am with child." Looking up, I asked, "What did you say?" Exasperated, Lina slowly annunciated each word. "I am with child."

"You are what?"

"I am going to have a baby."

"You are?"

"I am."

Putting down my quill, I nervously pushed back from my desk, stood and walked to my wife. Kneeling before her, I asked, "How do you know? Are you feeling well? Shouldn't you be in bed? We need to get someone to care for you. When?"

"Axel, I am fine. Are you not happy?

I was stunned by her question.

"Dear Lina, of course I am....I truly am, yes...." Clasping her hands in mine, I looked up at her. "I am glücken....I, mean, happy. Tell me how you feel. When will our child be born? How do you know you are with child?"

"A woman knows these things. The child is due in seven months."

"We need to think of names. I need to find someone to come to be with you. I shall...."

"Axel, calm down."

Standing, I paced back and forth across the room. My mind began to dwell on what could happen. On the possibility of Lina having difficulty, of her dying, or the baby dying. The more I thought about it, the greater became my anxiety.

"Axel. Stop pacing!"

1

I returned to Lina, knelt again before her and professed my joy and happiness.

We have been married for three months. Seven months from now would be February, 1834. I am to become a father! Will it be a son? A daughter?

Today is July 24, 1833. I opened my bank on the first floor of my new building in June. Two weeks later our apartment on the second floor was completed. Our child will be born in our new home.

"Lina, what shall we name our child?"

"We have months to think about names, Axel."

"What do you mean, names? Are you expecting twins?"

Laughing, Adelina shook her head. "You are really a ninny. Everything will be fine."

"But we need a name."

"If it is a boy, I should like to name him after you. I have to think of a name if we have a daughter."

"If a son, Lina, could we name it after my baby brother. He died as an infant."

"How old were you?"

"I was born four years after him. He was born in 1811 and lived only eleven months. My mother spoke of him when I was going to leave to come to America. I never saw her cry before."

Softly, Lina urged, "Axel, come sit down. Tell me about your family. I know so little. Tell me about your parents. Do you have siblings besides Anna?"

Sitting next to my wife, I was silent for some time. Calming my excitement about our child to be, I began.

"My grandfather was Eldric Heinrich Konrad. My grandmother was Elsa Hagen. They had only one child, my father, Heinrich Eldric Konrad.

"My grandfather was the overseer of an estate belonging to Danish Prince Frederick. The Prince no longer lived on the estate. He seldom visited it. The Danish royal family relied upon Germans to both run their estates and be their political advisors. Prince Frederick's father, King Christian VII, was of limited capacity, perhaps even mentally imbalanced.

"In the absence of Prince Frederick, my grandfather, I have been told, ran the estate. He was very successful in his management. He treated the workers with respect and dignity. My father told me they admired him. He paid them and provided for their well-being. The result was a very productive estate."

Interrupting, Lina asked, "Did your grandparents live in Denmark or Germany?"

"The Prince's estate was in the principality of Schleswig, part of Denmark. Schleswig is very popular with Germans. Many live there. The principality is just north of the German states.

"My father was ten when tumult developed. Peasants were resisting the other landlords. The French, under Napoleon, were attacking the nations of Europe. My grandparents were so concerned they sent my father to live with my grandmother's oldest brother, Lorenz Hagen, and his wife, Katrina. Their estate is near Bodden, Germany."

"Axel, I was born near Dobbersen."

"I know. Dobbersen is just west of Bodden. We lived so close to one another."

"Did your father ever go back to live with his parents?"

"No. He never saw them again. They were brutally killed by the French. Lorenz and Katrina raised my father. Lorenz and Katrina had only one child, Rikert. They sent him to a boarding school when he was very young. He seldom visited his parents.

"My father calls himself Henry rather then Heinrich. As a young man, he met Margaretha Broch at the church in Bodden. They fell in love and married. She moved to live with my father on Schlosshagen, my aunt and uncle's estate.

"They had six children. My sister, Margaretha Marie, the oldest, married Volker Schiller. Next there was a stillborn baby. He was followed by my brother, Juergen Karl Konrad. He is married to Maud Appel. Then came my brother Paul Heinrich, who died at the age of eleven months. Then my sister Anna, was born."

"Axel, I hope I meet Anna some day. She and I have something in common. Both of us were attacked by your cousin Rikert. I hope she does come to America as she wishes. Who was next?"

"I am the youngest.

"Uncle Lorenz's overseer was despised by the laborers. He was mean and resented my father. Increasingly my father, as a teenager and then young adult, assumed more and more responsibility. He eventually replaced the overseer when my Uncle Lorenz dismissed him.

"I was fifteen when I finally met Rikert. It was during one of his rare visits home. He was drunk and treated me and my father with utter contempt. He accused my father of trying to steal his inheritance.

"Rikert was so violent and vicious toward my father and me, Uncle Lorenz ordered his son to leave and not return until he had changed his ways and become a decent human being. Rikert's mother, dear, sweet Aunt Katrina, was so overcome she became seriously ill and was confined to her bed for months until her death. Uncle Lorenz, who was almost twenty years older than Katrina, was crushed by her death. He became despondent, withdrew and completely relied upon my father.

"As I grew up, my father trained me in the management of the estate. Every few months he introduced me to another aspect of being an effective and respectful overseer.

"When Uncle Lorenz died, his attorney sent a notice to Rikert to return home for the reading of the will. We waited two months. He did not show up. I shall never forget the reading of the will. My father was to inherit the entire estate with the exception of the manor. Rikert was to receive the elegant residence only if he ceased his immoral and abhorrent behavior.

"My father's management was very successful. Each year the estate earned greater and greater profits. From the profits, a substantial allowance, at Lorenz's direction, was sent to his son, Rikert. The balance was invested in the bank. By the time of Lorenz's death, the account had grown quite large. In his will, Lorenz directed half of the funds to go to his son, Rikert, and the other half to my father. Rikert's share, plus the residence, were only to be given to him if he changed his behavior.

"You know the rest of the story. Rikert finally returned. He attacked my sister Anna. In defending her, I pulled Rikert from her. He tried to fight me but was no match. He tried to kill me with a pitchfork. I succeeded in knocking it from his grip. It fell to the barn floor. He tripped, fell and was impaled on the tines of the pitchfork. He nearly died.

"My father, our lawyer and our minister, all felt I needed to leave the estate. Although I was innocent of harming Rikert, it was feared if he died, I might be found guilty of murder. So I came to America.

"As tragic as this was, it was on the *Deutschlund*, crossing the Atlantic, that I met you. The happiest day of my life – until today."

"Axel, I am so sorry it took such sadness to bring us together. Here, at last, we are safe from Rikert. Our child will be a new chapter, a happy chapter, in our lives."

Chapter Two

How blessed I am to have Lina as my wife. I could not endure if I lost her. I can't believe we are married and she agreed to come live in Chicago. It is a small, crude village. Yet Lina is thriving. She arrived with me from New York two months ago. Perhaps the biggest surprise for me upon my return to Chicago was to learn the news of Philo Carpenter.

Philo was one of the men I traveled with from New York to Chicago via the Erie Canal, then on Captain O'Flaherty's *Princess Rose* the length of Lake Erie and finally by stagecoach from Detroit to Chicago. Philo is a druggist. He lost his wife a month after they were married. Following several years of grief, he closed his pharmacy in Savoy, Massachusetts. He has opened one here in Chicago in the same cabin where Doc Wooten has set up his medical practice.

The day after Lina and I arrived in Chicago, I went to pick up my mail. John Hogan, the Post Master, greeted me. He was eager to catch me up on the local news as he gathered my mail and handed it to me.

"Biggest news, Axel, is the vote to be held in August to decide whether or not to incorporate Chicago. No, I'll take that back. The biggest news is about Philo. Just days after you left to go to New York to marry, Philo followed you. He married an old flame of his and beat you back to Chicago. Pretty little thing. Name's Ann Thompson. Philo told me he asked her to marry him four years ago. Guess her father didn't approve of Philo. She refused to marry him. Philo wed Sarah Bridges instead. She's the one who died."

John went on to tell me more of what has been going on.

I interrupted. "John, is it my imagination? Everything seems busier. More people walking about. I saw several new buildings going up."

"Damn right, Axel. Look at my wall of bins. Had to take down the old boots I had nailed to the wall to sort the mail. I built this more orderly system of wooden dividers. Each time I have them all alphabetized, I have to add another bank of slots and change all of the labels. More than fifty families have come to live here since the ice melted in the lakes.

"They're coming now the Indians are moving out. They heard a lot about Black Hawk back East. Hell, the government toured him around. You know he even met with President Jackson. He's a hero. He's taken the fear out of Indians. Folks feel it is safe to come here now."

Going through my mail, I was pleased to see letters from my father and sister.

Walking back home, I stopped to admire my building. I had hired Helmut Hummel from New York to design the two-story brick building. The bank's on the first floor, our apartment on the second. I contracted with Tyler Blodgett. He had just built a kiln. He employed Heinrich Lampmann, a brick maker from Germany, to operate his brickyard. I requested red brick. Herr Lampmann assured me, "I make the finest brick possible. The clay here is good. I brought red coloring with me from Germany."

It is a relief when I can talk with someone in German. My English is improving but I still need to concentrate to think of the right words and the right order to place them. Lina is struggling to learn English. I try to help her but we slip into German when we are alone. She is determined not to be like many of the German women she met in New York.

"The German wives I met rarely spoke English. Their husbands learned because they must speak it on their jobs. The wives have no life outside of the house other than trips to the shops where only German is spoken."

Holding my letters, I climbed the stairs to our apartment. Lina must have seen me coming. She opened the door and joyously greeted me.

"Is that mail I see you holding?"

"It is. Here, would you sort it while I change my clothes?"

When I entered our sitting room, Lina was excitedly reading a letter from her mother. Minnie lives in New York and works as a maid.

"Minnie sounds lonely and sad, Axel. She doesn't say so but I can tell."

"Should we ask your mother to come and stay with us until the baby is born?"

"No. You must stop worrying about me. We can have Mother come when the birth is near. Until then, I want you all to myself. You are already spending too much time at the bank."

"Are you sure? I worry about you when I'm not here."

"You need not."

It was such a pleasant day. The air so fresh. The constant hammering and sawing which had assaulted our ears for weeks had finally stopped. I was already thinking about our next home. It would be away from the noise of taverns and businesses. I dream of a fine house on one of the grassy lots I purchased last year.

Relaxing, I said, "Lina, you've never told me about your grandparents."

"I don't know much about them. I never met my grandfather or my aunts and uncles. They live in Eastern Prussia. Only my mother moved from Prussia to Mecklenburg."

"Were they Polish or German?"

"German, of course, Axel." Lina said incredulously.

"I meant no disrespect, Lina. Eastern Prussia was once part of the ancient nation of Poland. Some centuries ago, the Poles invited Germans to come and help protect them from Russia. With time, the number of Germans grew until they dominated the western part of Poland. Poor Poland eventually ceased as an independent nation."

Lina relaxed. "My grandparents were German. They spoke German. Their parents before them came from Germany to settle in Poland."

"Why did your mother move away from her parents?"

"Whenever I asked my Mother, she would blush and say nothing."

"If you were born in Dobbersen, did you ever meet your grandparents?"

"I never knew my grandfather, Christian Lueck. He died before I was born. He was much older than Matilda Kopf, my grandmother. My mother and father took me to meet my grandmother before we left for America. My grandparents had seven children. My mother is the youngest."

"Do they all still live in East Prussia?"

"Yes. Most of them live in or near the Village of Lobsens, east of the City of Schneidemuehle.

"My grandmother Matilda was 68 when I met her. She is short and stout, has a gentle smile and is very quiet. I never heard her say more than a few words. She has never overcome the loss of her husband."

"Your mother really hasn't told you why she left home?"

"She finally did, during our crossing.

7

"My father, Gerhardt, lived near the eastern border of Mecklenburg, not far from East Prussia. He was an itinerant peddler and often crossed the border into East Prussia. My Mother told me he was very handsome. Blushing, she added he was very forward. On his last trip, the deepest he had ever penetrated East Prussia, he stopped in Lobsens and set up a booth in the square. My mother went to the market, stopped at his booth and became enthralled. They spoke well into the afternoon. It was too late for him to move on to the next village. Minnie invited Gerhardt to come stay with her family for the night.

"Smitten with Minnie, he agreed. By then, most of mother's brothers and sisters had married and moved to places of their own. We had empty bedrooms. Grandmother was pleased to welcome him for the night. Father and Mother spoke for hours, well into the night.

"In the morning, while eating breakfast, Minnie announced to her mother, she and Herr Gerhardt wished to marry.

"Two days later, they were. My grandmother shed tears. Mother thinks they were of relief. That night my parents shared a bedroom and the next morning they left for Gerhardt's home in the German state of Mecklenburg."

"What about your father's parents?"

"My father was an orphan. When I asked him about his parents, his face would tighten and he would change the subject. Just before we left to come to America, he told me about his mother. Her name was Ermalinda. She was a dairy maid on a large estate. She was very pretty and taught him how to read and write.

"Ermalinda and my father lived on an estate owned by Baron Haushee and the Baroness. Father remembers how kind the Baron was to him. My mother never spoke of her father. When my father was ten, the plague struck the estate killing not only my grandmother but many others including the Baron. Life for my father changed dramatically. The Baroness hired Herr Rauh to replace the overseer who had also died of the plague. Herr Rauh quickly took control, imposing harsh measures including whippings for any infraction to his rules. Father was unprepared for the abuse. Herr Rauh apparently used father to show there would be no favorites. After a particularly horrendous whipping, my father ran away.

"I am ashamed of my thoughts, but have often wondered if the Baron might have been my grandfather."

"It is possible, Lina. All in the past now. Your mother and father loved you and that is all that matters."

"Thank you, sweety. I have never told anyone before."

8

"Can you hear my stomach growling?"

"Axel, you are always hungry. How can you eat so much and stay so thin?"

"My parents are thin as well. Do you have any of your potato salad left to tide me over to supper?"

"I do." I followed Lina into the kitchen and ate while we continued talking about her family.

"How many brothers and sisters do you have?"

"One brother, one sister. My brother, Wilhelm, is married. He and Clothilda live on a small farm with their children. It was my parents' farm, where I was born and raised.

"My sister Clara is single. When my parents announced they were going to America, Clara refused to come. She owns a small bakery in Dobbersen."

"Since your father died, has your mother ever expressed the desire to return to Germany?"

"She says she will never go back. I'm not so sure. I sense uncertainty."

"Just think of our child trying to figure out all of his aunts, uncles and cousins. Perhaps some day we can take him back to Germany to meet them all."

"Axel, we might not have a son. Will you be disappointed if we have a daughter?"

"Never. I shall cherish her as much as I do you."

Recalling the news John Hogan had told me, I told Lina about Philo.

"Did you know he was planning to get married?"

"No, I didn't. The old fox."

"What is her name?"

"Ann."

"Axel, we must go make a call to welcome Ann to Chicago. I should like to be her friend."

"How about tonight, after supper?"

"Tomorrow evening would be better. It will give me time to bake something to take."

Looking down, I saw my letters. Opening the one from my father first, I quickly read through it to assure there was no bad news. I didn't want to cause Lina any grief which might hurt the baby. It was all good news.

I read the letter again, this time out loud for Lina. "Anna is really coming. Axel, we must pack and go to New York as soon as possible."

"No. You must not travel."

9

"Axel, once and for all, I am not fragile. I have looked forward to this day for months now. I will not break. I will go with you. Not another word about it."

I have never seen Lina this adamant.

"Alright. We can take the *Princess Rose* all the way to Buffalo. This time of year the lakes are calm. We can leave as soon as the *Princess Rose* docks. That should be in two days."

"It is a miracle, Axel. Your plans to bring Anna to Chicago are working out perfectly."

I opened Anna's letter and read it out loud. Her excitement made us both grin.

Part Two

The Bank

Chapter Three

Nothing is as fresh a delightful summer day. Drawing deep breaths, I felt like I was back home. Without thinking I said out loud, "ach du lieber." Looking around to be sure no one heard me, I smiled and felt like a giddy kid stealing an apple from the orchard. Climbing the stairway to our apartment, two steps at a time, I burst in shouting, "Lina, would you like to take a walk?"

Smiling, Lina simply said, "Let me put on shoes and fix my hair."

Minutes later we descended the stairs. Opening the door to the outside, I took a deep breath. How fresh the scent. The street, unusually quiet, was free of the incessant early spring and late fall mud. A few of the businesses are beginning to plant flowers to attract customers. Mark Beaubien had ordered several fruit trees from Buffalo to decorate the front of his hotel and tavern, the Sauganash.

As we walked, Lina grasped my hand. Noticing my smile, Lina asked, "What are you thinking about?"

"We are like young lovers, holding hands."

"We are, Axel."

"I guess we are. I do love you Lina."

Standing on the bank of the river, where it splits, half going north, half south, we looked across at the endless prairie.

"Can we cross the river and walk in the prairie, Axel? It reminds me of the fields I could see from my bedroom back home."

"There is only the swing bridge, dear."

"I have taken it before, Axel. I went across with Mark Beaubien's eldest daughter. It doesn't bother me in the least."

Walking slowly, so as not to rock the rope strung boards, we giggled as we swayed back and forth. My Lina is afraid of little. She's not a pale, artificially panicky woman putting on airs. Lina is of hearty stock yet delicate and beautiful in appearance.

Once across, we walked leisurely into the tall grasses, blooming corn flowers and budding thistles and teasels. The field was white with Queen-Anne's lace. Picking one, smiling, Lina held it up to my nose.

Expecting a pleasant sweetness, I inhaled deeply, sneezed, grimaced and pushed it away. It smelled rancid.

"My Mother calls this 'piss-in-bed!'"

"I can't imagine Minnie saying such a thing."

"Mother is not nearly as rigid and stuffy as you may think. You have only seen her during the discomforts of crossing the Atlantic and here, in America, during her grief over the death of my father. She is terribly anxious about the future."

Coming to a rise, perhaps the same one where Chief Robinson and I had hunted last summer, we sat, our legs stretched out. We embraced. I kissed Lina.

"Axel, you devil."

A soft breeze caressed us. It bowed the flowers toward us. Grasshoppers flew in all directions while song birds serenaded us. A quail came toward us through the grass and flowers until it sensed danger and clumsily took flight. We were, after all, intruding on its homeland. Butterflies flitted from flower to flower. The rainbow colored, double-winged dragonflies soared more purposefully.

I lay back and watched the wisps of clouds slip slowly by. I forgot my worries about the bank. I fell asleep, not to awake until I felt the light touch of Lina's kiss.

"Axel, we have to go back now. I must start dinner."

My mind snapped awake, quickly regrouping, recalling the many demands on my time.

"This has been nice, Axey. Can we do it again tomorrow?"

About to recite all I had to do, I paused. "I would like that."

Back home, Lina climbed the stairs to our apartment while I entered the bank.

"Have you been busy, Reinhold?"

My only employee somberly responded. "Four customers since you and Frau Konrad left for your walk." Reinhold misses nothing. He gave me the ledger.

"Thank you. Ah, another deposit from Johann Wellmacher. It is satisfying to see how his bakery is thriving." The last entry was from a new customer, John Stephen Wright.

"It is good to see Herr Wright's name."

"He wishes to see you. He needs your advice on a financial matter. I offered to help him. He insisted on talking with you. He is so young." Reinhold stopped, his face reddening with embarrassment. "I beg your pardon, Herr Konrad. I meant no disrespect, Herr Wright being close to your age."

"Most men are young on the frontier."

I was fortunate to have hired Reinhold Schwoup. He is more than twice my age. Judge Lockwood recommended him to me, assuring me of his honesty and diligence. I have tried to reassure Reinhold of my confidence in him. I have asked him to call me Axel in private. He is of the old school, formal at all times, unyielding in his demeanor .

"Reinhold, why don't you leave early. I can close up today."

"Thank you sir." Taking off his eyeshade and sleeve protectors, he put on his coat, hat, bid me a good evening and left.

I sat down at his desk. Each time I look around at my bank, I am awed by what I have accomplished. I worry about the decision to make the bank elegant and substantial. My office, my desk, Reinhold's desk, the counters, the doors, the beamed ceiling, the window frames, everything is of golden oak. The floor is of marble tiles cut in squares and separated by thin brass strips. The kerosene lamps have green glass shades. On a sunny day, such as today, the oak glows as if gold. The chairs by the desks for the customers, also of oak, have green velvet seat cushions and backs.

I told my contractor of my belief Chicago would grow as would the flow of money into the city. I want the bank to reflect my confidence in the city and convey an image of permanence and safety.

I wish I had been here for John Stephen Wright. I had met with John and his father, John Wright, Sr., some weeks earlier. When they entered the bank, Reinhold had guided them to my office.

"Mr. Konrad, I am John Wright. This is my son, John Wright, Jr. I own the general store."

Standing, I walked from behind my desk. Shaking hands with both, I invited them to be seated in the semicircle of chairs by the hearth. I much prefer sitting with my customers rather than behind my desk.

"I have seen you at church. Lina and I should have introduced ourselves. How may I help you?"

Mr. Wright, Sr., began, "You are fortunate to have your wife with you. My wife and other children are still in Massachusetts. I am leaving to fetch them. I will return with them as soon as I can sell my business and home.

"John will remain here to run the store in my absence."

15

"I am curious, Mr. Wright, how did you choose to come to Chicago to live?"

"I first came west in 1815. On horseback at the time. I found Chicago unpromising. Not much here then. 1815, that's the year little Johnny was born."

"Pa, please, it is John and I'm not little."

"Sorry, son. No, you're not.

"To answer your question. Why did I come to Chicago? In recent years, who hasn't heard of Chicago? I had to see it again for myself. Ever since I visited seventeen years ago, I have felt cooped up back home. My store was doing well. One by one, my wife and I have been blessed with more children. Still I was dissatisfied. I craved the excitement and challenge of growing with Chicago."

Nodding my head in agreement, I said, "I understand. I felt trapped in New York, although I spent only a year there after coming from Germany. I wanted freedom to choose my future, not what was expected of me or, with my poor English, what I was permitted to do. I have not regretted coming here.

"How may the bank help you?"

"I have complete confidence in John to run the store. I would like to deposit operating funds with you which he can tap as he needs them. The bank is where he can bring his receipts. Most of all, if you will, I'd like him to be able to discuss with you personally any questions he may have concerning business. I have found it vital to my own success to talk over major issues with someone I respect before making my decisions."

"I appreciate you placing your trust in me. I will be honored to help in anyway I can." Turning to John, Jr., I said, "Mr. Wright, please never hesitate to talk with me. I, myself, seek advice as your father does. It is not that you and I are too young to make wise choices, rather, it is that we have not yet gained experiences which can guide us in our decisions."

Mr. Wright, Sr., stood, and, to the surprise of his son, announced, "I shall leave the two of you now and begin my journey east."

John Jr. and I stood. Father embraced son, kissed him, and shook my hand and left.

I could only imagine the conflicting emotions John was feeling – both freedom to be truly on his own and fear of making mistakes.

"John, you were born in 1815, I, in 1816. If I could establish this bank, you can certainly manage your store. Now, let's get down to business."

"I would like to open an account." John, Jr., handed me a note for $7,500 drawn on the City Bank of New York. I called Reinhold in. He established the account and gave John, Jr. a receipt.

That was several weeks ago. The Wright deposit was the largest one the bank had received so far from a local business. Just as I was about to close up for the day, John entered. Although close to me in age, John appears much younger. Lina often tells me others see me as older than I am. "You are so tall and sure of yourself, you give the impression you are well into your twenties rather than being eighteen."

"John, come in. Not a bad day, is it, for late July?"

"Folks tell me, Mr. Konrad, Chicago can get uncomfortably hot in July and August."

"I would prefer you call me Axel." I walked to the door, locked it, pulled down the green shade and turned to John, "Now, how may I help you?"

"I need to hire staff to run the store. Initially with me present, but soon to be in charge, so I can open a second store. Can you help me find honest men to hire?"

"I shall try. When do you anticipate opening the second store?"

"As soon as I hire staff. I am very busy. More folks keep coming to Chicago. I am convinced two stores will increase my overall sales."

"Do you need to write to your father for his guidance?"

"No." Reaching into his pocket, John handed me a letter. "Before Father left, he gave me this letter granting me full authority to make all decisions without his concurrence. As you can see, he even suggests the idea of the second store."

Reading it, I returned the letter to John.

"Besides staff, I could use advice on where to locate the second store."

"To give you the best advice and help available, I would like you to meet with my Board of Directors. There are six on the board, including myself. The others are Mark Beaubien, Philo Carpenter, Chief Alexander Robinson, Johann Wellmacher and Dr. Charles Wooten.

"Our meetings are informal. Everyone is free to express their opinions and recommendations. I think you will find them most helpful."

"When next will you meet?"

"We meet whenever there is a need. If you like, I could arrange for a meeting tomorrow. Would two o'clock be acceptable?"

"Yes. Thank you. Also, I have a deposit to make. Sales have been very good."

John gave me a sack filled with coins, some script on eastern banks, several gold nuggets, notes drawn on a bank in Cincinnati and notes from several individuals in Chicago who have accounts with me.

After John left, I entered his deposit in the books and put the sack and records in the vault, closed it and spun the dial.

Behind a concealed door, I entered the stairs to our apartment. I could smell dinner. Another blessing of my dear wife, she is a wonderful cook. She can make traditional meals which taste as they should but are not as heavy as typical German food can be.

Chapter Four

The next day the Board of Directors met in the dining room in our apartment. Lina insisted on preparing a luncheon before the meeting. She served potato salad with a light touch of vinegar, bits of bacon and thin slices of cucumber. She served fresh bread right from the oven with apple butter. Also small warmed sausages. All with coffee. I did not serve beer or liquor. Coffee, I hoped, would keep everyone alert.

"Gentlemen, last week, I sought your opinions on defining our purpose. Thank you not only for your ideas but your willingness to take time from your businesses to help me establish and operate my bank.

"I have written a statement of purpose. This reflects your suggestions. Lina wrote out copies. Here, please take one. First, the name. I propose The Greater Bank of Chicago. If I may, I'd like to read my proposal.

> It is the purpose of The Greater Bank of Chicago to provide:
>
> > A safe and honest place to secure funds and valuables entrusted to the bank by its clients
> > Advice and guidance to individuals, families, businesses and institutions
> > Gracious and friendly service to all clients
> > Safe and secure investment of deposits
> > Invest in loans which will improve the lives of Chicagoans and the economy of the City
> > Assure integrity of the staff and Board of Directors
> > Grant loans for only moral purposes

"Before giving your reactions, I would like you to meet with a major new client. Last week I reported on the financial status of the bank. I suspect some, if not all of you, found it tedious. I could tell from your reactions, the most interesting part was when I mentioned the meeting I had with John Wright and his son. They opened an account with substantial funds.

"Yesterday, John Stephen Wright came to see. He prefers to be called John Stephen rather than 'John Junior." He brought his first deposit of funds from the store. More importantly, he asked my advice on his plans to open a second store.

"I have invited John to meet with us this afternoon so he can explain what he is seeking. After we have met with John, I would like us to discuss the paper on the purpose of The Greater Bank of Chicago. This will give us a real case against which to evaluate the statement."

Philo spoke first. "Excellent idea. Do you think Mr. Wright will be put off if we ask him questions?"

"He expects you to do so."

Reinhold entered the room. He said nothing, waiting for me to acknowledge him. He stood just inside the doorway, erect as if at military attention. His closely cropped gray hair, his gaunt face, wire-rimmed glasses and thin body, remind me of a retired Hessian officer.

"Please come in, Reinhold."

"Sir, John Stephen Wright is here. Are you ready for him?"

"Yes. Thank you."

John was dressed in a suit. It reminded me of the two suits I had made for me in New York on the advice of Horace Morgan. I have not worn either since my visits to New York when I met with bankers to solicit advice on establishing and operating my bank. The only other time I wore a suit was during my wedding to Lina. No one wears a suit in Chicago.

I walked to greet John. "Welcome, John. Please sit by me.

"Gentlemen, this is John Stephen Wright. Starting with you, Philo, please introduce yourself, briefly tell of your background and current employment."

Philo began by asking, "John, may I call you John?" Young Wright nodded ascent.

"I am Philo Carpenter, a druggist from Savoy, Massachusetts. I came to Chicago about this time last year. I share a cabin with Dr. Wooten where we both conduct business. I recently returned from a visit East to marry Ann Thompson and bring her back to Chicago.

"I conduct a church school every Sunday. You are most welcome to attend. It's held at the Presbyterian Church. Been a month now since we founded the church."

Blushing, John responded, "My father has attended. I'm afraid I have not."

Mark Beaubien was next. "Glad to see you again, John. As you know, I own the Sauganash. I was born in Detroit. Came to Chicago in 1826. My wife, Monique, and I have five children. We're expecting our sixth any day now.

"Built my place two years ago. Used to have only the cabin next door. Still chuckle when I think of how three years ago they told me my cabin was in the middle of the street. I had to move the damn thing out of the way."

Mark managed, as he always does, to evoke a laugh. It eased the formality of our meeting.

"I'm Johann Wellmacher. Don't speak well my English. I make das brots und der kuchen..." Realizing he had slipped into German, Johann explained, "I baker. I make breads and cakes. Came here in eighteen and thirty. Baker at Fort first. Now have own place and doing well. You can do gut too."

Next was Chief Robinson. "I am Alexander Robinson. Some call me Chief 'cause my mother was part Indian. I was born in Mackinac. Been here since1812. Done many things in my life. Try to help Indians and gove'ment get along."

"I'm Doc Charles Wooten. Glad to meet you John. Born in Virginia. Worked in New York before coming here. Set up business when I arrived here in 1832. That's when Philo, Axel and I arrived together along with Seamus O'Shea. Hope you get to meet Seamus. He's a good fellow.

"Don't hesitate to come see me if you need a doctor."

"Thank you gentlemen. John, I came here from Germany. The day I arrived I met Seamus O'Shea in New York. He arrived on the same day. He came from Ireland."

Never one to hold his thoughts, Mark Beaubien snickered, "O'Shea ain't no German, that's for sure."

No one commented. This time it was out of place.

Waiting a minute, I continued. "After an adventurous year in New York, Seamus and I concluded it was not for us. We decided to follow the Lewis and Clark trail to Oregon. By the time we got to Chicago, we had our fill of traveling. I suppose it was the Indian attack in the Michigan Territory which discouraged us from going on.

"John, I have told the board of your request for advice. Could you tell us of your plans and ask the questions you put to me."

Sitting up straight, John spoke firmly and confidently.

"My father, John Wright, and I came here last October from Sheffield, Massachusetts. Together we set up a general store. He has gone back east to settle his affairs and return with my mother, my siblings and more merchandise. Since he left, I have concluded there is enough business for me to open a second store. I am so busy I can get no rest. Running the store, keeping the books and ordering more goods leave me no time to seek help to hire or to find a location for another store.

"My father gave me full authority to start up a second store. My lack of time has overwhelmed me and may be clouding my judgement.

"Mr. Konrad suggested I make a list of questions to ask you."

John withdrew a piece of paper from his pocket, unfolded it, took a deep breath and read it.

"How do I know it's right to open a second store?

"Where should I locate a second store?

"How can I find hard-working, honest men to work for me?

"I would appreciate your advice. Mr. Konrad told me you may wish to ask me questions. I shall do my best to answer them."

After a period of silence, Mark Beaubien began.

"Damn me, John. Nobody was here for me to ask if I should build a bigger, better place. Just jumped in when I knew in my gut it was time. Hell, I needed more room too for all my young ones.

"How did I know I could afford it? There's more than one tavern and inn in Chicago. Look around. This place is growing. Figured if I didn't expand, they'd go somewhere else.

"Is your store so crowded folks have to stand around until you can wait on them? Hell fire, most of the day my tavern was so crowded, I couldn't serve them fast enough to make room for others. One day I saw a good friend leave in disgust. There was nowhere for him to sit. That was the day I knew I had to expand.

"That your situation?"

"It is, Mr. Beaubien. Just yesterday I had trouble walking around to get goods for a wife from the Fort. There were so many customers waiting for me.

"The bell on the door rang so often, I couldn't tell if it was someone coming in or leaving."

Philo asked, "How are your receipts? Are your sales greater than your costs?"

"Mr. Carpenter, as best I can tell, my profits are growing each week. They seem to far exceed my costs. Without time to keep books, I can't be more precise."

"John, as a doctor," Doc began, "I can't be of much help. Few of my patients are able to pay me money. Most give me a dozen eggs, or some beets from their fall harvest, preserves or, my favorite, a pie or pot of stew. Axel can attest to my lack of money. Since he won't accept eggs or butter and I have no ready cash, I have yet to make a deposit. I figure as long as I am well fed and have a roof over my head, I don't need to keep financial books, just records on my patients."

Johann was next. He turned to me and asked, "Axel, could I talk to you in German? You tell John what I say?"

"Yes, Johann."

He launched in impassionedly. I took notes. Johann is a very bright man. Often, when we meet someone of a different language who struggles to speak English, we assume they are ignorant. Such is usually not the case. When Johann had finished, I translated into English what he had said.

"Johann said, I came here to find freedom. I bake cakes, cookies, pies and breads. When someone comes in for the first time, I don't charge them. They always come back. I am doing well. Seldom have anything left at the end of the day.

"I don't over charge. Just enough to put some money aside. I come each week to Axel and deposit my savings. I have almost enough to send for my wife and children to come join me.

"Before Axel opened the bank, I saved my money each night in a can buried under the floor. Each morning I dug it up to be sure it was still there. Much better now with the bank.

"Should you open a second store? I don't know your trade. I have been wondering how I could expand my bakery. I am running out earlier and earlier each day. I try to bake more but I don't have the space or the time. As it is, I begin my fires at three in the morning and am baking by four. I am so exhausted, I go to bed at nine, sometimes eight.

"I don't want to expand until I have sent money to my wife. When she arrives, I can talk to Axel about a loan.

"Sounds to me you are feeling the same thing. Were I you, I would open the second store. As I said, however, I don't know your trade."

I called on Alexander, "Chief."

"Axel likes to call me Chief. I prefer Alexander. John, I have done many things in my life, mostly working for someone else. I have never run a business. I work hard. Ain't never had cash to spare. No account here at the bank. Mystery to me why Axel has me on the Board. I can't offer you any advice on opening a second store. I think I can help on your other two questions."

"John, it is my turn. As you can see, my bank building was expensive. Before I began, I accumulated investments from several important men in New York. I am also fortunate to have a father who has funds to spare. None of that, however, assures success. I must be prudent in managing my resources. If I make bad loans, I will soon run out of funds. If I make wise loans, the repayments plus new deposits will assure the health of the bank.

"Should you open a second store? Knowing your father will return with funds from the sale of his properties back east, and his suggestion you open a second store, I see no reason for you not to proceed. Were you to request funds from the bank, it seems the board members would vote to approve a loan.

"Now to your second question, where should it be located? John, I presume we all know where your store is, but would you tell us to be sure?"

"It is located on Randolph just west of the courthouse."

"Alexander. Mark. You both have been here much longer than the rest of us. What are your recommendations?"

"On the north side of the river," Mark suggested. "Although there are fewer people living on the other side of the river, the area is beginning to be developed. Crossing the river is not easy. At first the store might not do as well as your current one, but that will change quickly."

"I agree," said Alexander. "While fewer people live just north of the river, there are many farms and homesteads further out who would come to a store on their side."

"I was thinking the same thing." John Stephen Wright asked, "Who would be best to see about purchasing a building or lot?"

Mark asked, "Billy Caldwell owns some land that way, doesn't he Alexander?"

"He does, Mark. Does Billy still come into the Sauganash? "
"Yup."

Not shy, John Stephen Wright requested of Mark, "Next time Billy Caldwell comes in your place, Mr. Beaubien, could you ask him to come see me about buying some property?"

"I will."

24

"I'd appreciate it."

Moving on, I asked, "Any recommendations for Mr. Wright's staff."

Everyone made suggestions. John made a list, then quizzed us on each name, scratching out those he rejected.

I asked "Is there anything else you wish to discuss with us, John?"

Smiling broadly, making his face even more youthful, John said, "I have nothing else right now. This has been very helpful. Thank you."

After shaking our hands, John left and I reopened the board meeting.

"In light of what we just did, I'd like to return to my draft statement of purpose of the bank.

"First, what do you think of the name I am proposing for the bank?"

"I like it," said Philo. The others all concurred.

Irrepressible, Mark asked, "Axel, who is this statement for? You, your staff, the board or your customers? I guess it's fine for us. Too fancy for ordinary people."

"I agree," Alexander said. "I got confused, no, bored, after I read the first couple of lines."

Philo and Doc concurred.

Doc suggested, "If you want something for the people, it needs to be simple and direct. How about "We're safe and rock solid.""

Philo added, "A bank you can trust."

Mark came up with, "Come grow with us as Chicago grows."

Alexander suggested, "I like combining them all. How about, "A bank you can trust. We're solid as a rock. Come grow with us.""

There was consensus.

"I will put that in my next flyer. The first one, announcing the bank was open really brought in customers. Time to try something else.

"Before we close, I have one final piece of business to put to you.

"Lina and I will be leaving for New York in a week or so. We are going to meet my sister Anna who is coming from Germany. With the uncertainty of the crossing, we may be gone a month or more. I need your approval on how I plan to keep the bank running in my absence.

"I propose to make Reinhold Schwoup an advisory member of the Board. Have him attend all meetings from now on and run the bank in my absence. In doing so, I would like him to meet at the end of each day with a minimum of two of you to discuss the day's business and seek concurrence in his actions.

"Is this acceptable or can you think of an alternative arrangement?"

Philo, as usual, was the first to speak.

"Have you discussed this with Reinhold?"

"No, I wanted to ask the board first."

Philo stated, "I'm impressed with Reinhold and accept your judgement on him. Is there someone you could hire to work with him so he is not overburdened? You know how many hours you work. I think it is unfair to expect the same from him."

Doc Wooten agreed. "It's a big leap of faith to turn the bank over to Reinhold without support."

"I agree," I concurred. "But who?"

Mark suggested, "There is a new lawyer in town. He is very impressive. Name's John Caton. It would give him a chance to meet many of our most upstanding citizens. Perhaps he could be persuaded to work a few hours each day. It would give Reinhold time to keep the books and meet at the end of the day with two of us during banking hours."

"Philo and Mark, would you two meet with Mr. Caton?"

Both agreed.

I asked, "If you are satisfied and he is willing, could you make the necessary arrangements, involving Reinhold, of course?"

"I think you need to talk to Reinhold first," said Philo.

"You all agree?"

Approval was unanimous.

"I shall do so this evening and get word to you in the morning. In the meantime, if there is no other business, we can adjourn."

Chapter Five

As the directors left, and before I went to talk to Reinhold, I stepped into our kitchen. I paused, marveling at my wife who was looking out the window. The sun highlighted the delicacy of her profile, her fine cheek bones, her glowing light brown hair, her long eyelashes, her lips slightly curved upward in the hint of a smile. Before Lina entered my life, I was blind to such observations. There was no one on the estate in Germany or in the nearby village who had caught my eye the way Lina has.

Lina had not heard me enter. As I stood there, she reached up to her hair, her slender fingers putting a wisp into place. She seemed content. I spoke quietly.

"Lina, would you be willing to have Reinhold join us for an early dinner this evening? The Board has approved my proposal to make him an advisory member of the Board. They have also approved placing him in charge of the bank while we go east."

Turning slowly toward me, her smile broadened.

"You wish to tell him over dinner? What a nice touch. I have a simple dinner planned. There will be more than enough for the three of us."

I walked to her, took her in my arms and kissed her. "Thank you darling."

Taking the inner stairs, I opened the door. Reinhold was working at his desk. No customers were present.

"Reinhold, it is such a nice day, I would like to close the bank early so we can get to the books well before dinner. Would you put the closed sign on the door and come to my office when you have posted today's business?"

"Yes, sir."

When he was ready, Reinhold laid out the books and receipts of the day's transactions on the small table where we met at the end of each business day. With the good weather, business had been light.

We first looked at the deposits. I compared the receipts to the entries in the books. There was a perfect match. Then I compared the withdrawals. Again, a perfect match. Next I counted the cash taken in during the day and compared it to what was on hand at the start of the day. Again, a perfect match. We then looked at the list of loan payments due. Of the loans made to date, only two called for monthly payments of interest. The terms of the others stipulated interest payments twice a year. The two monthly payments were due at the end of the month, several weeks off. Finally, I reviewed Reinhold's tally of assets. Loans made totaled $10,500. Funds on hand, $75,550.27.

"Thank you, Reinhold. Everything is in perfect order."

Reinhold gathered up the documents and cash.

Sliding aside a section of the wood paneling in my office, I opened the bank's safe. Reinhold placed the books, receipts and cash inside. I closed the heavy metal door, twirled the dial and put the panel back in place. As Reinhold began to leave, I extended an invitation.

"Lina and I would like you to come to dinner this evening. It would give us a chance to get to know you better."

"I would like to."

For the first time since I asked him to work for me, he smiled.

We took the inside stairway up to the apartment.

Lina warmly greeted Reinhold, blushing when he took her hand and gently kissed it.

"How sweet."

I led him to our sitting room while Lina finished preparing dinner.

"May I offer you a glass of apfelwein?"

"Yes."

I opened the small carved wooden cabinet and took out one of the bottles of cider I had brought from New York. Filling a glass for each of us, I gave one to Reinhold, and returned to my chair.

"This is refreshing. I have not had a glass since I came to Chicago."

Without realizing it, our conversation had shifted to German. It seemed to relax my guest. It is still easier for me to express myself in my native tongue. I don't have to search for words or ways to express my thoughts.

Our conversation took no particular direction. This was our first informal talk. We probed each other for some common ground other than the bank. I stumbled across such a subject when I mentioned how I used to go hunting with Chief Robinson.

"Where did you go, sir?"

"The prairie just west of the river. We'd go once a week my first summer in Chicago. Mostly rabbits and quail and an occasional pheasant. Do you hunt, Reinhold?"

"I do. I go south of here. I favor pheasants. Does Frau Konrad roast the game you bring home?"

"Actually, when I hunted with Chief Robinson, it was for Mark Beaubien to serve at the Sauganash. I have not been hunting since I married. Do you roast your catch?"

"I do. I would like it if you and Frau Konrad would come for dinner when I have shot a pheasant or two."

"I'll take you up on that. I have not tasted pheasant since I came to America."

"Do you fish, sir?"

"I haven't done so in America."

"Would you like to join me next time I go, sir?"

"I would. Where? The river?"

"No, too busy. I found a secluded spot on the shore of Lake Michigan, north of the settlement. I go just before sunrise. I catch mainly perch and bluegill. When lucky, I catch trout and even salmon."

"I hate to interrupt your conversation, but dinner is ready."

Lina led the way into the dining room. She had cleaned up from the board meeting, reduced the table to a more intimate size and put out a white linen table cloth and our best silverware.

I don't know how she does it, but Lina had found time to make pigs-in-the-blanket, boiled potatoes and sliced cucumbers in cream sauce.

Lina has a remarkable way of making our guests comfortable. Her questions, were I to ask them, would seem intrusive. Lina is non-threatening. She soon had Reinhold talking about himself.

"I was born in Bavaria near a small village just north of Munich. My father owned a farm. It wasn't large but it was his. His brothers were not as fortunate. They were laborers on estates. Being a landowner, even of a small farm, gave us more freedom. I was able to go to a good school."

Lina asked, "Are your parents still living on the farm?"

"They are. I often dream of going back to visit them. I doubt I will ever be able to do so. Letters must suffice."

A lull in our conversation seemed the right time for me to bring up the Board's decisions.

"Reinhold, I have something good to ask of you. What I am about to tell you has met with the unanimous approval of the Board.

"I would like to make you an advisory member of the Board of Directors. With your agreement, of course. In this capacity, you would prepare reports for the Board on the status of our assets and liabilities. Also, your analysis of each loan request. This would greatly enhance the basis for their discussions and ultimate decisions."

Reinhold looked confused. I had taken him utterly by surprise.

"Would you be willing to become an advisor to the Board? I will double your salary."

"I am willing, but do you think I can do it?"

"Yes.

"I have a second request. Lina and I need to go to New York to meet my sister, who is arriving from Germany in a few weeks. While we are gone, I would like you to run the bank."

Reinhold gasped. The blood left his face. He looked terrified. I have not seen such a reaction since Judge Lockwood confronted Erasmus Jeremiah Fitchen about his embezzlement from the Illinois and Michigan Canal Commission. No, that is too harsh a comparison. His look was more that of a young child, frightened by a nightmare.

"Running the bank has involved both of us. It is unfair to expect you to do it alone. I would like you to join Mark Beaubien and Philo Carpenter when they interview John Caton, a lawyer, to see if he would be an able assistant to you in my absence. If the three of you are satisfied he can do the job, he would work several hours at the end of each day to spell you so you can complete the daily books, reconcile the cash on hand and finalize all records.

"After hours, you would meet with two of the directors to brief them on the day's business. This would be in place of meeting with me. The directors would rotate, so over the time I am gone, they would each have the opportunity to meet with you.

"Is this acceptable to you?"

"Frankly, sir, I am... how should I put this? I...well, do you really believe in me? I try to do my best each day." His voice diminishing almost to a whisper, he muttered, as if to himself, "I don't know. I don't know."

"I have complete faith in you. Is there a reason you feel inadequate?"

Looking at Lina, I thought he wished to talk only with me. When she moved to get up and leave, he asked her to stay. Always the ultimate diplomat, she responded,

"Forgive me, I was going to get dessert. Axel, would you like to offer Reinhold a glass of Korn. It would go well with the apple strudel."

I poured three glasses of Korn, my favorite schnapps. Lina served the strudel warm. Sitting down to enjoy the dessert, Lina refused the glass of Korn, telling me afterward, she didn't want the baby to grow up a drunk.

Lina turned to Reinhold, "I am sorry I interrupted you. Please continue." I so admire Lina's sensitivity. She had afforded him a chance to think through what he wanted to say.

"I came to America almost ten years ago. I fled Germany when I was accused of cheating. I worked in a grocery in Munich. It was owned by a couple. Three times a week my Father takes his horse and wagon into the city to sell his goods to the grocer. I often rode along. He set up a booth in the market in Marian Platz.

"Every Wednesday, a grocer we got to know well, would come and purchase eggs and produce. When I was fifteen, the grocer asked my father if he could hire me to work for him. He and my father negotiated terms of my employment while I stood there in silence, my excitement mounting at the thought of living and working in Munich.

"I was growing up. I was beginning to notice girls. Many stopped at our booth in the market. I never spoke to them but liked to look at them." As Reinhold was telling us of his past, he relaxed, his usual stiffness of speech loosened. His emotionless manner slipped away. He became warmly human. When he spoke of noticing girls, he blushed.

"My mother didn't approve of me working and living in Munich. I was an only child, she said. Father was adamant. The following Monday, I packed. We left early. Father first drove to the grocery and dropped me off. He was anxious to set up his booth. Our goodbyes were brief. Father never shows emotion.

"I sat in front of the grocery for several hours before the owner came down from his flat above the store. When he opened the door for business, he was surprised to see me. He hesitated. I panicked. Had he hired someone else? How would I find my way to the market? I remember that day as if it were yesterday.

" 'Reinhold! Have you come to work for me?'

" 'Yes, if you'll have me.' Not wanting to anger him, I did not tell him my name was Reinhardt, not Reinhold.

" 'I thought your father had decided he could not spare you. Come in. Bring your bag. Do you have a place to stay?'

" 'No sir.'

" 'Till you do, you can sleep in the back of the store.'

"I followed him across the store and through a curtained doorway. The back room was filled with poorly arranged shelves stuffed with boxes, pans, pots and jars, some filled, some empty. There were items of clothing, sloppily folded, hats, stacked one atop another. There were boots and shoes, the laces of each pair tied together. The upper shelves were so jammed, the array of items overflowed, threatening to fall down.

"There was a small desk and chair. A ledger, quills and an inkwell were erratically placed on top of the desk amidst a scramble of papers. Hanging from overhead were links of sausages, hams and wire baskets. One was filled with eggs. I thought, perhaps the ones he bought from Father last week. Also hanging from hooks suspended from the beams overhead were cloves of garlic, onions, herbs, turnips and something I didn't recognize. Several unopened barrels lined the back wall. On top of one was a large, wax coated wheel of cheese.

"I found the fragrance of the room pleasing. Lying on the cot each night, I would concentrate, trying to pick out individual scents which made up the essence. I found it comforting and would always fall asleep still guessing.

"In the corner, near a door to the outside, was a small cot with a lumpy mattress. Straw was poking through a hole in the ticking. A cracked chamber pot was tucked under the cot. The floor was rough hewn boards, as in the store proper. Strewn here and there were bits of paper, a broken box, dust balls and dirt, and stains from spills.

" 'You can sleep here.'

"I put my bag on the straw mattress as Herr Feinkost asked me to come into the store. For the rest of the day, between customers, he pointed out the locations of items for sale. There was absolutely no logic to how he had arranged his store. While cleaner than the room in back, it was anything but orderly.

"My job was to keep the displays and shelves in the store stocked, replenishing them from the storeroom in back or from the market or vendors who came to the back door.

"During my first day, Herr Feinkost's wife, Frieda, came into the store and demanded to know who I was. Herr Feinkost explained he had hired me. She glared at me, said nothing, huffed, turned and left. Herr Feinkost was ruffled by the encounter, sighed and continued instructing me.

"That night, after the store was closed and Herr Feinkost had retired upstairs, I lit a lantern I found and spent several hours going through the store, memorizing the stock and where it was located. I was concerned I would not satisfy Herr Feinkost. Or, for that matter, Frau Feinkost.

"I need not have worried. As I became more and more accustomed to the stock, the customers and the Feinkosts, I began to put the stock room in order. I saved my money by not finding a place of my own. I bought a better mattress. It took Herr Fienkost some time before he noticed what I was doing in the stock room. He stormed out of the back room one afternoon, shouting for me. I thought I had done something wrong. I cringed. He confronted me, he had a huge smile. He was pleased, noting how much easier it was to locate stock.

"Sheepishly, I suggested I could do the same thing with the store, making it more appealing to the customers. He told me to go ahead, just not while the store was open. It took me months. To avoid confusion, I moved slowly, always putting the place back in order before going to bed. It would have been easier if I could have emptied a whole section at a time. It would, however, have made movement around the store even more difficult.

"Once a week I drew a floor plan showing the new arrangement. This helped Herr and Frau Feinkost know where things were. I learned the second day that Frau Feinkost worked in the store when her husband went to the market. She was pleased with the new order and the more appealing displays I arranged. She never voiced her pleasure but I could tell. She no longer looked at me as something evil.

"It was a week after I started before I met their daughter, Rosamund. About my age, Rosamund was very pretty. Early on, I sensed she was trouble. She liked to tease me. Smiling wickedly, she'd call me a street urchin. Other times, she would come close to me, smiling seductively, asking me if my bed was big enough for two. Although she bothered me, I never showed my reaction, always saying I was busy as I walked away from her.

"Once a month I would meet my father at the market and go home to visit. The next morning I hitched a ride with a neighbor back into Munich.

"The months stretched into years. It was eight years after I started when trouble hit. Rosamund no longer teased me. She ignored me. One evening, after taking off my shirt and trousers, as I was about to go to bed in my underwear, there was a knock on the back door. I opened it to find her standing there. She quickly slipped inside, pulled me toward her and wrapped her arms around me. I could feel her shape pressing against me. The temptation was great when she asked if she could go to bed with me. Luckily, my mind governed. I took her by the shoulders, pushed her from me, turned her around and firmly guided her to the door and outside. All I said was, 'Rosamund, I am not worthy of you.' In a voice I had never heard before, she cut me to the quick, 'You damn fool. You will regret this.'

"I thought about leaving Herr Feinkost's employment. There were no apparent repercussions from Rosamund's visit. Not, that is, until four months later when Frau Feinkost came storming into the store, shouting for Herr Feinkost.

"Her face was not only a fierce red, it was twisted in rage. Herr Feinkost asked what was wrong. Her reply still haunts me.

"Pointing directly at me she growled, 'That animal. Get rid of him. Immediately. Get him out of here. He has had his way with Rosamund against her will. That foul boy has soiled our daughter. She is with child. If I had a knife I would make sure he could never do that again.'

"Herr Feinkost turned to me. His face a mask of doubt. 'This isn't true, is it Reinhold?'

" 'No, sir. It is not. I have never been with your daughter.'

" 'He is lying. Rosamund told me,' raged Frau Feinkost. 'Rosamund was afraid to tell us when it happened for fear he would harm her. Now that she is showing, she had to tell me. Get that beast out of here! NOW!'

" 'Go upstairs, dear. You and Rosamund need to be calm. I shall take care of this.'

"Once gone, Herr Feinkost spoke to me, his voice mournful. 'I am sorry, son. I know you did not do this. I know who did but I cannot prove it. He is the son of the Mayor of Munich. Were I to accuse him, I could well lose the store.

" 'Nor can I tell my wife. She would never believe me. If she knew the truth, she would deny it even though she would be pleased to have her daughter marry the Mayor's son.

" 'I am deeply sorry it has come to this. I must ask you to leave. You will never know how much I regret this. You have not only put my store in order, you have developed an excellent accounting system for my books, saved me money and increased my trade several fold.'

"I packed my few things, accepted a gift of money from Herr Feinkost and left. I was not ashamed of crying that evening as I tried to go to sleep in a nearby inn. The next day being Wednesday, I went to the market, found my father's stall, explained it all and went back home with him that evening.

"A week later, the police came to our farm. I was in the field, working. I did not see the police and knew nothing of their visit until I came in for supper. My father was angry. My mother ashen.

" 'Wash up son.'

"When I returned, Father took me to the parlor.

" 'The police came today looking for you. I said you no longer lived here. They searched the house and barn, even the chicken coup. Since the field you were in can't be seen from the house, they accepted you no longer live here.

" 'They said you have been charged with embezzling funds from the Feinkosts. Apparently Frau Feinkost made the charges, her husband said nothing. I defended you. The police were unwilling to listen to me. They said I needed to bring you to them and you would go on trial.

" 'I am going to visit Herr Feinkost in the morning and demand he withdraw the charges.

" 'Please, Samuel, leave things alone,' my mother pleaded.

" 'Mother, I did not do this.'

"I told of the daughter's pregnancy and her mother's accusation I was the father. I said I was never with her. How when she tried to seduce me, I refused. I said I think even her visit to my room as all a way to cover up for her pregnancy. Her father told me she had been with the Mayor of Munich's son on repeated occasions. I knew Herr Feinkost was afraid of his wife. She was seeking revenge. This was her way. I told my parents it would be best if I left.

" 'Where will you go, Reinhardt?' My mother was in tears. Fleetingly, I smiled to hear my correct name. Strange the accommodations I have made for others, even my own name.

" 'I don't think I will be safe anywhere in Bavaria. I don't know. I will need to think.'

"Mother served dinner but we were not hungry. After mother went up to bed, my father and I talked it through. He suggested America, saying it would give me a fresh start. With the money he gave me and the money from Herr Feinkost, I had more than enough to pay for my passage to America. I ended up in Cincinnati, a city of many German immigrants. There I worked in a bank as a janitor until they discovered I was a hard worker and good with numbers and books. I worked for several years as a teller. I was eventually made a junior officer.

"Out of the blue, I was demoted, even though my work was constantly being praised. The owner's daughter had married and insisted her new husband work for her father. I was replaced. I found the owner's son-in-law ignorant and totally unaware. Frankly, he was disinterested in banking. He saw me as a threat to his career. It became intolerable. I left and came to Chicago."

Chapter Six

The day began a week of whirlwind activity. Philo, Mark and Reinhold were very impressed with John Caton. He agreed to work for the bank on a temporary basis. Reinhold advised me Caton would begin in two days, just days before Lina and I leave for New York. Meanwhile, Lina has been packing and re-packing. Could possessions be a curse? It seems to me we worry more the more we have.

I could tell Lina was worried, which was uncharacteristic. I found her reading and rereading the letters I had written to Captain O'Flaherty and his responses. I had arranged for him to arrive in Chicago with the *Princess Rose* at the end of July. The Captain's wife, Rose, and daughter, Molly, would make the trip with him. I had sent a note to Seamus to tell him. Seamus, who is sweet on Molly, said he'd come from Peoria right away. Lina and I will take the *Princess Rose* to Buffalo. Then the Erie Canal to New York City.

Lina also reread my letters to my father and my sister and their responses concerning Anna's journey to America. She reread my letters to Captain Mahler, of the *Deutschlund*, and his responses. He agreed to adjust his schedule so he could bring Anna to America.

It has always been my habit to draft a letter before finalizing it and sending it on its way. I keep the original copies so I can remember what I have written.

Lina had the copies of my letters and the responses spread out on the kitchen counter together with a worksheet she had drawn up showing the schedules for the ships. I guess it was to satisfy herself there would be no hitches.

I met with John Dean Caton the day he was to begin working at the bank. He arrived precisely on schedule. John is tall and very handsome. He has a dignified presence. Formally dressed, he appeared to be about my age.

I could see Reinhold smiling when he greeted John. I walked into the bank proper, extending my hand. "Welcome to the Greater Bank of Chicago, Mr. Caton. Please step this way to my office so we can get to know one another." John's voice is deeply resonant. There is a gracious confidence about him.

We sat by the hearth. Lina had placed a steeping pot of tea on the small table together with thin sugar cookies. I poured and passed the plate of cookies. John took several, a man after my own heart. I began.

"Mr. Caton, I appreciate your willingness to help me out while I go to New York. I presume Mark, Philo and Reinhold told you why my wife and I are making the journey."

"Yes, Mr. Konrad. I understand you are to meet your sister coming from Germany. I can think of nothing more important than you being there upon her arrival."

"John. May I call you John?"

"Yes, Axel."

I briefly told of my background and the purpose of the bank and its assets. "While in New York, I will once again call upon my financial supporters and meet others to seek additional funds. The more they invest in the bank, the more good I can do for Chicago."

"Very impressive, Axel. I look forward to working with Reinhold. He seems very capable. It will give me an excellent way to learn about Chicago and meet important leaders."

"Would you mind telling me about yourself?"

"Not at all. I was born in Orange County, New York, in 1812. I gather we are about the same age?"

"Not quite. I am four years younger."

"Remarkable. I thought surely you were older than me.

"My grandfather was born in England, of Irish descent. He came to America long before the Revolution. I am the fifteenth of my father, Robert Caton's sixteen children. My mother, his third wife, is Hannah Dean, hence my middle name. My father joined the Continental Army as a youngster and served with distinction. He died two years after I was born. Mother managed to assure I received a sound foundation in education. I taught school while studying for the law with a firm in Utica, New York.

"I decided to make my future in the west. I took passage on a steamer to Detroit. Still not knowing where I was to settle, I took a stage to Ann Arbor in the Michigan Territory. Pushing on westward, I had the good fortune to meet, purely by accident, my cousin's husband,

Irad Hill, who is a carpenter. Dr. John Temple had hired Irad to build a home for him in Chicago. The two of them were in White Pigeon getting lumber. I joined their rafting party which transported the lumber down the St. Joseph River where it loaded onto a schooner. I rode with them and the lumber to Chicago. That was some weeks ago.

"Since then, I traveled to Pekin and back by horseback to obtain admission to the Illinois Bar. In Pekin I met Judge Lockwood who encouraged me to pursue the law in Chicago. I have just returned. I deem your offer to work for you as most prophetic. I feel I have been led to Chicago by the Good Lord for a purpose I must be patient to understand."

"I know Judge Lockwood well." John nodded. "He recommended Reinhold to me. Reinhold is very capable and hard working. I have complete faith in him. He is excited to have you assist him.

"Lina and I will be gone, at the most, for two months. I hope it will be less. Travel is always uncertain.

"I shall call a special Board meeting for tomorrow so you can meet the members. It will give you the opportunity to ask any questions you may have. Don't hesitate to do so. I am closest to Dr. Wooten and Philo Carpenter. If you run into any complications, you will find both of them wise and thoughtful."

Two days later was a day of arrivals. First, Seamus O'Shea. Just hours later, the *Princess Rose* docked. Lina invited Seamus and the O'Flaherty's to join us for dinner. She also asked Philo and Ann Carpenter and Doc Wooten.

Seamus, who we had not seen since May, was so beguiled by Molly, he never took his eyes off of her. While the rest of us talked, Molly and Seamus quietly conversed with one another. They were completely oblivious to their surroundings. After dinner, Lina, Ann, Rose O'Flaherty and Molly excused themselves and went into the parlor while we men sat around the table talking. I almost laughed at Seamus's sad cow eyes as Molly left the room.

Doc brought up the subject of van der Weel and the Indian attack in Michigan. We four, along with Lieutenant Grege and van der Weel, had taken the stage from Detroit to Chicago. Camping one night, west of Marshall, four Indians attacked while we were sleeping. Despite Grege's warning, van der Weel had moved to sleep near the campfire. When the Indians attacked, van der Weel stood in panic. Silhouetted against the fire, he was struck by arrows and would have been scalped but for our slaying of the Indians by rifle shot. It sobered all of us and was the main reason Seamus and I decided to settle in Chicago rather than continue on to Oregon.

Lina had served riesling wine with dinner. Philo and Doc had imbibed. Seamus had not. I offered glasses of obstier after dinner. I knew Seamus swore never to drink alcohol because of his dreadful experiences with his drunken father. Yet in courtesy, I offered him a glass of the finest German brandy. He declined. Philo and Doc, who also frown on drinking, each accepted a small snifter of obstier. I poured myself a small glass as well. Everyone refused a second glass.

Our laughter grew when Seamus recalled how we had to push and shove the coach across the Calamic once we were in Illinois. "I was afraid the water would be over my head. Hell, I had come all the way from Ireland, survived the ocean, New York and the damn mosquitoes. All I could think of, as the water got deeper and deeper, was what a disgrace to drown in a creek."

Everyone teased me about my working for Mark Beaubien, serving meals at his Sauganash Tavern and Inn while Seamus got a job working for Lieutenant Grege.

"Axel," teased Seamus, "I was working for the government writing reports as Black Hawk and his warriors were battling the United States Army and you were serving settlers."

It was Doc Wooten who countered, "Seamus, you might have to move to Peoria to get away from the clutches of Josie."

On a serious note, Philo lamented the lack of culture in Chicago and, more importantly, the lack of any churches. "Have you gentlemen heard of Reverend William See?"

Doc Wooten asked, "You mean the damn charlatan? He's a fraud!"

"Exactly," agreed Philo. "He claims to be a Methodist preacher. I attended one of his services at the Point. He is filthy. So unwashed I could smell him although I sat in the back of the cabin. I'd wager he has not washed his hands for months. He looks ghastly in his green frock coat. It accentuates how tall and thin he is.

"He knows little of the Bible. He presents himself as earnest, but is an exhorter rather than preacher. He makes up in lungs what he lacks in learning. He loudly lambasted those gathered, exhibiting a remarkable lack of education or knowledge of the teachings of the Bible.

"I doubt he has ever been ordained or had any formal education. He berated and bemoaned everything under the sun. I wondered if he was intoxicated. After an hour, I left, so incensed by his hypocrisy. Once outside in the fresh air, I could not rid myself of his stench or of my anger over his dreadful drivel.

"Gentlemen. We need a real pastor and a real church."

"There are your Sunday school classes, Philo. They are excellent," Doc attested.

"Thank you, Doc. We need much more than what I can provide."

The conversation, having become serious, dampened the frivolity we had enjoyed just moments before. In an effort to lighten our musings, I attempted to tell a joke. Not my forte, I looked to Seamus.

"It is something Seamus and I have remained friends in spite of our heritage. Our pastor back home liked to compare the Irish to the Germans. He'd say: 'It is difficult to get the Irish to work and even harder to get the Germans to stop working.'"

Seamus responded, "I have been around Axel so long now, I am enjoying working as hard as he does or perhaps even more so."

With a sly smile, Doc told of a couple that had come to see him.

"The wife was very distressed. She asked me, 'Can you do a test to see if my husband is really German?' I told her there is no such test and asked her why she doubted him. She angrily replied, 'If he is German, why is he so lazy?'"

Captain O'Flaherty, laughing, added, "You know, we Irish love to fight. It is said: put an Irishman on a spit and you will always be able to find another one to turn it."

Smiling, I responded, "Have you been filling my wife with your stories, Seamus. She keeps telling me to slow down and take time off. She even said it is amazing she is with child, since I am always working."

Everyone's laughter stopped abruptly when Lina entered.

"Axel. I never said such a thing!" I blushed, stuttering in my embarrassment.

Behind Lina, stood the other women. Rose O'Flaherty announced, "Farrel, it is time we leave so Lina can get some rest."

"Yes, dear. Remember, dear, when aboard my ship, I am in charge. Gentlemen, we must leave. It has been a good evening."

Chapter Seven

The next day, while Lina entertained Rose, the Captain oversaw the cleaning and loading of the *Princess Rose*. Seamus and Molly discovered Chicago together. I spent time in the bank. John Caton arrived at one to meet with the Board of Directors. It went extremely well. He and Reinhold seem very comfortable with one another. I felt the bank was in good hands and would be well managed in my absence.

Late afternoon, several of the Captain's crew came for our luggage. An early morning departure was planned. I suddenly found myself idle. All was under control. I was only getting in the way at the bank and at home.

I went to spend the afternoon with Philo. While there, Rev. William See came for advice from Doc about pain in his feet. As soon as he entered the combined pharmacy-doctor's office, the air became putrid. I have never smelled anything so awful. Not even in steerage on the *Deutschlund* crossing from Germany. When Doc had Rev. See remove his shoes, I felt like gagging.

Although Doc closes a curtain for privacy with his patients, with the close proximity to the pharmacy, there is no barrier to sound or odor.

Seeing Rev. See out after his exam, Doc turned to Philo and me, lamenting, "That man is not just a disgrace to the church but to all mankind. I doubt he has washed himself or taken off his shoes in a year. His feet are black with dirt and rot. His flesh is being eaten by mold and filth as well as tiny worms. I told him to throw away his shoes, stay off of his feet for a week, and wear nothing on them. He is to soak his feet three times a day in warm, soapy water until he can see the pink of the flesh and then come back to me for treatment. I doubt he will heed my advice. It is likely his soles are covered with bites and sores.

"Thank God, true faith does not require we abuse ourselves."

Philo suggested, "Not bathing must be See's version of wearing a hair shirt."

Shaking my head, I said, "Doc, I don't know how you do it. I am not squeamish but that was too much. Or how do you deal with patients who complain but won't tell you their real symptoms."

"In some ways it's no different for me," Philo injected. "Folks come wanting a tonic or a physic but all they tell me is they're off their feed. I have to guess. More often than not, I give them a harmless tonic and they feel better. I have one which has a bitter taste. The more disagreeable the taste, the better they think it works.

"So many of them prefer the peddler who comes to town selling a brown bottle of tonic which claims to cure anything from gout to gallbladder, from blindness to ulcers. They all have high contents of alcohol. No wonder it makes them feel better – for a few hours.

"When they have finished the bottle, the peddler is long gone and their symptoms have usually gotten worse. That's when they come to me or Doc for help."

We chatted on until another patient came to see Doc. It was Josie. I could hear their conversation.

"Doc, I have met a man. I am in love with him. He is so much older than me. Can he give me babies?"

Doc spoke in a low voice, so I could not hear his answer.

That's when I got up to leave. Philo stepped out with me and said, "As you said, Axel, I don't know how Doc does it sometimes."

The diversion had worked. I stopped in the bank to say goodbye to Reinhold and John. I went upstairs to find Lina resting. I stretched out next to her and was soon asleep. When we woke, it was dark. After a light supper, I read the Bible out loud in German. We freshened up and went to sleep for the night.

The next morning, after a cold breakfast, dressed in our traveling clothes, we walked to the dock and boarded the *Princess Rose*. Seamus was already on deck with Molly. When the Captain began to shout orders to his crew, Seamus quickly kissed Molly and nimbly made his way down the gangplank. He waved to Molly. The sailors unhitched from the dock, scrambled up the plank and the schooner slowly slipped into the lake.

Our passage up Lake Michigan and around to Detroit was uneventful. We ate our meals with the O'Flaherty's. There were only two other passengers, an elderly couple, heading back to England, having decided America was not what they expected.

In Buffalo, I handed Captain O'Flaherty more than the amount of just our fare and confirmed the date we would once again take the *Princess Rose*, this time with Anna, heading back to Chicago. I hired a carriage to the Canal office. Within two hours we were on the barge, heading to New York.

I have now taken the Erie Canal six times. This was Lina's second time. We sat on deck watching the lush green countryside leisurely slip by, seldom seeing any humans except in small villages. We held hands, saying nothing, both of us relaxed and contented. The bustle and noise when we disembarked snapped us back to reality.

I hired a carriage. The driver loaded our luggage on top. What a contrast to my arrival in New York from Germany two years earlier. Then I spoke not a word of English, quickly lost all of my money and met Seamus who, in retrospect, I realized saved me from God knows what.

The driver knew of the Eagle, once again proving its fine reputation. When he came to a stop in front of the small but elegant hotel, a smiling Oscar, came out to help us. He took our luggage. August enthusiastically greeted us. Within an instant, the dining room staff came to shyly nod to us and Mamie Baruth came from her office, all smiles, kissing Lina and hugging me.

Once I saw Lina safely in our suite, in spite of Mamie's assurance the *Deutschlund* had not yet docked, I hurried out to the carriage I had requested wait for me, and directed him to take me back to the dock. I had him wait. I rushed to the Harbor Master office. Quint Barns was at his desk and recognized me. He just couldn't think of my name. He showed me how to look at his ledgers to search for the arrival of the *Deutschlund* back on July 2, 1831. Then I was anxious to find Lina. This time I asked if he had any word when to expect the *Deutschlund*.

At first he looked at me as if I was insane. Noticing my fine clothing and serious demeanor, he asked if I were Mr. Konrad. Assuring him I was, he said he had received word from the New Jersey coast where the *Deutschlund* had stopped to send word they would be arriving the next day. I suspect between Anna's excitement and Captain's knowledge of my anxiety, he had made the stop and paid a rider to come as quickly as possible to send this word to me.

The driver took me back to the Eagle where I joined Lina for a quick nap. We had a fine dinner in Mamie's apartment with James Dowling and a surprise, Mamie's son. The five of us talked nonstop. James looked the picture of health. It was neither the time nor place for me to ask any specifics, but he appeared to have recovered from his earlier illness.

Mamie was Mamie. She was gracious and obviously very proud of her son Carsten. I had never heard of him before. He is quite trim and good looking. I would guess perhaps twenty-five years of age. He had come to America with his parents when quite young. His early years in New York were spent living at the Eagle which his parents had founded. It was well established when Herr Baruth was killed in an accident. A few years later, at the age of twenty, Carsten struck out on his own, moving to the German community of Cincinnati in Ohio. There he became a lawyer, reading for a kindly old judge. We were to learn later that Mamie had asked him to come visit her without telling him the reason. Her intention was for him to meet Anna who, she thought, might just be a good match.

I was impressed with Carsten. As our conversation turned to the immediate past, the news of Chicago and Lina's pregnancy, he quickly and sensitively grasped what we were saying. He showed his interest without being in the least bit intrusive. I warmed to him. When we returned to our room for the night, Lina's feelings were the same. She took it a step further, as women will. "Axel, might Anna like Carsten?

Never perceptive in these things, I got it this time. "She just might be. She deserves happiness, as I have found, in marriage."

Part Three

Josie

Chapter Eight

Josie loved to sing as a little girl. Each day she sang, filling the small cottage with her sweet young voice. When she was old enough to go outside by herself, she sang. When she was old enough to go to school, she sang whenever entering or leaving the classroom. The teacher couldn't stop her from singing. Early on, Josie was seen by the teacher as a discipline problem. The teacher was one of those rare individuals who disliked music. The sound hurt her ears. Music, to her, was as jarring and brain numbing as fingernails scraping across a slate writing tablet.

Josie's voice was sweet. She could naturally carry any tune. All she had to do was hear it once and she knew it by heart. Josie's mother loved to hear her daughter returning from school each day. Hearing her clear, lilting voice assured her Josie had safely made it through another day.

Josie's father died when she was only one. She never knew him. She had no siblings. Her father had been the village blacksmith. He owned their cottage free and clear, so mother and daughter had a roof over their heads. There was a small garden plot in back which provided much of their food. A single cow yielded milk for drink and butter.

Shaylin Durst, Josie's mother, worked hard to provide. An excellent seamstress, she opened a shop, converting the small parlor for her business. The money she earned plus the produce from the garden and the cow were enough for the two to live comfortably.

Besides having a beautiful voice, Josie was very pretty. So pretty she attracted attention. This too, seemed to aggravate Josie's teacher. Hardly a day went by without Josie being punished for some indeterminate offense in the classroom. At first, Josie accepted the punishment with a smile and grace. This further angered Miss McGing.

A shriveled up, gray haired woman, Miss McGing was unpleasant in appearance, with several large moles on her chin from which prodigious amounts of hair sprouted. Behind her back, the other students made fun of their teacher, even calling her a wicked witch. Josie never participated in their meanness.

On the last day of school, Josie skipped happily while singing, wearing a new dress made by her mother. Josie was excited. Most days she wore one of her two plain dresses. Her mother made sure they were always clean and pressed.

Now ten, Josie had begun to attract the attention of the boys, particularly those too old to go to school. They would comment as she passed by. It made her blush, inwardly pleased. The contrast with the daily insults and abuse from Miss McGing, made her look forward to walking by the boys.

When the students entered the room for the last day of school, Miss McGing commanded Josie to the front of the class demanding to know why she was showing off with such a dress. Miss McGing hovered over Josie, pulling on a sleeve of the dress. Josie panicked. She knocked Miss McGing's arm from her dress, turned and fled the class in tears. No one made a sound. Miss McGing ordered Josie to return to her seat. Josie kept going. She ran all the way home, not hearing the cat calls and whistles. The door was open to the cottage. A customer was with her mother. Josie ran to her own bedroom, closed the door, took off the dress and sobbed and sobbed.

Shaylin quietly came in after the customer left. Sitting on the side of Josie's bed, she took her head into her lap, brushed back her hair and wiped away her tears.

"Hush, my sweet. Hush."

"Oh mother, I hate myself."

"Don't say that, child. Has Miss McGing been mean again today?

"She...she...tried to rip my dress...She hates me."

"I know. Perhaps it is time for you to stop school. Heaven knows few boys go to school at your age."

"Could I stop? I don't think I can keep going."

"When school starts up again, you can stay home and help me."

The next four years were a blessing. Each night at dinner, mother and daughter took turns saying grace. Thanking the Lord for the abundance they had. Josie's favorite was: "The blessing God put on the five loaves and fishes, may He put on this food." It made her feel God was with them, making the food special.

When fourteen, tragedy struck. It was 1828. Shaylin had a stroke and died. Suddenly beautiful Josie was alone. She no longer sang. She no longer smiled. She tried to keep up her mother's sewing business, the cow and the garden, but her heart wasn't in it. One by one, customers stopped coming. Josie's cottage was near Dublin. Her priest became concerned about her. He suggested she work as a maid for the O'Flaherty family.

"Farrel and Rose Kathleen O'Flaherty have three daughters. There's Rose, she's the oldest. Then there's Amber, she's the middle one. And Molly, she's the youngest. You would be more of a companion than a maid. Farrel O'Flaherty is a sea captain. He is gone for months on end, crossing to America and back. The women are kind and very friendly. Would you like to meet them?"

"I've never been to Dublin. Would I like it?"

"I could write a letter of introduction and give you their address. The grocer sends his helper into Dublin twice a week to buy supplies. He could take you there."

"Would I come home each night or live with them?"

Smiling, the priest said, "You would live with them. You could keep the cottage until you are comfortable in Dublin. Later on I could arrange to sell the cottage and give you the money for your dowry."

Josie instantly liked Rose Kathleen and the girls. The family had a cook and several maids. They didn't need another servant. Rose Kathleen offered Josie a room of her own and all of her meals if she would be a companion to her two younger daughters. Rose, the oldest, was engaged to be married.

Josie so liked her new home and companions, she was soon singing again. She brought joy to the family. The girls enjoyed putting on plays, ones they made up. There was always a part for a famous singer which was for Josie.

Josie went to church with the family, to all festivities and family gatherings. She became part of the family. The arrangements were perfect. Perfect, that is, until Josie went home to gather the few things she had left behind in the cottage. The priest had been unable to sell it although he had to admit to himself, he never put his mind to it. Not sure why.

Josie rode home with the grocer's helper. He dropped her off at the cottage and continued on. It was dusk. Josie entered, opened the shutters and was startled to find a man sleeping in her mother's bed. Getting over her fright, she gazed at him. He seemed clean. He turned in his sleep, his face becoming visible. He was strikingly handsome. Josie guessed he was around twenty.

Ever since the boys in the village had expressed their appreciation of her beauty and, at times, suggested things she didn't understand but sensed were not appropriate, she had been confused. When the younger O'Flaherty girls discussed boys they knew, they began to put meaning to what she hadn't understood. She, like they, began to dream about love and marriage.

Quietly as possible, Josie walked back into the kitchen and sat at the table. She did not understand why her heart was pounding so. She felt flushed. She thought of leaving, but something held her there. The sun set, the room became dark, the embers in the fireplace cast an eerie light. Josie nodded off.

"Is this a dream or has good fortune finally come to me."

Josie woke with a start. The voice was deep and sensual. There before her was the man from the bed. Josie jumped up, ready to flee.

"Don't leave, I shan't hurt you."

Mustering her courage, as firmly as she could speak, she demanded, "Who are you? Why are you sleeping in my house?"

"Your house? Now that's a kettle of fish. Damn young to own a house. Besides, its been empty for as long as I know."

"Ask Father Brennan. This is my house. I live in Dublin. If you want to buy the house, go see Father Brennan."

Laughing heartily, he sat opposite Josie, the table between them. He introduced himself. "I am Manus Costello. What is your name?"

"I am Josie Durst. My parents are dead. My mother left the cottage to me. Please explain yourself to me. How long have you been living here? Where did you come from? Who exactly are you?"

"Slow down, child. I'll answer you. I am...."

Angry, Josie said, "I am not a child! I am not afraid of you."

"I am sorry, Miss Durst. It is Miss?"

"Yes."

"I was in the Dublin guard. I was injured in a skirmish and can no longer serve. I have been staying here while I decide what to do and where to go. I can no longer use my left arm. I once was a groomsman but can no longer care for horses.

"I have a small amount of food. Could I make supper for us?"

"Fine, but then you must leave."

Josie became comfortable, especially when Manus said he would leave in the morning.

Josie slept in her childhood bed, the door closed for safety. In the morning she woke to the scent of bacon. She found Manus at the fire, making breakfast. His left arm was, she noticed, immobile at his side. He served the food and they both ate with relish. Their conversation was easy. Josie became less aware of their difference in age. Josie innocently told Manus he could stay longer, if he promised to keep out of sight so no one would think evil of her.

Another day became several. Early on, Josie went to see Father Brennan. He promised to find someone to purchase her cottage so she could return to living with the O'Flaherty family. He found her distracted and pondered the cause but came to no conclusion. He suggested confession. Josie said she had no time, perhaps another day.

Well into the third night following Josie's return to the cottage, there was a thunderstorm. She woke. The storm was very intense. Josie became restless. She could not stop thinking of Manus. She was surprised she thought of him holding her and kissing her. Finally, her heart pounding, she went to his room, intending just to look at him in his sleep. Opening the door slowly to make no noise, she stepped into the dark room. A flash of lightning revealed him, in her mother's bed. She did not move. She knew she should leave. She came to a start when he spoke.

"Josie, do you wish to be with me?"

His deep voice was gently inviting. The next flash of lightning showed he was sitting up, his muscular torso exposed, his injured arm shriveled from the shoulder to elbow. It so startled her she turned and began to leave, determinedly saying, "We should not be here together. What if someone finds out?"

"Is that all that worries you, Josie?"

"It is not proper."

"Josie, you are very beautiful. I love you."

"Stop. Leave! I won't sin with you. Not with any man."

"Ah, Josie, not even your husband? You wish me to marry you?" Manus' voice had changed. It was taunting. There was a hint of challenge.

"Get out! Get out now!"

"Why are you so angry? Don't worry your pretty little head. I love you."

Josie was frozen with fear. Manus walked slowly toward her until they were face to face. With his good arm, he pushed the door shut, violently grasped Josie arm and pulled her to the bed.

What followed was a blur. Josie thinks she screamed. She vaguely remembers struggling with all of her strength. His weight was too great. It seemed to go on for hours. She cried. Hot tears streaked her face. She refused to open her eyes. It was worse than a nightmare.

Her resistance was answered with vicious blows to her face and body. She lost consciousness. Later, still in her mother's bed, Josie endured the experience again. When she tried to flee, he repeatedly hit her. The pain was dreadfully intense. She blacked out again, slipping into a deep sleep.

When Josie woke, the storm had passed, the sun was up, the night was over. Her body was racked with pain. Her head felt as if it would burst. Her face seemed fat. When she put her hand to her cheek, it evoked a sharp pain. There was caked blood on her cheeks, her lips, her forehead.

Fearing a repeat, she cautiously sat up. Her eyes were nearly swollen shut, open just enough to see she was alone. The bedroom door was open. It took a great effort to get up. She sat on the edge of the bed, waiting for her swirling head to still. Finally, she stood. The spinning and swirling would not cease. She waited, her hand on the wall to steady herself. Slowly, carefully, because of her instability and also her fear, she made her way to the doorway. He was not in the kitchen. The cottage was silent. His coat was not on the peg near the outer door.

Making her way to her room, she threw herself on her bed, sobbing. Her sobs racked her body causing further pain. She deserved all that had happened. She curled up into a ball, sobbing. She was ruined.

After many minutes an inner strength surged up in her. She went to the washstand, carefully cleansed her wounds. She washed her body over and over. Tears of rage replaced those of pain realizing she would never be able to wash away her sin. Not even God would forgive her. Josie's sweet song was gone forever.

Chapter Nine

It took days for Josie's face and body to heal. Manus never returned. Josie lived in fear he would. She wanted to go to Father Brennan to seek forgiveness and to tell him of Manus, but was too ashamed. Besides, on her way to the church, everyone would see her face and know she had sinned. She was haunted, reliving the nightmare over and over again. On the third day, she had exhausted the food Manus had stored. She ate the few vegetables she could find in the deserted garden.

Each morning, Josie went to her mother's mirror to study the wounds on her face. The swelling was subsiding. The cuts were still very evident. She didn't worry about the bruises on her arms, legs and torso. Her clothing covered them. She studied her body the first day, never after that. She felt nothing but bitter revulsion when she saw herself naked. She lamented, Oh Mary, Mother of Jesus, I have sinned. She immediately regretted having uttered the words. She was unworthy to ever again plead to the Virgin Mary. That is when it struck her. I am no longer a virgin! Once again she sobbed, her body shaking, the blows hurting more intensely.

After a few more days, her hunger was too intense to ignore. She had to go into the village. She had money. That was not the problem. It was the wounds on her face, both those that could be seen and those she felt in her heart. Another day passed before she thought of using the bit of flour in the tin to put on her face to cover the bruises. She applied it lightly, looked in the mirror and applied more. She looked deathly pale.

It was a sunny day. She put on her mother's large gardening hat. Like her mother, Josie was naturally pale and burned easily. The combination almost disguised the evidence of the beating she had taken. She put on an old dress and walked into the village. It was not a long walk. It still hurt to move. Several old friends greeted her and asked how she liked living in Dublin. She responded as sweetly as possible, avoiding conversations.

She went to see Father Brennan. Not for her soul but concerning the sale of her house. He was at prayer. Josie waited. He was shocked by her appearance. He showed no reaction.

"How are you my child?"

"Fine, Father."

"Have you come for confession?"

"No, Father. I have come to ask you not to sell the cottage. Not just yet. I want to be sure I wish to stay in Dublin. Thank you for watching over the cottage for me."

"Are you sure there is nothing you wish to tell me? I am here to help."

"No, Father. Perhaps on my next visit."

After another try, Father Brennan sighed and walked Josie out of the church. As he watched her, he noticed a slight limp. He worried. The poor child. Something awful has happened to her. I have never seen her so despondent. She has changed. Jesus, I pray you will watch over Josie. May she be poor in misfortune, rich in blessings, slow to make enemies and quick to make friends.

Walking back into the church, Father Brennan felt tired. He cared too much to not take upon himself the grief and sadness of his flock. When he felt weighed down with their problems, he found comfort realizing how much greater the load the Blessed Mary, Mother of God carried. Think how many burdens are laid at her feet. How does she manage?

After another week, outwardly healed, Josie returned to Dublin and the O'Flaherty household. She did her best to be joyous, though her heart was aching. She, Amber and Molly did their plays, the sisters shared their dreams of boys, love and marriage. Whether they noticed or not how she had changed, they never spoke to Josie of her underlying sadness.

Two days after Captain O'Flaherty came home from his latest voyage to America, he called the girls, including Josie, to his study to meet with him. Their mother was present when they entered.

"I have made a decision. I have discussed it with your mother and she agrees. We are moving to America to live."

There was a long silence.

"Mother, I am to be married in a week. Must I go?"

"No, Rose. We will see you joyously married and set up in your new home before we leave."

"Mother," Amber was next. "I don't want to go to America. Where will we live? Are there not heathens there? Father, why?"

"I have found the Atlantic crossings increasingly more difficult for me. Most of my tonnage is taking Irish immigrants to America. They can ill afford the passage. The vast majority cross in steerage which is abysmal at best. Some die on each crossing. The stench, the disease, the lack of food have become intolerable to me. I can no longer do it."

"I have worried about your father for some time now," added Rose Kathleen. "I would like him to be home with us more often. More than just a few days every three, four months."

"What will you do for work, Father?" asked Amber.

"The Erie Canal has opened. Thousands of settlers are moving west. They take the canal from New York City to Lake Erie. From there, boats take them west on the lake. I have purchased a schooner to sail Lake Erie. It is clean, the voyage safe, just a few days the length of the lake. There is better money to be made. Best of all, my time away from home will never be more than a week. I regret how you girls have grown up without me."

"Where would we live, Father?" asked Molly.

"We have choices. We could live at one end or the other of the Erie Canal – either New York City or Buffalo. Or we could live in Detroit near the western end of Lake Erie, or in Chicago, the farthest point. Your Mother and I are leaning toward New York City."

It was much to absorb. The girls lapsed into silence. Rose Kathleen noticed how distraught Josie appeared. She asked, "Are you not feeling well, Josie?"

"I'm fine. I have a question. Would you take me or must I go back to my cottage?"

"Poor child, I hope you will come with us." Rose Kathleen said lovingly. "We think of you as one of our daughters. Unless you would prefer to move back to your cottage."

No one noticed Amber's quick smile when she thought Josie would not be going with the family. Amber tried to mask her feelings. She had begun to resent Josie. She seemed different ever since she returned from her weeks away. She had become distant, almost unfriendly. Perhaps what bothered her most, Josie was closer to Molly than to her. Josie, the fun Josie, no longer sang. She was often sullen. Rose Kathleen seemed to be treating Josie with more favor. Amber resented it.

"I should like to come with you. I never wish to return to my cottage."

Josie spoke bitterly. Molly, the closest to Josie, was puzzled. Before her recent visit to her beloved cottage, she described it as a bit of heaven. Molly had an image of a fairy tale cottage surrounded by a flower garden, with a thatched roof and stone chimney. She could picture a half door with Josie's late mother leaning out the upper half, a big smile on her face.

What had happened? Had she been sick? Was that why she stayed longer than planned? She was pale when she returned. Molly vowed to ask Josie when they were alone. She never had the courage to do so.

Captain O'Flaherty turned the house over to his banker to sell. A week later, their daughter Rose married. The packing done, the family and Josie headed to the docks in a carriage. Four large wagons with all of their possessions had preceded them and were already stowed away. The family boarded Captain O'Flaherty's ship. He, for the last time. He had sold it in New York. Looking at the ship, he always regretted he had not changed the name. It was the *Black Devil* when he purchased it. He never got around to revising the registration. The name had always made him uncomfortable.

The crossing went well. The girls got over their seasickness quickly. Rose Kathleen suffered for a week before she could keep any food down. Josie was fine the first few days before coming down with motion sickness. She found no relief for three days. Just as suddenly as it began, it stopped. Josie never told anyone she did not have what the others had endured. She was pregnant. Just before she left Dublin, she had slipped away and purchased a potion. The shifty druggist on a back street charged her a goodly amount. She felt it was much more than it should have cost. She was desperate. She waited until she had been aboard the *Black Devil* a few days before she began to take the daily dose as he had instructed her. Nothing happened. She was in anguish, worried she would begin to show.

The cramps finally began. The taste of the potion was almost intolerable. She didn't even try to eat. By the third day, the cramps were so intense she thought she would burst open. It happened during the night. She soiled herself. The druggist had told her to have towels nearby. Quietly, Josie got up in the dark, slipped out of the nightgown and wrapped it in one of the towels. She had been lying on another. Luckily, as best she could tell, it had kept the bed linens clean. Putting a third towel against herself, she put on an old pair of trousers she liked to wear as well as a jacket. She slipped into her shoes and made her way down the passageway and up to the deck. It was dark. She crossed to the guard rail and tossed the towels and, with regret, the fetus overboard. There was no noise. There was no ceremony. The last visible stain of her sin was gone. Josie crawled back to her bed and slept almost to noon. When she awoke, she was ravenous, startling everyone with all she ate for the next two days.

The women were excited to see New York. Captain O'Flaherty guided the *Black Devil* to an empty dock. They stayed aboard until all the passengers had disembarked. Their household goods were next, along with their trunks of clothing. Finally, the new owner came aboard and the transfer of the *Black Devil* was completed. Farrel and Rose Kathleen, the girls and Josie walked down the gangplank. Farrel never looked back. He was too emotional to do so.

They stayed at a moderate hotel, some blocks from the dock, where the street noise was acceptable. Farrel went with an agent to find a home not too far from the terminus of the Erie Canal. The prices were lower than in Dublin. For two days, he and the agent looked. They found nothing for sale that was acceptable. As their carriage was returning to the inn where they were staying, Farrel saw the perfect house.

The agent said, "But sir, it is not for sale."

"Everything is for sale for the right price, my good man. Coachman, please stop in front of the red brick house."

The agent had to hurry to keep up with the Captain. Farrel vigorously tapped the door knocker. An old, white haired man answered, "Yes?"

"May I speak with the owner of the house?" asked Farrel.

"I am the owner. What do you want?"

"I would like to buy your home."

"You must be Irish. You certainly have the attitude of one."

"As are you, I suspect."

The old man smiled broadly. "Please come in. We can talk terms." Walking through the large entrance hall, he led them into his library. "Would you care for a brandy?"

"If you don't mind, why don't we wait until we have concluded our business."

The agent was speechless as the two Irishmen negotiated. Each tried to outfox the other. They exchanged insults and praise so rapidly the agent was totally lost. After endless haggling, the two men stood and shook hands.

"Now, sir, a brandy?"

"Now."

"I didn't even ask you your name?"

"Nor did I ask yours."

Both laughed, the agent shook his head in disbelief and downed his brandy in two swallows.

A month later, the O'Flaherty family moved in. Decorators were still freshening up the downstairs. They had first redone each girl's room to their taste. Life settled into a new pattern. Farrel rode the Canal boat to Buffalo and took possession of his schooner. It had never been named. He hired a sign painter who, hanging over the sides, inscribed *Princess Rose* in gold letters. After stocking the hold with provisions, the galley with food and hiring and training a crew, Captain O'Flaherty took on his first passengers and trade.

So many were heading west, there had been no need to advertise for business. He would never cease to be amazed at the endless demand for passage. From Buffalo he sailed non-stop to Detroit. Usually, after an overnight lay over, he resumed the voyage up and around the Michigan Territory to the tiny settlement of Chicago. Each time he approached Fort Dearborn on the eastern shore of Lake Michigan, he noticed the settlement had grown. Home after his maiden voyage, his family agreed with him, they liked America.

They especially liked the winters when the lake became impassable. Farrel was home from late November to sometime in March.

For Josie, New York City was a welcome change. She rid herself of the fear of Manus appearing to wreck her life. When the proceeds of the sale of her cottage reached her a year later, she bought herself some new clothes. Also gifts for each member of the O'Flaherty family. They said it was unnecessary. Josie could tell she had pleased each of them

The family found a Catholic church to attend. Josie never went with them. She still felt unworthy to enter a church. Her sins were too egregious to ever be forgiven. She missed praying to the Blessed Mary. She had no one to tell her secrets. In the midst of such a happy and vigorous family, she felt alone.

Chapter Ten

The next few months passed quickly. After he mastered the lake currents and patterns of trade, Farrel invited Rose Kathleen and the girls to join him on one of his trips. Josie refused to go. In coping with her past, she had reached the stage of denying herself anything which might give her pleasure. She knew deep down she could never be forgiven, especially if she knowingly agreed to anything enjoyable.

Molly never gave up on Josie. She included her in her prayers. She tried to find books she thought Josie would like. The girls no longer created plays. Amber was too old now for, as she put it, "such nonsense." One day Molly complained to Josie how Amber no longer talked to her as before.

"She just seems to snub her nose at me. Like I am a child and she is an adult."

Josie tried to explain. "Molly, as we grow up, we all change. The child in us leaves or we suppress it. We try to behave like adults even though deep in our souls, we are still naive children. Be patient with Amber, she has not forgotten her love for you. When you both are grown, you will once again be the best of friends."

Mustering up her courage, Molly asked, "Josie, is that what happened to you back in Ireland when you left our home for several weeks to visit your cottage? Did you become an adult?"

Josie felt panic surge through her. She became hot all over, wanted to flee. Taking several deep breaths, thinking of what Molly had said, she responded, "Yes, I suppose in a way, that is what happened."

"But you still talk with me and are still my friend. Amber seems mad at me. Why?"

Josie felt trapped, fearful the conversation would overwhelm her barriers and she would tell Molly what had happened to her. Just then the dinner chimes rang. The two never resumed Molly's questions.

In mid-December, the Great Lakes became dangerous with ice flows. Most travel ceased in the winter. The Captain docked the *Princess Rose* in Buffalo and hired his most trustworthy crew member to live on the schooner all winter. He provided him with funds for fuel and food in exchange for him protecting the ship from vandals.

Taking the Erie Canal to New York, Farrel was thrilled to be home for Christmas and to welcome in 1832 with his family. After the holidays, Farrel became restless. He was not accustomed to idle time. Rose Kathleen tried to interest the Captain in the charity work she was engaged in at church. He rejected it as women's work. Rose Kathleen had to admit to herself there were only women doing it.

She tried to get him to make improvements around the house, but he didn't have either the skills needed or the patience. She even tried to get him to do carving, suggesting sailors were known for their beautiful wood and ivory carvings. His response was an angry, "I am not a sailor, I am a Captain."

Now and then, Farrel reached his limit and went out to the local pub for a pint. One evening he met Black Jack, a fight promoter. Black Jack told the Captain where to find his place. A week later, with snow on the ground and the boating season still at least a month or more off, Farrel decided to go see Black Jack's establishment.

Over the years, the Captain had seen fights, usually on the docks. Once, in his early years in London, he watched an organized fight. Two men faced one another and hit each other with their bare fists until one of them was knocked out. He found it bloody and tedious.

At Black Jack's, the fighters were within a roped in square. Screaming, shouting men sat in raised tiers of chairs around the square. A haze of cigar smoke hovered over the boxers. Farrel worked his way close to the square, paying for a seat. He had just settled in when a burly boxer hit a lesser but quicker man in the face. He was right in front of Farrel. The smack was so hard, the sweat on the man's face flew into the crowd, even onto the Captain. Wiping it off, he was riveted as the larger boxer pounded the man senseless until he slid off the ropes and crumpled down onto the canvas platform.

No sooner had he been carried out, than another pair climbed in and began slugging. Farrel was disgusted. He stood to leave when his name was called. Turning, it was Black Jack, motioning to join him. Farrel made it to the aisle and followed Black Jack to his office. The crowd noise was only slightly muted so the two had to almost shout to hear one another.

"How do you like it, Captain?"

"I must admit, it is interesting but I am afraid I find it disgusting. Is it always this brutal?"

"That's the point. It can go twenty, forty, even a hundred rounds. It brings in money. Men love to bet on the outcome. I get a big share of the take. Very profitable. Care to invest in my operations?"

"I don't think so. Right now I have all of my money invested in my schooner and house."

"I guess investing in ships is as much a gamble as boxing. Just more acceptable to the do-gooders."

When Farrel returned home, Molly greeted him with an unladylike sound upon smelling her smoke, sweat scented father. "Where have you been, Father, a pig pen?"

"No. Almost the same thing."

In late April, Josie finally acquiesced. She agreed to go with Rose Kathleen and Molly for a trip on the *Princess Rose*. She was won over with the understanding she would go as their maid and not as family.

In spite of her determination not to enjoy herself, she was excited. The canal ride was peaceful. She and Molly were inseparable the first day. That evening at dinner, the family joined several men on their way to Chicago: a doctor, a pharmacist, a soldier in uniform and two handsome young men. One, a tall German. The other, a very cute, red-headed Irish lad. She liked him. She sat next to him at the table. They chatted. She sensed he was younger than she and inexperienced, which made him appealing. She felt she could trust him not to take advantage of her.

Josie was unsure how to behave. She was shamed by even thinking of a young man finding interest in her. She was soiled. Yet, she was alive.

After dinner, the two went for a walk in the dark on the deck. Stopping along the railing, Seamus, that was his name, took her hand. Steeling herself for revulsion, Josie was surprised she found him attractive. She found herself tongue-tied. Her brains flew out of her head. She had never been so before. Seamus looked baffled. Determined to make an impression, Josie leaned in and kissed the young Irishman. At first he responded. As she pressed the kiss, he backed off and excused himself.

Unable to understand what had just happened, Josie decided she was being punished by God for her sins. She wanted another chance. What had she done wrong? Was he so inexperienced? Or too

61

experienced? Or was she unattractive? That had never been her problem.

The next day, Seamus avoided Josie. Her bewilderment turned to shame and then to anger. Who did he think he was?

When the *Princess Rose* landed at Detroit, the men, including Seamus, decided not to stay aboard, rather to take a stagecoach across the Michigan Territory to Chicago. The following day, Captain O'Flaherty was to continue, heading north, then west and down Lake Michigan to Chicago. After Molly was sound asleep in her bunk, Josie, who had packed her things before going to bed, arose, dressed and left the cabin with her bag. She slipped up to the deck, and walked boldly down the gangplank to the dock.

Once on land, her bold plan crumbled. She had no idea where to go. She didn't know where Seamus might be staying. Lights in windows guided her to several inns. Loud voices and laughter burst from each. Walking on, she found a secluded wooded area. Entering, she put her bag down, sat on it and began to regret leaving the schooner. She could go back. For what? She had not felt right living with the O'Flaherty family ever since the cottage incident.

Moving further into the woods, Josie found a fallen log and sat. She was tired. Using her bag as a pillow, Josie stretched out on the forest floor and went to sleep. Sun streaming down through the leaves woke her. Sitting up, she took a brush from her bag, undid her upturned hair, and began her morning ritual. She stroked her hair one hundred times. She pulled out a few dry twigs. Without a mirror, she could not turn up her hair. She ran her hands down her dress, a futile attempt to flatten out the wrinkles.

Putting her shoes on, she retraced her steps, coming out on the street with the inns. Ahead, she watched as Seamus and the other men climbed into a stagecoach and it drove off. She was too late. Now what?

Chapter Eleven

Standing on the edge of the street, Josie looked like a lost waif. Her wrinkled dress was dirty from her night on the forest floor. With her bag at her feet, she looked lost and afraid. What should she do? Where could she go? When honest with herself, she wanted to follow Seamus. How? He said he was going far beyond Chicago. She had money to take a stagecoach but was afraid to be with a group of men. She also wondered if there was anything to Molly's fear of heathens. She was hungry.

The street was deserted. There was no sign of life anywhere. It was very early. Josie fleetingly feared coming upon Manus. That worry, as it now always did, quickly shifted to anger. The anger emboldened her. Picking up her bag, she stepped forward and turned to her right, to look for a place to eat.

Far ahead of her was a fine looking young man leading several horses. Approaching, he warmly smiled at Josie, tipped his hat and greeted her.

"Good morning, Miss. You are up early."

There was something about him that instilled trust. Josie responded, "Good morning to you, sir. Might you know a place where I could get breakfast?"

"I do. I am heading to the St. Clair to stable my horses and get a warm meal. If you would like, you could walk with me. I should consider it the blessing of the Lord's day if you would break your fast with me."

Stopping in front of the inn, the young man introduced himself.

"My name is Brock Walton, recently from Ireland. May I have the pleasure of knowing your name, Miss?"

"I am Josie Durst, also from Ireland. Almost a year now."

The door of the St. Clair opened and a half-asleep stable boy came down the front steps and asked, "May I stable your horses, sir?"

Handing the reins to the boy, he nodded yes, and gave him a few coins.

"Thank ye kindly, sir."

Offering his arm to Josie, Brock Walton led her up the front steps, across the lobby to the dining room. The tables were empty. A waitress seated them.

"This morning we have fried ham slice, eggs, apple pie and hot coffee."

Brock nodded and the waitress went to the kitchen. He must be someone important, Josie thought. He merely nods and everyone acts.

"Is that acceptable to you, Miss Durst?"

"Yes." As soon as she said it, Josie realized her voice sounded frightened.

"May I ask where you were heading when we met?"

"For something to eat," Josie said, still cautious.

"And after you eat?"

"Chicago."

"You are of few words."

Josie did not reply.

"Ah, you are not sure about me. Is that it?"

"I don't know you, sir."

"Hmmm. That is so. I am of a wealthy Dublin family. My father has sent me to America to learn all about it. He believes a fortune can be made in the former colonies."

The waitress brought the hot food. Josie tried to eat slowly and ladylike. Her hunger won over her intentions. She was relieved when she noticed Brock ate with as much gusto as she.

When the waitress came to be paid, Josie reached into her bag.

"I invited you to break your fast with me. It is proper I pay for your meal."

Brock handed the waitress a gold coin. The waitress held it in the palm of her hand, not knowing what to do. It was many times the cost of the meals. Smiling, Brock said to her, "May your day be as bright as the coin. It is yours."

"Miss Durst. May I ask how you intend to go to Chicago?"

"I haven't decided?"

"Are you accustomed to horses?"

Stiffening, Josie replied, "I have ridden a horse before, if that is what you are asking?"

64

"I have three horses. One for myself. One for my baggage. One to spare. You may ride to Chicago with me if you wish."

"I am not sure it would be proper for me to be alone with you for so many days."

Suddenly blushing, Brock replied, "Quite so."

"If I found someone to join us, would you be more comfortable?"

"I suppose."

"If you are willing to wait here, I shall make inquiries."

Brock left as a couple entered. They appeared content with one another. The waitress seated them. Josie concluded the couple was married. Would she ever marry and be happy? Would any man have her?

Brock returned, sat down, "The clerk advised me a couple is leaving by carriage this morning and looking for someone to join them for safety. I believe it might be the man and woman at the other table. If you wish, I could introduce myself and see if they would like us to join them."

Smiling warmly, Josie assented.

Brock joined the couple. As he spoke to them, the couple looked to Josie and smiled at her. An hour later, the four were comfortably in the carriage, pulling away from the St. Clair Inn. Brock's three horses followed behind, the stable boy riding one, holding the reins of the other two.

The ride across the Michigan Territory was delightful. While some of the accommodations along the way were less than clean, Brock and the Blackwells made light of the discomforts. The three found much in common, their conversation was uplifting. Reverend Blackwell was a Presbyterian minister. He and his wife were missionaries. They were heading to Chicago to work with the Indians.

Josie seldom entered the conversation. When she did, her comments were usually questions about what was being discussed. At times, she felt waves of overwhelming shame for her past. Each night she had a room to herself. When the door could not be locked, she moved whatever furniture was in her room against the door. Nothing untoward occurred.

Arriving in Chicago, Josie was relieved. The *Princess Rose* was not among the few docked boats. Her hope was to find a place to stay before it arrived, if it had not already come and gone. Everyone stayed the first night at the Tremont House. Rev. Blackwell had a letter of introduction to Chief Robinson. They were directed to John Hogan, the Postmaster, for directions on how to find the Chief. They decided to make the Tremont House their base.

Brock Walton, anxious to get back with his horses, rode out of town the next morning, heading north to the Wisconsin Territory to observe Indian settlements.

Once again, Josie felt adrift and alone.

Chapter Twelve

Josie continued to stay at Tremont House. With the money from the sale of the cottage in Ireland, Josie was able to pay for her room and meals. After several days, however, she realized she was running through her money quickly. She immediately looked for a position. From the moment she had arrived in Chicago, she watched for Seamus. One day she saw Axel Konrad. Not sure why, she avoided contact with him. It gave her hope Seamus was still in Chicago.

She was cautious in her inquiries for employment, still racked with guilt over her sin in the cottage. One person told her to tell the Postmaster she was looking for a position. John Hogan, although courteous, seemed put off by Josie. She again leaped to the conclusion no one wanted anything to do with her. She was convinced Mr. Hogan knew she was a fallen woman.

Her eyes filled with unwanted tears. Josie fled the post office, embarrassed and ashamed. Would this never end? Walking hurriedly, she collided with a woman.

"Watch where you are going, child!"

Startled, Josie mumbled an apology to the older woman. Noticing how well dressed she was, she repeated herself.

"I am dreadfully sorry, Miss."

"I haven't been called Miss for a long time. Are those tears in your eyes, child?"

Although Josie's dander got up being called a child, she controlled herself. Wiping her eyes, "No, just must be dust in my eyes."

"Why don't you come and I can give you a cup of tea."

The two walked to a log cabin with a porch. Inside, the woman urged Josie to sit at the small table while she warmed the water for tea.

Josie watched the woman. She moved with grace, her full skirt swishing from side to side. For the first time, Josie noticed the bodice was quite low cut, revealing much of the woman's ample bosom.

"What is your name?"

"Josie. Josie Durst."

"You are the age my daughter would be now. I haven't seen her since she was only three."

"Why?"

"Her father took her from me. We never married. He came from a family who would not accept their son marrying a maid. I think he loved me. He wasn't able to rebel against his rich parents."

She placed a lace cloth on the table, then cups and saucers and a plate of cookies. Pouring hot water into the teapot, she put a spoonful of tea in a small basket on a chain and dipped it into the pot, placing the china lid on top.

"Do you like sugar in your tea?"

"Yes, if you have some."

"I haven't seen you before. Have you just arrived in Chicago?"

"Four days ago. I have been looking for a position. No one will hire me."

"Where are you staying?"

"At the Tremont House, but it is too expensive. I need to find work and a place to stay."

The woman studied her intensely.

"Josie. Would you stay with me? I have a spare room and could use someone to clean and cook and do the laundry. I couldn't pay much. You would have a roof over your head and three meals a day."

"I don't know. I would like to but, well, there is something in my past. Once known, it would ruin your reputation."

The woman burst into laughter. "Ruin my reputation! Hardly. Do you know who I am, what I do?"

"No."

"I pleasure men for money."

Seeing the expression of confusion on Josie's face, the woman said, "Child. I am a prostitute. Men come to me and pay for sex.

"And you think you could taint me? I haven't had a good reputation for years. At least not the kind you are thinking of."

Josie was silent, struggling to grasp the meaning of what the woman had said. The woman had the wisdom to say nothing. To let Josie figure it out. She got up and refilled the teapot with hot water. Passed the plate of cookies to Josie. Finally, she spoke.

"What have you done that is so bad?"

"I have told no one," Josie whispered, choking back a sob.

"No one should carry a burden all by themselves, Josie. You are too young to be anchored in the past. You need to move on. To find a new beginning."

Josie wrestled with herself. She began to shake. She wanted to tell so badly, she felt as if she were a dam holding back the water of the world. This woman, with her gentle kindness, had opened a small fissure.

"You will feel better if you share your grief. I will hold it forever in my confidence."

"I sinned while still in Ireland. So badly, I can't be forgiven."

"Did you kill someone, child?"

"No."

"Did you harm someone?"

"No."

"Did you steal something valuable?"

"No."

"Did you tell a lie that seriously hurt someone?"

"No."

The woman reached out and took Josie's hands in hers. She looked into Josie's eyes and asked, "Did you sleep with a boy?"

"Not a boy. A man," Josie whispered.

"How did it happen?"

The memory of that horrible night found its way through the tiny hole in the damn. Slowly, painfully, Josie relived her cottage nightmare. At first her words were jumbled. Eventually they became lucid. The woman continued to hold Josie's hands, her face both reassuring and compassionate. When Josie would pause, the woman said nothing, just squeezed her hands.

It took many minutes for Josie to describe the terror of the night. When, at last, she finished, she pulled her hands from the woman's, put her arms down on the table and buried her face in them, softly crying.

The woman did nothing. She waited. As Josie's weeping subsided, she placed her hand on the back of her head and stroked her hair. Patiently, lovingly, she comforted the distraught girl.

The feel of the hand on her hair was the same as when she came home from school after Miss McGing had abused her. Her mother would hold her and stroke her hair, softly hushing her. When Josie looked up at the woman, for a fleeting moment she saw her mother's face.

"I don't even know your name."

The woman smiled, the worst for Josie was over. "I am Lotus."

69

She again took Josie's hands in hers.

"Josie, I have an extra room. You can stay here as long as you wish."

"Won't I be in the way?"

"We can work it out."

"Do I have to be with men?"

"Absolutely not! Never. Not while you live with me. I shall treat you as my lost daughter."

Just then, there was a hard knocking at the door. Without waiting, the door flew open and a rough looking man entered. Seeing Josie, he grinned and asked, "Lotus, this a new girl?"

"Get out Hoss. I am not open for business today!"

His grin turned to a scowl, he shrugged his shoulders and left, closing the door behind him as noisily as possible.

"What I do with men like him is a sin. What happened to you was not a sin. You foolishly entered Manus's room. Why? You were curious. When he welcomed you and then forced himself upon you, he was the one sinning. You tried to escape his clutches. You were a victim, not a sinner.

"You must forgive yourself, Josie Durst. You did nothing wrong."

It was like her mother used to talk to her. When Josie came home from school, after Miss McGing verbally abused and humiliated her, her mother would reassure her she had done no wrong; always reassuring her it was Miss McGing who had done the wrong. Her mother always told her, "You must forgive yourself, Josie Durst. You did nothing wrong."

Josie moved her few belongings from the hotel to Lotus' home. The cabin had four rooms. The small parlor where they had their tea. Behind it was a kitchen with fireplace. Off the parlor to the right, a large bedroom. Off the kitchen to the left was a smaller bedroom which became Josie's. Besides the front door on the parlor, there was a back door in the kitchen. Josie used the back door to come and go. Lotus' clientele entered and left by the front door.

Chicago was growing. Men of more substantial means were arriving each month. Only a few brought wives with them. Some of the men came to see Lotus seeking Josie as well as the feminine surroundings. They enjoyed the finer things. Some demanded exclusivity. They demanded regular, preset days and times. They were more than willing to reimburse Lotus many times more than someone like Hoss.

With time, Lotus catered increasingly to the more refined patrons. Josie helped her furnish both the parlor and business room in tastefully elegant trappings.

Lotus refashioned several of her older dresses to fit Josie. They were more colorful and frilly than Chicago women wore. She also helped Josie wear makeup, particularly coloring her lips.

"You are so pale, you need some rouge to brighten your face. And your hair needs to be more stylish."

Josie, not realizing just how she looked, felt good about herself. No longer needing to hide in drab clothing, Josie was proud, now, to walk around in Chicago.

Almost a year later, in May, 1833, Josie saw Seamus O'Shea on the street. He was with Captain O'Flaherty, his wife and daughter and with Axel arm in arm with an attractive young woman. Excited and confident in herself, without thinking, Josie ran to Seamus. Unabashedly, Josie hugged and kissed Seamus. Totally bewildered, he pushed her away. Seamus mumbled something she did not comprehend in her confusion. She tried not to run from her embarrassment, but walked as quickly away as she could. Josie's cheeks were redder than the rouge.

Part Four

Anna Konrad

Chapter Thirteen

Lina and I watched as the *Deutschlund* slowly inched its way to the dock. It seemed to take forever to come to rest. I agonized at the slow pace to lower the gangplank. It has been almost a year since I received my father's first letter suggesting Anna wished to come to America. Standing there, next to Lina, I finally voiced the gnawing worry which had been chewing at my mind for weeks.

"What if Anna didn't make the ship? What if she succumbed to shipboard disease? What if she died? Or was attacked?"

My agitation surprised Lina. I am usually calm and confident. I rarely voice my feelings. I have always tried to mask my emotions except now, when alone with my wife. Here, on the dock, surrounded by others, I jolted her with my outburst.

"We will see her shortly, Axel. She is fine."

"Just how do you know that?"

Lina was surprised with the severity of my tone. I could tell from the reaction on her face. She said nothing further. Grasping my hand, Lina held it firmly.

"Look, there is Captain Mahler!" I spoke so loudly, everyone around me looked where I pointed.

Captain Mahler was near the opening at the top of the gangplank. He was waving. A moment later, a young woman came to his side. She waved.

"Anna! Anna!" I shouted, waved, turned to Lina, kissed her, turned back and shouted, "Anna, this is Lina."

We pushed our way to the bottom of the gangplank. Dropping Lina's hand, I ran up the ramp to Anna, leaving Lina behind.

"Anna, you are here!"

Staring at me, Anna responded in German, "Axel, have you already forgotten German?"

I teased in German, "Just giving you your first lesson in English."

I turned to Captain Mahler, gave him a bear hug, thanked him for bringing Anna safely to me. "I received your message, Captain. Yesterday."

"Axel, it is good to see you looking so well. Will you be staying in New York for a few days?"

"Yes, we are staying at the Eagle. I hope you can join us."

"I intend to. It will be good to get a few days rest. I'll send Anna's luggage to the hotel. Now go."

Taking Anna's hand I almost dragged her down the gangplank to Lina.

The two women, their faces wreathed in smiles, instantly enfolded one another in their arms, their words of greeting muffled. I stood wordless, my pride welling up in me. The two chatted as if they had known one another all their lives.

I led them to the carriage. I helped each in and sat opposite the two women. I gazed with admiration at their beauty. Anna, several years older than Lina, is more solidly built than my slender wife. How quickly the two talked of their common interests and experiences. Occasionally, Anna looked away to see the passing buildings and people, commenting, questioning, then turning back to continue the chatter as children do.

I made no attempt to enter the conversation. Now, at last, Lina has another to talk with as much as she wishes. I am just not very vocal. Lina suggests I am too sparing with my words. I work at it when it comes to bank business. I find social speaking uncomfortable and often superfluous.

The Eagle put out a warm welcome. Oscar must have been told to watch for our arrival. He opened the carriage door almost before we came to a stop. Mamie Baruth was at the door to greet us. James Dowling was in the lobby. Even Kiefer Küche, the chef, was in the lobby. August had abandoned the desk to be part of the receiving party.

Introductions complete, it was agreed we would freshen up and rest before joining Mamie and James for dinner in Frau Baruth's apartment.

Anna's room is adjacent to our's. There is a connecting door. Anna reached into the large carpet bag she had carried from the ship and pulled out letters for me and presents for Lina. Being anxious to read the letters, I immediately went to the desk in our suite. Anna insisted Lina open the presents.

"These are belated wedding gifts for you and Axel. I know he will not mind if you open them. This one is from our parents. It was our grandmother's. One of the few items salvaged from our grandparents' home after they were killed by the French."

Lina opened the small package wrapped in heavy brown paper. Inside, it was wrapped in velvet with a ribbon. Carefully undoing it, Lina opened the box. Set in more velvet was a diamond and pearl broach which opened to reveal a tiny portrait of a couple.

"My Father said they are Eldric and Elsa, our grandparents."

"This should not be given away. Your father should keep this."

Grinning, Anna said, "Father thought you might say that. He has another. A large oil of his parents."

Anna gave her another gift. "You should probably wait for Axel to open this one together. It is from Mother."

At my desk, I opened the packet of letters. There were six. I sorted through and read the one from my father first.

It was the thickest. Carefully lifting the wax seal, I unfolded the parchment. There was a long letter together with another letter of credit for a staggering amount. Humbled by it, I wondered whether or not I should continue soliciting funds from more New York businessmen.

I quickly scanned the letter to determine if there was any troubling news. Finding none, I began at the start and read with growing relish, always finding my father's thoughts worthwhile and timely. I was warmed as familiar images of home leaped from the pages. I visualized the manor, the fields, the hands, the horses, even the wonderful aroma of the barn and stables. When I thought of the stables I involuntarily shuddered. Will I never be able to move past the memory of my cousin Rikert attacking Anna? My fight with Rikert is still so vivid. I can so clearly see Rikert falling on the tines of the pitchfork. It nearly killed my evil relative. Now, at last, Anna is safe from the vile, vicious, depraved, vengeful monster.

The next letter I opened was from my mother. How loving and positive her sentiments. So like her. I pictured her as I read. She is so beautiful, so gentle in manner yet firm in her beliefs. Her letter was sweet as she wrote of the beautiful gardens around the manor.

A knock on the door interrupted. It was Anna's luggage. I directed Oscar to take it to Anna's room. Coming back through the suite, Oscar paused. I found a gold coin for him. Oscar handed it back.

"Not necessary, Herr Konrad. You are family."

He did not make a move to leave. I asked, "Is all well here at the Eagle?"

"The staff is worried about Frau Baruth. We think she might be taking ill. Otherwise, why did she ask Herr Baruth, her son, to come visit?"

"She is fine, Oscar."

"Thank you sir. We all pray she is well."

I finished reading my mother's letter which ended with instructions to give the enclosed letter to Lina.

I joined the ladies and handed the letter to Lina. She opened it as Anna and I watched. As Lina read the letter, she began to smile.

"Axel, Anna, I must read this out loud."

Dear Lina, My Dearest Daughter,

Henry and I welcome you to our family. How we long to meet you and shower you with our love. Axel has written to tell us of you. By now I am sure you know Axel is never very vocal in expressing his feelings. In his letters, however, he has told us enough about you so we know you are precious to him. His love of you comes through, even in his somewhat cryptic wording. He also describes you as pretty and wise.

We send our love to you with Anna. And our prayers that you and Axel will continue to find peace and joy in one another.

Please come to visit us. Heinrich and I long to kiss you, hug you and surround you with our love.

Your loving Mother
3rd of June, Year of Our Lord, 1833

"Axel, your parents have sent us a wedding gift. Sit down and open it with me."

I tried not to show my desire to return to my desk and read the rest of my letters. I sat down, telling myself, don't be so ungrateful.

The package was not very large. Removing the brown paper and next the silk wrapping revealed a small, finely crafted wooden box. The dark walnut wood's satin finish glowed. Together we lifted the hinged lid. Inside, nestled in dark purple velvet were a small cup, spoon, fork and rattle, all of silver. Tucked to one side was a small piece of paper. Opening it, Lina read aloud:

To our future grandchild,

These, child, were your father's when he was your age. Bless you. May God be your guide. May your life be rich in joy and always filled with purpose and the love of your parents.

Love, your Grand Papa and Mama
3rd of June, Year of Our Lord, 1833

"Axel, were you ever so small? Anna, what was he like as a baby?"

"Loud! He was so noisy, I think he used up his voice so that now he never speaks for very long."

I joined my ladies who were laughing. I made some appropriate remarks, I suppose. My mind was elsewhere. I could not believe how impatient I was to get back to my letters. Why do I anticipate so for something and then, when it happens, want to move on. For months, no years, I have longed for letters from my family. I have worried to no end that Anna would not arrive safely. Yet now, at last, she is here with word from my parents and all I can think of is to get back to Chicago. Can Lina read my mind?

Sweetly, Lina said, "Axel, do you have more letters to read? Would you mind it if Anna and I talk some more while I help her unpack?"

"Not at all."

I returned to the desk in our room. I picked up the letter from Reverend Steinhoff. He is our family's pastor, the only pastor I have ever known. His letter, filled with prayerful thoughts and God's blessings on Lina and our marriage, touched on the departure of Rikert from Schlosshagen.

"I am afraid your father's cousin left in anger, threatening revenge against you, my dear Axel. I understand he left Germany and has gone to America. I pray the Lord protects you and your wife from the evil of which Rikert is capable."

Rikert no longer dominates my days or evokes nightmares. Since Lina and I had arrived in Chicago, I finally felt out of Rikert's grip. Pastor Steinhoff's warning sent a shiver up my spine. Could Rikert's evil still know no bounds?

Lina brought me back from my dark thoughts.

"Axel, I have insisted Anna take a rest before dinner. I am going to lie down as well. Come join me." I did and fell sound asleep. Lina was up before me, dressing, when I woke.

Chapter Fourteen

Dinner was exquisite. The table in Mamie's dining room had been expanded. Six places were set. Mamie introduced her son, Carsten, and directed the seating arrangement. Lina was next to Anna who was next to Carsten Baruth. I was bracketed by Mamie and James. Wait staff entered, filling our wine glasses and placing course after course before us.

The conversation, at first, was awkward. I began telling Carsten how James Dowling's grandson, Seamus O'Shea, was my best friend in America. Lina urged me to tell how Seamus and I met. I surprised even myself. I mesmerized everyone telling about losing my bag with all of my money. About Seamus' attempts to get me to become a fighter for Black Jack. The Indian attack in Michigan and our early days in Chicago. Not sure what loosened my tongue. For me, I was actually eloquent.

Anna asked Carsten when he came to America.

"I was only four years old. We landed in New York on July 11, 1811."

"When did you move to Cincinnati?"

"That's a long story. Sure you want to know?"

Anna said, "Yes, if no one else minds."

No one objected.

"We lived at the Eagle. Father had bought it from an elderly German couple. They had the same high standards as Father."

Intrigued, I asked, "What was your father's name?"

"Joachim Christoph Baruth," answered Mamie. "I was nineteen when we were married. Joachim was forty three. He was a man of means and determined to come to America. He bristled under the restrictions imposed by the government. He insisted Carsten grow up in freedom."

"I was sixteen when I moved to Cincinnati. As much as I loved the Eagle and my parents, I could not see myself running a hotel. I wanted adventure. I was appalled by slavery in the south. I read about Cincinnati as a gateway to the north. Part of the underground railroad."

Anna interrupted. "What is the underground railroad?"

"Slaves are owned by plantation owners. Slaves are whipped. Wives are taken from their husbands. Slave children are taken from their parents. Slaves have no rights. They are beaten if it is discovered they are learning how to read. It is a living hell for them. Abolitionists in the north help slaves escape. Routes and safe houses have been established to help them to freedom. The network is known as the underground railroad.

"If they are caught along the way, they are returned to their masters where they are lashed to within an inch of their life. Abolitionists along the route are taking great risks. The southern states consider them to be breaking the law.

"Cincinnati has a significant German population. Once there, I realized I needed a skill. I found a position as a clerk for a lawyer. He was so impressed with me he encouraged me to read for the law. Cincinnati is in Ohio, a free state. It is across the river from Kentucky, a slave state. Cincinnati is an important portal to the underground railroad.

"I am now an attorney. I have tried a broad range of cases including one in a Federal court concerning an escaped slave who was being held in a Cincinnati jail to be returned to his owner in Georgia. I became known as an abolitionist. My life was threatened."

Carsten paused, looked at his mother, and continued.

"Mother, I have never told you this before. Upon leaving the courthouse one day, I was assaulted by two men in masks. One had a piece of pipe, the other a knife. I was fortunate they were not very capable. When they came at me from opposite sides, I ducked and lunged forward. They struck one another rather than me. I ran back into the courthouse, leaving the two sprawled on the pavement.

"The next day the newspaper reported two men were found outside the courthouse. One knifed to death, the other staggering away, blood dripping from his head. He was arrested for murder but acquitted for lack of evidence."

I looked at Mamie to see her reaction. Rather than concern, she was clearly proud of her son.

Anna asked nothing further.

The last time Lina and I had seen James Dowling he had been so ill we feared for his life. I told him I was pleased to see him looking so well. "I feel wonderful. Dandiest thing. The doctor I had been seeing had misdiagnosed my fatigue and discomfort. Foolishly, it took me many months before I associated the aggravation of my symptoms with his treatment. He would come to my suite and bleed me. For days afterward I was hardly able to get out of bed.

"I should give credit to Mamie. One day, after not coming downstairs for three days, Mamie observed how I seemed worse after each time the doctor came. It didn't take me long to doubt the efficacy of bloodletting.

"I found pamphlets which argue for and against the letting of blood. Those arguing against it make more sense. The next time the doctor came to visit, I shared my observations and questioned his intent to once again let my blood."

"Excuse me for interrupting, Herr Dowling. How is bloodletting done?" Lina asked.

"A good question. It is not a pleasant subject for dinner conversation. Perhaps another time."

Anna urged James to continue.

"There are two methods. One is to place leeches on the body and allow them to feast on the patient by sucking out blood.

"The other, more sophisticated method, is to cut the vein in the arm and catch the blood in a bowl. The flow of blood slows as the body attempts to close the puncture. The doctor may need to make a second, even a third cut. For me, by the time the doctor decided a sufficient amount of blood had been lost, I felt exhausted and usually fell into a deep sleep.

"Some go to barbers who use their razors. I shutter to think of letting a barber purge my bad humors. The more I thought about it, I could not even accept we have bad humors. What if someone has no sense of humor. What would the doctor do for them? One pamphlet suggested instruments used in the procedure may be unclean and introduce disease into the patient.

"When I challenged the doctor, he flared into anger. He became defensive and demanded either I agree to him letting my blood or find a new doctor.

"I decided to test my belief the bloodlettings were the cause of my illness. I did not seek a new doctor. Week by week, my health improved. I began to take my daily walks again, my appetite returned and I am now heathier than I have been in years."

A lull in the conversation followed until Carsten asked Anna, "How was your crossing, Fraulein Konrad?"

"It was comfortable and calm. Captain Mahler paid special attention to me. I ate all my meals in his cabin and had a first class room. The seas, he told me, were unusually serene. I never felt ill from the motion. I did feel nauseated, though, when the wind was still and the stench of the poor passengers in steerage rose up.

"I asked one of the crew to take me below to see steerage. He tried to dissuade me. I insisted. I took down the bundle of food mother had given me. It was like descending into living hell. I wept openly with what I saw. My bundle was just enough for only a few families for two days. There were so many more I wished I could feed. From then on I saved half of the food served to me at the Captain's table and took it down to steerage.

"I got to know several families. Perhaps the saddest moment was on one of my visits with a couple I enjoyed. They had a one year old daughter. I have never seen such large, lovely eyes. I held the baby on each visit. She would smile at me and melt my heart. One day the couple was alone. I asked where Lila was. The mother told she had died and the Captain insisted the baby be buried at sea.

"I am ashamed to say I could not return to steerage for some days. Axel, how did you endure it? No wonder poor Horst died."

"You get used to it. Besides, I had Lina to talk with and look forward to seeing each day. Steerage became much more tolerable after we met. All of which reminds me, Mamie. Captain Mahler said he would be staying a few nights here at the Eagle before returning to Germany."

"He usually does. I would expect him tomorrow, once he is sure his crew has things under control." As she spoke, Mamie looked at me with pleading eyes and asked, "Axel, tell us about Seamus."

I soon had the table regaled in laughter, exaggerating my Irish friend's antics. When Mamie winked at me, I knew I had done as she wished. I had lightened the mood of our gathering. It was time to tell about our baby.

"Lina has some wonderful news."

I guess I caught her off guard. Lina was momentarily flustered before regaining her composure.

"We both have wonderful news. We are going to have a baby in February."

The mood definitely became more positive.

After dessert, we reluctantly retired for the evening. Anna and Carsten lingered behind, talking.

Chapter Fifteen

Anna divided her time between Lina and Carsten. Mid-week, Lina told me, "Anna has fallen in love with Carsten. From what she tells me, she thinks he is interested in her. Would you accept him as your brother-in-law some day?" Lina just brushed me aside when I responded, "But they just met."

"Axel, didn't you tell me you fell in love with me the first time we met?"

"That was different."

"How?"

"I suppose it's possible."

"You haven't answered my question. Would you accept Carsten as your brother-in-law?"

"I would."

Lina took Anna to meet her mother, Minnie. Lina and I showed Anna some of New York. It was my only full day with my sister. I spent most of my time visiting Horace Morgan and the rest of my bank investors as well as new prospects. I gave each my latest financial report. By the end of the week I had collected another $250,000 of investments in the Greater Bank of Chicago.

Each evening Mamie had Lina, Anna and me for dinner with James, Carsten and, at times, with Minnie Albrecht. The evening when Captain Mahler joined us began somewhat strained. I suppose we all were reliving the horrors of our crossings. Lina melted our hearts by telling charming stories of her childhood. She soon had us laughing as she described her lessons to learn how to play the church organ.

Our evening dinners were joyous times, conversation flying from topic to topic. On the last evening, when Lina, Anna and I went upstairs, I announced it was time we head to Chicago.

"So soon? Can't we stay longer?"

"Anna, you sound just like I did when I was a child and didn't want to go to bed at night."

"Just think Axel, I was the one who convinced you it was time, little brother."

Lina giggled. "Not your little brother anymore."

"I shall miss Carsten. Will I ever see him again?"

"Anna, he will follow you to Chicago," Lina assured her. "He is taken by you. Trust me, he will come to you."

Anna blushed, shyly saying, "Do you really think so?"

In an attempt to convince Anna, I said, "If he does not, I shall go to Cincinnati and drag him to Chicago!"

"Don't you dare."

"Axel, don't tease your sister. This is a serious matter."

I retreated, mumbling I had notes to write.

The next morning we said our goodbyes. Carsten, bless his soul, told Anna he would like to call upon her if that was acceptable to me. I told him he would be more than welcome.

Our return trip to Chicago was uneventful. Captain O'Flaherty and his wife were gracious hosts. Anna marveled at all she saw, commenting on the beauty of the countryside.

Days before our arrival, my mind was on the bank and my plans for the wise investment of the additional funds I had acquired. With the new monies, I had more than tripled the assets of the bank. I could make a significant impact on the growth of Chicago.

Lina walked Anna, Rose and the Captain to our home. I stopped off to see John Hogan and collect my mail.

"You have several letters, Axel."

I could tell he was eager to talk.

"There was a murder while you were gone. A man was found with his neck cut from ear to ear. Don't know who he was. Big argument over who did it. Was he killed by an Indian? But he wasn't scalped. Doc Wooten looked over the body. Found three strange punctures in the man's back. He thinks he was stabbed in the back with a pitchfork. Says punctures match the tines perfectly."

I didn't hear another word John said. Tines of a pitch fork was all I needed to hear. Just like Rikert's fall on the pitch fork back in Germany after he attacked Anna. Afterward he was near death for weeks. Was the murder a coincidence? I would not let myself think the impossible.

When I became aware John had stopped talking, I thanked him and walked to the bank. Reinhold jumped up.

"Welcome back, Axel. Frau Lina stopped in to introduce your sister to me. I can see a strong resemblance to you."

"It is good to be home. I shan't ask if all is well with the bank. I know it must be."

"It is, sir. Shall I arrange for a board meeting for tomorrow?"

"Yes. I have a good report to make as well."

The bank indeed did well in my absence. There were more deposits, although none of great amounts. New loan requests had been received. Some were approved, some denied and several pending my return.

Reinhold told me about a loan request by Lotus. "She wants to improve her quarters. Presented it as a way to cater to more refined gentlemen. She appeared before the board to plead her case. We treated her with respect, as best we could, voted and unanimously turned her down. She didn't like it and vowed to find money elsewhere."

I went to the Sauganash and asked Mark Beaubien, "What do you know about the pitchfork murder?"

"Strange. Doc feels the man died from the neck slicing and the pitchfork stabbing was done afterward. Some kind of signal according to Doc. Not sure what he means. No one knows who the man was or who killed him. Twas talk around here every night for days."

Mark talked about other comings and goings until I suspect he realized I was no longer listening. I must learn to mask my impatience better. I finally excused myself, eager to get home.

Chapter Sixteen

The board meeting was my first with Reinhold presenting his summary report on transactions, assets and liabilities. I was delighted with the thoroughness of his presentation. The directors asked good questions. They were comfortable with Reinhold. He was at ease responding. I found myself relaxing. I was no longer a one-man show. It was amusing to listen to their comments on the appearance of Lotus before the board.

"She was dressed in what I am sure she felt was her finest," Philo offered.

"Finest? Looked darn cheap to me," Mark commented.

"You hypocrites," Doc said. "Every set of eyes around the table, including mine, were focused on her swelling bosom."

"Them beauties nearly popped out of her dress," Alexander chuckled.

I tried to change the subject, without success.

"She had more paint on her face than a Potawatomi warrior," said Mark. "And that dress, ain't seen nothing like that before."

Johann complained, "She had much toilet water. I almost gagged."

Smiling, Mark said, "That's called French perfume, Johann."

"Gentlemen," I asked, "How much did she request?"

"$2,000!" said Reinhold."

"What did she want it for?"

Referring to his papers, Reinhold read: "Purchase a larger building, carpets, large brass bed with canopy, damask wall coverings, chandeliers, velvet sofas and chairs, fine china, silk-lined drapes, Chinese vases, French kerosene lamps, a gross of scented candles, oil paintings with gilded frames, supply of wines and liquors, crystal glasses, silverware. Frankly, it was at that point I stopped recording the details of her request."

It was too much for me. I broke out into a hearty guffaw which provoked an outburst of laughter. It became so infectious we soon had tears streaming down our cheeks.

"Did you approve Lotus' loan request?" I asked.

Like a practiced chorus, together they soundly said "NO!"

Reinhold next listed the other loan requests and the decisions made on each.

"Charles Cleaver requested a loan to open a factory to make soap and candles. We approved it.

Mark commented, "He stayed at my place when he first arrived. Came from England. He speaks kind of funny. Very hoity-toity."

Somewhat disgustedly, Philo said, "That is how the English speak. They think we sound crude the way we slaughter the King's English."

After the laughter settled down, Reinhold continued.

"We approved a loan for $500 to establish a lumber yard and mill.

"There was a request for a blacksmith shop. We turned it down. Chicago already has four. We suggested the request be resubmitted next year if population growth continues.

"We turned down a request for $5 for a groom to pay for a wedding ring.

"We turned down a request by a perpetual drunk for money so he could purchase liquor.

"We approved a request by Lieutenant Jefferson Davis. He asked the bank to handle the deposit of funds approved by the Congress in Washington City. The appropriation is for $25,000 to improve the harbor on the lakefront.

"There are three loans pending: a request to build a jail, a request to build the First Baptist Church and a request for funds to establish the Chicago Temperance Society. This last request was received just today."

"Excellent report. Thank you, Reinhold. Listening to all the business transacted in my absence is truly impressive. It proves the bank is not only needed but respected."

Beside himself, Mark laughed loudly. "Good thing," he struggled to say amidst his laughter, "we turned down Lotus. We'd have lost all respectability had we funded her request."

None of us could resist, breaking once again into uncontrollable chuckles. Once decorum was restored, I reported on my trip to New York.

"While in New York, I called upon each of the bank's investors and some potential new investors. As you know, the purpose of my trip was to meet my sister. She brought an additional letter of credit from my father. All told, I return from New York with a total of $250,000 to invest in the bank."

Everyone spontaneously broke into applause.

Mark shouted, "This calls for a stiff drink!"

Nodding agreement, I went to the cabinet, pulled out my bottle of schnapps, poured and handed a glass to each. Mark, Johann and Alexander accepted a second glass.

After the meeting, I went upstairs where I found Lina and Anna drinking coffee. They were engaged in a discussion of Christmas.

"Did you believe in Saint Nicholas?" asked Anna.

"Of course, don't all German children?"

"I did," Anna said.

"When did you learn the truth?"

Looking up at me, Anna said, "When I was seven. My mother made me promise not to tell my little brother."

"Really?" I interjected.

"When did you learn?"

"Father told me when I was five. I promised not to tell you Anna since I thought you still believed. Seems like a cruel hoax to play on children. First parents tell their children a lie and then fluff it off when they learn the truth. I think we should not lie to our children."

"Axel!" Lina was incredulous. "Every child deserves the joy and excitement of St. Nicholas. Didn't you look forward to him each year?"

Anna asked Lina, "Who did you think put up the Christmas tree?"

"Saint Nicholas! He came when we went to church on Christmas Eve. How eagerly I looked forward to the walk back home. Especially when snow was falling. I loved to enter the house and smell the pine scent."

"Did you search for the pickle?" Anna asked.

"What do you mean?"

"Lina, didn't your parents put a pickle on the tree?"

"Anna, it would have smelled awful."

"Not a real pickle. A glass pickle."

"No. Why a pickle?" Lina was perplexed.

"Our parents hid it on the tree. When we got back from church, the children raced to see who could be the first to find the pickle. We had so much fun searching for the pickle, we'd almost knock over the tree. The lucky child was given an extra special gift left by Saint Nicholas."

"Anna, we had no glass ornaments. Father always said they cost too much and were frivolous."

"Not this year." Getting up, Anna went to her room and came back with a small package. She handed it to Lina. "I was going to save this until Christmas."

Lina carefully unwrapped the tissue and held up a green, slightly curved glass pickle complete with characteristic bumps. "I can't believe it. This is a pickle. I can't wait to put it on our tree.

"Axel, we will have a tree, won't we?"

"Yes, dear."

"What did you do last year, little brother?" Anna asked.

"It did not feel like Christmas. I felt particularly lonely. I pined for you, Lina. I missed our parents and you, Anna, and Christmas back home."

"Did you at least go to church Christmas Eve?" Anna asked.

"No. There is no Lutheran Church in Chicago. The first church was formed a few months ago. It's Catholic. That's not for me. Philo Carpenter holds a Bible class. There are no Protestant church services."

"That is unacceptable, Axel." Anna said adamantly. "I will not live here without church. Are there no other Germans in Chicago?"

Lina offered, "There's Johann Wellmaker, the baker, and Heinrich Lampmann who runs the brick yard."

"Surely there are others," suggested Anna.

"There's Reinhold!" Lina added.

I interjected, "I know of several other Germans here in Chicago. There's Friedrich Lobbeke. He claims to be the first German to settle in Chicago. Mathias Meyer disputes this, claiming he was the first. The other Germans I know of are John Van Horne, Johann Planck and Daniel Vaughan. I don't know their faith. Some might be Catholic. Go see John Hogan. If anyone knows, he will."

Excitedly, Anna asked, "Lina, can we go see this Herr Hogan tomorrow?"

"Yes. It will give me a chance to show you our little village." Lina paused for a minute before addressing me. "Husband," I knew there was no arguing when Lina began with that. "Even if it is just us, we shall hold church services this Sunday. We can use your bank conference room. You don't object, do you?"

I replied meekly, "No dear."

Four days later, there we all were, in the conference room. Besides Lina, Anna and me, sitting around the table were Herrs Wellmaker, Lampmann, Lobbeke, Meyer, Planck and Christian Ebinger. I had never met Herr Ebinger before. Herr Planck knew him and had invited him to join us.

John Hogan had given Lina and Anna the names of other Germans, all of whom he believed were Lutheran. Eight showed up as well. The Escher brothers, Jacob and Martin, George Gross, Jacob Ott, the Stanger brothers, Daniel and Christoph, and Adam Knopp. George Gross said Johan Rehm would come next week as well as Jacob Schaebele.

Christian Ebinger offered to lead the service.

I was apprehensive until he opened with prayer and a hymn. We sang "A Mighty Fortress Is Our God." We didn't sound at all bad. When Ebinger offered to preach, I was even more dubious. I should not have been. He spoke from the heart, his brief sermon based upon Matthew 18:20 – "Where two or three are gathered together in my name, there am I in the midst of them."

His closing prayer touched on us, the future of the Indians and, finally, on the vote to be held in early August. He prayed everyone would vote to incorporate our settlement as the Village of Chicago. He asked for guidance for the voters to make the right decision so Chicago may grow with God-fearing people.

Thus, the German Evangelical Lutheran Church came to Chicago. Informally, but sincerely. It would be ten more years before First St. Paul Evangelical Lutheran Church was founded.

I voted for the incorporation of Chicago as a village. I was one of thirteen who gathered at Mark Beaubien's Sauganash. We cast our votes verbally. I was disappointed so few voted. Even so, the outcome was legal and decisive. Twelve voted for and one against incorporation. Why only thirteen when there are close to 350 people living here? That's only four percent of the population. We need to do better. We can do better.

Part Five

Expulsion

Chapter Seventeen

The Village of Chicago was under siege. It had been for several days. The deafening noise was terrifying. Women and children were locked in their log cabins. Frightened mothers forbid their children from peeking out their unglazed windows, yet they themselves could not resist looking. Indians were everywhere. Naked, but for loin cloths, their bodies covered with paint. Their black hair pulled into knots on the tops of their heads. A profusion of hawk and eagle feathers sprung from their topknots. Their faces were painted with hideous decorations. Foreheads, cheeks and noses were covered with curved stripes of red, edged with black points. It turned their entire faces to horrid grins.

Some wore bells on their ankles, others feathers. Many beat small drums or hit sticks together. Their chants and shouts pierced the air in a maddening rhythm. The crescendo was unrelenting.

Tomahawks were swung overhead, the blades glistening in the sunlight. Bows were thrust upward toward the blue sky. Rifle fire punctuated wave upon wave of sound.

The tops of some spears had scalps fastened near the sharpened stone tips. Clinging to a few were bits of flesh, the blood turned a dull brown.

Here and there white men could be seen. They appeared calm although they carried rifles. Lotus cursed the celebration as bad for her business. Traders and half-breeds drove wagon loads of goods to the prairie southwest of the village, emptying everything on to a growing pile. There were bolts of cloth, colored beads, pots, pans, knives, axes, barrels of whiskey, gunpowder, clothing, hats, scarves, pins, needles, used boots and food stuffs.

For days, members of the Potawatomi tribe arrived, gathering on the prairies surrounding the village, setting up camp. They had come for the first annual annuity promised the tribe in the treaty with the United States government. The annuity was in exchange for the Potawatomi ceding their remaining lands in Illinois.

Seamus had closed the Illinois and Michigan Canal Commission office. Today, September 26, 1833, he joined Colonel Grege to observe the distribution of the goods.

"There must be over four-thousand natives," estimated Grege.

"They could become violent." Seamus asked, "What has the fort done to protect the village?"

"As usual, the Army is ill-prepared. For the most part, they are hunkered down in the fort."

Passing the Greater Bank of Chicago, Seamus waved to Axel who stood in the open door.

Further along, they passed Mark Beaubien standing with Chief Robinson in front of the Sauganash Hotel and Tavern.

The weather was warm and sunny. A beautiful day with a hint of autumn in the offing.

"Just think. We arrived in Chicago one and a half years ago," Seamus commented.

"I know. It's already been over a year since the Black Hawk War ended," responded Grege. "I still struggle in my mind with the brutality of the United States Army. The slaughter of so many innocent women and children still makes me angry. I still feel rage for the stupidity of the military ignoring Black Hawk's repeated flags of truce."

"Time moves quickly on the frontier," Seamus lamented. "There is so little time to stop to think."

"Have you thought about my offer to come west with me?"

"I don't know. I would have to leave my position with the Canal Commission."

"Would they give you a leave of absence?" Grege asked. "The money is good. The experience will be something you can tell your grandchildren."

Seamus took a while to respond. "It's intriguing. How soon would we leave?"

"As soon as the dust settles after this," Grege said, swinging his hand, indicating the Indians.

"I will think about it over night."

Coming to the hill of goods, Grege and Seamus pushed their way through the crowd of Indians. Seamus whispered to Grege, "If we get covered with much more war paint, they'll think we are one of them."

Looking down, Grege was surprised to see war paint was rubbing off on them from the closely packed Indians.

"As one of the drivers heading west," Grege commented, "I have been asked to help maintain control. Guess the Army still looks upon me as an officer."

Major Whistler of Fort Dearborn and a few of his troops were present.

Billy Caldwell stepped forward and shouted to the traders and half-breeds. "Start the distribution!"

They picked up items and handed them to the closest natives. They refused to give more than one item per Indian. The natives in the back anxiously pressed forward, threatening the traders. On the verge of chaos, Caldwell climbed onto one of the wagons. He shouted in the Indian tongue, warning they would halt the distribution if order was not restored. He had to repeat it several times before the mob settled into an uneasy calm. As each Indian received something, he unhappily turned and pushed to the back of the mass.

There was no design to the distribution. Each was randomly given whatever the trader or half-breed happened to grab from the pile. Happy were those who received gunpowder or alcohol. One Indian, given a bag of beads, angrily threw it to the ground. After glaring at the half-breed and reaching for his tomahawk tucked in his loincloth, he turned when a trader pulled out his pistol.

The pile of goods ran out before all Indians had received something. Tension grew as those in the back saw they were to get nothing.

Major Whistler ordered, "Draw your weapons but do not, I repeat, do not fire. This must end peacefully."

Seeing drawn guns, the unlucky natives turned, grumbling and left.

Walking back to Fort Dearborn, the Major stopped along the way to talk to clusters of citizens. His message was the same to each. "Be on your guard tonight. Some of the Indians may decide to attack, demanding more."

Several hundred Potawatomi returned after dark. Leonora Hoyne ran in panic from the back door of her parent's cabin to their neighbor. She pounded on the Collins' back door until it was opened. She quickly stepped inside.

"Mr. Collins, I don't know what to do. Poor mother is crazed with fear. She is lying down on the bed with a pillow over her head complaining she can still hear the fiendish yells of the red devils."

Leonora paused to catch her breath. "They're dancing in front with tomahawks and knives. Each time they shoot their guns Mother screams, begging me to stop their horrid noises.

"I don't know what to do. Father is not home. There must be hundreds of the naked heathens. I don't want to be scalped." Exhausted, Leonora stumbled to a chair and collapsed.

"Hush, Nora," said Ma Collins. She turned to her husband. "Pa. Go next door and see what you can do. Jimmy's old enough to keep us safe."

He left. Lenora followed close behind.

Morning found the village quiet, the Indians back in their camps. The warriors, exhausted from their night of dancing, anger and drinking, were sprawled out where they had fallen in their drunkenness. As the morning wore on, they began to stir, their eyes bloodshot, their war paint so smeared the once grotesque images were blurry smudges. Slowly, they moved twelve miles west to their main camp on the Des Plaines River.

Grege and Seamus met for an early breakfast. They joined Christian Dobson and the others he had hired to transport the Indians west of the Mississippi. Dobson read aloud the terms of their contract with the government.

"Each of you will be paid five hundred dollars for the use of your team, wagon and your time driving to and from the reservation."

"We will pick up the Potawatomi at the Des Plaines River. Meet me with your wagons and teams south of the Forks. We'll cross the branch at the ford."

Grege asked, "Seamus, I have a second wagon and team. Will you be taking it or should I find someone else?"

"I'll take it."

At the Des Plaines, it took a day to load the tribes' belongings, small children and oldsters. Clans clustered together; the warriors on horseback, their wives and older children on foot. Christian Dobson, satisfied order was best he could achieve, the caravan moved out, heading west.

The first night, the wagon drivers and Christian camped a short distance from the tents the Indian women erected. Seamus was impressed with their efficiency and precision. Campfires were started, food prepared. He fell asleep to the sound of mournful singing and chanting coming from the tents.

How like the Irish back home. When Seamus fled Ireland, his lot was no better than the Indians he was escorting out of the state. The British wished Ireland to be free of the Irish Catholics. Their harsh tactics were just as cruel and unjust as the American government wanting the Indian lands for white settlers. Seamus felt he was part of this disgrace. He was aiding and abetting the expulsion of the Indians from their land. Stripping them of their heritage. Sleep was now impossible. He became so anguished with what he was doing, he decided to turn back in the morning. His mind made up, Seamus finally fell asleep.

He had forgotten the discomfort of sleeping on the ground. His body ached all over. Pounding his boots upside down to rid them of any crawling creatures, he pulled them on, stretched and stood. Slim, for that is what he called Grege, squatted by the fire, frying bacon and slices of bread in the grease. A coffee pot was balanced on several rocks at the edge of the fire.

He watched Seamus limp to the fireside.

"Morn'n, Seamus. Breakfast is ready." He handed him a tin plate and cup. "Help yourself."

He poured himself a steaming cup, the smell heavenly. The coffee was thick, black and hot. It never tasted as good as when sitting aside a campfire. Between sips, Seamus took several hefty slices of bacon and two pieces of bread. Sitting on the ground, he bit into the bacon and bread. Nothing could taste better.

"Slim, I have decided I don't want to be part of this rape of the Potawatomi. I can't agree to stripping them of their native homeland. Sorry, I hope you can find a replacement. I can go no further."

Grege said nothing. The two men chewed and drank in silence. Seamus saw a young Indian boy standing nearby. He was in his mid teens, muscular for one so young. Seamus wondered how long he had been there.

Seeing Seamus had discovered him, the youth asked, "May I talk with you?" His English was quite good.

Grege openly drew his pistol. "You may."

"I come in peace."

"Sit. Would you like coffee?" Grege's voice was friendly, yet his gun remained in view.

"I would." Grege filled a cup and handed it to him.

"Would you like something to eat?"

"No, sir."

"What did you wish to say?"

"My father is dead. My mother and I are alone."

"When did he die?"

"When I was young."

The youth said nothing further. Grege did not prod him. He waited for him to speak when he was ready.

Refilling his cup, the youth spoke.

"How long will it take to get to where you are taking us?"

"Ten, twelve days, if all goes well."

The youth did not respond. He squatted, sipping his coffee. The three sat for some moments in silence.

"I heard you talking."

Grege again waited.

Looking at Seamus, the boy spoke. "You said you don't want to help move us from our land."

Seamus looked to Grege, who said nothing. His pistol was still visible.

Seamus finally said, "That is true."

"If my father were alive, I might think differently." The youth spoke with no anger. "I hear our warriors speak. They want to attack you. They want to turn back and demand their land. They would lead us to more bloodshed. I do not agree."

Seamus, taken aback, asked, "Don't you feel we have taken your land? Is it not wrong?"

"I do but we are tired. We have no choice. We need you to help us find peace."

Putting down the tin cup, he walked off, his head held high.

Grege said nothing.

Seamus simply said, "I'll go on with you."

Chapter Eighteen

The sun had not been up long before the caravan once again moved out. There were over thirty wagons, nearly one hundred warriors on their horses and maybe five hundred women and children on foot. The confusion coalesced into a long column of humanity moving west. Seamus was fascinated by the single horses with a pair of harnessed poles dragging behind. Hides were sewn together and stretched between the poles. The hide travois were loaded with more of the Indians' belongings. Several carried elderly. Some held children, too young to walk any distance. More than a few squaws carried babies on their backs. The women performed the manual labor. The men assumed haughty postures on their horses.

Seamus had seen a parade in New York celebrating some event. Catching only a glimpse, Seamus had felt the excitement and happiness it evoked in the people lining the route. Looking back from his buckboard, he could not see the end of their parade. This one, however, was not happy. He was part of a caravan leading the Indians into exile. Each day blended into the next until Seamus felt as if he had been taken back to Biblical times when Moses led his people for forty years in the wilderness.

Around the camp fire each evening, Seamus and Grege chatted. They recalled their weeks as observers to what was now called Black Hawk's War. It too was a sad journey for the Indians. Back then, the Americans, both regular Army and local militias were determined to kill as many of Black Hawk's forces as possible.

The first night out, Grege asked Seamus, "What have you been doing?"

"Working for the Illinois and Michigan Canal Commission. Can thank Axel for the job. He'd heard about it. I don't think I would have been hired but for you." Grege frowned, "Me? How?"

"The training you gave me writing your reports during the Black Hawk War. I work in the land sales office. Congress in Washington City granted land for the canal right of way. They authorized sale of the adjacent land to help pay for the construction."

"You like working in an office?" asked Grege.

"It's a job. Hard for an Irishman to find work. Have you ever seen the damn signs in New York, *Help Wanted, Irish Need Not Apply?* First few days working for the Canal Commission were confusing. Then frightening."

"Why?" Grege asked.

"I got scared when I discovered the director was stealing money. Axel convinced me to tell Judge Lockwood. That's who Axel talked to about the job for me. The Judge had Axel and me prepare a report for the Commission. The director stole several hundred thousand dollars.

"T'was a thing of beauty to watch the Judge confront Fitchen. He was the director. Judge got him to provide his records. We recouped most of the money the fool had taken. Rest he'd spent on ladies. Judge had Fitchem escorted to the Mississippi. Warned him never to return to Illinois or he'd go to jail."

"No trial?"

"No. Publicity would have hurt the plans to build the canal."

"So you've been working for them since?"

"Afraid so."

"Don't like the work?" Grege asked.

"I prefer fresh air."

"What'll you do when we get back to Chicago?"

"Don't know. Invest in something or other. Just have to see."

The third night out, Seamus asked Grege, "What became of Black Hawk?"

"You don't know?"

"No."

"It's an unbelievable story. You and I last saw Black Hawk when he and his son, Whirling Thunder, surrendered to the Army.

"He, his son and several of his followers were taken as prisoners down the Mississippi to Jefferson Barracks. That's just south of St. Louis. They were held there for eight months. Their treatment was harsh.

"In April of 1833, on orders of President Jackson, they were taken east, first by steamboat, then by carriage and part way by railroad. Along the way, settlers and citizens came out to see them. At first the crowds were hostile. Further east, they were greeted by thousands of curious, even adoring Americans.

"The friendly crowds restored Black Hawk's dignity. He responded to the adoration with pride, waving in acknowledgment. Newspapers reported his progress. His reputation as a vicious warrior didn't match the old man parading by.

"In Washington City, he was invited to the President's House. He met with Andrew Jackson and Secretary of War, Lewis Cass. It is reported they treated him with respect. Had I been present I would have had trouble not calling the President a charlatan. Every fiber in his body is hostile to the Indians. He has ordered their removal by any means necessary, including warfare and indiscriminate murder.

"From the President's house, Black Hawk and his closest followers were taken to Fortress Monroe in Virginia. There they were once again held as prisoners. They were treated as if they were a carnival sideshow. Artists vied to paint their portraits. Black Hawk has been quoted as saying, 'How smooth must be the language of the whites, when they can make right look like wrong, and wrong like right.'

"One of the artists impressed me. George Catlin is traveling across the Great Plains to sketch Indians in their native settings. I have seen his work. It is honest, portraying a noble people. His painting of Black Hawk captures his dignity and pride.

"I have heard none of this," Seamus said. "Where were the crowds when Black Hawk waved his white flags? Will Americans ever know the truth?"

"I have given much thought to Black Hawk," Grege moaned. "It is not easy to understand the motives of either Black Hawk or the Americans.

"By 1832, the year of the Black Hawk War, most Indians east of the Mississippi had reluctantly accepted their fate. They realized they could not win a war against the Americans. Besides, they were becoming addicted to the white man's alcohol and guns. They were being exposed to white man's diseases. It ravaged their health and will to fight.

"Black Hawk felt betrayed. His land was being taken without his permission. He never accepted the treaties signed by others. It is debatable they even understood what they were giving away.

"Black Hawk is a wise man. Did he truly believe he could regain what had been taken from him and his people? I don't know. Could not the same thing be said of those who fought the War of Independence from Great Britain? They too were a rag-tag, undisciplined force fighting against a mighty nation. Yet they won. I doubt Black Hawk knew of them. Was he any different than them? I don't know."

"Where is Black Hawk now?" asked Seamus.

"After leaving Fortress Monroe in Virginia, they toured the east coast. It was a spectacle everywhere they went. Huge crowds turned out in New York, Baltimore and Philadelphia. He was greeted as a hero. Heading back west, his reception began to change. By the time he reached Detroit, he endured a crowd which hung and burned effigies of him."

"I find this all hard to believe," Seamus said. "Where is he now?"

"West of the Mississippi. Not far from where we are headed."

Seamus shook his head in disbelief. "Slim, but for the Good Lord and luck, this could have been the story of my life. Back home, the English are waging the same war of expulsion against Catholic Irishmen. Does the desire for land really justify murder?"

"The latest I have heard is even more incredulous," Grege continued. "I understand Black Hawk has told his life story to a government interpreter by the name of Antoine LeClaire. It is now being edited by a newspaper reporter named Patterson. It's to be published."

Two days later they reached the Mississippi. There, it took boats several days to ferry everything across. Some drivers chose to return to Chicago rather than risk the water crossing. Christian Dobson hired wagons and drivers on the west side to replace them. Grege and Seamus went on. The crossing was torturous, especially for the loaded wagons and horses.

The second day on the west side, Christian rode ahead to meet with the Indian Agent. He and the agent came back to escort the caravan to the lands promised. It would be the Indians's new, permanent home. As the agent and Chris rode into camp, Seamus could not believe his eyes. The Indian Agent was none other than Erasmus Jeremiah Fitchen!

Nudging Grege, Seamus pointed to the Indian Agent. "That's the bastard who stole from the Canal Commission! That's Fitchen!"

"Are you sure?"

"I'll never forget him. How'd he get appointed?"

"Probably bribed someone."

"Slim, we have to do something. He'll rob the Indians blind."

"We'll talk to Dobson."

The column reformed and moved on west. Two hours later they reached their new land. The prairie and patches of woods offered some hope. The drivers clustered the wagons. The Indian women set up their tents. Some of the warriors rode out to seek game. By sunset, temporary camp had been established.

Grege and Seamus sought out Christian Dobson. He and Fitchen were conversing by a fire. Seamus stood back in the shadows while Grege approached Dobson. Seamus could not hear them, but whatever he said, Dobson followed Grege to where Seamus stood.

"Seamus, tell Christian what you told me about Fitchen."

The tale came tumbling out. Chris' usually calm face reddened. He clenched and unclenched his fists. Seamus ended his report.

"I need to think about this. I don't have the authority to remove him. Perhaps I can borrow a page from Judge Lockwood. Meet me in the morning to plan the best way to do this."

In the morning, the three men rode to Fitchen's agency post. Seamus stayed out of sight. As they had planned, Chris introduced Grege as Chief Agent from Washington City.

"Mr. Fitchen, this is Chief Agent Grege."

Grege looked puzzled and asked Fitchen, "What is your full name?"

Confidently, he responded, "Erasmus Jeremiah Fitchen, sir."

"What happened to Herman Joost? My records show he is the Indian agent for this post."

Fitchen was caught off guard but regrouped. "Herman Joost died. I have been appointed in his place."

Grege demanded, "May I see your commission papers?"

"They were burned in an Indian attack?"

"Indian attack! There has been no report of an attack," Grege challenged. "Exactly who appointed you?"

"I can't recall his name." Fitchen looked as if he was seeking an escape route. He was sweating. He moved to the door. He froze. Blocking his way was Seamus.

"Still stealing, Erasmus?" Seamus mocked. "How much have you pocketed so far?"

Fitchen turned back to face Dobson and Grege. "Who is he to speak that way to me?"

Seamus laughed. Grege grabbed Fitchen by the collar and shoved him outside. Not letting go, he forced Fitchen to the agency barn and had him saddle his horse.

"You have exactly one minute to mount and ride out of here. If I see you again, anywhere, I will shoot to kill."

Fitchen had difficulty stepping into the stirrup. It was comical to see him shaking so he could not lift himself up and mount. Grege pushed him up and slapped the horse's flank. The horse jolted forward and galloped off. Fitchen shouted, "What of my belongings?"

Seamus could not stop laughing. Grege turned, "I will follow his tracks tomorrow and put a real scare into him."

The three men searched the agency post. Seamus found Fitchen's account book.

"Once a fool, always a fool. Just like before, he has recorded every penny he has stolen. He's been here only two months and already has taken over $8,000.

"The money must be here somewhere."

It didn't take long before they found a loose board in the floor. Lifting it, they pulled out a carpet bag filled with gold and notes.

Later in the day Chris asked Grege, "Would you be willing to serve until a new agent can be appointed?"

Grege was surprised by the question. "Let me sleep on it."

Chris added, "I am sure you would be paid for the duration of your service. We'll talk in the morning."

Grege and Seamus were at their campfire when the young Indian, who had visited them back on the prairie in Chicago, appeared. He asked if he could speak.

Grege invited him to sit. He did not draw his gun.

"I have given much thought to what you said. I shall never forget. I do not know the future but I can go into it knowing there are some good white men."

With that he stood and walked into the dark.

The next morning, Seamus joined Grege. They saddled two horses from the agent's corral and rode a short distance in the direction Fitchen had taken. Grege stopped, dismounted and began to walk, carefully studying the ground.

Puzzled, Seamus asked, "What are you doing?"

"There were too many tracks near the agent's post. By circling I am looking for Fitchen's tracks. One of his horse's hooves has a peculiar mark making it easy to identify. There, see it?"

Seamus could not even see the hoof track, let alone the mark.

Pulling up, Grege turned north and set out. Seamus followed. Within an hour, they heard screaming.

They dismounted, hitched their horses in a grove of trees and began to cautiously walk toward the sound. In minutes they came to a dip in the prairie. At the bottom were a dozen or so young Indians. They were performing some sort of ritual. The screaming rose from their midst. Lying in the grass on the edge of the hollow, Seamus and Grege silently watched until the Indians seemed to lose interest and began to leave. Their horses were on the far side. They had left behind a bloody carcass.

Grege gasped, "It's Fitchen. He's tied down to stakes. They have been cutting strips of flesh from his naked body. The Indians have had their fun. Either Fitchen has died or passed out. It explains the end of the screaming.

"We need to wait until we are sure the Indians will not return. There were more than the two of us can handle."

After what, to Seamus, seemed an eternity, Grege pointed to the sky. "Those are vultures. They are circling to be sure it is safe to land. When they do, we will know it is safe for us as well and we can see if we can save Fitchen."

In minutes, the grotesque birds landed and walked awkwardly toward the carcass. Jumping up, Grege ran down into the dip, throwing small stones at the birds. They took flight. Kneeling at Fitchen's side, Grege felt his neck.

"He's dead."

Seamus was standing back, sickened by the bloody body. His scalp had been viciously cut off. All but his face had been mutilated. Flies abounded on the flesh. Fitchen's face was frozen in a grimace, his mouth gaping, caught mid-scream.

"The vultures are circling above us," Seamus whispered. "What should we do?"

"Not much we can do. If we go back to the post to get shovels, by the time we get back, only his bones will be left. There are not enough rocks to cover him. I don't want to take the time to dig a grave with our hands. We need to get out of here before we have an encounter with any Indians. The bucks seemed quite young. They may bring warriors back to see their handy work. Not the way I want to introduce myself to my new responsibility."

"So you have decided to accept Dobson's offer to become the Indian Agent?"

"I have. It's an opportunity for me to try and make amends. I can't change the past but perhaps the future."

Chapter Nineteen

Seamus had slept in the empty wagon on straw to be used to feed the horses. It was his best night since leaving Chicago. He had woken during the night. Overhead the beauty of the stars reminded him of his mother and the night he woke, frightened. He was five or six. He went to his mother. She calmed him and took him outside into the blackness of night.

"Look up, Seamus." He had never been up so late. The sky was a sea of sparkles. They were like dew drops on the fields capturing the morning sun, only brighter.

"Seamus, the stars are always above. We can't see them during the day, but they are there. We can't see them on cloudy nights, but they are there. When things are dark for you. When you are afraid. When you are lost. Remember, the stars are always with you. They are one of the signs God has to remind us he will always be with us." As when he was a child, Seamus went back to sleep.

The smell of the campfire and bacon combined with the sunrise woke Seamus. He put on his boots, brushed off the hay and joined Grege.

Grege greeted him with a question. "Would you be willing to stay and help me?"

Conflicted, Seamus was silent.

"I know you have a job back in Chicago. You could send a letter back with the returning wagons asking for more time. I could use your help establishing the financial records. And to help me think through how I will help the Indians adjust to the new land. How to parcel it out? Or perhaps let them tell me. I have complained about our government's treatment of the natives. This would be my chance to do better."

Still, Seamus was silent.

"You could stay for just a month or so. By then, I might well be replaced. Or the Canal Commission may demand your return. Or you might find you don't like the situation here.

"I need your honesty, Seamus. Not just in handling money, Lord knows how important that is. But to challenge me and my thinking. My years in the military have made me rigid about following rules and procedures. This demands new ways of thinking. You can help me see the new ways."

Reluctantly, Seamus agreed to stay a month.

Christian Dobson was delighted. He spent an hour going over what little he knew about the Indian Agency. He promised to write the government as soon as possible to explain the situation and recommend Grege for appointment as the permanent Indian Agent. He then excused himself to organize the wagons and drivers for their return. The wagon train pulled out several hours later, leaving Grege and Seamus behind.

"Seems like he wants to get out of here before you change your mind," Seamus observed.

"Probably so."

The two went through everything in Fitchen's office. They found the paper appointing Herman Joost as Indian Agent. They found the orders he had received which described in agonizing detail the functions of an Indian Agent. They found a box with directions, rules, regulations, forms and manuals. Their heads spun the more they read.

They also found a journal Fitchen had written. It began with his dismissal as director of the Canal Commission by Judge Lockwood. Seamus stopped to read it. His face grew almost as red as his hair.

"Listen to this." He read from the Fitchen's journal.

After three years of faithful service in managing the business end of the Illinois and Michigan Canal Commission, I was unjustly forced from my position as Director. My creative and tenacious work was twisted to appear as fraudulent. The charges leveled against me by Judge Lockwood are so false they can only be compared to those which led to Jesus being crucified. Never has anyone since then been so wrongly treated.

I was forced to leave Illinois. I was taken by guards to the Mississippi River. I was manhandled onto a ferry with my horse and taken across the river into the Iowa Territory.

After several days in Iowa, I came upon Herman Joost, who had been appointed as Indian Agent for the area. He showed me his letter of appointment, very proud of his new position. The fool invited me to join him in his journey west.

He had several pack horses to carry his belongings including, I was to discover, a cache of gold. That very night, after we had bedded down, I went through his bags. That was when I found the gold. Just as I put my hands on it, he confronted me with his gun in his hand. I tried to explain my curiosity. He would have none of it and ordered me to mount my horse and leave.

I rolled up my few items in my blanket. As I placed the bundle on my horse, I pulled my pistol, turned and confronted him. He had the temerity to fire upon me. He missed. I did not. Mine was a lucky shot – pierced his heart. He fell dead.

I stripped him of his gun, wallet and fine boots. We had camped aside a stream. I pulled his body to the edge, pushed him over the bank onto the soft sandy bottom. I used my horse to stomp the high bank down over his body, completely burying him.

I lay down for a good night's rest. In the morning I headed on to the Agency post. Joost had shown me the map so it was easy to follow. No one was present, the door unlocked. I unpacked, and now am the official Indian Agent.

I stopped reading. Scanning ahead, the rest consisted of daily events leading up to our arrival. I turned to Grege and said: "I can't believe his greed, his evilness. When we came upon where he had been tied to the stakes by the Indians, I had felt sorry for him. After reading this....I feel..."

Grege finished, "He got what he deserved."

Picking up the papers they had been reading before Seamus found Fitchen's journal, Grege commented on the rules and regulations for Indian Agents.

"This all is Washington City's way of protecting themselves from any blame for what an agent might encounter," Grege said, rubbing his forehead.

"Seems so," Seamus said. "Slim, I think the Commissioner is confused. Must be difficult to try and describe the right thing for an agent to do when the President doesn't want the right thing done."

Grege nodded, put down the papers and said, "We need to eat. Looks like the place is well stocked."

In an attempt to encourage Grege, Seamus offered, "When they get the message of your name, they'll appoint you. With your military history, they'll trust you. A military man knows how to keep the Indians under control. They will expect you won't mollycoddle them. They will presume you will follow the rules rather than do what is right. By the time they discover what you are doing, one of two things will happen. You'll either be removed or kept on. Either way, this is your chance to try."

"You may be right, Seamus. In the meantime, we need to divide the work. I'd like you to set up the books, write my reports and attend every meeting I have with the chiefs. I need you to hear them so you and I can discuss options.

"I will spend as much time as I can with the Indians. To walk the land with them. To learn their way of thinking. They need to learn to trust me and you."

It was three weeks before a message arrived from the Chairman of the Canal Commissioners, encouraging Seamus to stay in Iowa to assist Grege as long as it is necessary. Mr. O'Malley concluded his letter saying, "Seamus, you are a valuable asset to the Commission. I pray you will return to work for us when your work in the Iowa Territory is finished."

With each day, Seamus and Grege made progress in their meetings with the Indians. At first, communication was difficult. That was until an old Indian guide turned up at the Agency. Neither Grege nor Seamus could understand or pronounce his name. It was Seamus who first called him "Our old man." He spoke English and was willing to serve as a translator. The Indians called Grege, "Stern Good Man," and Seamus, "Fire on Scalp."

Not a day went by without Seamus thinking of Molly. Had she written to him? At last, although he found working with Grege both satisfying and exciting, he decided to return to Chicago. That night, after dinner, he told Grege, "As much as I wish to stay, it is time I go back home."

"I knew this day would come, my friend. None of what I have accomplished would have been possible without you at my side. I shall miss you, Fire on Scalp."

The next morning, Seamus left. Riding east, several times he saw groups of braves. The second time he realized they were guarding him, a sign of their respect. A week later, as he approached Chicago, Seamus reflected on his role in helping the Potawatomi adjust to their new home. Grege's words haunted him. "This is not the final move. As more Americans move west, they will want the Iowa Territory freed of Indians as well. And so on until....until, I don't want to think of the end for our friends."

Part Six

Winter

Chapter Twenty

The winter of 1833-1834 was severe, even for those used to the rough winters of the past. Snow began to fall in late November and continued on and off for months. There were no thaws to tease of warmer weather to come. In early January a sleet storm coated the blanket of snow, forming an almost impenetrable surface. Children delighted in walking atop the piled high snow, coming upon familiar objects, and looking down at them. Down at the barely visible hitching posts in front of the Sauganash. Down into windows usually too high for them to see through. Down at the Frog Creek sign, barely poking up through a drift.

Little Joey was popular with his friends since he had a sled his father had made for him. He would climb up to the top of one of the largest snow drifts and gleefully slide down the side, coasting some distance before coming to a stop. It was a challenge climbing back up to the top on the slippery, sleet-coated mound. His friends laughed as Joey's feet could find no purchase and he glided backward. Temperatures had dropped after the sleet storm so the surface was not only icy but rock hard.

It was Joey's turn to laugh when each of his friends tried to scale their mountain, only to find it nearly impossible. It was Buck, a half-breed, who came up with the solution. He ran to get a long rope. Tying it to the trunk of the tree on the far side of their snow pile, the boys could pull themselves to the top, teeter the sled on the peak, lay down on their belly, let go of the rope and have the ride of their lives.

The boys argued over who had glided the farthest. Buck slammed his heel into the surface to mark how far he had ridden. Joey tried to beat him, using his hands to "paddle" his way farther. He succeeded but Buck argued he had cheated. Stony, a very large child who had difficulty balancing on the sled, sided with Buck. "Ain't fair to use ya hands," Stony declared. Marty sided with Joey. The four argued for some minutes, until it was Stony who announced, "I'm going home. I'm cold and hungry." Realizing he was losing his ally, Buck said, "This taint fun no more," and left as well. Marty, shivering, also left. Joey tried one more run but without his friends it was no longer fun. He too went home.

Seamus had been watching the boys from the window of his small cabin. He wished he could have done that when he was a kid. He never saw snow until he came to America. Shrugging, he sat near the fireplace for warmth. His wood supply was dangerously low. His funds were nearly gone. He had tried to cut down the tree out back. He could not. It was as frozen as everything else. Seamus had returned from the Iowa Territory in late November. He had reopened the Canal Commission's Chicago office. The influx of new settlers had ended for the winter so there were few sales of Canal lots to handle. He was paid only a fraction of his salary during the winter months. Not even enough to pay for three meals a day.

Seamus had withdrawn the last of his money from the bank. On his last visit to the bank, Axel had invited him to his office.

"Seamus, I understand you have closed your account. Where did all your money go?"

Seamus stiffened. "What business is it of yours? Must I explain my needs to you?"

Axel was surprised with Seamus' reaction even though he realized that as a banker he had overstepped his bounds.

"I am sorry for the way I sounded. I asked as your friend, not as your banker. Can I help you?"

Calming down, Seamus responded, "I suppose. I am on one-quarter pay for the winter and can't find work."

Cautiously, Axel asked, "When you left for Iowa, your account was quite substantial. It should have been more than enough for your needs."

"Damn it, you Kraut. It's none of your damn business how I spend my money." With that Seamus stood and angrily left the bank.

Reinhold, having overheard the exchange, came to Axel's office. "I think I can answer your question, Axel."

Waving his hand for Reinhold to sit down, Axel said, "Please do."

"Twice, while he was in Iowa, Seamus wrote to ask me to send him half of his funds. In his second letter, he made reference to giving it to Colonel Grege to set up a special fund for the Indians. I kept a small amount in his account before the second withdrawal. I had a chat with him the other day. He feels so sorry for the Indians he wants to help them any way he can."

"Has he now used the small amount left?"

"Yes."

"Any suggestion how I could help him?"

"Might ask Frau Konrad to invite him for dinner now and then"

Smiling, Axel said, "I shall. Any other thoughts?"

"Well, yes. When he was coming in to take out small amounts since he got back from Iowa, I never told him he was out of money. We could put money into his account and I tell him I made a mistake in our record?"

"Don't you think he will see through the action?"

"He might, Axel, but he is desperate and it would allow him to save face."

"Please add money from my personal account. Could you find a way to tell Seamus?"

"I will."

"Any other suggestions?"

"Can you think of someone who could hire him for a few months?"

"Good thought. Johann Wellmacher or John Wright might need help. I'll talk to them."

A week later, Lina succeeded in getting Seamus to come to dinner. Anna had not really had a chance to get to know Seamus. Her English was still limited. Seamus spoke in his rudimentary German with help in translating by Lina and me. It was a pleasant evening. Each time she sensed Axel was about to talk money, she quickly intervened.

Seamus entertained everyone telling of his Iowa experiences. Lina encouraged and praised him. When he talked of contributing his funds to the Indians, she celebrated his kindness.

When he told about Erasmus, he left out the torture and the killing of Herman Joost. "He was evil to the core. Hard to understand what drives men to such vile acts."

Dinner with Lina and Axel became a regular event. During their third dinner, Seamus asked Axel how his bank was doing and what happened in his absence. Lina listened carefully, to thwart her husband from turning to Seamus' need for funds.

Axel began, "It has been an unusual autumn and winter so far. Autumn was mild and seemed reluctant to leave, only to be followed by this unrelenting snow. Business has slowed down at the bank. It has given me the chance to visit many of the businesses to assess their needs. I have also been in correspondence with our representative to

Congress to learn of any pending Federal actions which might impact Chicago.

"The bank has approved several loans for exciting projects. Do you know John Planck?"

"Can't say I do."

"He's a German immigrant. Member of our German Lutheran group. The bank approved a loan for him to open a tavern in Dutchman's Point."

"Where is that?"

"Northwest of Chicago. Not too far."

"A tavern? You in favor of taverns now?"

"One of the conditions we imposed is it also be an inn. I am convinced it is a solid loan. Need some of them to keep the bank running.

"Also approved a loan to a group of business men to establish a water company to haul fresh water to residents. We'll have to see how that goes. Good water is needed but I am not sure this is the route to take.

"The Village of Chicago has also asked for a loan. This is a first. Should be a solid investment for us.

"We approved a request by two men for a loan to start their business to build wagons and carriages.

"We have approved loans for both the Presbyterians and the Baptists to build their first churches. These I really favor. We need to expand the number of churches in Chicago to try and counterbalance the growing number of taverns.

"I recently had the pleasure of meeting a new Chicagoan, Nelson Norton. He arrived in November and within weeks came to see me for a loan. He will be building a drawbridge at Dearborn Street to replace the ferry the village approved last summer. The bridge will further boost growth of Chicago north of the river."

Anna, who had been patiently sitting through all this, interrupted. "Little brother, should you be sharing this information with us. Shouldn't the bank's business be confidential?"

Seamus laughingly teased, "Little brother? Anna, Axel is anything but little."

"To me he shall always be my little brother."

Axel, suppressing a smile, responded. "I trust the three of you not to speak of these loans. Just catching Seamus up on all that has happened while he was chasing Indians."

Seamus turned to Lina. "When is the baby expected?"

"In the next few weeks. He is very rambunctious, kicking, eager to be born. Impatient, just like his father."

"A boy? How do you know?"

"Anna and I know," Lina said, blushing.

Walking back to his cabin, slipping and sliding on the icy path beaten down after each snow fall, Seamus looked up at the stars and said a prayer to his mother asking her to put in a good word for him. The stars, her stars, were being hidden for the most part by the rapidly passing clouds.

Back at his cabin, he stirred up the embers, added two small logs, settled down by the fireplace and reread all of Molly's letters. When he had returned from the Iowa Territory, John Hogan gave him five letters from Molly. Since then she had written three more times. He was not nearly as faithful in responding. He found expressing himself in writing much more difficult than in person. This evening, however, he was so moved by the stars, he went to his makeshift table, and wrote a long letter to Molly.

He began by telling what his mother had told him about the stars and compared it to his love of Molly even though they were apart. This was the first time he had so expressed himself this way. When he read what he had written so far, he almost threw it into the fire. Seamus decided to finish the letter in the morning and went to bed.

In the morning, he read what he had written. It was almost poetic and exactly what he had intended to write. He resumed writing, telling of his news, his dinners with Lina, Anna and Axel. He described the sleet storm and the snow. By this point, he realized he was searching for things to write and ended his letter and walked it to the Post Office to send it on its way.

John was excited. "Remember last summer how an unknown man was found dead, his throat cut and what appeared to be wounds from a pitch fork in his back? I think I know who it was. Got a letter addressed to the Postmaster from a Mr. Hesbitt of New York. His son is missing. He left New York in July, intending to come to Chicago. His son wrote to him from Detroit. He had spent the night there before continuing the lake route to Chicago. The father wrote to me, the Postmaster, asking if I had seen his son."

Seamus asked, "You think the son was the man who was killed? How can you know for sure?"

"The father described him. His son has one finger missing. He lost it when a cable snapped and sliced right through it. The dead man was missing a finger."

"That doesn't prove it was his son. The father write anything else?"

"Yes. Son also had a long scar on his left cheek, also from the cable. The dead man had such a scar."

"Father say how old his son was?"

"Twenty-five. I asked Doc. At the time he had estimated the body being in his mid-twenties."

Seamus asked further, "What became of the body?"

"He was buried on the river bank after a few prayers were said. Grave site wasn't marked since no one had claimed the body."

"You written back to the father?"

"Not yet. Not sure what to say."

Just then Axel entered the post office. John quickly told him the same story.

Axel suggested, "I think we should ask Philo and Doc to compose a letter since Doc examined the body and Philo said the prayers when the body was buried.

Further, Axel suggested, "Seems to me we need to belatedly investigate the murder to see if the culprit can be found."

Chapter Twenty One

Seamus, John and I burst into Philo and Doc's cabin, hot to pursue the murder. Luckily both were there, neither was busy. After telling of the letter from Mr. Nesbitt seeking his son and John's conclusion he was the unknown man murdered last August, we all calmed down. Doc was first, asking John for Mr. Nesbitt's letter so he could concentrate on the description of his son.

Doc seemed to take forever. He then went to his files and pulled out the notes he wrote at the time he examined the unidentified body. He spread them out on the table as we all hovered around. His notes included a detailed drawing of the severed neck and another of the back, showing the multiple puncture wounds in a precise row. He even had measured the distance between each wound, noting they were equidistant from one another. He had a third drawing of the face with several sketches of the long scar on the left cheek. Finally, he had a drawing of the full torso, neck and hand showing a finger was missing.

Doc again read the letter. It seemed clear to me the drawings were Mr. Nesbitt's son. Doc carefully put his notes and drawings back in their folder and returned them to his file. Turning to us he said, "I have no doubt whatsoever the body was that of Mr. Nesbitt's son.

"Doc," Seamus asked, "Which happened first, his neck being cut or the pitchfork stabbing him in the back."

"The neck. The pitchfork punctures were inflicted sometime later, as they drew very little blood. Most had been lost from the vicious neck wound. In fact, the neck was so deeply cut the head was almost severed from the body."

"Sounds like the murderer was either very angry or insane," Philo observed.

I remained silent. At the time of the discovery of the body, I had been plunged into deep anxiety. Could Rikert be in Chicago? Was this a signal to me he was still chasing me? Was he intent on harming me? Or, worse yet, Lina?

"Why would the murderer stab the man in the back after he was dead?" asked Seamus.

The question just hung in the air. We all remained silent.

After what seemed an eternity, during which I was ready to burst, Philo spoke. "I think we should present this to the village officials for their guidance."

I asked, "Do either of you recall precisely where he was buried? The father said if his son was dead, he would like to take his remains back to New York for burial in the family plot."

"I think I could find the location but not until the snow is gone and the ground thawed," Philo replied.

My anxiety was resurrected. The village officials expressed remorse but provided neither guidance nor took any initiative. It was left to us. Philo wrote to Mr. Nesbitt. Doc included a brief description of the body, writing in only general terms, omitting any mention of the wounds. Philo wrote the body could not be exhumed until the spring. Finally, he stated it was unknown who murdered his son or why.

From then on I never went anywhere without watching for Rikert. If he was in Chicago, I wanted to know so I could protect Lina, Anna and myself. I decided not to tell my wife or sister. I certainly didn't want to excite Lina now that the baby was about to be born. Nor tell Anna who came all the way to America to flee the nightmare of Rikert back in Germany.

Simultaneously, I anticipated the birth of our son. The waning days of January brought even more snow. Anna was now in charge, doing the cooking, washing and housekeeping. Lina insisted she help. Anna gently pushed her aside or gave her sewing projects to work on. February began. Now was the time. Nothing. Each morning I prayed this would be the day. It wasn't. The first week passed, then the second, then, at last, the day came, February 22, 1834. Lina and Anna were calm. I was not. Anna took charge and told me to go to the bank. The minutes passed as if the clock were not moving. At noon, I went upstairs for lunch and was rather brusquely told by Anna to go eat at the pub.

I meekly went back downstairs, the sound of Lina moaning in the bedroom haunting me. I decided not to go eat. I might be needed. About three in the afternoon, Anna came down to tell me it was time to get Doc. I rather stupidly asked, "Why? Is something wrong?" Anna huffed, told me to get him and went back upstairs.

Doc came, would not talk to me, went upstairs and my wait continued. Reinhold knew enough not to talk to me. There was little business, in fact not much so far this year. The snow, cold and wind had virtually paralyzed our village. No one ventured out except for food, firewood or church. Mark Beaubien once told me he made his money between April and Christmas. "The winter months are deadly for business."

Half past six, Doc came down the inner stairway, smiling. "You may go up now to see your son. A healthy boy. Lina is fine. She did well and is asking for you. Congratulations Papa!"

Usually undemonstrative, I hugged Doc, thanked him profusely and ran up the stairs. I made it halfway up before coming back down to let Doc out and relock the bank door. Upstairs, I burst into the apartment. Anna was there to slow me down.

"Now, little brother, you need to learn to be calm and patient. Your son is resting."

I tiptoed into the bedroom. Lina was propped up, looking remarkably fresh, smiling. At her side was our son. He is beautiful with wisps of blond hair, his face soft and angelic, his eyes closed in sweet sleep.

I bent over and kissed Lina on the cheek and whispered, "I love you."

Lina replied, "This is your son, Paul Heinrich Konrad."

All I could think was his name was bigger than he. We decided to call him Henry. For weeks, I had no thoughts of Rikert. I forgot all about him until April when another corpse was found. This time an older man shot in the chest several times. He was found near the site of where the corpse of Jerrod Nesbitt's body had been buried.

Mr. Nesbitt had come to Chicago as soon as lake traffic had resumed. He had his son exhumed and took him back to New York. The whole incident drew folks to the site and the digging. Mr. Nesbitt was stoic as tears ran down his face unabated. There was nothing we could do. It was not easy for any of us.

Then, just weeks later, the old man was found. Right where Mr. Nesbitt's son had been. Whoever killed the old man was deliberate in the placement of the body. When Doc examined it, he found the signature puncture wounds in the man's back.

This time I told Doc, Seamus and Philo the story of Rikert and his near death at my hands. Doc confirmed the man had died almost instantly from the gun shots and the stabbing in the back was inflicted much later. When I finished telling of Rikert, the three were ashen. They agreed with my conclusion that Rikert must be behind the murders. It was Seamus who suggested, "Could it be Rikert is not in Chicago, and has hired someone to come here and commit these murders?"

Philo said, "I suppose it is possible. If Rikert is as insane as you describe him, I would think he is here to relish the acts of violence and their impact on you, Axel. You have not seen him here in Chicago?"

"No, I haven't. Back in August I was constantly on the lookout for Rikert. With each passing month I calmed down. I can understand not seeing Rikert over winter. None of us have been out more than absolutely necessary. If he was here last autumn and now here this spring, he is making himself scarce."

"I think you should tell your wife and sister," Philo said. "I'm serious, Axel. Not only you need to be watchful. They also need to be alert to possible threats, especially to your baby son."

That evening, after dinner, when Henry had been put to bed, I brought up Rikert.

"I am very sorry to shatter our bliss." I measured my words carefully. "I need to tell you of a possible threat to our lives. Last August an unidentified man was found dead. His throat had been cut. When Doc examined the body, he discovered a row of wounds in his back. They were made after the man had been killed. Doc measured them and concluded they had been made by the tines of a pitchfork."

Anna gasped. Lina turned pale.

"At the time I worried the man might have been killed by Rikert. I became very concerned and looked at every man in town twice to see if any might be him. After a month or so, I was convinced it was a coincidence and put it out of my mind.

"Recently, John Hogan got a letter from a Mr. Nesbitt of New York asking if his son, who was headed to Chicago, might have been seen. He described him. John realized the description given by the father matched the unidentified man. John, Seamus and I went to see Doc who pulled out his file on the corpse. His sketches and details were the same as given by the father in his letter.

"You may recall that just a few weeks ago, Mr. Nesbitt came to retrieve his son's body. Philo had answered his letter suggesting he not come until the spring. The body was exhumed and taken back east by Mr. Nesbitt.

"Yesterday a second corpse was found. This time an older man who had been shot in the chest. When Doc examined him, he found the same wounds on the back done by a pitchfork. What makes it even more sinister, the body was found on the river bank where Mr. Nesbitt's son had been buried.

"I am convinced Rikert is behind both murders. I believe he is using them to send a warning of some sort to me. Since I have not seen Rikert in all these months, it is possible, I suppose, he is still in New York and has hired someone to commit these heinous acts on his behalf to terrify us. I am afraid, however, it is more likely Rikert is here in Chicago.

"We must be extremely careful. I don't want either of you to go out without the other, or with someone else to escort you. We must always keep the doors to our apartment locked and never open them without knowing who is calling.

"I know you left home, Anna, to get away from Rikert. I am so sorry he followed us to America. His vile acts are most likely intended to frighten us. They have done just the opposite. They have warned us and put us on guard. We all have an inner strength and faith in God which will see us through this.

"If you see anything which frightens you or you suspect anything, tell me. Together we can defeat Rikert once and for all.

"Until we do, I have talked with several men I trust implicitly to guard us day and night. They will not intrude on our daily lives."

Lina responded, "Thank you for telling us, Axel. Anna, I am so sorry this must still haunt you. Perhaps I am being selfish to be more thankful than ever you are here."

Anna, who had hardly moved or blinked while I had talked, seemed to mentally shake herself and said, "Lina, Axel, please don't worry about me. I am strong. No matter how long it takes, even years, if he is here in Chicago, we will find him and rid ourselves of this ungeheuer."

Chapter Twenty Two

In mid-January, 1834, a few days after Seamus' first dinner with Lina, Anna and me, I found work for Seamus. I first went to John Hogan to see if he could use help. John was sympathetic but needed no assistance. Next, I asked Johann if he could use Seamus in his bakery. Johann immediately responded he needed someone who spoke German. I told him Seamus spoke German. Johann just stared at me, his face slowly reddening. When I asked him if he was not feeling well, Johann angrily responded, "I won't have no damn Irishman." I was shocked with both his vehemence and his prejudice. I wanted to argue with him. Remaining silent, however, I left after buying a cookie to make amends.

I had success with John Wright. He had opened his second store on the north side of the river and was in need of help in his original store on the south side. He got excited when I described Seamus' experience in keeping books, writing reports and at ease with people.

"Business is slow up north. I need to spend more time there to train staff and drum up customers. I could use a good worker for the days I am in the new store."

After Johann's reaction to hiring an Irishman, I felt I needed to tell John Wright about Seamus. "Seamus is from Ireland. Does that make a difference to you?"

A puzzled look came to John's face. "Why, should it?"

"It shouldn't, but many refuse to hire the Irish. At least that was the way it was in New York."

"Not here. Not with me."

"Thank you, John. One thing. Seamus is proud and might feel offended if he knew I was looking for a job for him. Would you mind asking him directly?"

"I will. I don't know him. How can I meet him?"

"Every Wednesday evening Seamus has dinner with us. If you would be kind enough to join us this week, you could bring up the need for help and go from there."

"Sounds good. What time?"

The evening went perfectly. John and Seamus hit it off. Afterward, Lina tickled me, which always makes me giggle and laugh. "You are crafty, Axey. You invited John just so he could ask Seamus to work for him."

"How did you figure it out?"

"I could tell. You are a very good man."

Several weeks later, John stopped to make his latest deposit in the bank. "Thank you for recommending Seamus. He works hard and has brought laughter to the store. Customers love him and are buying more. Seamus has even figured out what items aren't selling and put them together on a small table with a sign that reads: 'Sale. All prices drastically cut.'

"I can't believe how the customers are buying the items. Not sure they need any of them. They can't resist a sale. Your friend is a natural."

At the end of the day a week later, as Reinhold and I went over the day's transactions, he told me Seamus had been in the bank. "He deposited twenty-five dollars. He told me he has a job at Wright's store and has more money than he needs."

"That is good news."

Reinhold smiled and asked, "Did you arrange for Seamus to be hired by John Wright?"

"Lina invited John to our regular dinner with Seamus. John was taken by Seamus. It went from there. Speaking of Seamus, did he ever question the money you put in his account when he had drained all his funds from the bank?"

"He didn't ask any questions. I guess I was believable expressing my embarrassment admitting I had made a mistake in his account balance. I think the clincher was when I asked him not to mention it to you or you might dismiss me."

"Reinhold, you are getting as crafty as I am."

Impulsively, when we closed the bank, I invited Reinhold to join us for dinner. Lina never fusses when I do, always welcoming him warmly.

After a hearty meal, I announced, "Lina, this evening is my weekly meeting of the Lyceum." I noticed Lina fleetingly frown before quickly masking it.

"Dress warmly, it's cold and snowy."

As Reinhold and I descended the stairs to the outside, I said, "Why don't you join me. You might enjoy the meeting." Reinhold agreed. Walking to Cook's Coffee House, he asked me what the meeting was about.

"Philo and I, together with several others, began the Lyceum last month. There are a dozen members so far. We meet weekly to discuss issues of the day. Tonight's topic is the relationship between Chicago and the State of Illinois. What are the responsibilities of each?

"Each week we select a topic for the following week and name who will lead the discussion. Tonight it will be David Hall."

The wind and snow were fierce as we walked. I slipped on the ice-covered board walkway and almost fell to the snow below. Reinhold's quick grasp of my arm saved me from harm. The heat from the fireplace welcomed us as we entered Cook's.

David Hall greeted Reinhold, "I don't believe I know you."

Reinhold extended his hand. "My name is Reinhold Schwoulp. I work at the bank."

"Come join us near the fire." He introduced Reinhold to the Lyceum members, including Philo and Doc.

"Before we begin our discussion of issues between Chicago and the State, Philo would like to bring up an issue. Philo."

"I suggest the Lyceum create a library. I have a few books I would like to contribute. On nights like this, I find myself reading my books for the third or fourth time. If we all contributed our books and advertised for others, each of us could expand our reading options."

John Noble responded vigorously. "I agree. I have read my books so often, I can quote some passages verbatim. I have five books I'd be glad to add to the collection."

Doc said, "I have some."

Anson Taylor asked, "Medical books? Not sure I'd read them."

"No, some solid literature."

I agreed and asked Philo, "You mentioned advertising. In the *Chicago Democrat*?"

"Exactly."

"If we are in agreement, gentlemen, could I see a show of hands?" David asked. It was unanimous, including Reinhold.

Our discussion of the topic of the night was one sided. There was general agreement we wanted Chicago to be independent of the State except when we need the State to fund improvements such as paving the streets, building bridges over the river and keeping the peace in the settlements beginning to develop outside of Chicago.

After the meeting ended, Reinhold told me he found it interesting and would like to attend in the future. Bracing ourselves against the wind and snow, we had walked only a short distance before I noticed flames rising from Lotus' cabin. I shouted, "Fire!" I ran to the front porch. Reinhold and several others were right behind me.

The heat was already intense. I kicked on the door. It didn't move.

Shouting against the wind, I attempted to ask, "Does anyone live here since Lotus moved to the Sands?"

Turning around, all I saw were blank faces. No one knew.

"We need to be sure there is no one inside."

John Noble called against the roar of the wind and fire, "Help me pull the hitching rail free." Several men grabbed hold and dislodged it. Taking the rail, they rammed it into the door which swung inward. The fire was raging at the back of the cabin. I pulled my coat over my head, entered and looked into the each room. I began to inhale smoke. It made me choke and gag. My eyes watered and my skin felt as if it would melt. The noise of the flames deafened the shouts of the others.

In the small room to the right, I saw a body on the floor. Kneeling at its side, I could not tell if the man was unconscious from the smoke or already dead. I lifted him up, staggered, overcome by the smoke. It took Doc and Reinhold to pull me out, along with my load.

My coat was on fire. Without any hesitancy, they knocked me off my feet and rolled me in the snow. The body fell to the side, smoldering, having caught fire from my clothing.

My mouth was open as I gasped for air. As I was rolled over, a second time, my face pushed into the snow, filling my mouth. What a blessing. The cold soothed my parched mouth and hot cheeks. Behind me, the roar increased in intensity. Sitting up, I watched with the others as the porch fell, the roof collapsed and the flames lit up the sky. The logs burned well into the next day until all that remained was the stone fireplace and chimney.

I looked for the man I had pulled from the fire. He was to my left, steam rising from the singed clothing. Pointing at the body, I asked, "Doc, is he alive?"

"No."

"Doc, is he anyone we know?"

"I can't tell. He has been dead for some months."

Doc called to the others and asked them to help me to his office and to bring the corpse as well."

From that day on I became an avid supporter and member of the Washington Volunteers, Chicago's first fire department. When Gurdon

Hubbard proposed to sell a fire wagon to the city, I contributed much of the $894.38 cost.

I tried to minimize the event when Lina learned of my misguided heroism. Nothing, however, remains secret in Chicago. She chided me. I could tell she was proud of my concern for others even though, in this case, there was no one in danger other than myself.

Two days after the fire, I went to see Doc to ask about the corpse.

"Axel, I am afraid we have another pitchfork murder. No way to identify who the man was. I'm afraid there is no mistaking the pitchfork puncture wounds in his back. My guess is he has been dead between three to five months."

Counting backwards, I figured he was murdered sometime between last August and October. This makes the total of known pitchfork murders to be three. When will they cease?

Chapter Twenty Three

Lina had written to her mother in late December telling her the baby was due in February. She asked her to come be with us in the spring. Each of Minnie's letters after that included advice on pregnancy and birthing. Lina considered it all respectfully without being frightened by the warnings. Lina had not needed any of the remedies Minnie had suggested for when Little Henry would not sleep and cried a lot. Henry is a very happy baby. He is already smiling. Now with the worst of winter past and the days getting longer, we take him out for a ride in his carriage. It was Seamus who told us about a baby carriage for sale at Wright's General Store.

We couldn't go far. The mud came back with the first thaw. After our first outing, I began to laugh. "Lina, I can just imagine Henry coming home late from school, covered with mud and explaining he had been playing with his friends."

Much of the snow, which had hidden Chicago for months, was melted away by two days of torrential rain. The river rose three feet, flooding low-lying areas. Some had to move their homes. The streets, such as they were, became dangerous. The village leaders debated the need for laying wooden walkways. As they dithered with the cost, I worked behind the scenes to get several businessmen to secure lumber and begin constructing raised paths. I financed the cost with my own private funds. Everyone involved assumed the money was based on a loan. No one ever asked how the presumed loan was to be repaid.

In late March, Lina and I began to watch for the arrival of Minnie. I paid Joey to check the harbor each morning and evening for the sight of a ship. Late the afternoon of May 2, 1834, Joey came into the bank, breathless. He had run to give us the news.

"A ship is in the harbor. Unloading right now."

"Thank you Joey." I gave him a gold coin. He looked at it. Bit it.

"This is gold! Ain't never held gold. Thanks."

With that, Joey ran out.

I declared, "I will go to the dock to see if it's Minnie's ship which has arrived."

"Axel, I will go with you."

"No, dear. Not in this mud."

Not waiting for Lina to argue, I rushed out. The planked walkways were incomplete. I made good time until I would come to gaps where there still were no walks. Ahead was a carriage several blocks from the dock. Gurdon Hubbard was stepping down. I quickly asked, "Gurdon, might I ask your driver to take me to the harbor. My mother-in-law may be arriving and I would rather not have her walk to our home in this mud."

"You may. Boris, please take Mr. Konrad to the harbor and then to his home. Axel, don't hurry. I won't be leaving here for an hour or so."

The passengers were disembarking when I arrived. I was in time to see Minnie walking down the gangplank. To my surprise, behind her was Carsten Baruth.

I greeted my mother-in-law with a hearty hug. She kissed me on my cheeks. Her smile was as beautiful as my wife's. I welcomed Carsten. He asked me about Anna. He was nervous. He's going to ask Anna to marry him. Lina will never believe I, who never see romance, thought this.

Once their luggage was loaded and Minnie, Carsten and I were in the carriage, Boris took us home. On the way, the two nervously asked questions.

An anxious Minnie, asked "How is Paul Heinrich? How is Lina? Is she getting enough sleep? Is Paul Heinrich gaining weight?" She asked her questions so quickly, she did not pause for my answers. Carsten, politely waited but finally blurted out, "Do you think Anna will be pleased to see me? Does she ever speak of me? Should I not have come?"

I finally held up my hand. "All is fine. Everyone is well. Both will be very happy to see you."

Boris guided the carriage close to the elevated walkway in front of the bank. He opened the carriage door and helped Minnie out, then Carsten and finally, me. The coachman unloaded the baggage. In this flurry of activity, Lina and Anna appeared. Lina was holding our son. Little Henry reached his hand toward the horses. Anna was stunned, frozen, a smile emerging as she realized the significance of Carsten's appearance.

In minutes, everyone was in our apartment and Lina and Anna were serving coffee. Henry was delighted to be handed from Grandmother to Carsten to Anna to me and back to Lina. This was a good day.

At dinner, Anna asked, "You arrived in a fine carriage this afternoon. Is it yours Axel?"

"It belongs to Gurdon Hubbard. I borrowed it so Minnie and Carsten didn't have to slog through our mud."

"Who is Herr Hubbard?"

"An interesting fellow. He was born in Vermont. His father moved the family to Montreal where Gurdon worked in a hardware store. He came to Chicago at the age of 16 under contract to the American Fur Company. He was their agent here, trading with the Indians for furs. Married the young daughter of a Potawatomi Indian chief. They separated after the death of their two infants. Gurdon married a second time, four years ago. He and Eleanora moved to Chicago last year."

Anna interrupted to ask, "Is Eleanora also an Indian?"

"No, she's white. Gurdon now deals in real estate. As you can guess from his fine carriage, he is doing quite well. He has expanded his trading business into imported goods. He is currently building a warehouse. He is one of the bank's best customers.

"By the way, next month the harbor work should be completed. Ships will be able to navigate the Chicago River and dock inland from the lake."

Minnie asked, "Anna. How are you adjusting to Chicago?"

"I like it here. The people are friendly. I know enough English to have simple conversations with them. Lina and I go shopping together. We have a small group of Germans who attend informal German Lutheran services each Sunday. In its way, it is more meaningful to me than regular church services. I feel closer to God."

Curious, Minnie asked, "I noticed some rough looking men on the streets. They all had guns and knives hanging from their belts. Aren't you afraid of them?"

"Not really," Anna replied. "Some may not be very clean, but they all hold women in very high regard. There are so few of us, they treat us like one would a piece of fine porcelain."

Undeterred, Minnie asked, "I saw a woman dressed, ah, well, ah her dress was less than proper."

Lina, attempting to change the subject, asked if anyone wanted more berries and cream as she passed the bowl of strawberries and pitcher of cream.

Anna told of the general store with bolts of fabric to make one's own dresses. "They have some ready made items. Not very fashionable. We don't have occasions where we need a fancy dress. You asked how I am adjusting. I am comfortable here."

I asked, "Carsten, might I interest you in a brandy?"

He nodded yes, his expression indicating he would be happy to leave the women to their talk.

We sat in my den, relaxing as we sipped brandy.

"Axel, what do you do besides banking? I mean, are there any cultural events or societies?"

"There are. We have our first newspaper, the *Chicago Democrat.* First published last November. It has a political bias which sharpens the issues for me even if I don't agree with their stand. The owner is John Calhoun. If you can stay here for a few weeks, I'd like you to meet him.

"Calhoun does a good job reporting on the actions taken by the Village trustees. He has a sense of humor regarding their goings on. One of his recent reports was about an ordinance establishing a fine of two dollars for any hog found loose on the street without a nose ring.

"They passed another ordinance to stop river pollution. Calhoun noted it made no provision for detection or enforcement of the ordinance. Noble intention. I'm not sure it will achieve success.

"I am a member of the Chicago Temperance Society."

Smiling, Carsten lifted his brandy snifter in response.

"I know, I do drink on special occasions. I doubt the Society will achieve prohibition. No force will ever succeed in stopping all alcoholic drinks. If, however, the Society can cut down on excessive drinking, in my mind, that would be a victory." I paused before asking, "Tell me, do grocery stores in Cincinnati have sample rooms where men can imbibe in hard liquor to decide if they wish to buy a bottle?"

"Don't call them sample rooms. In Cincinnati, they're called backrooms. Really not much more than discreet taverns. Do you have any cultural events here in Chicago?"

"Up until recently, anything approaching culture has been limited to visits by traveling performers appearing in the Sauganash. Not long ago the Rialto on the west side of Dearborn Street between South Water and Lake was converted from an auction house to our first real theater. The name was changed to the Chicago Theater. It is owned and managed by Alexander McKenzie. His nephew, Joseph Jefferson, performs there whenever he is in town. I'll check their schedule to see when he is expected back. I'm told he is a good comedian with material suitable for the ladies.

"On a more sophisticated level, we have two discussion groups: Chicago Lyceum and Polemic Society of Chicago. I attend whenever I am interested in the topic to be discussed. Otherwise, most folks get their entertainment in one of the taverns."

I offered to refill Carsten's glass. He waved his hand no.

"Axel, I have a question to ask you. I understand your parents are still in Germany."

I nodded yes.

"You are Anna's only family in America. I could write to your father but it would take months before I would hear his answer."

Carsten paused. His face showed uncertainty. Sitting forward, he got to the point.

"I would like to ask Anna to marry me. May I have your permission to do so?"

How difficult to ask. It is a necessary ritual. It reduces men to stumbling awkwardness. My role, I realized, is to protect my sister.

"Carsten, nothing would make me happier. It is not my happiness that matters. Have you discussed this with Anna?"

"No, I thought I should ask your permission first."

"If you will, tell me your plans for the future. Would you live in Cincinnati? Can you support a family, should the two of you be blessed with children?"

"Would Anna and I live in Cincinnati? Only if she wishes to. I have been here for only a few hours and already sense the vitality and opportunity of Chicago. If Anna agrees to marry me, we would decide together where we should live.

"Can I support a family? I would do my best to do so. I have savings which are enough to establish myself and survive for a year or two. After that I will balance my goal to serve the poor with my need to earn money by serving the rich."

As Carsten spoke, his hesitancy melted away. He spoke with confidence and passion. I was pleased to respond. "I fully expect Anna will say yes to your proposal for marriage. I respect and admire you wishing to help the less fortunate. I, too, do my best help those least able.

"Anna will bring to your marriage a substantial dowry. Our parents have significant means. Barring an upheaval in Germany, I would expect our father would provide for both of you in the future, if the need arises."

Smiling, I added, "I probably should not say this. Anna is smitten with you. She talks of you each day and cherishes your letters. I wish you well and yes, you have my permission to ask Anna to become your wife. I appreciate you respecting me enough to ask for my permission."

The relief on Carsten's face almost made me laugh. Here I was, younger than he, yet he was nervous talking to me. I stood. He did. I reached out and offered my hand. He grasped it in a vigorous handshake.

"Carsten, I shall look forward to calling you brother.

Part Seven

The Sands

Chapter Twenty Four

S eamus, I would like to discuss your future with me. You have made my life manageable. Business at Wrights is booming. I know you came to work for me because of the slow down in your work for the Canal Commission in the winter. Your hours with them have increased with the arrival of spring.

"I guess what I am trying to say is, you will need to decide if you can continue to work for me or devote all your time to the Canal Commission."

"I know," Seamus responded. "John, I am not sure what I should do. I find working in the store to be more exciting than selling parcels of land. The Commission pays more. Could I think about it?"

"If you work with me, I would like you to take over and run my store on the north side."

"Run the store?"

"Yes. You would be in charge: order goods, set prices, hire staff, all it takes to manage the store."

"My pay?"

"Twenty five dollars a week. Eventually, I might be able to give you a share of the profits."

"Is the store making a profit now?"

"No. It is running slightly in the red as best I can tell."

Seamus ran his hand through his thatch of red hair, then tried in vain to smooth it out before he asked, "What is the amount of profit you are making on the main store?"

"It varies. During the winter months we're lucky if we make a hundred dollars a week. Last summer there were weeks when the profits were nearly five hundred a week."

Seamus did the math in his head. "When do you anticipate the northern store will begin to make a profit?"

"My guess? This summer."

Seamus extended his hand, saying, "Agreed. When do I begin?"

"Tomorrow. We can go to the store first thing in the morning. I'll introduce you to the clerks and show you the stock and books."

The next morning, mounting Tin Bucket, Seamus met John Wright at the main store and together they rode across the new bridge and headed north. Seamus had never ventured here before. There were far fewer buildings than south of the river. The land, for the most part, was either swampy or forested. Between the road and Lake Michigan was a sandy rise with tall grass. Just east of the road they passed a cluster of small cabins and shacks. Other than a few horses tied to hitching posts, there was no sign of life.

Seamus noticed the doors of each building were painted different colors or had decorative displays hung in their centers. Pointing to the hovels, he asked John, "What's all that?"

"The Sands. Unsavory businesses. Prostitutes mainly, some taverns, a few boarding houses. It's a blot on Chicago. Guess with so many men and so few women, it's inevitable. I heard such places follow the frontier. Hope they move on soon."

"Do any of them come into the store?"

"They do. Much as I would like to, I don't turn anyone away if they have money to spend. More than once I've had a gent come in after a night at the Sands, asking for credit. Hope that doesn't discourage you from taking over the store?"

"No. A deal is a deal. By the way, do you sell liquor?"

"I don't. Wish I didn't have to carry tonics. Many customers believe in tonic medicines. Another way for them to get their alcohol without thinking they are drinking.

"Here we are."

Seamus was surprised by both the size and sturdiness of the building. As the men dismounted and tied their horses to the hitching rail, Seamus studied the store. A wide porch stretched across the broad front with a roof, posts and three steps up from the road. There were several rocking chairs on the porch. The double doors were wide open. As they entered, Seamus breathed deeply. The fragrance of ground coffee, dill pickles and cinnamon was like perfume to him.

The board floor was spotless and the shelves neatly stocked. Behind the counter was a young man wearing a clean, white apron. Seamus entered ahead of John.

The clerk greeted him. "Welcome to Wrights, sir. May I help you?" Spotting John, the clerk quickly added, "Good morning Mr. Wright."

"Good morning Rupert. I would like you to meet Seamus O'Shea. He has agreed to help me out by running the store. Seamus, this is Rupert Rodgers. Rupert has worked here since I opened the store. He is invaluable and done well to establish the trade."

Seamus walked to the counter as Rupert stepped out from behind it. They shook hands, each a bit uncertain. Seamus smiled, saying, "I look forward to many good chats, Rupert. Afraid you will have to put up with my Irish humor and sayings. We should become good friends."

"Good to meet you Mr. O'Shea."

"Nay, none of that. Call me Red or Seamus."

John Wright interjected, "Rupert, would you mind answering Red's questions and showing him around. I need to get back to the main store. Nicky has decided to quit and go west. Not a total loss. I will need to find someone to take his place." With that, John left and rode off.

It was still early. There were no customers. Seamus suggested the two go sit in the rocking chairs and talk.

"I hope my becoming the manager doesn't sit wrong with you, Rupert."

"No, sir, it doesn't."

"None of that sir bit, Rupert. I'd wager you are older than me. Not 'til I'm fifty will it be time to be calling me sir.

"Let me tell you about myself. I don't drink. I am Catholic. I work hard. I am single for now. I've my wife picked out, just haven't asked her yet. She lives in New York.

"I like a man until he convinces me I should not.

"My mother used to tell me: As the old cock crows, the young cock learns. Rupert, you're not an old cock. I am young and need you to teach me everything about this store.

"Oh, I should mention, I will need a day or two off to go to Peoria and resign my position with the Canal Commission. I can do that next week. Canal business is slow in the winter. I've been working in Wright's main store. I have some familiarity with the business. I'll need your help and patience with me."

Rupert asked, "Were you born in Ireland, Red?"

"I was. Came to America in 1831. Best thing I ever did. Where were you born, Rupert?"

"Don't rightly know. I was raised in an orphanage in Detroit. Soon as I was old enough, I ran away and came to Chicago."

"I guess I'm sort of an orphan too. My Ma died when I was twelve. My Pa ran off when I was fourteen. Folks don't know how it is to have no Ma or Pa. My Pa was a drunk so I was alone as a kid, 'cept for my sisters."

"Your sisters here with you?"

"No, they're back in Ireland. I hope to bring them here soon."

"Here comes Miss Lotus. She lives in the Sands."

Seamus looked up. Though he never met Miss Lotus, he knew who she was and what she was. He was curious how Rupert would treat her.

"Good morning, Miss Lotus. You are up early. Our first customer of the day."

As Lotus came up the steps, Rupert introduced her to Seamus. "Miss Lotus, I'd like you to meet the new manager of Wrights. This is Red."

Seamus stood and took the hand Lotus offered. "Pleased to meet you Miss Lotus."

"It is a pleasure to meet you, Red."

Seamus was fascinated by her. Her dress was surprisingly modest. Her hand soft and gentle. Her smile engaging. Her hair neat. Her face was younger and less drawn than she had appeared when he last saw her from a distance.

After she left with her purchases, Rupert rejoined Seamus on the porch. Seamus asked, "What is she doing up north. Her business is on the other side of the river."

"Not any more. She moved up here some months ago. Her house is the finest, I'm told, in the Sands. First time she came to the store, she was not dressed like today. Something has happened. She seems more refined and subdued now."

"Interesting. Well, I suppose I need to get busy. Would you mind showing me the books?"

Inside the store, Rupert hemmed and hawed behind the counter until he pulled out a large box filled with many slips and scraps of paper. "I don't know how to keep books, Red. I have saved all the slips and bills and such. Dated them all. That's as far as I am able to go."

"Not to worry. John ever give you an account book?"

"Not sure." Again reaching under the counter, Rupert handed Red a large, leather-bound book.

Opening it, Seamus said, "Good. Do you have quill and ink and someplace in the back where I can work?"

"Follow me." Pushing aside a curtain, Rupert led the way through a storage area to a small office of sorts with a desk and chair and, thankfully, a window facing south.

"This is good," Red said. "I will get started sorting through your records and see what I can do to set up the account book. From time to time I will take a break so you can begin to show me the stock."

Seamus became so engrossed going through the receipts and bills, he was startled when a young woman came in with a tray.

"Excuse me, sir. Mr. Rupert sent me in with a bite for you to eat. Said to tell you it is well past meal time."

"Thank you. Who might you be, Miss?"

"Oh, I'm Tina. Tina Boland. I work next door at Miss Irene's Café."

"What do I owe you, Tina."

"Mr. Rupert put it on his bill."

Reaching into his pocket, Red handed Tina a coin. She blushed, curtsied and left.

After eating, Seamus went out to see Rupert. There were four customers, three waiting for Rupert to finish serving the first. Without a thought, Red stepped forward and asked, "May I serve whoever is next?"

Two men stepped forward at the same time, each saying, "I am." When each heard the other, they both stiffened, ready to fight. Red smiled, and said, "Gentlemen, this is a good afternoon. Wrights is pleased to serve both of you. Out of the corner of his eye he noticed Rupert had just finished with his customer.

Red said, "If one of you will tell me what you wish, Rupert with help the other."

The anger defused, one of the men stepped forward and asked Seamus if he would step over to the corner with him. He whispered, "I need underwear." Recognizing his embarrassment, Seamus whispered in response, "Forgive me, this is my first day. Do you know where the stock is kept?"

"Right behind you, you fool!"

Turning, Red said, "So it is. Thank you. Here, would you mind selecting the size you need. I'm a wee one. You being so big, you know what will fit you best. When I grow up, if I ever do, I hope I can be as tall as ye."

Relieved, the man smiled, reached to the shelf, selected two sets of long underwear and handed them to Red. "These is my usual. Now, I need some tobacky and couple bottles of Doc Luten's elixir tonic.

Red had noticed the tobacco in a jar on the counter and the elixir tonic in the store room. "One moment please."

Going in the storeroom, Red quickly wrapped the underwear in brown paper together with three bottles of the tonic. Back out, he said,

"Show me how much tobacky you want." With that, Red took the scoop in the jar and pulled it out full. "This enough?" The man nodded yes. Red put it in a small bag.

Knowing the stock from the main store, Red quickly jotted down the costs, added it up and said, "That will be a dollar and forty."

The man pulled out coins, carefully counted them out and handed them to Red who handed the bag and bundle to the man, whispering, "I put three bottles of the elixir in with your other purchase in the brown paper."

Smiling for the first time, the man thanked Red and noticed he had been served faster than the other man. As he left, he turned and said, "You know your business, Red."

Chapter Twenty Five

It was his fourth week at Wrights store near the Sands. Seamus enjoyed the work, the customers and the ride on Tin Bucket to and from the store. He and Rupert got along well. During slow times, they told each other of their pasts. Seamus, who was still only sixteen, almost lied about his age. He paused and finally said, "I'll be seventeen in December." Rupert did not react. He was eighteen. The two had a good laugh.

Thinking back, it wasn't until Seamus' third day that Clancy showed up. He was the other clerk. As Rupert rolled his eyes, Clancy made some lame excuse about his grandmother being sick. Red decided not to confront him about his absence, just made sure he docked his pay for two days.

Clancy was a large fellow. He was not very bright. Seamus guessed Clancy was in his mid-thirties. He seldom worked. Was so slow doing whatever Red asked of him, it got so Red stopped asking him. Of course, Seamus realized, that was just what Clancy wanted.

After a month, Red gave Rupert the day off, saying he had earned it. When Clancy showed up an hour late in the morning, Red said to him, "I presume when Mr. Wright hired you, he told you the days and hours you would work. Is that right?"

"Yes, he did."

"Do you realize you are expected to show up for work at eight in the morning?"

"Yes, I am."

"You didn't show up until quarter past nine this morning."

"I overslept."

"Your pay will be less for the hour you missed. I will excuse the fifteen minutes this time."

"Makes no never mind to me."

Later in the day, an Indian came in. Red was just coming out of the back. Since Clancy was behind the counter, he decided to see how he would handle the Indian.

The Indian stood patiently, waiting for Clancy to serve him. There were no other customers in the store. After ten minutes, the Indian turned to leave. Red stepped out and called to him, "May I help you, sir?"

The Indian turned and walked back, hesitantly.

In broken English, the Indian asked for ten cents of tobacco and a few pieces of candy. Red separately bagged the two items, asking for fifteen cents. The Indian handed him a beaver pelt. Red reopened the two bags and added to each, took the pelt and handed the bulging bags to the Indian who smiled slightly, nodded and walked out.

"Why didn't you ask the gentleman what he wanted?"

"He worn't no gentleman – he's a savage."

"That's it, Clancy. You don't work here anymore. Get out!"

Clancy didn't move. He got a vicious smile. "You and who else goin' to force me, you little Mick." As he growled his insult, Clancy moved toward Red until they stood face to face. Before he knew what happened, Red chopped Clancy in the neck with the side of his hand. With the other, punched him in the gut. When Clancy fell forward, Red struck him in the face with his raised knee. Gasping for air, Clancy straightened up, his face bloody. Stepping back, Red pulled a gun he had tucked in his belt.

"Now get out! If I ever see you again, I'll shoot you in the knees."

Clancy clenched his fists and rushed toward Red. The gun exploded. Red missed his knee, rather hit Clancy's left shin. He crumpled to the floor, howling in pain.

"Now get out!"

"I can't walk."

"Then crawl."

Tina came rushing in, stopped and asked, "You all right Mr. Red?"

"Couldn't be better. Just waiting for this scum to crawl out of here."

Looking back down, he watched Clancy, on his knees, crawl out of the store.

"Thank you for your concern, Miss Tina. Better get back to work in case Clancy gets someone to come back to cause trouble."

When Red told Rupert the next day what happened, he warned, "Clancy will want revenge. Better hire his replacement right away. Don't want you to be here alone."

"You know anyone who would like to work here?"

146

"Matter of fact, I do. My big brother, George, is looking for work."

"Have him drop in tomorrow."

Red hired George. The brothers were a good team. They made sure one of them was always present during store hours.

Almost two weeks passed before the next incident. Not the same thing. No blood shed or threats, just a very strange encounter.

It was in the afternoon. Business was slow when a man came in, an unusual man. He was somewhat bent over with an unpleasant face. Red decided he was in his late forties. He was well dressed. He entered the store with an arrogance his posture belied.

Red, in the office, heard the initial exchange between the man and George.

"Good afternoon, Mr. Unruh."

In a gruff, hostile voice, the man asked, "Is the owner here?"

"No sir. He doesn't work here. He works in the main store 'cross the river."

"You in charge here?"

"No sir, Red's in charge."

Red, standing at the entranceway to the backroom, asked, "How may I help you, Mr. Unruh?"

Reaching into his coat pocket, he pulled out a paper. "This is my list. Deliver it in an hour to my business in the Sands. Add it to my tab." As Red took the list, Mr. Unruh turned and left without another word.

George shook his head, "Now that's a nasty fellow."

"Not the most congenial, is he?" Red commented.

It took the two of them twenty minutes to assemble everything on the list. It made quite a pile on the counter. In setting up the books, Red had entered the name of Evert Unruh in the ledger with a number of unpaid bills totaling almost two hundred dollars. One of the first slips included his address. Not really an address, just a description of the brick building with the bright red door. Note said, "Can't miss it. Biggest building in the Sands."

Wrights had a horse and wagon. Red and George loaded the items and George left to deliver it all. Red had included a hastily written invoice marked "Payment due in ten days or there will be no more credit."

After George left the store, Red slipped his gun into his waist after making sure it was loaded. He was relieved when George returned with a handful of gold coins which paid the sum due plus fifty dollars in excess.

George eagerly told Red of his encounter. "I drove up to the house. Impossible to miss it. Sticks out like a sore thumb. Why would anyone want to live in the Sands? Knocked on the door and Miss Lotus answered. She had a darkie come help me unload the wagon. He was dressed in red shiny pants and white shirt with red buttons and necktie.

"You should see the inside of the place. Lots of candles and reds and golds. Carrying everything to the back, I passed rooms along the way. Most doors were closed. One was open. Lady half sitting half laying on this fancy couch, hardly wearing nothing. I was glad to get out of there. Just as I was nearing the door, Mr. Unruh came blustering in, shouting.

"'Damn fool! Don't ever come in the front door again. Go around back!'

"Miss Lotus tried to calm him down but I just got out of there.

"You ever been in the Sands?" When George saw the look on Red's face, he quickly added, "I don't mean to, well, you know, visit them places. Just meant, you seen the shacks? Even the air made me feel dirty."

"I have only seen it from the main road. You say Lotus was there. She had her business 'cross the river. Moved over here. Interesting. She must be running the business for Mr. Unruh. Guess two peas in a pod."

Chapter Twenty Six

What a perfect morning, Seamus thought as he rode Tin Bucket across the bridge. It was June 15, 1834. There was a gentle breeze coming off the lake. The sky was almost as blue as the water. Each breath Seamus took coursed joy through his body. Even the Sands looked better on a morning like this. Hitching Tin Bucket to the rail, Seamus looked at Wright's storefront. He thought, it would make the store more homey if shrubs were planted in front.

Shortly after Seamus and George opened the store for the day, John Wright entered. He greeted the two. After some small talk, he asked Seamus to join him on the front porch. They sat in the rocking chairs. Seamus wondered what might be wrong. Business had been good. The books were current. Each day there were more customers. Used to hard times, Seamus leaned back, gently rocked back and forth and decided whatever it was he could handle it.

"Seamus, or should I call you Red?"

"Either."

"Seamus, as you know, my father has returned from the East with my mother and the rest of the family." He spoke so seriously, Seamus was convinced he was about to be dismissed.

"My father wants to resume management of the main store and wants me to manage this store. After much debate and, frankly, some arguing, I convinced him to make you a partner. If you agree, you and I would manage this store together.

"Seamus, you keep excellent books and are better with the customers than I am. I have worked every day for almost two years now. If you agree to become a partner, it would give me the freedom to take days off. You too. You could work three days, I could work three

149

days and we could overlap the seventh day each week. What do you say?"

"Would I still be paid or just get my share of the profits if there are any?"

"It would work this way. Father has agreed to pool the profits from the two stores. He would get fifty percent of the total. You and I would each get twenty-five percent."

"So you mean I could end up getting a share of the profits of the main store plus a share of any profits from this store?"

"Yes."

"And I would only work four days a week?"

"Yes. Oh, and one other thing. When I built this store, I added living quarters above it. While my family was out East, I lived over the other store. My mother wants me to continue to live there with the rest of the family. If you wish, you could move in upstairs. It would save you whatever it is you are spending now for your cabin."

Without hesitation, Seamus said, "Agreed."

Two days later, on Seamus' first day off, he moved his few belongings and furniture to above the store. The following day he went to see Axel to tell him of his good fortune. They had lunch together at the Sauganash.

"How's Little Henry, Papa?"

"Good. He has grown. Life has changed for me. I have to be quiet when he is napping."

"That should be easy for you, Axel. You not being into talking much."

"Reminds me," Axel commented, " How would you like to attend the meeting of the Polemic Society next week?"

"What's that?"

"Members and guests debate an issue at each meeting. Sometimes it is of substance, sometimes it's silly. Next week we are going to debate if the Congress of the United States has the constitutional power to make internal improvements in the states."

"It's of no concern to me."

"Ah, but it is Seamus. The Chicago harbor needs dredging. We could use federal funds to do the work. Also, we could use better roads leading into Chicago. Some in Congress say it is unconstitutional for Washington City to pay for roads and harbors in the states. Others feel it is critical for the development of the nation. Want to come?"

"I'll see. Now that I will have free time, I'd rather attend the Temperance Society meetings. What are they like?"

"Frustrating."

"How so?"

"Everyone who attends is opposed to the making or selling alcoholic drinks. There is no debate on the issue just on how to achieve it. We talk over and over again about what to do. I am getting pretty tired of the same people saying the same thing each time we meet."

"Maybe they could use some Irish irreverence. When's the next meeting?"

Just then Mark Beaubien came over. "Irish irreverence about what?"

Sheepishly Axel said, "About the Temperance Society."

"That damn bunch of do-gooders. If they have their way, I'd be out of business." Slapping Seamus on the back, Mark laughed loudly, saying, "Temperance'll never happen. Men need to drink."

"How is business, Mark?" Axel asked even though he was aware of the increased sums Beaubien was depositing in the bank.

"Never been better. More gents everyday." Sitting down, Mark continued, "Seamus. I was surprised you quit working for the Canal Commission. You working up in the Sands now? You and Miss Lotus in business together?"

Never shy, Seamus asked, "You want a cut rate, Mark?"

"Not me. How is Miss Lotus? I miss seeing her around?"

"I think she's in a kettle of fish. I've seen her with some black eyes and bruises. Got the best place in the Sands. Seems to have a partner, though, a mean bastard. Whenever George or Rupert take an order to the house, they come back with more lurid stories. Best I can tell, Miss Lotus isn't working, if you know what I mean. She has a bunch of young girls for that.

"I have ridden by her place. It's large, two-story, surrounded by all the other places. They are nothing but shacks and flimsy sheds. Her place is like a palace. She and her partner must be making a handsome profit. Unruh, her partner, buys the best we have in food stuffs. He has us order real fancy items from back East. Some I never heard of before. Doesn't fret a bit about the cost.

"George has seen Unruh hit Miss Lotus. He said he wanted to hit the misshapen no-good. Suppose Miss Lotus sold her soul to him."

Surprisingly embarrassed with the Seamus' description of Miss Lotus' place, Mark asked Axel, "I hear your sister is going to marry the gent from Cincinnati."

"Word does get around. Yes, she is."

Seamus, surprised, asked, "When? Where?"

"This September. Here. Lina and Anna are planning a big shindig. I learned from my own wedding, I don't get involved. Just have to show up, properly dressed."

Just then Henry Gherkin entered the Sauganash. Looking around, he saw me and came over and asked, "Herr Konrad, could I talk to you? Alone?"

Axel moved to an empty table, wondering what the town's gravedigger could want. They sat down.

Speaking in German, Herr Gherkin said, "I need your help. I came here from Prussia a year ago. You know I make coffins and dig graves. With all the new people coming to Chicago, my business has increased. The problem is most of the dead have no families here and I don't get paid. Folks think my job is easy. Don't realize it's difficult to dig on the sides of the river. Herr Konrad, I need money. Can you give me a loan?"

Axel responded, "Come see me tomorrow at the bank. I'm sure I can help you out." Reaching into his pocket, Axel slipped several coins into Herr Gherkin's hand. "Have yourself a good meal. I will see you tomorrow.

Bowing Gherkin stood and walked from the tavern.

Returning to sit with Seamus, Axel said, "There are so many decent men and women in need. I must think of a way to help them."

Seamus said nothing. Axel, his mind elsewhere, stood, excused himself and left. Mark, who had come back, said, "There goes the most decent man I have ever met."

Seamus replied, "Yes he is. Too bad everyone is not like him."

Chapter Twenty Seven

Seamus entered St. Mary's, genuflected, sat at the back of the sanctuary and bowed his head in prayer. He and John Wright alternated taking Sunday off from working in the store. Since their partnership had been set two months before, Seamus had missed church every other Sunday. His prayer always began and ended with his love for Molly and pleas for the Good Lord to be with her, keep her well and safe. Perspiration beaded on his brow and trickled down his back, wetting his shirt. The church was hot. What else could one expect in August?

The Sunday service would not begin for another half hour. Seamus relished this brief period of peace and quiet. His prayer complete, he studied the interior of the church. He recalled when Father John Mary Irenaeus St. Cyr first arrived in Chicago on May 1, 1833.

The priest held his first service four days after his twelve day journey to Chicago. The Mass was held in a twelve foot square log cabin owned by Mark Beaubien. It was woefully inadequate, with dozens having to stand outside at the door and windows to worship. Not quite five months later, the first St. Mary's Church was completed. Mark Beaubien had paid $400 in silver half-dollars for its construction. It was here Seamus was deep in thought as the parishioners began to enter for Mass.

Seamus liked Father St. Cyr. He had met with him shortly after his arrival, seeking absolution for abandoning his sisters in Ireland. Absolution for his failure to stop the massacre of innocent women and children in the Black Hawk War. Absolution for his part in the murder of Fitchen. Absolution for his vindictive thoughts about Evert Unruh.

Father St. Cyr had patiently listened to Seamus. The Father had difficulty understanding English. St. Cyr was born in Lyon, France. It had been only two years since he arrived in St. Louis. He was ordained within a year and raised to the priesthood on April 6, 1833. Days later he was sent to Chicago. St. Cyr acknowledged the petition signed by 128 Chicagoan Catholics. They represented around half of the population. Among those signing were Alexander Robinson, Billy Caldwell, Mark and his older brother, Jean Baptiste Beaubien. Seamus was proud he had signed the petition as well even though it was written in French which he was unable to read. Many of the Catholics in Chicago were French, French-Canadians and converted Indians. Very few were Irish. The hand delivered petition was received in St. Louis on April 16. The Bishop approved and appointed Father St. Cyr the following day.

Responding in halting English, Father St. Cyr told Seamus he did not need absolution, rather accept his actions had been noble, his thoughts pure, his person wholesome. Father St. Cyr's words would forever be engraved on Seamus' heart.

"Seamus, my son, you had no choice but to leave your sisters in Ballynakill. The risk was to you and your sisters. Had you been captured, your sisters may have suffered imprisonment. Nor were you or Colonel Grege responsible for the actions of the Army. He tried to object, to no avail. Your reports and eyewitness observations told the truth. You two were innocent of any wrong doing. As to the death of Fitchen, there is no way you could have anticipated his capture and torture by the Indians. He chose to live cheating others. He caused his own violent death, not you. As to your vindictive thoughts about Evert Unruh, well those you need to cease. Pray for help in seeing the man as crippled, not only in body but also in mind. Pray for his redemption. Avoid him if you can, remain silent if you can't. Vengeance is the Lord's, not ours."

Thinking back to Ireland, Seamus remembered how, as a youth, he had no use for the church. He changed when he learned the English were trying to destroy Catholicism and had virtually enslaved the Irish Catholics. Smiling, he thought, there is nothing to convince a youth to want something more than to tell him he can not have it. The mysterious ways of the Good Lord.

Seamus put his thoughts aside and focused on the Mass. St. Mary's had filled up while he was recalling the past. He always found comfort and renewed energy during the service.

Departing after Mass, Seamus felt a deep tranquility. Leaving the church entrance at the corner of Michigan and Madison Avenues, he walked the few feet east to Lake Michigan's sandy shore. The sun sparkled on the nearly still water. The sands were blinding in their reflection of the sun. Seamus sat down on a low dune. What a perfect day. The peace he had felt during the service permeated his every fiber, his burdens dissipated.

Reluctantly, Seamus walked back to St. Mary's to retrieve Tin Bucket. As he untied his horse, he was shaken from his thoughts by a familiar voice.

"Seamus, I wish to apologize for my past behavior. Can you forgive me."

Looking up, there was Josie. Seamus felt a rush of anger. She had no right to intrude on his day. Calming himself down, he said, "Good day to you, Miss Josie."

Before this time he had seen her as an ignorant girl who had tried to seduce him on the *Princess Rose*. Before him now was a more refined young lady. Her dress was simple but well made. Her face was free of paint. Her hair was soft and stylishly set. Her expression was one of gentle pleading. Her voice was soft, not in the least harsh or demanding. She did not advance to touch him, but rather stood just far enough to make clear she was not seeking physical contact.

Softly again, Josie said, "I am so sorry for my past behavior. Please forgive me."

Nodding, Seamus spoke, "There is nothing to forgive, Miss Josie. We were both young and innocent. I regret I was so rude in rebuffing you."

Seamus, simply said, "You are looking well."

"I am."

"I have not seen you for months now. Have you moved?"

"Yes, I have. I live with Miss Lotus in her new establishment."

Seeing Seamus try to mask his shock and disapproval, Josie added, "Contrary to what everyone thinks, I am not a prostitute. I was desperate to find a place to live. No one would give me a job. No one cared but Miss Lotus. She has become the mother I lost when I was a child back in Ireland. She cares for me, feeds me and makes sure I come to no evil."

"I am happy for you." Still not sure of himself, Seamus asked, "Do you live in the Sands?"

"Yes, I do. But I am in no way involved in her business. Miss Lotus has told me you work at Wrights General Store."

"I do."

"Would it bother you if I came to shop there?"

"Come whenever you wish."

"Thank you. I always give my list to Miss Lotus. Well, I need to get back home." As Josie walked to a fine carriage, she turned and added, "Seamus, I saw you inside. I didn't want to interrupt your prayer. I come every Sunday. Perhaps I will see you next week."

"I can come only every other week. I shall look forward to church in two weeks. Do come into the store. Goodbye, Miss Josie."

"Goodbye Mr. O'Shea."

Seamus mounted Tin Bucket and rode off as Josie climbed into the carriage and sat next to a man. The carriage rode off.

Several weeks later, Josie entered Wrights General Store. Seamus was in the back, working on the books. Rupert was finishing up with a customer. As he left, Josie asked Rupert, "Is Mr. O'Shea not here today?"

"He's in the back. Would you like me to show you the way?"

Nodding yes, Josie followed Rupert, who pushed aside the curtain in the doorway and announced, "Someone wishes to see you, Red."

Looking up from his desk, Seamus masked his surprise. "Good morning, Miss Josie." Standing, he pulled over a second chair by the desk. "Please be seated."

Was it his imagination or did Josie look like she was gaining weight?

"Red? Is that what you are called now?"

"Just when here at the store. Got started by Rupert and I did not object. Do you have a special order?"

"I want to ask your advice. When we talked several weeks ago, I told you I am not working as a prostitute. That is true. I didn't tell you, I am with child."

"Congratulations!" Seeing sadness in Josie's eyes, he asked, "Are you not pleased?"

"I am, except there is a problem. I am not married. I thought I could not bear children. Then this happened." Josie was tense, speaking so slowly Seamus felt her words were difficult for her to utter.

"Seamus, when I was fifteen, a man forced himself on me. I became pregnant. During the crossing from Ireland to New York, I aborted the baby. Since then I have lived in shame and grief. Miss Lotus was the first person I ever told. She understood and convinced me I was not at fault. When I met you on the *Princess Rose*, I thought I fell in love with you. It was the first time I ever experienced such a feeling. I was ignorant about how to express myself. Even more ignorant of my own feelings. When I accosted you in front of Axel, the Captain and his family, I not only embarrassed you, I made a fool of myself.

"You were kind to talk to me outside St. Marys. I feel I can trust you."

"Miss Josie, should you be telling me all this? Shouldn't you talk with Father St. Cyr instead?"

"I have. It is he who suggested I talk with you."

"I trust his judgement. I will listen and help you anyway I can."

"I have lived with Miss Lotus since I arrived in Chicago. She keeps me safe." Josie paused, collecting her thoughts.

"A well dressed gentleman came to see Miss Lotus more than a year ago. After he returned several times, he suggested to Miss Lotus he would appreciate finer surroundings and exclusivity. She tried to get a loan from the bank but was turned down. Next time the gentleman urged her to improve her business, she told him she had tried to get a loan but was turned down.

"It was around then that he first time cast eyes on me. It was only for a brief moment. He decided he must have me. Miss Lotus threatened she would kill him if he came close to me. That did it. He kept visiting Miss Lotus until the day he told her he had built a new house for her in the Sands. He must be wealthy. The new place is very elegant and must have cost a pretty penny.

"Miss Lotus moved her business. She furnished the place with the finest decorations she could buy. He provided her with what seemed like an endless supply of money. When we moved, I discovered I had a private suite far from the business part of the building. I can access it without going into the business rooms. It has its own kitchen, albeit small, and dining room. Each evening Miss Lotus and I have dinner with Mr. Unruh. He has been very kind to me, like a father.

"That was until the evening Miss Lotus was not feeling well. Mr. Unruh and I had dinner without her. He is very charming. I was attracted to him. Not as love, rather as comfortable security. The evening was pleasant. He helped me with my chair. After dinner he bid me good night and kissed the back of my hand. That night my dreams were a swirl of the man in Ireland who had his way with me mixed with images of the charming Mr. Unruh.

"Miss Lotus was ill for over a week. She thinks it is something she ate. I am not sure. Mr. Unruh and I continued our evening meals in my private dining room. His charm was infectious. I began to have lustful thoughts of him at night. One night, when he kissed my hand, I took his and pulled him to me and kissed him on the lips. His response was quick. He embraced me, held me tight and kissed me deeply in return.

"Two nights later, he invited me to his suite. It is on the second floor of the building, in the back. I had no idea it existed. It is exquisitely furnished and decorated. He offered me a drink by the fireplace. I relaxed and felt safe and happy.

"He spoke of many places he had been. He came to sit by me. When he placed his hand on me, I moved away. His smile seemed innocent. I apologized and said it was time for me to leave. He showed no anger. The next evening, again after dinner, he invited me to his apartment. I should not have, but I agreed. This time when he reached for me, I did not resist. The child I am carrying was begun that evening.

"When I told Miss Lotus, she cried. She said it was her fault for not more carefully watching over me. She said she would demand Mr. Unruh marry me. I suggested I get rid of the baby. She was adamant, saying 'You must have the baby. It will give you power over Mr. Unruh.'"

"I am so sorry, Miss Josie. What do you plan to do?"

"I will have the baby. I refuse, however, to raise my child in such a place. What should I do?"

"Have you and Mr. Unruh married?"

"He refuses."

"Why?"

"He won't tell me. When I knew I was with child, I told him and asked if we could wed before I began to show. His reaction was frightening. First, joy. Not joy as you or I would show, but a sinister joy, if there is such a thing. He kept saying, 'I am to be a father. A son to continue my life's purpose.' Afterward, he scowled and stomped out of the room.

"He would not talk to me for days on end. One evening, when he finally allowed me to talk to him, I again asked if he would marry me. He looked sad and said, 'I am not sure you should have this child. His life will be one of hatred and misery.' He poured himself a drink, sat next to me and took my hand. He had not shown tenderness to me since the day he took me to his bed. He said to me, 'Josie, marriage would be a dreadful mistake for both of us. For me, it would needlessly tie me down. I can only thrive if completely free. For you, it would mean days of uncertainty and doubt, followed by an occasional day of my presence which you would soon come to fear. I am not a common man. My habits can only be described as vile. I have never felt love nor even commitment to anyone else. I cannot be a husband. Certainly not to some one as sweet and innocent as you.' As he spoke, the gentleness of his touch turned to an iron grip which was painful and brought tears to my eyes. He thought I was shedding my tears because he refused to marry me.

"He released my hand, saying, 'I am sorry, Josie. I wish I were a different person.' He stood and left.

"A few minutes later, Lotus came into the room. She found me softly crying. She asked why? I told her. She said, 'You poor child.' She asked if I wanted the child. I said I did. 'I will go talk to *him.*' Miss Lotus left without another word and went to see Mr. Unruh.

"When Miss Lotus confronted him about me, he struck her. Since then, any time she goes against his wishes, even if she is unaware of his wishes, he hits her. Life has become a constant horror for her."

Seamus asked, "How does Mr. Unruh treat you now? Does he demand his way with you?"

"No, he doesn't. He is afraid I will lose the baby if he takes me. I now see what Miss Lotus meant about controlling him. Each day I dread seeing him. I avoid him, no longer having dinner with him. I want to get away. I will not have my child born in a house of ill repute. I have no money. What can I do?"

"You say Mr. Unruh has money."

"Yes."

"Why not demand he build you a house far from the Sands. On the south side of the river. Or far north of the Sands."

"Why would he do that? He would never see me."

"Tell him you wish your son to have a good, safe, God-fearing life."

"Son! What makes you think it will be a son?"

"From all you have told me of the monster, he would be prouder of a son than a daughter. Take advantage of his weakness now, while you have the upper hand. Should you lose the baby or it be still born, he will either discard you or, well, you can imagine."

Josie was silent, thinking. Seamus got up and went into the store to give her time. When he returned, she got up, held out her hand to clasp his and quietly said, "Seamus, you are a very smart man. I shall see what I can do."

Shortly before Christmas, Seamus learned Josie had moved into a fine home of her own and had delivered a healthy son. The house is south of the river, overlooking the lake. Seamus rode Tin Bucket to see it. He had no intention of visiting, just to see it. When he found it, he felt compelled to see Josie. Tying Tin Bucket to a cast iron hitching post, he struck the brass doorknocker. A maid answered. He gave his name. The maid asked him to wait. He heard the baby cry nearby.

When Josie appeared carrying her son, her face was wreathed in a broad smile. "Seamus, I hoped you would come to see my son.

"Seamus O'Shea, please meet Nicolaus Durst. Nicolaus, this is your Uncle Seamus. He is my best friend."

Seamus was struck how Little Nicolaus is the perfect image of Josie. He is handsome for a baby, cooing and smiling.

"He likes you Seamus. As soon as he heard your voice at the door he stopped crying. May I call you his uncle?"

"You may. So may he as long as he wishes."

Josie placed the wiggling little bundle into his arms. The only baby Seamus had ever held before was Little Henry Konrad. To hold a baby, he thought, is truly a blessing.

"Josie, I thank Father St. Cyr for advising you to talk to me. It is good to be an uncle and your friend. You may always count on me."

"Would you like to see the rest of my house?"

"I would."

Josie led the way, pointing out the purpose of each room on the first floor.

"I even have a wine cellar. Evert bought the house from a wealthy New Yorker who had it built for himself. He had never been to Chicago. When the house was done he ordered it to be furnished. Even the wine cellar was stocked. He finally came to Chicago in the fall of last year. He stayed only two nights. He found Chicago primitive. He returned back East and ordered the house be sold including everything in it.

"Evert learned of the house. He brought me here to see it. I was apprehensive to be alone with him. He was disinterested in me. He stayed in the parlor while I walked through each room."

Climbing the grand stairway, Josie took Seamus to her bedroom suite.

"I love this room best of all. It is as if whoever chose the colors for the rooms knew what I liked.

"Evert had to meet only two times with the owner's real estate agent. The negotiations went well. The owner was anxious to rid himself of this beautiful estate. Evert held out for a very low price. He succeeded. I was able to move in a week later."

"Where did Evert get all his money?"

"I don't know anything about his past. Not long after he came to Chicago, he began to build his Palace of Pleasure."

"Excuse me, Josie. Palace of Pleasure?"

"Do you really need to ask me, Seamus? He toyed with naming it Lotus' Delight to entice Lotus to run it for him. He was aware of her desire to improve her place and cater exclusively to gentlemen, not drifters. She had no money so she jumped at his offer to build a larger, more elegant place for her business on the condition she would run it for him and get a percentage of the profit.

160

"I don't know where his money came from to build the Palace. Since it opened, he is reaping thousands of dollars both from the business with the girls and his gambling den."

"Where is that?"

"Under the house. Lotus told me it has a well concealed entrance. Evert is selective on who may enter. His only criteria is men who have a certain, minimum amount of cash or gold."

The tour of the house over, Josie asked Seamus to stay for tea. He declined, pecked Josie on the cheek, blushed and left.

Chapter Twenty Eight

There is a rough looking man at the door, Miss Durst. He's fierce angry. I didn't let him in. Left him standing outside." Tessa was flushed, her voice edged with fear. "Miss, he's rude. His clothes are torn and dirty. Skird me. I slammed the door and locked er' he could hurt me. Think he'll go away?"

"Tessa, is Terrence back from exercising the horses?"

"My no good husband? He just got back. He stopped for an ale or two. You know he does like his drink."

"Please ask him to join us."

Minutes later, Terrence entered the parlor, holding his cap, dipped his head and said nothing. Tessa walked around him and stood next to where Josie was sitting.

"Good day, Terrence. I have a special favor to ask of you. There is a rough looking man asking to see me. I would like you to remain with me, while Tessa allows him to come in. If he threatens me, I will ask him to leave. If he does not, I want you to physically force him out. Is that clear?"

"Yes, Ma'am."

"Tessa, if you will."

Josie could hear the door open, Tessa ask the man to enter and follow her. The man shouted, "I don't like being made to wait. Where is she?"

"This way," Tessa said tersely.

Upon seeing where Tessa was leading him, he pushed her aside, entering the parlor. His self-assurance weakened upon seeing Terrence. The two men were both tall and large. The stranger, however, looked almost insignificant before Terrence.

He stopped a respectable distance from Josie, startled into silence.

Softly and confidently, Josie asked, "May I ask your name and why you wish to see me?"

Attempting to regroup, the man spoke in a more placid voice, "I want a thousand dollars!"

"You did not tell me your name. Who are you?"

"Clancy, Herr Clancy Grob."

Tessa was impressed with Miss Josie's calmness.

"Why should I give you any money?"

"So I don't tell everyone the name of your bastard son's father."

The stern look on Josie's face remained unchanged.

"Is that a threat, Herr Grob?"

Taken aback by her calmness, he responded, "Do you want everyone to know the name of your son's father?"

"Herr Grob," pausing for emphasis, Josie softly said, "What makes you think the name of my son's father is a mystery. It is well known. It is not a secret. Leave my home immediately. Never bother me again."

Clancy looked confused. He clenched and unclenched his fists, trying to understand and to control his growing rage. "I know more about him. I'll tell if you don't pay me."

"Herr Grob, I have asked you to leave my home. If you have anything you wish to tell about Mr. Unruh, go see him and ask him for money. There is nothing about him worth one thousand dollars to me. Perhaps it will be worth it to him."

Turning to Terrence, Josie asked, "Terrence, please escort Herr Grob out. If he resists, you have my permission to use whatever force is necessary. Good day to you, Herr Grob."

Terrence swiftly stepped forward, grasped Clancy's right arm, twisted it behind his back and turned him around as Clancy's face grimaced in pain. When Terrence pushed him toward the hallway, Clancy tried to resist. He was no match to the former blacksmith whose muscles bulged under his tunic. At the doorway, Terrence gave a mighty shove propelling Clancy out of the house and tumbling down the front steps.

In a voice Josie had never heard before, Terrence shouted, "Never come back." He shut the door so vigorously, the slam reverberated throughout the house.

Rid of Clancy, Josie called to Terrence. He re-entered the parlor. Tessa was pale, Terrence red faced, Josie began to shake.

"Thank you both for protecting me. We will need to be watchful in the days ahead. I believe Herr Grob is unstable. I have no idea what it is he wanted to tell me. I don't care. By now you know Mr. Unruh and I have little contact with one another and then, only the few times he wants to see his son."

"Miss Josie, may I suggest you talk with Mr. O'Shea. He might have some suggestions for your safety."

Thinking for a minute, Josie said, "I agree. I will write a note. Terrence, could you take it to him?

"Yes, Ma'am."

Seamus dropped everything an hour later when he got her note. He immediately came to Josie. She explained what happened. He asked a few questions.

"I suggest you write to Mr. Unruh and tell him what happened. Emphasize Clancy's threat to tell you something about Mr. Unruh for one-thousand dollars."

"Seamus, I try to avoid Mr. Unruh as much as I can."

"I know. Whatever Clancy knows about Mr. Unruh will enrage him. I agree Clancy is unstable. Ask Mr. Unruh to make arrangements to protect you and your son."

Josie agreed, wrote the note and let Seamus read it. "This is perfect, Josie. Can Terrence take it to Mr. Unruh immediately?"

Terrence took the note. Seamus volunteered to stay with Josie until she got a response.

An hour later, Tessa opened the front door to the sound of the knocker. Josie and Seamus were still in the parlor. When they heard Mr. Unruh's voice, Seamus, as prearranged, stepped in the alcove, to listen without being seen.

Josie stood as Evert entered. "Thank you for coming so quickly, Evert." Stepping forward to meet him, Josie lightly kissed him on the cheek. Of all things, he blushed and smiled.

Before Josie could say anything further, Evert said, "I shall take care of Clancy."

Josie asked, "How can you assure he won't come back and harm either me or Nicholas?"

"I have my ways. Before the day is out, he shall leave Chicago for good. I am sorry he bothered you. I knew it was serious when I got your note. I am no fool. I know you prefer not to see me. Believe it or not, in my way, I care for you and our son. Nothing shall ever happen to either of you as long as I live."

Josie was about to respond, when Evert turned and left the house without another word. Seamus stepped into the room and said, "Interesting reaction."

Josie, nodding, said, "I think he is afraid to express tender emotions. He had to flee before he showed he could be human."

Seamus added, "He looked like he was about to say something but fled instead. He is a strange man."

"I thought about my situation the other day," Josie mused. "I guess I am what is called a grass widow."

"What's a grass widow?"

"In my case, an unmarried mother."

"Whatever embarrassment your situation may cause you, Josie, it is nothing compared to the horror of being Mr. Unruh's wife, forced to live with him and abide with his every whim and compulsion."

No one ever saw Clancy Grob in Chicago again.

Part Eight

Axel

Chapter Twenty Nine

apa! Papa!" I stopped. Little Henry walked toward me, as unsteady as a drunken sailor. "Lina, come quick! Henry is walking." I knelt down. My son fell into my outstretched arms. I hugged him as I lifted him up. His mother entered the room. "Lina, Henry walked to me. Here, let me show you." Putting Henry down, I pointed him toward his mother. Frowning, our little son plopped down, exhausted.

I tried to prod him to get up and walk. Alas, he was finished for the day.

"He'll walk again. Time for your nap, Henry." Lina took him to the nursery.

My wife had begun to show two months ago. Our next child is due in the summer, about four months from now. If all goes well, it'll be when Henry's sixteen months old. At the rate he is growing, he should be a little man by then.

Coming back into the room, Lina asked, "Did Henry really walk?"

"He did. I couldn't believe it. I am still getting use to him beginning to talk. Soon we will have two. Can you manage two?"

"Axel! Of course. You men think only you are strong. Besides, Anna helps."

"It is time for my board meeting." Kissing her on the forehead, I went downstairs and entered the bank. Reinhold had set up the room for the first meeting of the expanded board at two o'clock. I had just enough time to greet the new teller Reinhold had hired, a young Swedish lad. Carsten Baruth had urged him to come to Chicago and look me up. He had worked for a bank in Cincinnati and spoke English with a delightful accent.

"Welcome, Mr. Johansen. I am so glad you agreed to work for Reinhold. He tells me of the excellent letters of reference you gave him. You are in good hands, Anders, with Reinhold."

"I look forward to working for Mr. Schwoup and you sir."

The bank door opened and Gurdon Hubbard and Doc entered.

I greeted both, saying, "Doc, please show Gurdon to the board room."

One by one, the rest of the bank directors arrived.

I joined them in the board room. I was pleased to see the enormous table comfortably accommodated everyone, including Reinhold and myself.

"Gentlemen, I am pleased to call our meeting to order on this 21st day of April, 1835. First on our agenda is to introduce four new members to the board. I wish to acknowledge the absence of Alexander Robinson. He asked to be relieved of his position on the board. He served well and I hope in the future he might be willing to join us again."

After having everyone introduce themselves, I asked the new members to tell about themselves.

"As those of you who know me well, I am a person driven by precision and neatness. Therefore, I would like the four of you to speak in alphabetical order. Which means, John, you are first."

"I am John Calhoun. I'll begin at the beginning. I was born in Watertown, New York, where as an adult I attempted to publish the *Watertown Eagle*. It was a financial disaster. I arrived in Chicago in October, '33. Brought my printing equipment and two apprentices. The first thing we did was lath and plaster the unfinished building at South Water and Clark Streets. Once set up, I began printing the *Chicago Democrat*. Loan from Axel allowed me to print the paper for some months before it paid for itself.

"Six months later, my wife, Pamelia, arrived. She helps me with proofreading and printing. My goal is to give the news and to point out problems in our community in the hope it will help our citizens find solutions."

Philo Carpenter commented, "Are you aware how distressed John Hogan was with your editorial on the Post Office?"

"No. He must have missed the point."

"Actually he did," agreed Philo. "When he read it a second time, he liked it. So much so, he sent it on to the Postmaster General in Washington asking for funds to implement the changes you suggested."

"I'm glad you mentioned that, Philo. I find it painful at times to state my opinions, knowing someone will be hurt by them. I never publish an editorial unless I am convinced it is accurate and needed."

I nodded to John Caton.

"First, let me thank you, Axel, for asking me to be on the board. Also, for hiring me days after I arrived in Chicago. As you all may know, I am a lawyer. Working here at the bank while you went to New York gave me the opportunity to meet many Chicagoans. In fact, as a result of my working at the bank, I was retained to work on the legal aspects of the incorporation of Chicago. It also led to my prosecution of Chicago's first case of larceny.

"I don't mean to sound boastful. I just want to attribute my quick introduction to Chicago to the bank. My career has been further boosted by my election as the justice of the peace and my partnership with James Collins. On a more personal note, I will be returning to New York in a few months to marry Miss Laura Sherrill and bring her back here to live."

"Thank you both for agreeing to serve on the board."

"Colonel Grege, would you go next please." Grege had returned from Iowa where he had served as an Indian Agent for almost a year. As is his nature, he was very modest in giving his background. I was particularly pleased when he agreed to serve on the board.

"I am looking forward to learning some about the banking business. I have yet to decide what I will do with the rest of my life. After so many years in the Army, I knew it was time to get out. I'm not sure yet what to get into."

"Gurdon."

"I know most of you personally. I am Gurdon Hubbard, former fur trader, former husband to several, former member of the Illinois legislature and former resident of Danville, Illinois. I am now in real estate. It began by representing a cousin who lives in Connecticut. I have recently begun a new venture, meat packing. It's a rapidly growing business. Chicago is well positioned to become the slaughter house of the nation, shipping meat to the East."

"There, gentlemen, are our new board members. I appreciate the willingness of the rest of you to continue to serve on the board. Your advice and counsel have been critical to the success of the bank."

There was no need to outline the role of the board. I had done so when I asked each of the new members to join the board. I did the same thing with the returning board members. I feel it is important to once a year review why we do what we do and my overall goals.

171

"Before we get to today's agenda, Reinhold, please present your report on the current status of the bank." The picture he presented was of a healthy operation with assets continuing to grow and loan interest payments being made on time with only one exception. He next presented the new loan requests for our consideration.

"In February of this year, the state legislature authorized the governor to negotiate a loan of half a million dollars to begin the work on the Illinois and Michigan Canal. Mr. Konrad met with Governor Duncan and leaders of the legislature. The governor has submitted an application for $100,000.

"This would be a highly speculative investment on our part. I personally believe it is in our interest to seriously consider it in light of the profitable operations of the Erie Canal in New York and the Miami and Erie Canal in Ohio. Connecting Chicago with the Mississippi via the I & M Canal will open the Midwest.

"I have one concern. Repayment would initially be based on a tax approved by the legislature. The tax will be inadequate, however, to pay the interest on the loan. This would be a problem until the canal is constructed and in operation. At that time, the return on our investment will be substantial."

I interjected, "Reinhold, before we delve into this request, would you mind presenting the other loan requests?"

"Certainly.

"Next is a request by Lieutenant Jefferson Davis for the bank to accept funds appropriated by Congress to dredge the river and allow deeper draft ships and to remove the sand bar so ships can directly enter the Chicago River. While this is not a loan request, as such, it does represent some risk if the Federal Treasury is not timely in their disbursement of funds.

"The bank could be placed in the position of honoring contractor invoices which could exceed the funds transferred to us from the U. S. Treasury. To make the payments would, in effect, be temporary loans."

"What do we know of this Jefferson Davis? Have you met with him, Axel? Is he an honorable man?" asked John Caton.

"I have met with Lieutenant Davis. He is, I believe, an honorable man. He is eager to see the work on improving our harbor and river start. He is passionate about how it will improve our commerce. Lake boats will be able to dock much closer to our businesses. The contractor will hire many of our citizens to do the work. It would greatly increase our competitiveness with other ports on the lake."

"Do you feel we can trust Lieutenant Davis in his dealings with the contractors and the bank? What can you tell us about him."

I was pleased with John Caton's questions. He will be a worthy member of the Board.

"Davis was born in Kentucky. His family moved to Louisiana and then Mississippi during his youth. He graduated from the US military academy in West Point after which he was assigned to Fort Crawford, Wisconsin. He was back home in Mississippi during the Black Hawk War, returning in time to escort Black Hawk to prison. At the time, Chief Black Hawk made it known he liked Davis for his kind treatment of him.

"Davis is married to Sarah Taylor, daughter of Zachary Taylor, his commanding officer. Apparently they married over the objections of her father. She is not here with him in Chicago.

"I find Lieutenant Davis a compelling personality and yes, I believe we can rely on him to be fair and honest in his dealings with both the contractor and the bank."

Satisfied, John Caton said, "I don't know the procedures of the Board but based on what you have told us, I vote we approve Lieutenant Davis' request to accept the funds from Congress."

The other board members agreed. Reinhold resumed his report.

"We have a loan request from Nelson Norton. He is seeking funds to build the first ship here in Chicago for lake trade. His application states the proposed ship will be named *Clarissa*.

"The Lake House Association is seeking a substantial loan to build a three-story brick hotel to be elegantly furnished. The Association is made up of five prominent Chicagoans including Mr. Hubbard. When we discuss and vote on this request, I suggest Mr. Hubbard recuse himself from our deliberations.

"Next is a loan request by Thomas O. Davis so he may publish Chicago's second newspaper. It will be the *American*. I recommend Mr. Calhoun recuse himself from our discussions.

"We have a loan request to publish a directory of Chicago residents.

"Last, we have a loan request submitted by a lawyer from southern Illinois, Stephen Douglas. His intention is to purchase one thousand acres south of Chicago."

"Thank you, Reinhold. Before we analyze these requests, could you advise us of the assets presently unencumbered for us to consider committing?"

Looking at his notes, Reinhold found the exact figure. "We have ample funds to cover all of these requests, if that is your decision. In addition, the bank has adequate reserves to cover daily operations, future loan requests as well as monies to offset any possible defaults on outstanding loans."

I was quite pleased with the intense and intelligent discussion of the loan requests. After two hours, with Reinhold keeping notes, the board approved loan requests as submitted by the Lake House Association, Nelson Norton for the *Clarissa*, the Chicago directory and Mr. Davis' loan to publish the *American* newspaper.

The discussion on the I & M Canal loan request evoked debate over Chicago's recent rate of growth.

"The growth has been astounding," began Philo Carpenter. "There are buildings occupying most lots in the city causing new construction to expand south, west and north. One day I pass a vacant lot and two days later, when I once again walk by, I discover a building has gone up almost overnight. I wish I had the time to watch one being erected. How is it possible?"

"Not good work!" Johann Wellmacher blurted out. "Des buildings not last the winter."

Colonel Grege spoke, "The new buildings will last, Johann. I was so fascinated, I watched one go up in a day rather than weeks."

"Yah, das no gut. Not strong," Johannn argued.

Doc spoke to ease the debate. "Colonel, what is different?"

"Well. With hundreds pouring in each month, the carpenters were unable to build fast enough. Settlers had to live in tents or out in the open.

"I talked to one of the carpenters. He told me he builds what he called a balloon frame. He said it is a new technique. Saves on timber. Timber is scarce because of demand. A balloon frame depends on nails for stability and not wood mortised and pinned together with oaken dowels. So the frame can go up in a few hours. The sides are clad with clapboards. The whole structure can go up in a day. The old method takes weeks.

"Do you realize how our little village has grown more than tenfold since you arrived here just a few years ago?"

Johann silently shook his head.

Doc brought us back to the I & M Canal loan request. "Reinhold, I have come to respect your judgement. If you think this canal loan is good business, I am in favor of it."

"Growth of Chicago will continue. Each improvement makes it more attractive. I think the canal loan makes sense," Philo concurred.

The request for the I & M Canal was cut in half with the caveat to give a second loan when the basis of repayment is more assured. The loan to Mr. Douglas was deferred until I could talk with him personally.

"Unless there is anything else to discuss, I propose we adjourn. Hearing no objections, this meeting is concluded. Before you leave, I would like to give a personal invitation to each of you.

"Lina and I invite you to attend the marriage of my sister, Anna Konrad, to Carsten Baruth of Cincinnati, on May 5th. The Reverend Issac Hallan has graciously agreed to perform the ceremony at St. James First Protestant Episcopal Church. Anna and Carsten want as many of our friends as possible to attend.

"Lina tells me she will be sending you written invitations."

The meeting over, I went to my office. I had just sat down when Doc Wooten came in, closed the door and sat down. "Axel, there has been another pitchfork murder."

Chapter Thirty

I followed Doc to his office. Along the way, Doc said, "This time it's a young Indian. He appears to be only about twelve years of age. His heart was pierced by an arrow after which he was jabbed in the back with a pitchfork. His body was found in a stand of tall grass east of the fort. From best I can tell, he was killed some weeks ago."

We entered Doc's office and residence at the corner of Lake and LaSalle. He no longer shares a cabin with Philo. Each has moved to a larger building. Philo's pharmacy and residence are located on the southwest corner of Lake and Clark.

Inside, Doc led me into his office. The Indian lad was on his back on Doc's examining table. He was covered with a sheet. Pulling it back, Doc pointed out the bruises on his face and upper torso.

"He fought his attacker," Doc observed. "He put up a fierce fight."

I asked, "Was the arrow shot at him before the fight?"

"No. I believe he resisted his attacker until he was knocked unconscious. The arrow was taken from the boy's quiver and forced into his heart. He would have died instantly. As with the other three murders, he was not impaled with the pitchfork until hours after he died.

"Axel, I can no longer keep these murders secret. It is important we make them known to the officials and the public. I would like to talk to John Calhoun about this and the previous murders. The sooner the public is aware of what is going on, the sooner the killer will be caught."

I remained silent, uncertain. I must have looked panicked as I relived again the day I saved my sister Anna from Rikert.

"Axel, you do not need to tell of your encounter with your cousin back in Germany. We can keep your name out of this."

"That would be best. "

Doc and I went to see John Calhoun, publisher of the *Chicago Democrat*. He invited us into his tiny office. Closing the door for privacy, he observed, "The two of you look like you've seen a ghost."

Doc began, "John, a body was found this morning east of the Fort – an Indian lad. He was murdered."

"Any idea who he was?"

"No."

John asked further, "Are you concerned it will cause problems with the remaining Indians?"

"Possibly. Our primary concern, however, is the lad is the fourth murder by the same person."

"How do you know?"

I answered, "All four were murdered and then, hours afterward, jabbed viciously in the back with a pitchfork."

"How do you know the same person killed all four?"

Doc said, "The puncture wounds have all been in the exact same point of the back. The first died from his neck being cut from ear to ear. The second's remains were found in the ruins of a cabin destroyed by fire. The third man died from a gun shot to the chest. The Indian lad was most likely beaten until he was unconscious at which point an arrow was forced into his heart."

John had pulled out a pad and was writing notes as we talked. He asked, "Do you have any idea who might be doing this and why?"

Doc said nothing. I struggled and finally said, "I will answer that John, but only if you give me your assurance you will not repeat or publish what I am about to say."

Pulling on his beard, John looked at me long and hard. He finally asked, "Did you do this Axel?"

I was stunned. Doc emphatically said, "He did not do this! Absolutely not!"

John continued to look at me for what seemed to be an eternity before he said, "Axel, I trust you. You can trust me. I shall keep what you tell me in confidence."

I sighed deeply. "It all began back in Germany." I told of Rikert's attack which ended in his falling on the pitchfork. "Afterward, he lost his legal battle concerning his inheritance of his father's estate. It was left to my father.

"He followed me to America and paid to have someone kill me. Obviously without success. Next he had my intended wife kidnaped. She was rescued. I believe he has either followed me here to Chicago or is still in New York paying someone to commit these random murders. The pitchfork wounds are, I believe, intended to send me a message of fear."

When I began to tell of Rikert, John stopped taking notes. Seeing this, I told more than I would otherwise have done.

"Have you seen this cousin here in Chicago?"

"No."

Doc spoke. "Were this New York, I would urge Axel to go to the police. We have no law officials here."

John noted, "While we don't at the moment, we will in early August, when we will vote to elect constables. I have interviewed the leading candidates. I am impressed with John Shrigley. He is from England where he worked for the London police. Oremus Morrison is also standing for the position of constable. I am not as impressed with him. I can't see him vigorously pursuing crime considering his massive weight.

"Until the election, you are right, we have no law officials. If you agree, I can invite Shrigley to my office and outline the four pitchfork murders and seek his advice. I would make no mention of either you or your cousin.

"Unless Shrigley convinces me otherwise, I will do a front page story on the murder of the Indian lad. To keep my readers' attention, I propose to do follow up stories, one by one revealing the other murders. If your cousin is in Chicago, this will give him the impression we are getting closer to finding the murderer.

"May I proceed?" John asked.

I looked at Doc. He nodded encouragement.

I responded, "You may."

"We can talk after I meet with Shrigley. He might have some good advice."

A week later, the lead article on the front page of the *Democrat* was headed by "Search Has Begun For the Pitchfork Murderer." I did not bring a copy to either the bank or our apartment. I didn't want Lina or Anna to see it. Very naive of me to think neither would see the paper elsewhere.

Lina approached me several days later when Anna wasn't present. "Have you seen the article on the Pitchfork Murderer?"

"Yes."

"Is that why you didn't bring the newspaper home?"

"I didn't want to worry you?"

"It is better I know than you keep me in the dark."

"You are expecting. I need to protect you."

"Nonsense. You must always trust me and tell me. My father always preached, forewarned is to be forearmed."

"I also want to keep it from Anna."

"She will eventually hear talk. Or see the newspaper. She is getting very proficient in speaking and reading English. After supper this evening we must talk about it."

Nothing immediately useful came from Calhoun's conversation with Shrigley. If he is elected, he promised he will immediately begin an investigation. In the meantime, Shrigley vowed to go over Doc's notes on the four murders for possible leads. He will unofficially pursue any he identifies.

Over the next several weeks, Calhoun kept the story alive, asking citizens to inform him of anything suspicious. Nothing materialized. When Doc and I next met with him, he said he had again talked with Shrigley who told him he may have to wait for the next murder for fresh leads. John told him Chicago has grown so quickly, the vast majority of the over 3,000 residents are strangers to one another making hiding easy.

Each day, no matter where I am or go, I find myself looking at every face. It took me weeks before I asked myself, if Rikert is in Chicago, where would he hide? The Sands? If he is behind the murders, would he be foolish enough to commit them himself?

The more I thought about it, the more I became convinced he is hiding in the Sands. If there, he surely must realize he can't come into the business area. Accordingly, I rationalized Anna, Lina and Little Henry are safe.

Weeks turned into months without another murder. Slowly my anxiety seeped from my consciousness. I was able to genuinely celebrate the birth of our daughter, Adelina Wilhelmina, on July 10, 1835. Lina is happy and healthy. Our wee one -- yes, some of Seamus has rubbed off on me -- is pretty. I was just as anxious as I was when Henry was born. Our little Minnie is perfect, her delivery went smoothly. Lina was up and about two days later. I wonder if there is a man on earth who could endure the discomfort of being pregnant much less the pain of delivery. I am ashamed to admit I am thankful women rather than men bear children.

Elections were held on August 15. Three hundred pound Oremus Morrison was elected constable along with John Shrigley and Luther Nichols. In addition to his duties as constable, Morrison also serves as coroner.

A week after the election, Oremus Morrison and John Shrigley arranged to talk with Doc Wooten and me. We met in Morrison's office on the lower level of his home at Clark and Madison.

Oremus seemed gentle and kind. His girth is misleading. Although generous to the poor, he is fearless when dealing with anyone violating the law. He thanked us for coming.

"I am concerned about the Pitchfork Murders," he began. "This kind of story sends fears through our citizens. If it continues, word will spread around the country and the flow of newcomers will hamper the growth of Chicago.

"Doc, would you mind describing the conditions of each of the corpses."

"Not at all."

Spreading his files on the table, he carefully went through each. Oremus was particularly interested in Doc's sketches of the pitchfork punctures.

"Axel, may I ask why you are interested in these cases?"

Doc looked at me.

I hesitated, conflicted between my need for privacy and my duty. Oremus leaned back in his chair, puffed on his cigar and showed no impatience with my reluctance to respond. I finally began.

"As the law, can I rely on your discretion?"

Oremus turned to John, "Is this acceptable to you Shrigley?"

John asked, "Axel, what exactly do you mean?"

"I believe I know who might be behind these murders. I do not want the reason why I know made public."

Oremus leaned forward. "As long as you neither committed the murders nor aided and abetted the killer, I can assure I will never reveal anything you say to us today."

Uncomfortable but satisfied, I began with the pitchfork incident in the barn in Germany and continued on through Lina's kidnaping in New York. It never gets easier in the retelling. All I can hope is the murders will cease as a result of the efforts by the constables.

"I have several questions. Have you seen this Rikert here in Chicago?"

"No, I have not."

"Would you describe him for me."

"He's short, thin, in his early forties. He drinks to excess and can be very abusive. When sober he can be quite charming and dress elegantly. He never fully recovered from falling on the pitchfork. He stoops forward, unable to stand erect. When sober, he is usually clean shaven. He is unable to control his temper, even when sober. He often has vicious confrontations with anyone he thinks hasn't treated him well. His face can change from pleasant to hideous in seconds."

"Have you given any thought as to where he might be residing if he is in Chicago? The type of work he might be doing? They type of people who might be his associates?"

"I keep thrashing it over and over in my mind. Although I have never seen the Sands, I believe it would appeal to him. He thrives on drink and wanton women, although he would much prefer to live in finer lodgings than I understand exist in the Sands. What type of work he might be doing? I don't believe Rikert has ever worked a day in his life. His father gave him an excessive allowance which he wasted on debauchery."

John interjected, "Liquor and women, you're describing the Sands. It's a good place to start our investigation."

"One other thing." I added, "Rikert only associates with someone beneath him, who he can control and who will never question him. He instinctively resents and resists authority."

"Now that Shrigley, Nichols and I have been elected, I think it is time we make a very public visit to the Sands. I would like to enter each of the businesses, introduce the three of us and offer our services if they are ever in need of help. Might just meet this Rikert."

As Doc and I left and headed to our homes, we stopped to chat.

"How do you feel it went, Axel?"

"Doc, I am hopeful. What do you think?"

"I agree. Seems too simple, though. If Rikert is as crafty and diabolical as you describe, he won't be easily snared."

"You know, Doc, he has a huge opinion of himself. He might just like to challenge us all by meeting the constables head on and egging them to arrest him."

Chapter Thirty One

O remus's voice rose as he paced back and forth in his tiny office. Doc and I sat against the wall, mesmerized by the Constable's rage. His girth did not slow him down. His speech quickened the faster he walked. On the far side of the room stood his two assistants, Luther and John. Their faces were expressionless. I concluded they had seen Constable Morrison excited before.

"I knew the Sands was degradation at its worst. I never imagined how low society can sink in sin. It took us two days to visit every single hovel and shack. There are no streets, just beaten paths. The buildings are strewn around like dice thrown in craps. Some places are so flimsy, we could see through the gaps in the boards. One has no door, just a torn drape limply hanging across the opening. When we entered, we were confronted by two women in the midst of entertaining two men on bales of hay.

"No matter where we went, our presence evoked no reactions other than stupid grins on the faces of customers and shameless arrogance on the faces of the *hostesses.*"

John Shrigley interjected, "It became clear after the third *house* the word had gone out of our raids."

"I'd hardly call it raids," added Luther. "Scantily clad women stood outside and waved us in."

"They audaciously shouted obscenities at us or invited us to spend a dollar or two," John incredulously added.

"Axel, we saw no one who matched the description of your cousin. God knows we searched. It was the most disgusting two days of my life," Oremus growled.

"We didn't force men to show us their backs, if not already visible, or stand up to see how tall they were, so we may have missed him," Luther said in revulsion.

"From what you told us, Axel," Oremus asked, "is it likely Rikert would be so disgracefully and shamelessly engaged?"

"No. He may be a pig but I can't imagine he would want to be revealed in public."

"I lost count. There must be more than fifty shacks and shanties. Everyone of them had business no matter the time of the day. How could there be so many?" asked Luther.

Oremus answered. "I have been here two years now. The growth of Chicago in the past two years has been staggering. You've been here longer, Doc. What was the population when you arrived?"

"We were told about 150. No official number back in the spring of 1832," Doc responded.

"What is it now?" asked Orsemus.

"Over three thousand," said Doc.

John exclaimed, "That's over one thousand percent increase in three years!"

Doc continued, "Since there are still many more men than women, the Sands meets the men's needs. More and more men come see me with cases of the French Disease. Damn epidemic. Oremus, you should post signs throughout the Sands warning of the risk of catching the plague."

Oremus had stopped pacing and plopped himself into his chair. I held my breath, fearing the chair would collapse under his weight. Stroking his chin, he spoke.

"I'm sorry we have no progress to report to you, Axel. We visited the brick mansion in the midst of the hovels in the Sands. Miss Lotus was most gracious and invited us to tea. We declined. Did sit a bit in the parlor. She was very forthright in answering my questions, assuring me no man had visited her establishment who matches the description you gave to me.

"When I asked her who financed the construction of the Pleasure Palace, she said Mr. Evert Unruh. He is her partner and has a private apartment in the large building. I asked if I could meet him. She said he had gone East for a visit. I asked if he matched the description of the man we were seeking. She assured me he did not even closely resemble your cousin.

"I can think of nothing else we can do for now. I assure you, the three of us will pursue any new leads we get. Until we have further information or another pitchfork murder occurs, I'm afraid the case will have to be set aside."

I kept my disappointment from showing when I said, "I appreciate all the three of you have done. I pray there will be no further pitchfork murders."

I stood to leave. Doc did as well. Oremus slowly lifted himself from his chair, his weight requiring effort to do so. "Axel, our time at the Sands was not useless. As constables, we delivered a very clear message. While we can't shut down the Sands, we won't condone it. I told each establishment about the Chicago Board of Trustees passing an ordinance authorizing me to levee fines against brothels. We will begin fining on our next visit. Most just laughed when I told them the fine would be twenty-five dollars. Their profits must far exceed the amount of the fine.

"Some day, there will be enough good citizens to demand the destruction of the Sands. While tearing down the shacks won't bring an end to the illicit behavior, it might make it less brazenly present."

Two days later, Constable Morrison came to see me. I invited him into my office. Once the door was shut and we were seated, he spoke.

"Axel, there has been another pitchfork murder. This one even more gruesome. The body was found naked on the river bank. It was headless! The man's back has the punctures of a pitchfork. He was quite large and muscular. I had the corpse taken to Doc Wooten's. He confirmed my observation the man had been dead for several months. Doc feels the body was buried and only recently dug up and dumped on the river bank.

"I shall do what I can to investigate the murder. I'm not at all optimistic I will uncover the identity of the murderer."

Chapter Thirty Two

Not sure what has changed. My days are whipping by to the point I feel I am no longer in control of my life. Doc told me he feels the same sense of being caught in a rushing stream, watching the banks speeding by so fast, he can hardly distinguish what he is seeing. We were both bothered. I really had not thought about it until I spoke of my feeling out loud.

"I can't believe it's already October," I said. "It's almost 1836."

"I think I am overwhelmed by the number of immigrants arriving each day," Doc lamented. "The growth of our once tiny village has mushroomed beyond my comprehension. I no longer sit idly by waiting for a patient to come see me or a family member frantically bursting in, begging me to come to their home right away.

"Some days I have no time for my noon meal. Most days my waiting room is crowded. I am so focused on caring for others, I have no time to think about myself. My days are blurring together."

"That's it, Doc. It is all blurring together. The bank is busy. When I finally close the bank and go upstairs to relax in peace and quiet, I am instantly challenged by my children. Lina puts our little baby daughter in my lap as Henry runs to tell me his latest adventure. I dearly love them. If I could just have a few moments to relax and adjust.

"I can't understand how Lina can be so calm in the midst of a whirlwind of children, toys, naps and meals. By the time we put the children to bed, we are so exhausted, we no longer have time to just sit and quietly talk. All too soon, it is time to begin the next day."

Doc and I were in Mark Beaubien's tavern. It was mid-afternoon. We were sitting at a back table. Several others were across from us.

Suddenly there was music. Not Mark on his squawky fiddle, but the sweet sound of a piano. We looked up, astonished to see a piano standing in the corner. One of Mark's daughters was playing. She was playing what I recognized as Mozart. I had not heard it since I left Germany.

Our conversation ceased as Doc and I relished the sound. Mark and his wife came from the other room, standing off to the side, smiling with pride at their child. Becoming aware of their presence, she stopped, blushing.

"Don't stop, dear," her mother said. "You play so beautifully. I much prefer your music to the sounds your father makes."

Mark, pretending to be hurt, poked his wife. When she turned to him in disgust, he said, "I could not agree with you more, Monique."

Their daughter, embarrassed by the attention, got up and scampered from the tavern.

Mark came over to our table.

"How long have you had the piano?" Doc asked.

"Three months. Not surprised you don't know. I was beginning to think you were going somewhere else."

"No, just too busy," Doc mumbled.

"Last time I saw you two," Mark continued, "was at your sister's wedding, Axel."

"Guess that's right. Doc and I were saying how we have lost track of time."

"Speaking of time, I need to get back to my office," Doc said.

Shortly afterward, we left the Sauganash. Doc walked to his place, I to the bank.

In my office I reflected on Anna. Her wedding had been on May 5th, almost five months ago. It was the first church wedding since I came to Chicago. Weddings here are usually held at home. St. James was large enough to hold everyone we invited.

Anna carried a bouquet of spring flowers. She was aglow in her happiness. Her hair was pulled up, entwined with flowers and ribbons. Lina had helped Anna make her wedding gown. It was elegant. Carsten wore a dark suit and grey vest. He had a single flower in his lapel. Lina and I were witnesses. Lina was showing, the baby due in two months. She was lovely in a pale blue dress, a vision of beauty and grace. I, for the first time in Chicago, wore one of my New York-made suits.

Standing facing the altar, I listened carefully to the words spoken by the pastor. I had not heard anything said at my own wedding. I had been in a trance. Although I was ecstatic, I had been strangely withdrawn during our wedding ceremony. I had almost panicked. Not about becoming a husband, rather over the aura grasping me. Thankfully, I did not make a fool of myself and snapped out of it at the end of our vows.

At Anna's wedding, I looked at Lina and said a prayer thanking God yet again for blessing me with her.

The weather on May 5th could not have been better. I hired a number of carriages to take the guests to our home. Lina had asked Johann to bake special cakes, cookies and other delicacies. Mark Beaubien had blended a punch fit for the occasion. Seamus and Molly had arranged decorations in our home. Yes, Molly. She and her parents had come for the wedding. Lina's mother, Minnie, had come from New York along with James Dowling and Mamie Baruth.

I was so engaged in conversation with our guests, I did not notice Lina had disappeared. Dear Anna, always thoughtful and caring, even on this, her wedding day, came to me to say she had insisted Lina go to our bedroom and rest.

"Everything is fine, Axel. Lina needed to get off her feet. The past few weeks have been exciting but exhausting for her. When you can, go see her."

I did so immediately. I gently knocked and opened the door. Lina was sitting in one of our stuffed chairs, her feet propped up, a smile on her face.

"I knew you would come in a panic, Axey. I am fine."

I went to her side and knelt by the chair.

Lina took my hand and said, "This has been a wonderful day, my love. Now go back to our guests. I shall join you in a few minutes."

A little more than two months later, our daughter, Adelina Wilhelmina was born, healthy and adorable.

––––––––––

The evening following Anna and Carsten's marriage, Seamus, Ferrel O'Flaherty, James Dowling, Doc and Philo gathered with me in my library. We were all sipping brandy with the exception of Seamus who, true to his abstinence of alcohol, drank apple cider.

"Chicago is not at all what I expected," observed James.

"What'd you expect?" asked his grandson, Seamus

"A small village filled with log cabins, horses and Indians."

Somewhat defensively, Seamus objected. "Not any more."

"If you look hard, you will still see cabins and a few Indians," I offered. "There is a growing sophistication. Logs are no longer used in the village. Mine is no longer the only brick building. Boardwalks are beginning to lift us out of the mud."

Just then we heard several gun shots as if to disprove my claim of sophistication.

187

"It's sunset," Doc explained. "John Hogan, the Postmaster, still marks sunrise and the end of the day with his rifle. Doubt he'll be allowed to do it much longer."

"I suppose another measure of Chicago's maturity," Philo interjected, "is our Pitchfork Murder spree."

I cringed. Ferrel asked, "Pitchfork murder?"

I was thankful Doc responded, briefly telling of the four without mentioning me.

James Dowling, looking at me, commented, "Sadly, murder becomes more common the larger a city grows. Even sadder is how it becomes less shocking unless you know the victim."

Looking around the room, I realized everyone knew of my confrontation with Rikert back in Germany with the exception of Ferrel. With a slight nod at Doc, he answered Ferrel's question, telling the full story. He added the constables were pursuing the case without telling the public of the background involving me.

"I was unaware the nightmare followed you to Chicago, Axel. Have you told Lina?" asked James.

"I have. Anna also knows. Other than being on guard, there is nothing we can do. I have not seen Rikert. I don't know if he is hiding here in Chicago or orchestrating the murders from New York."

"I can only imagine the horror each murder has evoked for you," James' voice clearly tinged with emotion. "I wish I could help. I shall pray for an end to Rikert's scourge. I'm afraid prayers are the only weapons left to an old man."

Aiming to lighten the conversation, Captain O'Flaherty, with a very exaggerated Irish brogue, told of an elderly Irish man who died and went up to Heaven. He was greeted at the pearly gates by St. Peter who said:

"Before you may enter Heaven, I have a question for you. How many followers did our Lord Jesus feed with five loaves of bread and three fish?"

Smiling, the Irishman said, "Five thousand."

"Correct," said St. Peter. "You may enter."

Next seeking entrance was a German. St. Peter, said to him, "Before you may enter Heaven, I have a question for you. Our Lord Jesus once fed five thousand pilgrims with five loaves of bread and three fish. Can you tell me the names of each of the five thousand?"

After the laughter subsided, I asked, "Ferrel, is that because St. Peter is partial to the Irish or because he knew we Germans are good with details?"

Sensing we might be headed for a serious debate, James returned to his observations of Chicago. "I found our trip from New York delightful. The Erie Canal and Lake Erie gave me my first chance to see the beauty and enormity of America. The next time I come to Chicago, if I live long enough, it could well be by railroad."

Philo nodded in agreement. "I understand both here and in Germany, over a hundred or more miles of tracks have been laid. Do you really think railroads will be extended outside of the east coast?"

"I do," answered James. "It's just a matter of time. A railroad would significantly reduce the number of days to travel between New York and Chicago."

Seamus, bristling, jumped in. "They'll never replace ships and barges. Blimey, we are about to start construction on the Illinois and Michigan Canal."

James, ever the diplomat, hastened to say, "I agree, Seamus. Ships can carry much larger loads than today's somewhat feeble railroads.

"Tell me about this canal. I know you have been working for the Commission. Exactly where will the canal be located? When will construction start? Will you work on the construction?"

Seamus enthusiastically responded. "The canal is to start at the river, just south of Chicago, and run southwest to LaSalle on the Illinois River. When complete, it will connect Lake Michigan at Chicago to the Gulf of Mexico."

"How long will the canal be?"

I could see James was very proud of his grandson. I suspect he knew all about the canal but was asking questions to give Seamus a chance to explain.

"96 miles."

"Isn't the distance to the Gulf much greater than that?"

"Yes. The canal needs only to get to the Illinois River which connects with the Mississippi River which eventually empties into the Gulf."

Fascinated with the discussion, Ferrel asked, "What do you do, Seamus?"

"Right now, I'm selling land for the Canal Commission. The U. S. Congress allotted the Commission a wide right-of-way along the proposed route. The excess land is being sold to finance the construction. Sales are good. Speculators are buying land hoping it will increase in value. Some sell within a few weeks of their purchase, making a substantial profit."

Doc said, "I thought you were working at Wrights' General Store."

"I did, for the winter when canal sales dropped off. I am back in canal sales. When business tapers off, I'll return to Wrights."

"Your future sounds good, Seamus," Ferrel noted. "Are you committed to living in Chicago?"

"I am, sir. This is the happiest I have been since before my dear Mother died. I was only twelve then. Why do you ask?"

"Well, I wondered where my Molly might live after she marries?"

Blushing, Seamus said, "With me, I hope, sir."

"Are you planning on marrying my daughter?"

Seamus was speechless. It was as if he and the rest of us were frozen in silence. It seemed to me to be for minutes. It must have seemed like an eternity to Seamus. Finally, I suggested, "Why don't we leave and give Ferrel and Seamus privacy."

Having regained his composure, Seamus boldly said, "That won't be necessary. I love Molly. Sir, may I have your permission to ask your daughter to marry me?"

"How old are you son?"

"I am seventeen, nearly eighteen."

I thought back to when I met Seamus in 1831 on the docks of New York. I was sixteen then. He was only fourteen but told me he was twenty-one. This time he was telling the truth.

"Are you aware that Molly is only fifteen? Much too young to marry."

I looked at the others. Doc and Philo seemed as uncomfortable as I felt, being present for such a private conversation. James' appearance was that of a very proud grandfather, pleased to be witnessing the exchange.

"She is, sir. I shall abide by your judgment if only you will grant me your permission to speak to Molly of my love and desire to marry her."

The smile, which I felt was ready to erupt the moment the conversation had begun, came forth. Captain O'Flaherty's face broke into a grin. In a hearty voice, he announced, "Yes! Do ask her. Then her mother and I will no longer have to listen to her anxiously asking us over and over again, if we think you love her."

I proposed a toast. "To Molly and Seamus. May their marriage be as happy and fruitful as Lina's and mine."

Everyone stood to toast.

Seamus asked me, "Does this mean we are in competition to see who can have more children? Not exactly fair. You have a head start."

Our laughter filled the room.

When it subsided, Captain O'Flaherty shocked us all. "Seamus, I would like to discuss with you about taking over the *Princess Rose* after you and Molly are married."

Two days later, Seamus came to see me. "Axel, remember when Captain O'Flaherty mentioned the other night about me taking over the *Princess Rose*?"

"Yes. Have you two talked?"

"We have. He wants me to take over his business. To become the captain of the *Princess Rose*. He would retain ownership. We'd divide the profits, fifty-fifty. This would be after Molly and I are married."

"What did you say?"

"I told him I would think about it. Axel, I don't want to do it. Even though Lake Erie isn't like the ocean, it still frightens me. Ever since I nearly drowned off the coast of Ireland, I am afraid of lakes and oceans."

"Have you talked to Molly about it?"

"I have. She wants me to decline her father's offer. Do you think he will refuse to let me marry Molly if I say no?"

"No. I think he is so pleased with the prospect of you marrying Molly, he wants to entrust his ship to you, the grandson of Captain Myles O'Shea. Remember, Ferrel was the lad who told your grandfather of the loss of one of his ships. This might be his way of making amends. He might feel he caused your grandfather to die because he brought the bad news."

"Do you really think so? It wasn't Ferrel's fault."

"I know. He may not even be thinking what I suggest. You should do what is right for you and Molly. By the way, have you asked Molly to marry you?"

Smiling broadly, Seamus said, "I'm no fool. I asked Molly before I talked to the Captain. She and I have been talking about marriage for a long time."

"When are the O'Flaherty's leaving?"

"They did this morning. I told the Captain I will have an answer for him the next time he docks in Chicago. By then he will know Molly's feelings. Means I will be both looking forward to and dreading the return of the *Princess Rose*. That is if Mrs. O'Flaherty and Molly are aboard."

Part Nine

Seamus

Chapter Thirty Three

William Ogden was born in Walton, New York, on June 15, 1805. When his father died, he took over his real estate business, although William was only a teenager. Thinking he might want to be an attorney, Ogden attended law school. He left after a short time. He assisted his brother-in-law, Charles Butler, concerning a new building for New York University. In 1834, William was elected to the New York State Legislature.

Charles Butler invested $100,000 in land in Chicago. He did so, site unseen. In 1835 he asked William to go to Chicago to assess his purchase. Once in Chicago, William attempted to walk the site. He soon found himself standing ankle deep in mud. He could not believe Butler had wasted so much money on a swamp. He wrote to his brother-in-law: "You have been guilty of the grossest folly. There is no such value in the land and won't be for a generation."

Determined to make the best of it, William had the land drained, surveyed, streets laid out and subdivided into lots. Once dry, he advertised the lots for sale. His timing was perfect. Men were inundating Chicago, eager to purchase land being sold by the Illinois and Michigan Canal Commission. Speculative fever seemed to infect everyone. Within ninety days, Ogden sold one-third of Charles Butler's land for a sum greater than his brother-in-law's total investment.

During the buying binge of Butler's land and lots by the Canal Commission, William Ogden and Seamus O'Shea met. Seamus was once again in charge of the Commission's Chicago office. Ogden, thirty years of age, was captivated by the young Irishman. They met for the first time at the Sauganash where Mark Beaubien introduced them. Each had heard of the other and was wary of his competitor. Seamus quickly put Ogden at ease.

"I am glad to meet your, sir," Seamus said. "I congratulate you on your success. Your advertisements are very appealing. If I were seeking land to purchase, I would beat a path to your office."

"From your brogue, may I assume you are Irish, Mr. O'Shea?"

"Yes and damn proud of it, Mr. Ogden."

Ogden, every bit Seamus' equal in confidence, smiled. "Perhaps it is I who should come to your office. I hear your lots are selling faster than ice on a hot day." From that day forth, the two got together for dinner every now and then to compare notes.

"What are winters like here?" William asked.

"Can be very harsh. Sales trickle down to a halt. Not much to do for three, four months."

"What will you do then?"

"I'll resume managing Wrights General Store. Will you be going back to New York?"

"I've decided to make Chicago my home. I'm going to return to New York and wrap up loose ends. I also want to engage an architect to design a home for me.

"Seamus, what can you tell me about the proposed canal?"

"Why do you ask?"

"I had a hand in the Erie Railroad. The I & M might be a good venture for me."

"What would you like to know – it's history, the finances, design, schedule?"

"Everything."

"Asking an Irishman to tell you everything he knows is dangerous, Mr. Ogden. Hard to shut us up."

"I'll risk it, Mr. O'Shea."

"Why don't we go to my office. I have a map of the proposed route."

The two left the Sauganash and walked to the Commission office.

"Ain't fancy. The sign is almost bigger than the office."

Pushing through the line of men waiting outside, Seamus led the way into the office where several clerks were selling lots. The two entered Seamus' office which was behind the counter. On the wall over his desk was a handsome map.

"You heard of Louis Jolliet?"

"Was he the French Canadian explorer?"

"Yes."

"Did he make it to Chicago?"

"Jolliet and a Jesuit priest named Father Marquette came up the Mississippi and the Illinois River, hoping to get back to Lake

Michigan. They had to make a portage to reach the Chicago River. Jolliet was the first to suggest, according to the journal he kept, that a canal be dug to connect the Chicago and Illinois rivers."

"When was this?"

"1673! Only recently has his idea been resurrected."

"Why now?"

"Chicago is bursting at the seams. Farmers bring their grain here so we can ship it East. If they could load it on boats nearer their farms, it would save time and money.

"In 1822, the U. S. Congress made a land grant to the State of Illinois for a canal. Possible routes were surveyed. Two years later, Judge Lockwood arranged for a more detailed survey. They estimated the cost to build the canal to be somewhere between $600,000 and $700,000."

"Is Judge Lockwood still involved?"

"Might say so. Behind the scene, that is."

"Do you know Judge Lockwood?"

"Yes, he recommended me to the Commission."

"How is the canal to be funded?"

"In 1827, the U. S. Congress granted more public land to Illinois – a six mile wide pathway along the route. The cost to build the canal will be paid for from the proceeds of the lands sold. That's where I come in. I am selling the lots."

"Would you mind telling me how old you are?"

"I'm eighteen. Long story why the Judge wanted me hired. I can tell you some other day."

"I'll hold you to that. I'm curious, although the more you tell me, I'm not surprised."

"When will construction begin?"

"Next year, 1836, likely in the summer. Assuming, that is, the Commission can select contractors and hire laborers."

"I have been looking at the map on the wall. Could we look at it more closely?"

For the next hour, Seamus, at Ogden's urging, spelled out in great detail the route, the locks, the depth, tow path designs, the overall dimensions and preliminary construction schedules. Seamus told of the horrors Mrs. Duffy had described about the construction of the Erie Canal and the dreadful toll of lives including the death of her husband due to malaria. Seamus expressed deep concern for the men who would dig the I & M Canal.

Several weeks later, when the two talked again, Ogden told Seamus he had met with Judge Lockwood.

"The Judge has arranged for me to meet the Commission. Would you be willing to join me?"

"Why?"

"I would like to make a proposal that I be involved in the management of the construction. Through my connections back East, I can induce many of the workers who dug the Erie Canal to come and work on the I & M.

"Why have you join me? Most of the workers will be Irish immigrants. If you partnered with me, we could assure them better conditions. You could serve to be a liaison, representing the interests of your fellow countrymen."

The meeting with the Commissioners went well. They entered into an arrangement with William Ogden based in large measure on his assurance he would listen to and act upon Seamus' advice and counsel.

With the advent of winter, Ogden went back East and Seamus resumed managing Wrights General Store. His deposits in the bank grew significantly. His expenses were minimal. He looked forward to 1836. It would be a year of change: working in a new capacity for the Commission and his marriage. Seamus and Molly had agreed to get married in the fall of the year. He would be eighteen and she sixteen. The Captain and Mrs. O'Flaherty had granted their consent. Also in 1836, Seamus anticipated the arrival of his sisters, Briana and Nora, from Ireland.

Chapter Thirty Four

Late in the summer of 1835, Seamus wrote to Captain Liam Moore of the *Bonnie Jean* to make arrangements for Briana and Nora to come to America. It took months before he got a response. In his letter, Captain Moore outlined a tentative schedule of his voyages between Galway and New York. He offered to arrange for Seamus' sisters to safely travel from Ballynakill to the port on Galway Bay. Seamus wrote back with his choice of which date would be best. In his second response, Captain Moore wrote:

Seamus,

You can rest easy. I shall make sure your sisters arrive safely in Galway. I no longer go to Londonderry on my way to the United States as I did when you made the crossing. The demand here is sufficient to more than make up for the fares I made stopping in Londonderry.

I have talked to Father Bevan here in Galway. He sent a message to Father Garreth in Ballynakill. I am enclosing Father Garreth's letter which is most encouraging.

Once aboard the *Bonnie Jean*, Briana and Nora will be under my personal care. Their cabin will be adjacent to mine and they will eat all their meals with me.

I anticipate the *Bonnie Jean* will arrive in New York with your sisters around April 20th of 1836.

Hans and Chan Lee send their regards. When I mentioned you will be meeting your sisters upon our arrival in America, they both expressed their desire to see you.

Your friend, Liam Moore

Seamus read the enclosed note. It was, indeed, from Father Garreth.

Seamus, my son,

Your letters from America have brought joy and smiles to Briana
and Nora. They always let me read them. I am amazed with all you have
accomplished and with your genuine warmth and courage.

I have been blessed with a young priest assigned to help me fulfill
my duties. I have now been serving the church here in Ballynakill every
day since I arrived fifty-one years ago. It is time I slow down and do
some travel. Father Malachi is capable and itching, I can tell, to do more.
I have decided to travel to Galway Bay with your sisters. Were I younger,
I would continue on with them to America.

Nora and Briana are beaming with expectation. It will be good for
them to spread their wings. Macha has been baking and cooking, insisting
the girls will need food for the crossing. She is helping them sew new
dresses. I suspect Macha wishes she could come to America with them.
She considers them as the children she never had. She will, as will I, miss
them dearly.

The funds you sent are more than sufficient for their journey. They
will be safe. Do not worry, lad. May your days always be touched by a bit
of Irish luck, brightened by a song in your heart, and soon warmed by the
smiles of Briana and Nora. May the smile of God always light the three
of you in glory.

Go with God, Father Garreth

There was another letter enclosed. It was sealed with a smudge of
wax without an imprint. Running his finger under the edge, the minute
he saw the handwriting he knew it was from Briana.

My Dear Brother,

As I am sure Father Garreth has written, he is going to travel with us
to Galway. He claims it is to visit relatives but I think there is a more
compelling reason.

A month ago, I caught sight of our Father. I was shopping in the
Village. The square was crowded. As I made a purchase, I felt someone
watching me. I paid no never mind. At the next stall, it happened again.
This time I looked. It was father. He was close enough for me to be sure.
He looked very sad and was crying. Not sobbing, for he was as still as a
statue. Tears were streaming down his face.

I felt both fear and sympathy. I didn't know if I should run or reach
out to him. I bowed my head in prayer, seeking guidance for what I
should do. When I looked up, he was gone. I pretended to continue

shopping, going from stall to stall, looking for him. I did not see him again.

Since then, I have watched for him everywhere, in the square, in the shops, in church. I even went to the graveyard. He was not there, at least not when I visited. There were fresh flowers on Mother's grave.

Seamus, I have told no one. His clothing was clean. He looked healthy. He seemed no longer a captive of drink.

Could Father Garreth want to come with us to Galway to protect us from Father? Has he seen Father?

This is no way to end my final letter to you before I see you in America. I must know. You must know. When I was alone with Father Garreth, I told him of seeing Father. He showed no reaction. I finally asked if he had seen Father. He told me he had. Father has visited him at the church several times. Father Garreth told me he struggles with his duty as a priest and his duty as a guardian. As a priest, he told me, he should hear Father's confession and grant him forgiveness as would Jesus. As a guardian, he told me, he must protect Nora and me from the violence Father has shown in the past.

Together, Father Garreth and I decided not to tell Nora. When it is time for us to leave, we shall depart Ballynakill after dark to evade Father if he is watching.

Do not worry dear brother. Soon we will all be together and safe from the past.

My love and prayers, your sister, Briana

The months crept by slowly. His sisters and his father were never far from his thoughts. Seamus found absorbing himself in his work dampened his growing anxiety. He went to see Philo, Doc and Axel. They no longer met on a regular basis, only when one of them needed counsel. As he should have expected, each assured Seamus all would be well and his sisters would arrive safely.

William Ogden returned from New York. Seamus met with him to tell him he would be gone for perhaps a month when he went to New York to meet his sisters. To his surprise, Ogden not only expressed no objection but became uncharacteristically excited. He asked Seamus to meet with several Irishmen while he was in New York.

"I have been in contact with some of the Irish leaders of men who once worked on the Erie Canal. The timing of you being in New York is perfect. I will give you their names and addresses. Dominick Breen is the most important of the group. The others respect him. He has a good head on his shoulders."

"What would I be meeting about?"

"To convince them to encourage Irish workers to come to Chicago. We need laborers to start digging this summer."

Seamus left well before Liam's anticipated arrival of April 20th. He wanted to wait in New York rather than be tied in knots of worry in Chicago. In New York he could check each day to see if the *Bonnie Jean* had arrived. After checking the docks on his first full day in New York, Seamus found a place to stay nearby. The Royal House was anything but. His room was filthy. The food in the tavern intolerable. He put up with both so he could be near the docks.

Seamus could not sleep once the sun rose. He hurriedly dressed, choked down a minimal breakfast and rushed to the Harbor Master's office. After a few days, the Harbor Master recognized Seamus and would answer his inquiry about the *Bonnie Jean* before being asked. Seamus returned mid-afternoon to inquire again.

He had free hours each morning and afternoon. After a few days he went to see the Duffy family. The boys were taller and Nella more haggard looking than ever. He stayed for only an hour. He felt out of place.

Another morning he went to see Black Jack. When he got to the building, he didn't enter. He again felt out of place.

He finally went to see Dominick Breen. The minute they met, Seamus felt excitement and purpose. They talked for hours. Seamus explained, "I live in Chicago. I came back to New York to meet my sisters who are arriving from Ireland. When William Ogden learned of my trip, he asked me to talk with you.

"Digging is about to begin on the Illinois and Michigan Canal. Mr. Ogden would like you to convince Irishmen to come to Chicago and work on the Canal. I work for the Canal Commission."

Dominick tensed up when Seamus mentioned the canal.

"How can you sell your soul to a canal? Do you have any idea how many Irish died digging the Erie? Is that all Americans think we Irish are good for, to dig and die? I'll be damned if...."

Seamus interrupted. "I am well aware of the tragedies of the Erie."

"What, were you there?"

Seamus didn't answer, rather he asked, "Were you?"

"I've just been in America a year. Many have told me the Irish diggers were treated no better than Negro slaves."

"I've heard that too. When I came to America five years ago, I lived in New York with the widow of a canal worker and her two sons. I may not have worked on the Erie but from what she told me, I shudder to this day. I learned of her husband and the inhuman conditions of the workers. He had an agonizing death. His wife works nights so she can earn enough to pay rent for a tiny apartment unfit for humans. She struggles each day to provide for her children. When not working at a laundry, she spends much of her time ironing clothing and linens for wealthy customers. She is thin and exhausted. Each day I expected her to drop dead. I would not have agreed to ask you to send workers if I were not sure the conditions on the I & M will be better than on the Erie."

Dominick was convinced. Not by what Seamus had described, but by his passion. He probed him for more details. Seamus didn't know if he did this as a test or to learn. Whichever it was, Dominick shifted the conversation from opposition to questions about the number of laborers needed, the measures to be put in place to assure decent housing and wages and concern for the safety of the workers including medical attention. Seamus surprised even himself with the intensity of his own responses and his commitment to be a vigorous advocate for the Irish workers.

"I will begin immediately to encourage our countrymen to go to Chicago on one condition."

"What's that?"

"That I can give each of them your name and how they can find you in Chicago."

Taking a pad from his pocket, Seamus wrote down his name, location of where he lives and his office with the Commission. He handed it to Dominick.

Dominick folded it and put it in his pocket.

Unabashedly, Seamus asked, "How can I help our countrymen back in Ireland?"

Dominick asked, "Just what do you mean?"

"How can I help Ireland become free of the British?"

Glancing around the tavern where they were talking, Dominick studied Seamus for a long time, trying to decide if he could trust him. Finally he said, "Let's go outside. The trees have no ears."

At first Dominick spoke slowly, then gradually more rapidly with greater fervor.

"Are you Catholic, Seamus?"

Without hesitancy, Seamus said, "I am."

"I am as well. I lost my father and two brothers in Robert Emmet's rebellion of 1803. I don't believe we will ever be able to gain freedom from the British by force. They have the army, we don't. They have the arms, we don't. They have money, we don't. They own most of Ireland. A stone and a slingshot can't topple the British giant.

"Have you heard of Daniel O'Connell?"

"No."

"Where are you from, Seamus?"

"Ballynakill."

"Where's that?"

"Roughly halfway between Dublin and Galway."

"Ah, the countryside. Did you ever get news from Dublin?"

"No. We lived in the bogs, not in the village. I was fourteen when I fled. Who's O'Connell?"

The two were walking down a street of shops. They turned west, entering a street of modest homes. Much finer, Seamus thought, than the tenements where Mrs. Duffy and her sons live.

"O'Connell was born to a once wealthy Catholic family. His uncle, who was rich, tucked Daniel under his wing and saw he was educated, especially in France. He encouraged his nephew to study the law.

"When he was twenty-one, Wolfe Tone," seeing the expression on Seamus' face, Dominick paused. "You've not heard of him either, have you?" Seamus shook his head. "Up ahead is a park, we can sit there and talk."

Breen led the way to a clearing in the center of the heavily wooded park. Several benches surrounded a large pond. A pair of swans were gracefully gliding among the water lilies. Selecting an unoccupied bench, farthest from the only other one in use, the two settled down. The air was chilly. The sun warmed them.

"Theobold Wolfe Tone was born in Dublin. His father was a coach-maker and member of the Protestant Church of Ireland. Tone preferred to be called Wolfe. He studied law at Trinity College and qualified as a barrister at the age of 26.

"Tone was a dreamer. He proposed the British found a military colony in Hawaii. William Pitt rejected the idea. Disappointed, Wolfe became interested in Irish politics. He wrote pamphlets attacking the government. He became committed to the independence of Ireland from England. Enamored with the French Revolution, guided by their principles, he became an advocate for the British to abolish their restrictions against the Catholics. As a Protestant, he saw the Catholics as an ally in his goal of seeking independence for Ireland."

The man who had been sitting on a bench across the pond, stood and began to walk along the pathway around the water. As he approached Dominick and Seamus, he slowed down, coming to a halt in front of them. Dominick stopped talking, suspicious of the man. He tipped his hat and asked, "Are you gentlemen Irish?"

Without any hesitation, Seamus responded, "I'm from Chicago, sir. Are all New Yorkers as rude as you?"

Startled by Seamus' question, the man frowned and hurried on.

"That was strange," Seamus commented.

"Never know. I should have warned you, I am often under surveillance. The bias against the Irish has recently increased. We are seldom hired for other than the most menial jobs. Now the government has become concerned about Irish immigrants supporting revolution in Ireland. The United States favors the British against Catholic Ireland."

"I thought I had left all of that behind me," lamented Seamus.

Breen was seething with anger and determination about the struggle for their countrymen to gain freedom from, as he put it, " the blood-sucking British."

Nervously, Dominick said, "We have talked enough today. Where are you staying?"

"A cheap inn near the docks. Once my sisters arrive, we shall lodge at the Eagle Hotel."

"What is the name of the inn?"

Smiling, Seamus said, "The Royal House."

"I know it. May I call on you tomorrow. Say about noon? In the dining room?"

"If you call it a dining room. I'll be there waiting for you."

Chapter Thirty Five

After a fitful night, Seamus rose early, his body aching from the hard pillow and lumpy bed. Walking to the window, he looked out at the ships docked at the end of the street. He decided he would never get accustomed to living near water. Whether looking out, as now, at the endless expanse of the Atlantic, or in Chicago seeing the blue waters of Lake Michigan, he was uncomfortable with large bodies of water.

For the first fourteen years of his life, his view, in all directions, was of drab brown stretches of the bogs. No matter how often his mother pointed out the beauty of the sunrise, the mist or the far mountains, he could never escape the stench and sameness of the bogs. They surrounded their mud cottage. At an early age he had to help his father work the bogs, digging up large cubes of the peat, laying them out to dry in the sun, gathering them in the cart and pulling the cart to the market in Ballynakill. Once they sold all of their peat, the empty cart was easier to pull. The walk home seemed twice as long knowing he was returning to the bogs.

Yet the beauty of the ocean or the lake, frightened him. A fear born crashing in the sea off Ireland when he nearly drowned. Yet it was the ocean which carried his sisters to him.

Would today see the arrival of the *Bonnie Jean*? It was still a week before Captain Moore said they might arrive. All the sails were furled up on the forest of masts lined up along the water front. Seamus reflected on the many times, during his crossing when he overcame his fear and climbed up with the crew to unfurl the sails or take them up. The day he sat rocking in the crow's nest for hours seemed like yesterday. His patience was rewarded when finally he could call down, "Land Ho." So much had happened to him since then.

Dressing, he walked quickly to the Harbor Master's shed. He entered to see if they had any word from the *Bonnie Jean*. Quint Barns, shook his head no. They exchanged no words. Seamus walked back to the Royal House and had a meager breakfast. Each morning his hunger fled with the lack of news about the *Bonnie Jean*. Bored, he again walked to the Duffy tenement. Climbing the creaking stairs to their apartment, he inhaled the familiar foul stench. In the months he had lived here, he had become so used to the odor it no longer bothered him. Today, it did.

Nella opened the door in response to his knock. Her thin and haggard faced brightened into a smile when she saw him.

"Seamus! Come in! Billy! Cole! Come see who is here."

Cole ran into Seamus' arms. "Seamus! You here!" He was no longer a teetering toddler. Behind him came his older brother. Billy extended his hand to shake Seamus'. "I told Mother you would visit again."

"Kneeling down, he wrapped his arms about both boys. Billy tried to resist smiling, being the man of the house. Finally, his resolve melted and he grinned.

"Would you like a cup of coffee?" Nella asked. "Oh, forgive me, have you eaten breakfast?"

"I have." He handed a paper-wrapped package to Nella.

Blushing, she opened it. A warm loaf of bread, a sausage and a large piece of cheese.

"How wonderful. Now you must join us."

The four sat eating the fresh fragrant bread and slices of cheese and sausage. The boys sipped their slightly sour milk. Seamus and Nella sipped weak coffee. Nothing has changed, thought Seamus. I need to send more money to them. It has been months. I have neglected them.

Boys called from the street for Billy to come and play. He went to the window and shouted down he could not.

Seamus felt much more comfortable than during his visit days before. He asked each Duffy to tell him their news. The time flew by. Reluctantly, he said he had a meeting and left, promising he would return if he could.

Walking back to the Royal House, he noticed the clock tower. It was almost noon. Inside the sparsely decorated dining room, he found Dominick seated at the table in the corner farthest from the doorway.

"You are careful, Dominick. We can't be seen from the front window, although not much can be seen thorough the filth. Window hasn't been washed in years. Besides, no one likes to sit back here. Too far from the kitchen."

Dominick did not smile. He was tense. He spoke in a hushed voice. "Seamus, I have been thinking about our conversation yesterday. I have been less than honest. No, that's not right. I have not told you everything I should have. There is a warrant out for my arrest back in Ireland. I was involved in a failed insurrection three years ago. I was wounded by the British. All the others were killed. Several in battle, the others were hung. I escaped. I believe there are British agents looking for me. You may not wish to associate with me."

"Nonsense. Ogden said you have a good head on your shoulders. That's good enough for me. You were telling me about Wolfe Tone yesterday when the man interrupted us. You left off with Wolfe allying himself with the Protestants. What came of that?"

"Together with Thomas Russell, Napper Tandy and others, Tone formed the Society of the United Irishmen. It was a political union of Roman Catholics and Protestants. Their goal was reform, not armed revolution. They opposed violence. By 1794 the United Irishmen felt they could no longer achieve their dreams of universal suffrage and equality in the Irish parliament. They pegged their future on a French invasion. Their liaison with the French was arrested. Britain and France were at war at the time. This made the United Irishmen's negotiations with the French treasonous.

"Tone became involved in one scheme after another. At one point he was negotiating with the Dutch to support the French. Tone traveled to France on several occasions. Eventually he was captured in Dublin wearing a French uniform. He was tried, found guilty and sentenced to be hung. In prison, awaiting his execution, Tone cut his own throat and bled to death."

"That took courage, Dominick. I don't think I could kill myself. Besides, for me, it's against my Catholic faith."

"Tome's hatred of the British was greater than the fear of his faith."

"What has this to do with Daniel O'Connell?"

"Ah, yes, Danny. A French fleet actually entered Bantry Bay in 1796. Danny's uncle had warned him not to become involved with the French and Wolfe Tone. When the fleet invaded, Danny was caught in the middle. At the time he was enrolled as a volunteer sworn to defend the British government. The very government which was intensifying their persecution of the Catholic people. He was, you will recall, a Catholic himself.

"He was caught in a dilemma. He could not support the rebellion nor could he continue to actively support the government. He retreated into the practice of private law for ten years as tensions increased between the Irish and British. Eventually O'Connell could not restrain himself. He formed the Catholic Board with the express goal of Catholic Emancipation and the right of Catholics to become members of Parliament. He was relentless in pursuing the rights for the Catholics. He was challenged by a noted duelist. O'Connell mortally wounded him. Afterward he vowed to provide financial support to the widow and daughter. The widow refused to accept it but Daniel paid an allowance to the daughter until his own death more than thirty years later.

"His efforts for equality resulted in O'Connell's election eight years ago, 1828, to the Irish Parliament. To be seated, however, he had to take the Oath of Supremacy which is incompatible with our faith. Because he would not take the oath he was denied his seat.

"The outcry against this was so great, an uprising in Ireland was a real possibility. After all, eighty-five percent of Ireland is Catholic. A year later, the law was changed allowing the seating in Parliament of Catholics and, by the way, also Presbyterians."

"So Daniel O'Connell was finally seated?"

"No, it was ruled the change in the law did not apply to earlier elections. O'Connell had to run again. He was unopposed and finally seated in 1829."

"If this was so, why were we in Ballynakill still fearful because we were Catholic?"

"Nothing is easy for the Irish. Either in Ireland or America. Next came O'Connell's campaign to abolish the Tithe Tax."

"What's the Tithe Tax?"

"You really don't know, Seamus?"

Just then the waitress, who had served the two a bowl of stew with stale bread came to take their plates. Neither had eaten any. Brilliantly iridescent meat floated on a sea of thick, almost congealed grease. One look and their appetites had disappeared.

"Ain't ya goin' eat? If not, pay up and leave. I needs the table."

Looking around, Seamus angrily said, "What for? There's no one else here."

"Don't sass me you piece of horse dung. Now pay up or I'll call for help."

Dominick reached into his pocket and handed the waitress a few coins, saying, "Here, Miss."

He stood, grabbed Seamus' arm and urged him to leave quietly. Outside, he said, "Never draw attention to yourself in New York. Anyone hearing our accents will report us and we'll be arrested. Let's walk into a better neighborhood."

"I need to check with the Harbor Master, then find somewhere else to stay. That stew was the last straw."

"Come to my new place tomorrow." The two men parted. Seamus ducked his head into the Harbor Master's office and got the negative shake of his head. Returning to the Royal House, he gathered his bags and left. He walked to the Eagle. The walk calmed him down. Nearing Mamie Baruth's hotel, it hit him. He didn't know Dominick's address.

Chapter Thirty Six

Seamus berated himself for failing to ask Dominick his new address. As he approached the Eagle, Seamus struggled to put on a cheerful face. August greeted him warmly and asked if he wanted a room or would he be staying in his grandfather's room. Seamus was so distraught he had to ask August to repeat what he said.

"Do you wish a room or will you be staying with your grandfather, Mr. Dowling?"

"A room of my own."

"Would you like to be near his room?"

"Yes, that would be good."

Once in his room, Seamus emptied his bags, opened the window and shook each of his items outside. Bugs fell to the street below. A few bugs dropped onto the floor. Those he saw, he stomped on. When he undressed to wash himself, he searched his body for insect bites. There were none he could see. He chided himself for staying in a hell hole like the Royal House. He should have immediately come to the Eagle.

Redressing in fresh clothing, Seamus stretched out on the bed to relax and catch up on the sleep he had missed while staying at the Royal House. He could not. After half an hour he rose, straightened himself, tried to comb his thatch of red hair, gave up and walked to his grandfather's door. Knocking, he said, "It is your grandson, Seamus," His grandfather opened the door.

"Seamus, come in." Grasping him in a bear hug, James squeezed so vigorously he took Seamus' breath away. "You are early. I didn't expect you for at least another week. Too anxious to stay in Chicago?"

"I was."

"Have you registered? Did August tell you I expect you to stay with me?"

"He asked me. I chose to get my own room....didn't want to inconvenience you."

"Nonsense! My suite has two bedrooms."

"My real reason is I made a foolish mistake."

James' face turned serious. "Sit down and tell me if I can help."

"I have been staying at a hotel near the docks so I could check twice a day to see if the *Bonnie Jean* had docked. The place was a hell hole. I left, sick of the rotten food and the filth. When I unpacked here, my bags were full of bugs. I shook everything out the window. I don't want to infect you or your room."

"Is that all?

"Yes, sir."

"Go downstairs and ask for maids to fill my tub with steaming hot water. Go to your room and bring only what is essential. Have the maid take your clothing and burn it. I'll send a messenger to my clothier to come first thing in the morning. He'll arrange for a complete new wardrobe."

Before Seamus could voice an objection, James guided him to the door and said, "Now go and give August my requests."

Grandfather and grandson had dinner in the evening with Mamie Baruth in her private dining room. Each quizzed Seamus about news from Chicago. Mamie peppered Seamus with questions about Anna and Carsten. He repeatedly assured her they were healthy and happy.

"They have found a nice frame house near Axel and Lina. Carsten has opened his office. He provides legal services to the bank. Through contacts with Axel's clients and friends, he has many seeking his counsel. His days are full. Anna helps Lina care for her children."

Seamus said he wished to check the docks each day for news of the *Bonnie Jean.*

"I know someone who works at the money exchange office on the docks," Mamie remarked. "I shall send Oscar first thing in the morning to take a note asking him to send word the minute the *Bonnie Jean* is sited.

"I expect you to bring your sisters to the Eagle when they arrive," Marie continued. "I have already cleared the suite adjacent to your's, James. Herr Knapp has decided to return to Germany. He missed the homeland. His rooms are being freshened up and should be ready in a week."

"When did Lenz leave? Was it unexpected?" asked James.

"I knew he was planning on it for several months. He asked me to say nothing to anyone," Mamie said. "He was a very private person. I was obliged to honor his wishes."

"I never got to know him," James commented. "Over the year he was here, I rarely saw him coming or going, and even less in the dining room. I assumed he ate most of his meals in his room. I hope he finds the happiness in Germany he did not enjoy here."

When all the questions had been asked and answered, Seamus told of William Ogden and the I & M Canal. He told of Ogden's request that Seamus meet with several Irishmen in New York and why. Pausing, debating, Seamus cautiously mentioned Dominick and all he had told him about tumult in Ireland. Mamie and James listened, their faces expressionless. When Seamus had told all, including Dominick's worry about being caught, James spoke.

"You are appropriately concerned. Unless you wish me to, I do not feel I should give you my thoughts or advice. You have done well on your own. From all you have accomplished in Chicago, it is clear you are very capable of making your own decisions. Follow both your heart and mind. You will never go wrong if you balance and heed both.

"I clearly remember when I was confronted with a similar situation. I told my father of my indecision. He told me of an Irish lad faced with a challenge. He pondered it, trying to think of the consequences if he acted or didn't act. He carefully thought through his options. To save his friend he would have to climb over a high brick wall. He could go home and let the friend fend for himself. Besides, the wall's height was greater than the Irish lad. He didn't think he could get over it. If he were caught he could be arrested.

"He finally decided he could not abandon his friend. How could he possibly climb the wall? Impulsively he tossed his cherished hat over the wall. Heart pounding, he became determined to retrieve his hat. Without a further thought, he scampered up and over with no problem other than skinned hands and knees. He saved his friend and recovered his hat.

"There will always be times in our lives when we must ignore the odds against us and act on the side of the angels."

"Thank you, Grandfather."

Several mornings later, Seamus went to Dominick's address, the one Ogden had given him. This was how he had contacted him before. Mamie gave Seamus the use of the Eagle carriage and Oscar, her driver. At Dominick's original address, the landlady angrily said, "He left two days ago without paying the rent he owed me."

Seamus had Oscar drive him, one by one, to the other addresses William Ogden had given him. At the first, no one answered Seamus' knock on the door. A neighbor opened her door and said, "He ain't here no more."

They had no luck at the second address. At the third, a young woman answered. Seamus explained his plight. He showed her the list. By this time it was obvious to Seamus the men on Ogden's list had fled from perceived or real threats to their lives. There was something in Seamus' panic which convinced the young woman. She invited him in.

He told of his day with Dominick and his failure to get his address. He explained why he was seeking Dominick and the three other men. He even talked of Wolfe Tone and Daniel O'Connell. A baby was sleeping in a crudely made crib in the corner. It woke and cried.

"I am sorry sir, I must feed my daughter." Lovingly she lifted the baby and sat in a broken rocking chair. She draped a cloth over her shoulder, opened her dress and nestled the baby under to nurse.

"Mr. O'Shea, how do I know you are not the law?"

Seamus laughed so instantly and joyously, the last of the woman's concerns melted away.

"Dominick, my husband and the other two are now living in the basement of Our Lady of Peace Catholic Church. Tell Father Naal I said he can trust you."

"I don't know your name."

The young mother blushed, responding with a giggle, "I am Denice Lynch."

The church was three blocks away. Seamus told Oscar to go a block east and wait. He was concerned about calling attention to his presence. Seamus entered the church. A woman in the narthex guided Seamus to Father Naal's office. Accepting Seamus' story and the mention of Denice, the priest nodded and without another word, led the way.

They walked to the altar. Seamus' knelt and genuflected. Father Naal led Seamus behind the altar. Lifting a well concealed trap door in the floor of the narrow passageway, the two climbed down a ladder to the damp basement below. The foundation of the church was of large, roughly cut stones. It was dark. A dim light ahead cast a long shadow. They were walking on a hard dirt floor. Much like their cottage floor back in Ireland.

Images haunted him of the dead tax collector sprawled out on the cottage floor, blood oozing out of his smashed head. It took considerable effort for Seamus to suppress his growing panic. He feared he was walking into a trap.

214

Father Naal pulled on a heavy ring to open a plank door. In contrast to the near darkness through which they had walked, the candle-lit room was quite bright. At first, blinking, Seamus heard, rather than saw, Dominick.

"Seamus O'Shea. How'd you find us?"

Quickly recovering, Seamus smiled and teased, "The lovely Denice and her wee one gave me directions."

Laughing, Father Naal said, "I shall leave you now. May the good Lord give you wisdom and bless your undertaking."

Dominick embraced Seamus. Turning, he introduced the others who stepped out from the dark. They all sat down around a crude table.

Impatient to resume their interrupted conversation of several days earlier, Seamus asked, "Just what is the tithe tax?"

"You get to the point quickly, my friend. When did you flee Ireland, Seamus?"

"The Year of Our Lord, eighteen hundred and thirty one," Seamus replied.

"You lived in a small village in the center of Ireland?"

"I did."

"That explains it. Most living in outlying areas were unaware of the distinctions between rent owed to the damned English landlords and the tithe tax. In some areas, it was the responsibility of the landlords' agents to collect both. In other areas, government agents directly forced payment of the Tithe Tax.

"For Catholic Irish tenants, the Title Tax added insult to injury. I imagine your family barely eked out a living."

Seamus answered. "That is so. My father and I dug up peat and worked a small plot of land to grow potatoes. We rarely had more than potatoes to eat. Life was hell. We endured. Not until I came to America did I realize just how deprived we were of a decent life." Seamus' voice dropped almost to a whisper as he ended speaking, unable to go on, emotionally overcome by the memories.

Dominick explained, "To tithe is to give one tenth of what you have to the church. Many tenant farmers are forced to give a cow or produce to pay the rent, leaving nothing left to pay the Tithe Tax.

Looking at each of the men, Dominick said, "We are all Catholic. Almost nine out of ten tenant farmers in Ireland are Catholic. The government can't control everything so they allow the rural Catholic churches to exist. The loyal parishioners give first to the Catholic church and what is left to pay rent to the landlords. Afterward, few farmers can then afford to also pay the Tithe Tax."

Impatient, Seamus asked, "What the hell is the Tithe Tax? What's it for?"

"For the Church of England!"

"What?" Seamus shouted in his anger.

"That's right. The English government levies a ten percent tax on everyone in Ireland. The moneys and goods paid go to support the Church of England. Catholics, poor Irish Catholics, dying of starvation, have to pay to support the very church determined to eliminate Catholicism in Ireland!"

The first of the other men to speak introduced himself. I am Padric, Denice's husband. He spoke in a soft voice.

"I share your rage, Seamus. I could no longer survive. I felt I had escaped Hell on earth when I fled Ireland. When Danny O'Connell decided to work to repeal the Tithe Tax, I, along with my neighbors, joined his crusade by refusing to pay it. Danny preached we abstain peacefully. That only inflamed the English. They created the Irish Constabulary to police every province in Ireland. They were empowered to seize property in lieu of payment of the Tithe Tax. They took our family plot, leaving us homeless with no means to feed ourselves. My older brothers moved to Dublin. My widowed mother moved to the village and worked as a maid. I fled to America to avoid the Tithe Tax War. Here, I met Denice."

"The Tithe Tax War?" prodded Seamus.

Dominick continued, "Many could no longer follow Danny's non-violent stand. They began to arm and attack the Irish Constabulary. Although Danny refuses to support violence, he has taken on the defense in the courtroom of those arrested."

The second man spoke next. "I'm Cormac McCarrigle. I was there, in Carrickshock. I was there on December 14th. We fought and beat the British marionettes!"

Softly, Dominick added, "It was 1831."

Seamus noted, "I left Ireland in April that year."

"Before Carrickshock," Dominick said.

"What happened?" Seamus asked Cormac.

"A bunch of us attacked the tithe collector. Would have been easy except he was escorted by a detachment of the Royal Irish Constabulary. They had rifles. We had few guns, mostly stones, clubs and whatnot.

"Three of our men were killed when the constables fired on us. We killed twelve constables and the chief bastard. Many of our men were injured. I was winged." Rolling up his sleeve, Cormac proudly

216

showed the scar in his upper arm. "For weeks afterward, we had a watch system set up to warn if the Constabulary returned.

"Some months later, a local traitor turned over a list of names to the government of everyone who allegedly took part in the attack. The government took the first batch to court. I fled before I could be taken. Afterward, I learned Danny O'Connell, defended the first group in court and won."

"Do you regret having fled?" asked Seamus.

"Nay. Back there I would have joined the Tithe War which spread to much of Ireland. I can be of greater help here collecting money to send to our men in Ireland. Had I stayed, I might well have been killed, leaving my wee ones fatherless."

Chapter Thirty Seven

Thank you for trusting me. I am here to seek your help. Nine years ago the Erie Canal was opened. Many Irish immigrants helped dig the big ditch. I am well aware of how difficult it is for our countrymen to find jobs, especially the Irish Catholics. Digging the canal was a rare opportunity to work. It was brutal work. Some were smothered to death when the walls of the ditch collapsed on top of them. Many more died of disease. I know the widow of one such worker. She has told me of her husband's last days. He died in her arms.

"In Illinois, digging another canal is about to begin. I need to encourage our countrymen to come to Chicago to dig the Illinois and Michigan Canal."

After hearing of Daniel O'Connell and the Tithe Tax, Seamus finally was able to tell Dominick and the others why he wanted to meet with them.

"I hope I can make a difference in improving the conditions for the Irish who work on the I and M. I have been hired by the Canal Commission to represent the needs and concerns of the Irish workers. I believe the commissioners to be honest men who will do whatever they can to avoid what happened during construction of the Erie.

"William Ogden of New York has decided to settle in Chicago and work with the Canal Commission. He is an honorable man. I have worked with the Commission for several years now, selling land along the proposed route. The sale proceeds are to be used to finance the construction.

"If you are willing to encourage Irishmen to come to Chicago, I pledge to serve and protect them. I shall fight for their rights, decent housing, pay and medical care."

Dominick remained silent. Cormac challenged, "Seamus, I believe you are sincere and mean well. Do you really think Irish Catholic immigrants will be welcomed to Chicago? I have heard such promises before. All have been hollow, at best, most lies. The rich moguls see us no differently than pack animals."

Padric snickered. "Pack animals are more valuable to them than Micks."

"Micks?" asked Seamus.

Cormak, with a look of astonishment, responded, "You don't know we're called Micks?"

"No."

"You call yourself Irish?" shouted Cormak.

Dominick put up his hand. "Please. Seamus, we are derisively called many things. We're Micks to some because so many of our countrymen are McDonald this or McAllister that. Someone began to call us all, "Those Damn Micks.'"

Shaking his head, Seamus continued. "Cormac, I understand your anger. My father killed our landlord's agent when he came for the rent. My father was a drunk. I fled fearing I would be arrested for what he had done. I had worked at his side digging peat. When he was too drunk, I did it alone. We ate nothing but potatoes, day in, day out.

"Is what I am promising you hollow? Am I lying to you? Are my words worth less than horse droppings? No. Can I assure you I will give my all to defend and protect the workers? Yes. Can I assure you I will always succeed? No, but then no one can give such assurance."

Padric offered, "Seamus, please excuse Cormac. He is our firebrand. He says what the rest of us may be thinking but don't voice."

Dominick spoke next. "Gentlemen, I trust Seamus. Denice, with the instincts of a wife, trusted Seamus enough to tell him how to find us.

"Many of our countrymen here in New York are living in squalor, unable to find work. Each time I see an "Irish need not apply" sign, I want to throw a brick through the window. The worst that can happen to the men we urge to go to Chicago is they will find hard work for which they will be paid. For my part, I will do what I can to encourage men to go to Chicago."

The others nodded in agreement, even Cormak.

Emotionally, Seamus said, "Thank you. Now I have a question. How may I send money to Ireland to support the cause of independence?"

Dominick quickly said, "Funnel your money through me. I guarantee it will get to the right men."

Stepping outside the church, Seamus' mind instantly flipped to his primary reason for being in New York. When would Briana and Nora arrive? He directed Oscar to the Harbor Master's office. No news.

Back at the Eagle, he had dinner with Mamie and James. Each evening, after no word, James reminded Seamus, "It is not yet April 20th. Be patient. My granddaughters are in good hands."

The day finally arrived. Seamus insisted on spending the entire day at the docks. And the next day as well. On the third morning, at breakfast, he greeted his grandfather. "I should have returned to Ireland to personally bring my sisters to America."

Nothing would console him. Three days soon became three weeks. Seamus would listen to no one. He walked to the docks each morning, spent the day and walked back, exhausted and increasingly frantic. It was almost the middle of May. He was oblivious to the world around him. He didn't notice the delightful weather, or what he ate. His worry spiraled out of control whenever he added his father to the mix. Had he attacked Father Garreth and his sisters on their way to Galway? Were they even alive?

When word finally came the *Bonnie Jean* had been sighted entering the harbor, he questioned if it was true. James ordered the carriage. He and Seamus departed the Eagle. To Seamus, the carriage barely moved. Familiar buildings he had walked past each day for weeks seemed to slip by no faster than if he were on foot.

Only when he could inhale the scent of the sea did he become himself. Turning to James, Seamus said, "Are my sisters really arriving Grandfather?"

"Yes, they are."

The carriage slowed. The streets leading to the docks were crowded. The noise was familiar to Seamus. They passed the Royal House. "That is where I stayed. By now, had I not wised up and come to the Eagle, the bugs would have totally consumed my scrawny body."

During their ride to the docks, Seamus had so often run his hand through his unruly thatch of red hair, it was laying flat. Oscar called down to them, "This is as far as I can take you. I shall wait here."

Seamus quickly jumped down, gave his hand to help James alight. The two stood amidst the whirling throng, looking toward the harbor. They were still too far to distinguish one mast from another. Staring intensely, Seamus became woozy watching the masts rocking from side to side, out of rhythm from one another. Forgetting James, Seamus pushed his way through the crowd. Whether it was instinct or luck, he headed toward what he thought was the *Bonnie Jean*. Walking faster, he did not stop until he caught a glimpse of the gold *Bonnie Jean* written on the hull. They had arrived. Only then did he turn around to see if James had followed him. He did not find him in the montage of faces.

Walking on, Seamus arrived in time to see the gangplank being lowered to the dock. There, at the deck railing, were Briana and Nora. He jumped up and down and waved. They saw him and waved back.

Seamus was finally joined by James. He was out of breath having rushed to catch up with his grandson. First down the gangplank were several of the crew followed by an officer and then Briana and Nora. It had been five years since Seamus had seen his sisters. Briana was now twenty-two and stunningly beautiful. She was graceful and lithe, with smooth, pale complexion and flaming red hair to match her younger brother. She wore a dress of white linen embroidered with shamrocks.

Nora was sixteen. One of the things Seamus did during the long days of waiting, was to picture in his mind's eye how each of his sisters would look. Never did he imagine them being any older or different than when he left them. He could not see them in his mind's eye appearing older or so beautiful. Nora had her father's dark hair. She wore it in long curls tumbling down onto her shoulders. Her dress was pink, also with shamrock embroidery.

The sisters ran down the gangplank. Their feet seemed to hardly touch the wooden boards. Nora, first, flung herself into Seamus' arms and kissed him on both cheeks, her tears of joy wetting his skin. All she could say was, "Oh Seamus, Oh Seamus, Oh Seamus."

A more reserved Briana smiled. Her younger sister would not let Seamus go. Standing immediately behind her brother was a handsome older gentleman. She hoped he was her grandfather. Gently releasing himself from Nora's arms, Seamus reached out. "Briana, you are beautiful!"

"Am *I* not, Seamus?" asked Nora, pretending to pout.

"Of course, you are. Nona, Briana, our grandfather."

One of the crew asked, "Please move off to the side so others can get by."

More kisses and hugs followed.

"James, would you mind walking Nora and Briana to the carriage while I arrange for their luggage?"

Impatiently, Seamus forced his way up the gangplank, against the flow of immigrants, to the deck. He could see Captain Moore on the upper deck and made his way to him.

"Seamus, I have a mind to put you in chains for endangering my passengers on the gangplank."

Seamus blushed. He was silent for a minute before he realized Captain Moore was teasing him. The two greeted one another and made arrangements for the luggage to be brought to the Eagle. "Captain Moore, will you do us the honor to come stay at the Eagle and share a few meals before you must depart?"

"Tell me where it is and I'll come."

As Seamus was about to leave the Captain's deck, he remembered. Turning back he asked, "Where are Hans and Chan Lee?"

"In the galley."

Racing through the tumult, Seamus made his way below deck to the galley. There they were. His old German sail master and the ship's cook. Wordlessly, they gathered, embraced, and sat down.

Seamus broke the silence. "Hans, I met a German on the dock when I landed five years ago. The German you taught me helped both of us survive."

Chan Lee, who had never before shown a sense of humor asked, "Is she a beauty?"

"He is a man."

Seamus could not tell if Hans was serious or jesting when he asked, "You are close to a man?"

The three talked until Seamus realized he was holding up his grandfather and sisters. "Would you both come to the Eagle for dinner when the Captain comes?"

They looked at one another in surprise, nodded, and Hans said, "We will if the Captain orders it."

Leaving them, Seamus went up on deck and up to the Captain's deck. He quickly told of his invitation to Chan Lee and Hans, obtained Captain Moore's agreement and disembarked.

The next day, James Dowling arranged for dinner with Captain Moore, Chan Lee and Hans in his suite. It was somewhat awkward. Seamus soon had everyone enthralled with his stories of the West, especially about the Indians.

For the next several days, Seamus and his sisters talked to each other when ever they were awake, often in James' suite. They ate all of their meals with Mamie. Seamus took his sisters to see the Duffy family. They brought gifts of food.

Two days later, the three departed for Chicago. Molly joined her father on the *Princess Rose*, eager to meet her future sisters.

Nora sought the opportunity to speak with Seamus alone.

"Are you and Molly truly in love?"

"Have you spoken with Molly?"

"Don't be evasive with me Seamus. I'm the one asking questions, not you!"

"Why do you ask?"

"Seamus! Don't tease me."

Turning serious, Seamus asked, "Do you like Molly?"

"Seamus, answer me first! Are you in love with Molly?"

"Yes."

"Are you going to marry Molly?"

"Yes. I wrote all about this. Why are you asking me? Don't you approve of her?"

"Quite the opposite. I like Molly very much. Don't be flippant. I don't want you to hurt her. Are you getting married anytime soon?"

Seamus looked pensive. Finally he asked, "What day is this?"

"Tuesday."

"I mean what is the date?"

"May 11, 1836."

"We are getting married in four months, on September 3."

"Really?"

"Absolutely, little sister, absolutely."

"Does Briana know this?"

"No, why don't you tell her."

Smiling in triumph, Nora went looking for her sister.

When Axel and Lina met Briana, she greeted them, "Seamus has written so often about the two of you, I feel we are already friends. Whenever I had doubts about the voyage and Chicago, I said to myself, all will be fine. Lina and Axel will be there."

Part Ten

Radiant Sun

Chapter Thirty Eight

A year after the birth of our daughter, Adelina, we experienced tragedy. On August 15, 1836, Axel Heinrich arrived. Born early, he was tiny and pale. He never cried, only whimpered. He refused to take nourishment. Lina and Anna tried everything they had ever heard from wet nurses back in Germany. Nothing induced our third baby to sup. Three weeks later, he slipped away. I had resisted Lina's desire to name him after me. I had no reason, just felt we shouldn't. I acquiesced. Today, just the thought of his name intensifies my pain.

I have never seen Lina so sorrowful. She struggles to resume her normal routine. She cares for Henry and our wee Adelina, but without any joy. It is as if some of her life drained away with the death of little Axel.

Doc Wooten visits often. He tells me this is not unusual for a new mother to become despondent with the loss of a baby. I am angered each time he tells me, "Healing of the heart will come with time." His words don't help me overcome my anger and grief.

I shall never know if the visit by Chief Alexander was coincidence or somehow he heard of our loss and came to us with an Indian antidote. He entered the bank early in the afternoon on October 25th. He asked to see me. The Chief has no account with us nor has he borrowed money from the bank. I welcomed him to my office, doing my best to appear cheerful and gracious.

He asked about Lina and the children. I was surprised how unable I was to respond. As I sought an answer, Alexander sat stoically in silence. I said nothing. I just could not find the right words. I was still deeply wounded. I could not say all was well yet I did not want to burden him with our loss. I said nothing.

After many minutes, Alexander said, "I have come on a personal matter, Axel."

I nodded and the Chief continued.

"A child was left at our doorstep some weeks ago. He was clad in deerskin. I believe he is about three. We cannot find his mother. He is healthy. He speaks no English."

Alexander said no more.

Instinctively I knew he was not seeking money. I felt a calm come over me. Peace I had not known for weeks. I was astounded when I asked, "Could we give him a home?"

Alexander nodded, stood and said, "I shall bring him tomorrow," and left my office.

I went to see Doc and told of the Chief's visit and my surprising response.

"Mothers who suffer from depression after they have lost a baby often thrive when given a needy child. It's worth a try. You must know, it will not be easy to have an Indian child. Many will object and malign you. As he grows, he will face prejudice. He may seek his natural parents. You may be taking on heartaches greater than you are now feeling."

"Doc, are you saying we should not take this child into our home?"

"Not at all. You just need to go into this with your eyes wide open. While your feelings are important, it is Lina who must welcome the child wholeheartedly."

I sat for some time not saying anything further. I left only when a patient came into the waiting room with a seriously bleeding hand.

I am stubborn. Something about my reaction to the Chief puzzled me. Even more puzzling was my sense it was divinely inspired. I don't wear my faith on my sleeve. I don't talk about my faith. But I have never doubted my faith.

As a child, I wondered, of course. Reverend Steinhoff taught confirmation class. I have never been particularly good at memorization so was not the best in his class. I shall never forget his explanation of infinity.

"God's love is infinite," he told us. "The infinite is like a tiny bird who flies to the highest rocky mountain in the world to sharpen his beak. He does this once every hundred years. The time it would take the bird to wear down the mountain is not even be a second in infinity."

As an adult, I have put this into my own perspective. What is beyond the moon and stars? Is there something beyond? If not, what is out there? If there is a limit, what is beyond the limit? Where did the moon and stars come from? My mind aches whenever I think of this. Each time I conclude this is not for me, or any of us, to know. I have faith to accept what I don't understand.

So too is it with my acceptance of the Indian baby. This is meant to be.

I said nothing to Lina in the evening. Why? I don't know. I was not afraid of her disapproval. Just felt tomorrow would take care of itself.

I never left the bank the next day. I waited, strangely confident, anticipating something good. Alexander entered holding the hand of a handsome boy. "This," Alexander said, "is Radiant Sun."

Alexander softly whispered something to Radiant Sun.

Letting go of his hand, the lad walked to me and took my hand, saying something in his native tongue. Alexander, smiling, said he called me his "Tall Father."

Radiant Sun showed no emotion, neither fear nor delight. There was a presence of wisdom about him without arrogance.

In his other hand, Alexander was carrying a large deerskin bag. "This was left with Radiant Sun." He handed the bag to me, spoke in the boy's language saying, I presume, goodbye. Alexander left. Radiant Sun stood before me, waiting. I reached down, lifted him and gave him a hug. Several customers in the bank looked without warmth at the exchange. I walked to the stairs and carried the lad to our apartment.

Anna greeted me. Hearing my voice, Lina came from the kitchen. I had put Radiant Sun down. He was dressed in a deer skin jersey and pants and wore moccasins. His black hair was modest length, framing his finely chiseled face. His skin, a rich brown, set off his blue eyes.

Lina said nothing. She walked to Radiant Sun, knelt before him, took his hands and gently pulled him into her arms and kissed him on each cheek. Looking up at me with the first genuine smile I had seen since the death of our son, she whispered, "Thank you."

"Lina, we need a larger home. I can't stand the bickering between Henry and Radiant Sun. Henry resents his new brother sleeping in his room. We need more room."

Lina looked up from her sewing, smiled and said nothing. After three years of marriage, she allows me to let off steam, not commenting until later on, usually after I have eaten.

"I am going to go look at the lots I bought when I first came to Chicago. One might be just right for our new home. I prefer south of

229

town. The lots north of the river are too close to the Sands. I'll not have my family living anywhere near a den of iniquity."

I stood in the doorway, waiting for Lina to agree. She returned to her sewing in silence. If I am honest with myself, I admit she is wise not to respond to my rare outbursts. When I get an idea or get agitated, I am very impulsive, determined to take immediate action. I am trying to be more patient with myself. To give myself time to cool down or let an idea percolate and consider it in a more rational mind set.

This time, however, I know I am right. Thankfully, money is no problem for us. My insistence that we need a bigger house will not go away. I have been thinking about it for weeks. Shrugging my shoulders, I grabbed an apple from the kitchen, said goodbye and left.

I walked the two blocks to the stable where I keep Thor. I rubbed him behind his ears as he nuzzled me. He tried to reach the apple in my pocket and whinnied when he could not pull it out. I retrieved it. He took it from my palm. How can such a large creature be so gentle?

Smithy was not in his usual rocking chair enjoying the sun. I threw the blanket on Thor, lifted my saddle from the shelf, placed it on Thor, reached under his belly and tightened the straps. Thor became anxious with me. He kept turning his head to see why Smithy wasn't saddling him. Placing the bit in his mouth, I looped the reigns to the saddle horn and dropped the stirrups. I opened the gate to Thor's stall and led him outside. I tied him to the rail. I opened the fine leather bag Smithy had made for me, took out my pad of paper, pulled out my pencil and wrote a note to Smithy telling him I was taking Thor for a ride. I placed the note on the seat of his rocking chair and placed a stone on it. I have never come to the stable when Smithy was not present. I was mildly concerned. Unhitching Thor, I mounted and rode east.

At the main road into Chicago, I headed south. Before looking at the lots I owned, I gave Thor his head. To my left were the blue waters of Lake Michigan, to my right grass, marshes and woods. The breeze caressed my face. The fresh scent of the sand and grasses tickled my nostrils. Overhead puffed open cotton bolls hung from the blue sky. Thor and I were totally alone. We both enjoyed the freedom of our gallop.

I reluctantly reigned in Thor. "Sorry, fella, time to head back." Thor pranced as he sauntered at my command. He twisted his head around, as if to see if I was serious. Deciding I was determined, he slowed, turned around and headed back. Our pace was more leisurely. Nearly back to my property, Thor's ears perked up. He sensed something ahead. I saw nothing untoward. Thor slowed, clearly aware of something. I saw motion on the horizon. Pulling up Thor, I listened.

I heard singing. Advancing slowly, we came to the figure of a man sitting at the road side. He was singing in a deep voice. I dismounted, led Thor by the reigns as I felt for my gun which was concealed under my coat.

Assuming a relaxed manner, I picked a thin stalk of grass and placed it in my lips. The man stood as we approached. He was unusually tall and husky. On the ground, where he had been sitting on a slight ridge, was a large carpet bag, boots and a jug. He stopped singing. Even his head was large. He was much my age, dressed formally for someone barefooted. His shoes were the largest pair I have ever seen.

Stopping a few feet from him, I experienced the rare event of facing someone taller than me. I am six feet, two inches in height. The stranger had a good three or four inches on me.

"Have you lost your horse, sir?" I asked in a friendly voice.

The stranger laughed lustily.

"Hardly. I was so eager to get to Chicago, I didn't wait for the wagon I was expecting to ride, so I am walking. Just sitting a bit to enjoy the view before heading on."

He reached down and lifted the jug. I noticed his large hands.

I extended my hand in greeting. "My name is Axel Konrad. I live in Chicago. Let me be the first to welcome you."

He shook my hand so vigorously I felt his grip down to my feet.

"I'm John Wentworth, Esquire. Would you like a swig of whiskey?" He pulled the plug and handed the jug to me.

"Most kind of you. Not just now."

"Good thing. I need every drop left to bathe my blistered feet."

He stepped back to where he had been and sat. Pulling his right leg up, he crossed it over the other, twisted up his foot, so the bottom was upward. It was covered with festering blisters. Some had burst revealing raw red flesh. He slowly tipped the jug and poured a trickle of whiskey on his foot. He winced, shifted feet and repeated the procedure.

"Painful but gives relief."

My conscience tugged at me. "Would you like to ride Thor the rest of the way?"

Laughing again, he replied, "Not sure Thor would like that. No, I'll walk. I'm the one who decided not to wait, so I'm the one who has to bare the burden of my impatience.

"How much further do I have to go?"

"I'd say twenty minutes. Tell me about yourself, if I am not being impolite asking."

231

"Right neighborly, sir. Glad to.

"I was born in Sandwich, New Hampshire, twenty-one years ago. Taught school for a few years. Wrote political articles for some newspapers. Just graduated from Dartmouth College. Decided to come to Chicago. Hear there are great opportunities. Packed my sheepskin's in my carpet bag along with my belongings, grabbed my jug and started out west.

"Is it true you've a newspaper in Chicago?"

"Yes, the *Chicago Democrat.*"

"Wrote to John Calhoun. He's agreed to make me managing editor if I'd come to Chicago. So here I am. Hope to also complete my study of the law. Law's a good profession, don't you think?"

"Yes."

"What do you do, Mr. Konrad?"

"Banker."

"Not much for words, are you? Dutch or German?"

Suppressing my reaction to his comment, I responded, "I was born in Germany."

"Who do you work for?"

My indignity must have shown. Wentworth quickly added, "For yourself?"

"I own the Greater Bank of Chicago. Hope you will come visit me when you have settled in. I would appreciate your business."

"I will. Can you recommend the name of a lawyer who might consider taking me on as his clerk to read for the law?"

"I can. Carsten Baruth. He's a fine lawyer. I will talk to him if you wish."

"Yes, do. Is there a hotel you recommend?"

"The finest is the recently opened Tremont. For a less expensive hotel, you could try the Sauganash until you can assess your other choices."

The whiskey having dried, Wentworth yanked stockings from his coat pockets, pulled them on and put on his boots. I must have shown my amazement, as John noted, "Big, aren't they. My boots are fourteen inches long and six inches wide. Have to have my shoes specially made for me. These are new and not yet broken in, ergo the blisters. Another indication of my impatience. Too much to do, not enough time to do it."

Standing, Wentworth plugged his jug, grabbed his carpetbag and said, "Thank you for welcoming me. I'll stop by the bank tomorrow." Mounting Thor, I bid goodbye and headed north.

I stopped where I thought my lots might be. I dismounted and walked inland, watching for stakes the surveyor had placed to mark my property. He told me he had tied bits of red cloth to the top of each. Thor stopped and began to chomp on a clump of grass. I tied his reigns to a scrawny bush. Leaning over to do so, there, staring me in the face, was one of the stakes with the bit of red.

Orienting myself to the road and lake, I paced until I found the other stakes. After I had purchased the lots, I was mad at myself for not coming to see them first. I need not have worried. The sites are perfect. They are near enough to the lake so we will be able to watch the sunrise each morning. I own four lots, each hundred feet lake frontage and two hundred feet in depth. I will have my architect design the house, out buildings and the placement on as many of the lots he feels would be best.

I sat down, took a deep breath and relaxed. I seldom do so. I could hear Thor pulling up the grass and the waters lapping on the sandy shore. I lay back and watched the gulls overhead, their squawky calls inconsistent with their soaring flight. Closing my eyes, I happily recalled the first time when Lina and I had walked into the prairie west of the north branch of the Chicago River. Lina was not the least intimidated by the swing bridge of logs rocking on the two stout ropes.

Henry and Radiant Sun intruded my reminiscing. How can I help my two sons appreciate one another? I tried to put myself inside the mind of each. What caused their animosity?

Henry was king of the house before the arrival of Radiant Sun. He had to share his room with him. His toys. Our attention. We had taken pains to prepare Henry for the arrival of his sister. We had no time to ready him for Radiant Sun. He arrived with no warning.

Radiant Sun must be hopelessly confused and feel insecure. Perhaps it is his nature to fight back, to defend himself. What can I do now? I need to give this careful thought.

Getting up, I walked from one end of my property to the other. Welling up within me was pride with all of my accomplishments. I own a very successful bank. I am about to build a magnificent home. My pride quickly turned to guilt. My success, such as it is, is due to others. I just invested the monies my father and James Dowling gave me. I try to help others. Should I build the home I have been dreaming of or give more of my money to those in need?

Looking around, I realized the quiet and beauty would mean isolation for Lina. The pitchfork murderer was still lurking. Building my home here would place my family in danger. I need to think about my plans. Out here there would be no neighbors. The beauty and solitude, I was so enjoying a few minutes before, now seemed threatening.

I walked to Thor who pulled on his reigns. He happily nuzzled me as I freed him, mounted and headed home. He knows the way. When I saw men standing outside the stable, my faint concern of not having seen Smithy before now turned to fear. All looked toward me as Thor and I approached.

Doc stepped from the group and met me a few feet off. "Axel, Smithy has been killed! His back has been punctured with his own pitchfork!"

Dismounting, I dropped the reigns. Thor followed me. The men parted. Smithy was sprawled on the ground, face down. Thor walked up to him and tried to turn him over with his snout. One of the men guided him to his stall.

I knelt at Smithy's side. He had a piece of paper in his clenched fist. I pried his fingers loose and retrieved my note. At his side lay the rock I had placed on my note to keep it from blowing away. It was covered with blood. Doc helped me roll Smithy over. I was shocked to see his forehead smashed in.

I lifted Smithy and held his torso in my arms as I sobbed. Several patted my back to console me. It was, I thought, my fault. Finally pulling myself together, I stood and addressed the men.

"This is my fault. When I came to get Thor, Smithy was not here. He was always sitting here. He was missing. I should have looked for him. I might have saved his life."

Doc, at my side, spoke. "How long ago did you leave with Thor?"

"An hour ago."

"Smithy was killed early this morning. He was killed and brought here so you would see him on your return. You could not have saved him. He had been dead for three to five hours when you first arrived."

Constables Oremus Morrison and John Shrigley, just arriving, pushed their way to see Smithy.

"Another Pitchfork Murder! I thought we may have seen the last of them." Oremus immediately took charge. "I would like to interview everyone who has any information on Smithy's day, his routine and the discovery of his corpse.

"John and I will need to investigate the site of the crime. We will put a notice in the newspaper seeking information from any citizens who may have seen something. I am determined to get to the bottom of this."

Chapter Thirty Nine

Oremus and John asked me to join them in Smithy's small cabin adjacent to the stable. We sat at his small table. John took notes. Oremus asked me questions. I was aware of my surroundings, the questions and my deep sadness, yet, as I have experienced before in my life, I had a feeling of remoteness. It was as if I was watching myself from outside of myself. Oremus and John's voices sounded far off yet I could hear them perfectly. I have learned to accept these sensations, knowing I can fully function and that no one is aware of what I am undergoing.

"Axel," Oremus asked, "Smithy was murdered in his bed and carried out to the rocking chair hours later. Are you sure the rock we found covered with blood is the same one you placed on your note when you left with Thor?"

"How could it be? If you said the murder occurred long before I came to get Thor, the rock I placed on the note would be blood free."

"Exactly." Oremus was looking at me strangely. Was he suggesting I killed Smithy?

"Where were you at sunrise, Axel?"

"At home with Lina and the children."

"What time did you leave and where did you go?"

Oremus' voice was emotionless, his demeanor hostile. John Shrigley had stopped taking notes. His expression suggested he did not agree with Oremus' questions.

"I dressed, ate breakfast and went downstairs to the bank around nine o'clock. Reinhold and Anders had opened the bank as usual, at eight. I worked in my office until noon at which time I went back upstairs to have my noon meal with my family. Around one I went to the stable. I was gone for an hour. I met a stranger during my ride."

"A stranger?"

"A tall man walking to Chicago."

"Walking? What is his name?"

"John Wentworth."

"Anything unusual about this Wentworth?"

"He's from the East. He's very tall."

"What was he doing when you met?"

"Sitting at the side of the road."

"You say he was coming to Chicago?"

"Yes."

"Did he have a horse?"

"No."

"Where had he come from?"

I said, "The East."

Oremus' voice became even more hostile. "He walked here from the East Coast?"

"No."

"Mr. Konrad, is there such a person? Can he verify this? Can Lina verify when you left your home and Reinhold when you left the bank?"

I felt anger surging to the surface. Afterward, I decided it took such great control for me to maintain my demeanor it caused my sense of remoteness to dissipate. John Shrigley must have reached his limit. He spoke sharply.

"I do not feel it is necessary to verify Axel's statements. He is not the Pitchfork Murderer!"

Oremus turned on John. "I am in charge here and will conduct this investigation as I see fit. If you can't abide by it, leave."

John glared at Oremus. "I find your approach not only offensive but misguided, Constable. I have equal standing here and will not allow you to miss the obvious."

Mockingly, Oremus responded, "And what exactly is the obvious?"

"There clearly are two rocks. One used to kill Smithy and another to hold down the note. When the murderer saw the rock holding down Axel's note, he took advantage of the opportunity. He placed the bloody rock near the corpse after he carried it out to the rocking chair and put the note in his fist."

"Where is the second rock?" shouted Oremus.

"Go look outside, damn you, Oremus. There are rocks of all sizes all over the ground. Any one of them could have been the one Axel placed on the note.

"If you insist on diverting our energies to conduct interviews with the banker and his wife, I shall not be a part of it. I will have Luther assist me in interviewing everyone who might be able to shed light on the case and pursue the real Pitchfork Murderer, whoever he may be."

Before Oremus, whose face had turned red, could answer, Doc entered.

"I agree with John. The rock found at Smithy's side is not the murder weapon."

"How the hell do you know that?"

"The rock at Smithy's side has little blood on it nor does it have fragments of skull bone or flesh. From the depth and rough edges of the wound, the murder weapon has a sharp edge for it to penetrate as deeply as it did. The rock used to hold down the note and which was found at Smithy's side, is smooth and round. It is abundantly clear to me the killer took the rock holding down the note, rubbed it into the wound and placed it at the side of the corpse. I suggest you look under or around Smithy's bed for the murder weapon."

Oremus sat rigidly, stubbornly resentful of Doc's presence. John went into Smithy's bedroom to look around. He shouted. "Doc, would you come here please."

I followed Doc to the side of the bed. John pointed to the chamber pot. In the night fluid, which was a pale red, was a large, rock. Doc lifted the rock out. It was jagged and had fragments which Doc announced were pieces of bone.

Carrying it out to the other room, Doc confronted Morrison. "This, Oremus, is the murder weapon. I will compare it directly to the fatal wound. I am confident this is the murder weapon."

I went back to my chair and collapsed in it. I was drained. My anger gone. I looked at Oremus, waiting for an apology. At the moment he was incapable of uttering one.

John took over. "Luther and I will begin the interviews. It is best we do so immediately. Doc, could you send someone from outside to get Luther. Axel, could you select who you feel I should interview first and invite him in. Ask the others to stay close by for their turn.

"Afterward, I suggest you go home. This has been an ordeal which you didn't deserve."

I did as John asked.

The minute I walked into our apartment, Lina could see I was shaken. Before she could speak, Radiant Sun ran to me, reached out for me and said, "Up, Papa."

I sat, took him in my arms and he kissed me. His smile made me shed the tears I had been holding in. I felt foolish.

"Sad Papa." He said nothing more. Radiant Sun rested his head on my chest and instinctively sensed my need for comfort.

Lina came to my side and softly suggested, "We can talk after the children are in bed."

The investigation yielded little new information. The pitchfork was found in one of the stables. Doc confirmed the rock found in the chamber pot was the murder weapon. Mark said Smithy had not come to the Sauganash for either his usual breakfast or lunch. Several regulars, who kept their horses at the stable, each said they took their horses in the morning and noted the absence of Smithy. Each was able to explain where they had gone during the day.

Oremus never apologized to me. He made himself scarce for a week. I could not make sense of his obstinance, neither his belief I was the murderer nor his unwillingness to speak to me when he was so clearly in error.

After putting the children to bed, I explained everything to Lina. She listened, said she was sorry and, in effect, put me to bed as well.

In the morning, Radiant Sun woke me. He climbed up into our bed and lay down next to me. When he saw I was awake, he asked, "You better?"

Chapter Forty

Lina and I were sitting in front of the fireplace, the glow of the embers the only light in the room. The children were in bed. The first flakes of snow had fallen during the day. It was too soon to utter the word winter. Living so close to the lake can result in an early snow while just a mile or so west the sun still warms the air.

The waters of Lake Michigan have an impact on our weather year around. The water never freezes in winter except near the shore where the winds pile up mounds of ice creating beautiful formations and caves. On a winter day, our temperature can be as much as ten or more degrees warmer than several miles inland. In the heat of summer, the lake never warms up to match the air temperature so our highs of the day can be significantly lower than west of the city.

Only in the evening can Lina and I talk without interruption. Our children are truly a blessing, but they play havoc on adult conversation. During the daytime, we are unable to talk of what is on our minds. We try to spell out simple thoughts. Henry has begun to ask, "What talking 'bout?" We resist switching to German. Our children are Americans and should speak English. So as we relax before the embers, we each dig into the memories of the day to speak of what we have wanted to say since rising in the morning.

"Lina, I am concerned about Henry and Radiant Sun. Is it normal for two boys to fight with each other as they do? Radiant Sun is so sweet and gentle. Henry seems resentful of him. Is this what we should expect?"

"Perhaps we give too much attention to Radiant Sun making Henry feels neglected"

"Possibly." As I turned it over in my mind, Lina suggested another reason.

"Do you think Henry hates Radiant Sun because he is an Indian?"

"No. Henry's too young to think that."

"Why don't you take the boys out with you. Show them the bank. Take them for a carriage ride. Show them the lake. Take them to see Johann Wellmacher and buy each a cookie."

"It's worth a try."

So this morning, I took my sons downstairs to meet Reinhold and Anders and show them the bank. At first the boys were shy. They found courage through each other, holding hands, of all things. I showed them my office and then opened the vault to show them the coins, documents and gold nuggets in safe keeping.

Next I walked them to the bakery. Henry held onto my left hand, Radiant Sun my right. I slowed my normal pace to their little steps. When one boy pointed out something the other looked to see. They asked simple questions and delighted in the answers.

As we walked, passing men would greet me. Henry asked, "Who them Papa?"

Radiant Sun said little.

When I opened the door to Wellmacher's bakery, the boys smiled as they smelled the fragrant warmth of fresh bakery goods. Johann presented each with a large sugar cookie in a paper cone.

Radiant Sun asked Henry, "Eat now?"

Henry responded, "Show Mama."

"Me too."

Next we went to the post office. John gave me several letters and a package. He introduced himself to my sons. As we were turning to leave, a farmer entered. I'd met him. I couldn't recall his name. He looked down at the boys and asked me, "Where'd you get the injun? He escape from Iowa?"

I responded, "This is my son, Radiant Sun."

"Your son! You got a squaw on the side?" He laughed derisively.

"Lina and I are his parents."

Taking the boys' free hands I guided them outside.

Henry looked up at me and asked, "What injun Papa?"

"I'll explain when we get home. Now lets go to see Uncle Carsten."

Just then, Radiant Sun, who knew the man's comments were about him, dropped his cookie. He looked down at it on the ground. Looking up at me he said, "Sorry."

Henry picked up the paper cone to give it to Radiant Sun. The cookie had fallen out. To my surprise and joy, Henry handed Radiant Sun the empty cone, then broke his own cookie and gave half to Radiant Sun." Neither boy said a word.

Carsten's office is in a small building next to the bank. When we entered, he greeted us, lifted each boy and kissed them and marveled over their cookies. Aunt Anna was there as well. She was helping with the paperwork and bent down to kiss each.

The two boys proudly showed their cookies. Radiant Sun said, "Henny gave me."

A whimper came from the corner of the law office. Henry was the first to reach the crib where his baby cousin had awaken from his nap. "Baby. Baby wake. Come Rady."

Radiant Sun ran to his side. The two boys looked down at Theodore Baruth. Anna picked up her three month old son and let each boy touch his tiny fingers.

While Anna and the boys were engrossed, Carsten and I sat and talked.

Carsten commented, "In the year we have been here, there has been great change. Chicago is growing rapidly."

"It is. Over four hundred lake ships have entered the harbor so far this year. They've brought more settlers and over 28,000 tons of goods."

"Any idea how many live here now?" Carsten asked. "I understand the town board is having a count made."

"The count is complete. Board's to announce the total in a few days. My sources say it is 3,820. That's over a twenty-fold increase since Seamus and I arrived here five years ago. When the numbers are officially reported, they'll show more than eighty percent have been here a year or less."

"Explains why chaos abounds," Carsten commented. "It's good for my business. Speaking of business, I took on an interesting case yesterday. Client wants me to sue the town board for the lack of a good school."

"What's wrong with Ramsey School?"

"Not good enough."

"Doesn't he like the location? Madison and Dearborn is prime land. For Chicago, its darn good. Two stories, several class rooms. Better than rural schools."

"He says it's not like schools back East."

"He want a private school?"

"Not sure. I just got the case yesterday."

"There are other choices. There's the Infant School. It was founded several years ago by Eliza Chappell. She went on to marry the Reverend John Porter. The school is highly regarded. There are several other schools. I'm only vaguely aware of them. Why don't you come to the next meeting of the Lyceum Society. We could suggest schools be raised as a topic for the following meeting's discussion."

"Let others do my research for me?"

"Why not. Save you time."

"I'll talk to my client and suggest he also come to the meeting."

"Radiant Sun and I ran into our first incident of prejudice. A farmer suggested Radiant Sun was the illegitimate son of my squaw mistress. I had not thought the ugliness would start so soon."

"I'm sorry, Axel. I'm afraid you, Lina and Radiant Sun will have to endure this sort of thing from now on. I pray it is never more than verbal abuse. The day will come when you will have to explain Radiant Sun's heritage to him and tell of his birth parents. I admire the two of you for embracing him as your son. Your position in the community should dampen the worst of it. Have you considered giving him a Christian name?"

"Henry may have already done so. He calls his brother Rady."

"I had an interesting experience earlier this week. I went to look at the lots I own south of town. Thinking of building a home. On the way I met a giant of a man. He told me he was walking to Chicago. Taller than me by four inches and I'd guess outweighs me by a good fifty pounds. Of all things, he was bare footed. Had his boots, a jug and carpet bag at his side. He was singing.

"As we talked, he sat on the roadside and poured whiskey on the bottoms of his blistered feet. Jolly man. Just graduated from Dartmouth College. He said he wants to read law here in Chicago. I gave him your name. I think he's going to go far. Might be a good help to you."

"What's his name?"

"John Wentworth. Hope you don't mind I gave him your name."

"Not at all. I could use the help."

"Papa! Papa!" cried Rady as he ran to me. "See baby."

Grabbing my hand, Radiant Sun urged me to come with him. I followed my son to the side of Theodore's crib. "See?"

Henry, standing by the crib, pointed to my nephew and said, "Papa, Teddy."

Carsten had followed me. Reaching into the crib, he lifted Teddy out of the crib and went back to sit, while Henry and Rady traipsed to his side.

The boys and I left shortly thereafter.

Part Eleven

The Canal

Chapter Forty One

Taking out his handkerchief, Seamus mopped his brow. The bit of cloth was already sopping wet and did nothing but spread his sweat across his face. Trying not to be conspicuous, Seamus squeezed the handkerchief until drops of moisture fell to the parched ground. He again wiped. He felt no drier. The speeches were endless. The blazing sun loomed overhead in the cloudless sky. So much for all the days of worrying it might rain. Since he had been in America, Seamus could not recall a single Fourth of July that wasn't hot and dry. He had come to think of the Fourth of July as the start of summer.

Seamus was embarrassed he had been asked to sit on the platform which had been erected for the occasion. He didn't want to be there with all the politicians and bigwigs. Besides, after several hours of speeches, he had reached his limit. To distract himself from his growing impatience, he tried to name each of the men on the platform. There was, of course, William Ogden, one of the men in the front row. He had already spoken. Seamus found his words fascinating. Especially when he touched on his background and philosophy.

Seamus knew, of course, the three Canal Commissioners, also in the front row: Gurdon Hubbard, William Thompson and Colonel Archer. Oh God, Seamus thought, the commissioners haven't spoken yet. The crowd kept growing as the speeches went on and on. Sitting next to Seamus was Oremus Morrison, his girth oozing over the side of his chair, encroaching on Seamus' space. He tried to shift to his right to break contact with the constable's massive thigh, only to encounter the other man who immediately grumbled. Droplets of sweat trickled inside Seamus' shirt down his back.

Axel had declined a seat on the platform. Working for the Canal Commission, Seamus had no choice. He was unsuccessful in locating

Axel in the crowd. Axel had told him he would delay his arrival until two hours after the scheduled start of the ceremonies. As Axel put it, "I don't need to listen to all the windbags take credit for something most of them thought and still think is a boondoggle. They will jockey for positions on the platform just in case the Canal is a success so later on they can say they were responsible for it."

William Ogden insisted Seamus be on the platform to symbolize to the Irish workers that he was in a position of importance. Seamus didn't need to show off except when he delighted in exercising his inherent Irish confidence and bravado.

So far he had also identified his close friends, Philo Carpenter and Colonel Grege. There, in the back row, was Billy Caldwell. Seamus had to wait until the men in the rows in front of him turned their heads to one side or the other to be able to see who he might know. A noise behind the platform caused many to turn around, giving Seamus a full view of their faces.

In that brief instant, he recognized John Wright, John Caton, Archbald Clybourne, John Hogan and John Calhoun. The rest were strangers to him.

Seamus' concentration was interrupted by applause at the introduction of Governor Joseph Duncan. Seamus had never seen him before. He concluded he was present since he had signed the legislation endorsing the Canal and providing State of Illinois funds. Seamus tried to concentrate on the governor's remarks. He was unable to. Like all the others, the Governor was excessive and pompous. Seamus soon blocked out his words and looked for people he might know in the audience.

Off to his left, in the back, was a large group of Irishmen from New York drawn to Chicago to dig the canal. Looking intently, Seamus could make out faces he knew. One young man, for whom he had arranged to give emergency food and money, jumped up and down to get Seamus' attention. Without thinking, Seamus half waved, half saluted in return. A twitter rippled through the crowd. Anything to break the monotony of the speeches was welcomed. Just think, Seamus thought, how they would react if he began to sing.

More applause snapped Seamus' attention back to the platform. The governor sat down. Another local man of the cloth offered another prayer. This was the fourth. Seamus decided this was to make sure none of the churches of Chicago felt slighted. Finally, the commissioners were asked to speak. Gurdon Hubbard was brief. His bits of humor brought more laughter than warranted. Another sign the crowd was restless for relief. Next came William Thompson. His speech, Seamus thought, was what Americans call a real stemwinder. He managed to rouse the audience. Colonel Archer was finally introduced. He was brief and to the point. When he finished, he stepped down from the platform and walked to a roped off area. He was to ceremoniously turn the first shovel of dirt.

Those on the platform gathered around Archer, with the audience crowding behind them, straining to see what was going on. The shovel Archer was to use had been stuck in the ground. Archer pulled it up. To his surprise, it was a pitchfork, not a shovel.

Archer turned to Gurdon Hubbard, "This isn't a shovel." Gurdon, just as surprised, offered, "The ground is baked dry. Someone must have decided the pitchfork would make it easer for you to turn over the dirt."

Colonel Archer, never at a loss for words, gave yet another speech, briefer than his first, but still longer than necessary. Seamus scolded himself when he found he was comparing the day's ceremony to the agony of burying the dead back home in Ireland.

Mark Beaubien and several other tavern owners had brought kegs of beer and barrels of whiskey to celebrate. Some in the crowd had already been imbibing which explained the boisterous voices in the back of the crowd. It was Judge Lockwood who surprised everyone next.

With the aid of a young man, the Judge tapped a barrel of whiskey and the two tipped it at the edge of a nearby spring and emptied it into the water. Decorum crumbled. The crowd burst into celebration. Watching the reckless abandon as men rushed for their alcohol, Seamus said a prayer of thanksgiving that he did not drink. He never wanted to become a drunk like his father.

The formalities complete, Seamus sought out the large group of Irishmen. He pushed and shoved through the throng looking for them. The heat was intense, the stench of sweating men overpowering. No one looked familiar. Seamus decided to make his way out of the mass when someone tapped his shoulder. Turning, he was startled to be face to face with Dominick Breen.

"Looking for me?" the New York Irish immigrant asked.

"I didn't know you were here," gasped Seamus. "Is it safe for you to be here?"

"You tell me. Is it?"

A familiar voice said, "I think so." Standing behind Dominick were the men Seamus had met in New York: Padric Lynch, Cormak McCarrigle and the third man who had not spoken..

"I have a horse and wagon if you'll join us," Dominick invited Seamus. "We can go to our lodgings."

Seamus climbed up in front. Cormak drove the wagon. Dominick, Padric and the third man climbed up and settle on a load of straw in the back of the wagon. They traveled the short distance to the buildings and shanties being erected for the canal workers.

Cormak pulled up in front of one of the few sturdy buildings. He jumped down and hitched the reigns to the post.

"We have rooms here. Food's simple. Run by John Scanlan and his wife." Dominick noted. "Cormak was especially drawn to the place. Scanlans are Irish. John told us when they first opened, his wife rolled a cask of whiskey out front. She borrowed two glasses and a tin cup from their nearest neighbor, hung up a crude sign and set up business."

The five men met in the Scanlan's back room. Once seated, looking at the man who had never spoken when he met them in New York, Seamus asked, "Might I ask your name?"

In a raspy voice, barely audible, he said, "My name is P. J. Londra."

"Happy I am to meet you, P. J."

Padric explained, "P. J.'s voice was lost when the British tortured him. Beat him repeatedly to get him to accept the Church of England and denounce Catholicism. During the torture they hit him a vicious blow to the throat, seriously damaging his ability to speak. He rarely does. It is painful for him to do so."

Reaching across the table, Seamus extended his hand. P. J. grasped it.

"Thank you, P. J., for honoring me with your name."

P. J. smiled as their grasp loosened.

Dominick began, "Enough of this. We're here, Seamus, to check out conditions. Did you see the shanties as we rode into this area? You call these acceptable?" Before Seamus could answer, Dominick continued. "What will the workers be paid? What about adequate and decent food? Medical care? Doesn't look to me like you're keeping up your end of our bargain.

"Almost two hundred Irishmen have already arrived in Chicago at our urging. More are on the way. My reputation is at stake. Damn it, Mr. O'Shea, are you about to stab me in the back?"

Seamus showed no reaction. He sat silently as Dominick questioned him. Padrick looked down. Cormak leaned forward, as if ready to strike Seamus. P. J.'s face was blank.

Seamus spoke softly and slowly. "I, too, am concerned with the appearance of this area. So far, no one has been hired. I am working with Ogden and the Commission to establish a hiring office and the terms of employment. At times I am the lone voice making demands on behalf of workers. I am stubborn as a mule. I am against heavy odds. I don't know how much I can accomplish."

"I thought so," snarled Cormak. "You are as phony as a I thought you were."

"I never promised you success, just my total energy on your behalf."

"Nonsense. You sound no better than the British. Sweet talk us to give up our faith and then piss on us when we refuse." As he spoke, Cormak stood and leaned across the small table, looming large in Seamus' face.

Padric placed a hand on Cormak's back, urging him in a firm voice, "Sit down Cormak. You are acting like a spoiled child. Seamus, what do you recommend?"

Dominick had not flinched during Cormak's outrage. He looked at Seamus without any expression.

"Would the four of you be willing to attend my next meeting with Ogden and the Commission to voice your concerns? Am I correct in assuming none of you wishes to work on the canal?"

Each said that was correct.

"Then you could voice your convictions without fear of retaliation of not being hired. This would reinforce what I have been saying. Are you willing to do so?"

In a much more civilized voice, almost as meek as a supplicant, Cormak asked, "Do you really think they would listen to us?"

"Listen? Yes. Totally agree with your demands? No."

Dominick asked, "When would you propose we meet with them?"

"I will speak with William Ogden and Gurdon Hubbard within the next two days. I have great respect for both men. They will convince Commissioners William Thompson and Colonel Archer to agree. I may also invite Axel Konrad to be present."

"Who is he?" asked Padric.

"President of Chicago's largest bank and my best friend. He will aggressively support your demands, if you speak respectfully and with civility. He is a very decent man."

Dominick said, "I will attend. Padric, will you?"

"Yes."

"Cormak?"

"I will."

"PJ?"

He nodded yes.

"I will let you know the time and place," a very relieved Seamus said, "Please don't drink before the meeting. And remember, be civil."

Two days later, Seamus met with Axel and Gurdon. Both agreed to talk to Thompson and Archer and convince them to listen to the Irishmen.

"Can you tell me about Colonel Archer?" asked Seamus, once agreement had been reached.

"Gurdon, you know him better than I do. Would you mind?" Axel asked.

"Of course. Archer's grandparents came to America from Ireland half a century ago. Their son, Zachariah, fought in the Revolutionary War. William was Zachariah's third child. William was born in Kentucky, moved to Ohio and eventually moved to Illinois. He's been a member of the Illinois legislature, most recently, the Senate.

"He recruited volunteers to fight in the Black Hawk War. He's never spoken of fighting in the war. Must have done something significant, to end up a colonel.

"He and Governor Duncan are colleagues. They laid out the Town of Marshall. They were successful. Sold all the lots in eleven days. Soon afterward Archer, came north to Chicago. He's persuasive and uses contacts to further his career. I don't expect him to continue his interest in the Canal once it gets going.

"For now, he's pushing the improvement of Widow Brown's Road. He's having the portion from Chicago to where we were the other day for the dedication planked-over to make it more passable. He makes good use of his friendship with Governor Duncan to get things done.

"If we can convince Archer to listen to your Irish friends, Seamus, Thompson will agree to listen to their demands as well."

Chapter Forty Two

This is our last visit before the wedding," Molly said to Seamus. They were sitting on a rise of sand facing Lake Michigan. It was a month after the Fourth of July, 1836, ground breaking for the I & M Canal. "There is still so much to do to get ready. September 3rd seems so far off yet is coming too fast. I don't know what to do first. I want everything to be perfect."

Gently placing his fingertips to Molly's lips, Seamus whispered, "Hush now, love. You will be there. I will be there. That will make it perfect. Nothing else matters."

"Oh, Seamus, thank you." Taking a deep breath, Molly complained. "My mother continues to raise questions. She is distressed we are not following Irish traditions. Father hasn't met your parents to see if they are acceptable."

"Molly, we have been over this before. My dear Mother has been gone lo these twelve years. I don't know where my Dad is. Besides, he's a drunk. I haven't seen him since I fled Ireland. How could your father meet with either? He'd have to go to Heaven to see my Mum. By now, he might have to go to Hell to see my Dad."

"Seamus, how terrible. You told me Briana saw him and he looked better."

"He may be. Would your father go back to Ireland to look for him? Why? My father doesn't care about me. Do you want me to talk to your Mother to explain it to her?"

"No, I'm sorry." Pausing, Molly asked "Will we have straw boys?"

"Do you want to follow old traditions?"

"I don't know."

"Why don't we arrange for Lina and your mother to talk about all this?"

Throwing her arms around her intended, Molly gleefully said, before she kissed Seamus, "Yes! Do."

They sat quietly for a while, each with their own thoughts. The water was perfectly calm. A deep blue. A bird was chirping nearby. A lazy bee was flitting from one grass stalk to another, frustrated none had nectar. A large, brown beetle scurried by, a wiggling caterpillar in his ugly jaws. The breeze carried the sweet fragrance of a flowering tree.

"I love it here, Seamus. I can't believe this will be my home in just a month. Tell me more about the canal ceremony."

"The festivities on July 4th broke more than the ground. After the ceremony, I met with Dominick and his friends. It began on a sour note. Dominick laid into me about not watching out for the Irishmen he was encouraging to come to Chicago."

"How could he say that?"

"In his shoes I might have thought the same thing. My work with the Commissioners had not achieved any solid agreements on behalf of the workers."

"What did you say to Dominick?"

"I listened and then suggested he and his friends meet with the Commissioners to present their demands. Working with Axel and Gurdon, I arranged a meeting. It went well. I don't expect all of Dominick's demands to be met. After the meeting I told him this.

"Dominick looked at me and said, 'You gave us the chance to make our case. They listened to us. I have never seen Cormak so calm and so brilliant. From the questions the Commissioners asked it was clear to me they understood. Now they must balance our demands with their expenses.' "

"Seamus, you are a genius."

"Hardly, my love. The clincher, I think, was when P. J. spoke. He can hardly talk. The British tortured him. They hit him in the throat and damaged something.

"P. J. was so impassioned, I could see the impact on the faces of everyone in the room.

"More than four hundred Irish workers have arrived so far and more are coming every day. I have set up an office at the site of the groundbreaking where I am registering the workers. My assistant and I record their names, ages, next of kin and local addresses. I have several doctors with me each day. Doc Wooten organizes them. Each recruit is examined by one of the doctors. They screen out anyone not fit to work. Canal digging is demanding. It is hard physically. Inevitably the swamp disease will strike. The Commission has agreed to have a doctor present at the site at all times.

"I arranged for Doc Wooten to examine P. J. He said there is nothing he can do and suggested P. J. speak only when it is absolutely necessary. He suggested he carry a pad of paper and pencil and write notes to express himself. P. J. was resistant until I figured out he can't read or write. I have arranged for him to be taught. He is making good progress. It has lifted his spirits.

"On another matter, Axel is assisting me in working with Chicago and Cook County building inspectors. Many of the workers are living in a growing settlement which is fast becoming a miserable place. The inspectors will condemn the worst hovels. Axel has set up a group of Chicago men with the means to have decent housing built. It is a daunting task which will not abate until the canal is finished."

"Does this place have a name?"

"It does, a very descriptive one – Hardscrabble. As the worst of the shacks are replaced with tolerable housing, I hope the name will be changed."

"Has work begun on the canal?"

"It has. I visit the workers each day. They are digging. My presence seems to calm them down. I take notes on anything I feel needs attention. Once a week I send a report to the Commissioners together with my recommendations."

"I am very proud of you, my love."

Again, the two lapsed into silence.

Molly reached for Seamus' hand. "Lina told me about the Pitchfork Murders. It's horrible. What can you tell me about them?"

"Don't worry your pretty little head, my wee one."

"Stop that right now, Mr. O'Shea. I am neither your wee one, nor am I some frail thing."

Seamus was silenced by Molly's outburst.

"You men are all alike. Lina said she has to take Axel to task every now and then for his tendency to treat her as a fragile flower. Neither Lina nor I want to be set aside like a piece of porcelain. If that is what you are wanting for your bride, we had better call off the wedding right now."

"Now, Molly."

"Don't 'now Molly' me. Either you tell me everything when we are married or I will go after you with my frying pan."

Looking into Molly's eyes, Seamus thought he saw a bit of mischief. Taking the chance, he leaned over, tickled her in the side and when a smile began to emerge, kissed her. Molly pushed Seamus away, after she returned his kiss. Molly said, "Now mister. Do you promise to treat me as your partner in all we do or not?"

"I shall, love. I will always. It's just, I see it as my responsibility to protect you. If that means not telling you something, so be it."

"What about the Pitchfork Murders?"

There was no escaping it. Seamus told all he knew including the pitchfork instead of the shovel at the groundbreaking.

"How many murders have there been?"

"Five, over a period of three years."

"Who is doing it? Lina seemed afraid to tell me."

Seamus told her about what occurred in Germany and the kidnaping of Lina in New York. When Seamus finished telling all he knew, Molly hugged and thanked him.

"See, that wasn't hard to do."

Abruptly shifting subjects, Molly asked, "How many children should we have?"

"As many as you want."

"What kind of answer is that?"

Blushing, Seamus said, "As many as we can. I love you, Molly and want to love you as often as I can."

"You're blushing," Molly giggled.

"My mother died giving birth. I could never forgive myself if that happened to you. My father fell apart when my mother died. I have often wondered if he felt it was his fault. The price for a brief moment of pleasure."

"That's nonsense. The Good Lord wants us to have as many children as we can. I aim to honor God as long as I can."

"Molly, I want you to meet Dominick, Cormak, Padric and P. J. They are doing God's work, both by getting work for Irishmen and supporting the push for a free Ireland."

"I would like to meet them. How are they supporting freedom for Ireland?"

"They are collecting money which they send to Daniel O'Connell back in Ireland. He believes he can get the British to lift their ban on Catholicism. He opposes violence and needs money to get others to follow him. I want to send him money."

"What little I have read about Danny O'Connell, I agree with him. If you are asking my permission, do send him money. Just save enough for us to have a place to live, food to eat and clothes for ourselves and our children."

"There may be some danger doing so, Molly. Dominick believes he is being watched in New York by the government. The British are so obsessed they have asked the American government to help them stop the flow of money and arms to Ireland."

Jutting out her chin, Molly said, "Well that's a risk you and I need to take."

Chapter Forty Three

Seamus looked forward to his morning ride with Tin Bucket. Since Smithy's brutal murder, Seamus had moved his horse to the stable behind Wrights General Store. He was still living above the store. For weeks he chided himself each morning for not finding a more suitable home, one worthy of his soon to be marital status. Last week he finally acted. He would be moving in a few days to live on Washington just east of Dearborn. It was a well-built, frame home with a small barn in the back. Tin Bucket pranced in his stall when he heard Seamus open the stable door.

"Top of the morning to ye. You going to miss this place?" For the first time, Seamus realized Tin Bucket might miss the other horses in Wrights' stable.

Rubbing Tin Bucket's nose, Seamus asked, "Ready for today's adventure?"

Before heading to the Commission office, the two went north and raced for several miles. As quickly as Chicago was growing, north of the river still had little new development. Seamus was always glad to get past the Sands. Much of the land was swampy. The frogs, their chorus so thunderous at night, were now quiet. Both man and horse relished the wind in their faces. Reluctantly, Seamus pulled Tin Bucket to a halt and turned back south.

"Time to face the day. Lets get to work."

Land sales continued to be at a feverish pitch. In recent weeks, some who had purchased canal lots were standing on street corners offering their parcels at inflated prices to any takers. New arrivals fell for the hawking pitches shouted out. Passing their naive customers, Seamus was tempted to encourage them to come to his office for lower prices. The inflated prices were often two, three times their value.

Seamus thought of the huge profits he could make if he were to purchase the most attractive lots and then resell them. He talked briefly with Axel about the possibility and why he felt it would be immoral. Axel agreed. Seamus felt such a scheme would make him almost as bad as Fitchen, the corrupt Commission Director he had uncovered.

In his office, this August 10th, Seamus sat at his desk in the back room, assembled his notes from the week and began to outline his report to the Commissioners. One note made no sense to him. He usually took the time to write down exactly what he had observed. This note, however, read only, "McPeake angry."

Putting it aside, Seamus identified six issues he wanted to address. None were major. The weather had recently turned cooler which eliminated many of the worker's complaints. It was Barnaby who had grabbed his arm and said, "Been prayin' for cooler weather. Guess St. Pat heard me and put in a good word."

"That's it!" thought Seamus. Praying. Jimmy McPeake had complained about some of the workers calling the Irish "Potato Heads" and "Damn Papists." Seamus decided to put this at the top of his list. Anti-Catholicism was not new in America. The English settlers had brought their strong hatred of the Irish Catholics with them to America. He knew he couldn't stop it among the canal workers. He hoped to nip it in the bud before it got out of hand.

Why was there such hatred of Catholics? Damn Henry VIII and his fight with the Pope. If only his first wife had given him a son, England would still be Catholic and the Irish would be a free nation.

"Sir, Mr. Konrad would like to speak with you."

Jumping up, Seamus greeted his good friend. "Come in and take a load off your feet."

Sitting down, Axel's expression was quite serious.

"Has there been another murder?" Seamus asked.

"No. I am here on another matter. It's personal. In reviewing the bank records this morning, I noticed you have withdrawn a substantial sum from your account. Are you in trouble?"

Seamus, immediately bristled. "Is it customary for you to pry into private matters?"

Axel instantly realized he had been awkward in the way he put his question.

"No. You are my best friend and I want to help if I can."

"Do you ask your other customers how they spend their own money?"

"No. Forgive me Seamus. I don't mean to intrude on your financial decisions. It's just that, well, I understand you came into the bank with a stranger, withdrew hundreds of dollars and gave it to him."

"Damn you, Herr Konrad! Leave my office." Seamus stood up, walked to the door, opened it and rigidly waited until Axel left.

Slamming the door shut, Seamus returned to his desk. His rage grew rather than subsided. He could no longer concentrate on his report to the Commissioners. What right did Axel have to question how he spent his money? Should he move his account to the new bank? Getting up, he paced back and forth, five steps, turned around, five steps back, turned around, five steps forward, until he felt like smashing his fist into the wall.

Pulling on his coat, he stomped out of the building and walked in an uncontrolled rage, mindless of where he was headed. Tin Bucket, hitched in front of the Canal office whinnied when ignored. Nor did Seamus return the greetings of friends he passed. His face was red with tension and fury. His pace quickened until he was close to running. He had no idea when he turned south. Not, that is, until he finally noticed his surroundings. The street had come to an end. When he stepped onto soft ground, he finally paused. His pique was too justified to suppress.

Axel had no right to interfere. Is that what made him so mad, or was it his lingering doubts about giving the money to Dominick? Seamus felt a surge of pride when he did. Proud he was helping in Ireland's struggle with England. Proud his money might ease the life of someone living in a mud hut, fighting to survive because of the English. So what was bothering him?

Just hours after Seamus gave away hundreds of dollars, Dominick left Chicago. Was he to be trusted? Seamus began to wonder. He resisted the thought. It kept gnawing at him. Two days later, Seamus had talked with Cormak and Padric. They seemed uneasy when Seamus asked why Dominick had left. When he mentioned the hundreds of dollars he had given him, they looked surprised, as if they knew nothing about it. Or was he misinterpreting their reactions to reinforce his own doubts?

He hadn't given away all the money he had withdrawn from the bank. He used the other half to purchase his new home. He was confident it was a wise investment. But the O'Connell money? Would it actually get to him?

Continuing to walk further into the prairie, his mind flipped back to his anger with Axel. His question had touched a raw spot, Seamus' growing doubt. Just like when he had done something naughty as a little boy. Somehow his mother always seemed to know. She would gently probe with questions until he either blurted out what he had done and cried or he became angry with his mother.

He remembered the time his father talked with him about his anger. By then, Seamus had realized his anger was really with himself and not with his mother. He had failed himself by doing something wrong. Just like giving his money to Dominick. He was ashamed to admit his doubts to Axel, so he covered it up with his indignation and rage.

Now what? If he was honest with himself, he had to admit Axel was worried about him as a friend. Still, he needed to respect boundaries in their friendship.

Seamus tripped over a stake in the ground with a bit of red cloth tied to it. The tall prairie grass had obscured it. The stake was the kind used by surveyors to mark out property. Seamus had fallen to the ground. There, before him, was a dead body. He jumped up in revulsion. The corpse was face down. Looking down, Seamus saw puncture wounds in the man's back. Stepping away, Seamus struggled to decide what to do. Regaining his composure, he went through the man's pockets. They were empty. He needed to report the latest Pitchfork Murder. A lone tree was twenty paces away. A large outcropping of rock was in the opposite direction. With these markers he would be able to find the spot again.

Back in Chicago, Seamus went to the constable's office to report the murder. To Seamus' relief, John Shrigley was on duty. He hitched his horse to the official wagon. Seamus got Tin Bucket and stopped for Doc who was in and willing to join them. Doc rode with John. Seamus led the way.

Doc concluded the man had been dead for a day or two. He helped John lift him into the wagon. They took the corpse to Doc's office for him to make a thorough examination. Doc wrote down his observations, including sketches of the pitchfork wounds and the gunshot wounds to the abdomen.

"Unlike the others, this man was killed where we found him. He would have suffered a slow death from the wounds to the belly. He was still alive when stabbed in the back by the pitchfork."

John asked, "How can you tell?"

"By the large pool of blood when we rolled him over. It had soaked into the dry ground. If he had been killed elsewhere, the blood would have been much less, which tells me he was shot and then pronged by the pitchfork."

"Would he have been conscious?"

"Yes."

Seamus excused himself before he became ill. He mounted Tin Bucket and rode further south. Adding to his confusion over whether or not Dominick was trustworthy, he felt he had been wrong in questioning Axel's behavior. Finding the latest victim of the Pitchfork Murderer hit Seamus hard. It was more than his shock at seeing the corpse and his anger over someone's life ending in such a vicious way. He now appreciated, as never before, how the terror each murder must impact Axel in ways he could not imagine. Axel must fear for his wife, children and sister every waking hour and, yes, his close friends, including Seamus himself.

Remorse and guilt washed over Seamus as he raced south. He had been dreadfully wrong in lashing out at Axel. Making a wide circle Seamus guided Tin Bucket west to the site of the canal work. He slowed Tin Bucket down as he rode along side the growing ditch. It was sixty feet wide and four feet deep. Men were down at the bottom working west, jamming their shovels into the clay. They threw it behind them where other men scooped it up and filled buckets. Up on the banks, men pulled the buckets up by ropes and dumped them a few feet back from the edge. There, still others spread it evenly to form what would become the tow path.

Surveyors were on either side of the ditch to assure the bottom had a slight downward pitch to the west. Measurements were made from the bottom up to the tow paths to assure they were level. When the ground surface rose or fell, the banks were either cut down or filled in so the tow paths would be easily passable for the donkeys or horses to pull the boats along the finished canal.

Seamus rode along the ditch greeting workers by name. Progress was being made to construct a temporary office where records would be kept and medical emergencies could be handled. It was an unusual design. Rather than being anchored to a foundation, it was built on a large sled so it could be moved along as the work progressed.

Workers leveling the tow path stopped to greet Seamus. They patted Tin Bucket who thrived on their attention while pretending not to notice it. Further southwest, another surveyor was laying out stakes to mark the precise route of the canal. Seamus was pleased to see P. J. sighting through the transit and signaling his rod man to set stakes. It was Seamus' biggest success so far, placing an Irishman in a professional position. Since surveyors use hand signals rather than shouting, P. J. was well-suited for the job. He had an assistant who held a slate and chalk. When a command had to be called, P. J. wrote it down and the assistant signaled the command. Happily, the assistant was also Irish.

Some of the workers began to sing. Others joined in. The Irish melody threatened to bring tears to Seamus' eyes. He pulled on the reigns and headed back. Less than an hour later, he was sitting at his desk. Picking up his notes, he quickly completed his report to the Commissioners. Sitting back, he pondered his dilemma. He knew he should go see Axel and apologize. His pride got in the way. He just could not get himself to do so. Axel owed him an apology.

His uncertainty over Dominick haunted him. He could not accept the possibility he had made a mistake. Unable to admit an error blocked him going to see Axel. The image of the corpse he found in the prairie entered his hodgepodge of thoughts. It became more confused by the memory of the tax collector lying on the floor of their cottage in Ireland, his head badly crushed by his father. This explained his reaction to the pitchfork victim. Seamus felt hot all over. Sweat on his brow flowed into his eyes, the salt burning them.

"Sir?"

Seamus involuntarily jerked up his head.

"Sir, are you alright?" It was one of the clerks.

"Yes. Yes. What is it?"

"Sir, Mrs. Konrad would like to talk with you."

Getting up, Seamus stepped from his office. It was getting late in the day. There was only one customer seeking to purchase a canal lot. Lina was standing demurely near the outer door. Seamus walked to her.

"Good afternoon, Lina. Please come into my office."

Seamus hoped he sounded normal. He certainly didn't feel like himself.

"If you are busy, I can come back another time."

"After the day I've had, I could not wish for anything nicer than a visit from you."

"Seamus, Axel told me about his inexcusable behavior this morning. He is wrought with anger at himself. I have never seen him like this. You are his best friend and he is worried he has lost your friendship forever.

"He's a very proud German. Too proud to admit to you he made a mistake. He sets very high standards for himself. He has failed and is wallowing not only in guilt but in self-pity. I have urged him to come see you and apologize. He just got angry with me, stomped out of the house and has been out riding Thor ever since.

"Can you forgive him?"

Smiling, relief flowing through his very being, Seamus reached out and took Lina's hand. "You are an angel, dear Lina.

"I, too, went for a ride. I, too, am stubborn. I, too, feel I was rude and treated Axel as an enemy rather than my best friend. I have been sitting here trying to get my bonnie body to get up and go tell Axel I am sorry.

"We are acting like two small boys fighting over a stick. Pretty pathetic, isn't it?"

"If you truly feel that way, would you come for dinner this evening? I won't tell Axel so he doesn't get his German dander up."

"Are you sure?"

"Please come. Shall we say at seven. I'll have the children ready for bed. They always love to see their Uncle Seamus."

"I accept. You are indeed an angel."

Chapter Forty Four

Seamus hesitated at the foot of the stairway. Part of him wanted to leave. What if Axel became angry and ordered him to leave his home. He could understand if he did. That is, after all, what Seamus had done when he demanded Axel leave his office. He trusted Lina. Could she control her husband when he was determined and mad?

Nonsense. His friendship was worth eating humble pie. Seamus began his assent, one foot slowly stepping up after the other. The door opened. The two boys came tumbling out onto the landing.

"Unc Seamus! Unc Seamus!"

Kneeling down, he enfolded Henry and Rady in his arms. They wiggled free and pulled him into the apartment where Lina greeted him.

"Axel is freshening up. Come in Seamus."

The boys ran around the room, giggling and laughing.

"I have something for you boys."

Running to him, they tried to climb up into his lap. Henry was first, leaving no room for Rady. He unsuccessfully pulled on Henry's foot, only managing to pull of his shoe. Rady laughed, holding Henry's shoe over his head. Henry tumbled down and raced after Rady.

Seamus reached into his pockets and pulled out two small parcels wrapped with string. Seeing them, the boys returned to their uncle, who handed one to each.

Pulling on a loose end, the string bow loosened. Henry watched what Rady had done and did the same thing. Simultaneously, they ripped off the paper. Out fell a gold coin from each package.

"Money," shouted Henry.

Rady bit his coin and announced, "Gold!"

The boys ran to their room. Lina explained, "They have banks. You are the first to give them money to put in them."

An awkward silence filled the room, making Seamus aware for the first time of the delicious fragrance coming from the kitchen. Lina left to tend her cooking, leaving Seamus alone.

Moments later, Axel entered the parlor, stood stock still upon discovering Seamus. The Irishman stood. He and the German faced one another, neither wanting to make the first move. Lina returned, observed the two.

"Axel. Have you forgotten how to welcome our guest?"

Neither man spoke nor moved.

Taking Axel's hand, she gently pulled him to the middle of the room. She walked toward Seamus who began to laugh.

"I can imagine my dear mother up in Heaven looking down at us saying, "Your feet have brought you where your heart is." As he spoke, Seamus walked toward his old friend.

Standing toe to toe, Axel's stern face melted into a wide smile. "I am sorry," he said in an emotion laden whisper.

"It's my fault, Axel. You meant to help me and I rejected you." Seamus grabbed his much taller friend and gave him a hug, squeezing him until he relaxed. Axel put his arms around Seamus, lifted him and twirled around and around until the two, dizzy, fell to the floor.

The boys ran from their room and piled on top of the two men.

Her goal accomplished, Lina called to Henry and Rady, "It's time for bed." After their objections failed to sway their mother, they kissed their Uncle Seamus and scampered off to their room.

"Axel, please put them in their beds and say their prayers while Seamus helps me put the dinner on the table."

Seamus began the dinner conversation with an exclamation.

"I have thought through my reaction to your visit this morning. I withdrew money from my account for two purposes. First, to purchase a home for Molly and me." Axel was about to interrupt, stopped, seeing Lina shake her head. "It's on Washington, just east of Dearborn. I paid for it outright. I gave the rest of the money to the man you mentioned.

"His name is Dominick Breen. I met him in New York. William Ogden wanted me to go see him to ask him to encourage Irish immigrants to come to Chicago to build the canal.

"Dominick and his friends are supporters of Daniel O'Connell who believes he can achieve independence for Ireland through peaceful means. I abhor violence. I saw enough of it during the Black Hawk War. Killing is not the answer. It only hardens opposition."

Lina could see Axel was bursting to comment. After another look at Lina, he resisted.

"That was several days ago. Shortly afterward, Dominick left town. When I confronted his friends they seemed surprised. Should I have trusted Dominick? Has he run off with my money for his own use? When you came to visit me I was stewing about it. You touched a raw nerve and I reacted in anger. I am sorry."

"Seamus, you taught me English. Every now and then I am asked if I am Irish. Guess I picked up more than the words. I have a bit of an Irish accent as well.

"Anyway, you once said something to me which I often repeat to myself. 'Lord, clothe me with the robes of innocence.'

"Daily, Henry and Rady become more and more aware of the world around them. They face each new thing with innocence. As adults, we become more and more cautious. Cautious not to be hurt. Not to be made a fool. These are things we learn. Unconsciously, we limit ourselves and our joys for fear of getting hurt. By doing so, we miss the happiness of youth.

"I admire you, Seamus, for your trust and innocence. If William Ogden trusts Dominick, you should as well. You made your decision because your heart led you to. Trust yourself, my friend."

Sensing the need to change the subject, Lina asked Seamus to describe his new home, after which, Axel spoke of Stephen Douglas.

"Douglas borrowed money to purchase 1,000 acres south of Chicago. He is from downstate in Jacksonville. He stopped by this past week to make his first interest payment. We had a nice conversation. Fascinating person.

"Small in stature, he's a firecracker in drive. Came from Vermont in 1833. Opened a school and charged three dollars per pupil. Gave it up and studied the law. Named state's attorney for a local county a year later. When we approved his loan last year, it was based more on faith than fact. I have to admit, I was relieved when he made his first interest payment. Not sure where he will get the money to pay off the loan in four years."

"What does he intend to do with so much land?" asked Seamus.

"He's convinced Chicago will grow so fast, his land will soon be in demand."

"Axel, have you been told of the latest murder?" Turning to Lina, Seamus added, "Sorry Lina. Perhaps I should not talk about it now."

Lina answered with a question, "Is it another Pitchfork Murder?"

"Yes."

"Lina, would you like to excuse yourself?" asked Axel.

"No. I want to know everything as it happens."

Seamus continued, telling of his discovery of a body earlier in the day. When he described the location, Axel exclaimed, "The surveyor's stake marks one of the lots I own. Bought them when I first came to Chicago. I have been thinking of building our home there. Decided just the other day the area is still too undeveloped to be safe. I'm surprised no one has come to tell me about it."

"How could they? You have been out riding all day," Lina commented.

"How many victims now?" asked Seamus

"Seven."

Lina rose to clear off the table. By the time she brought in dessert, Axel had changed the subject.

"I am very concerned about the wild speculation here in Chicago. Prices are becoming more inflated each day. Several of my investors out East have written to me expressing concern. The economy is soaring out of control. Many are reckless in their investments. The Treasury is frantically printing paper money without sufficient gold to back it up."

"I see it every day, Axel, what the prices canal lots are going for. Even worse are the sidewalk sales. Unsuspecting newcomers are paying two, three times the cost we are selling lots for. They turn around and sell them for even higher prices. They are not worth it. Maybe someday, but not now. How will it end?"

"I'm not sure. I read a recent article in one of the Eastern papers. It could all crash. Men who have borrowed to purchase property will suffer the most. Values could drop precipitously. Loan amounts will exceed the lower values. Speculators will be left in debt, unable to sell their property. It could be devastating to the entire economy."

"If your loans can't be repaid, will you have to close your bank?"

"No. I have been increasing our reserves for two years now. I had to order a larger vault to hold all the gold I have accumulated."

"Time for you to stop all this gloomy talk and enjoy your dessert." Lina brought in a warm cheese cake and bowl of cherries in sweet sauce. Cutting a large piece of cheesecake for each man, she covered them with the cherries and sauce and a puff of whipped cream on top. She served herself a much smaller piece. She poured cups of steaming hot coffee.

"Lina, thank you for writing to Molly's mother about the wedding. She has ended her criticism of our plans. Molly was getting so distressed, I worried she would postpone the wedding."

"I can't appreciate Irish traditions. I wrote how distraught my Mother became trying to serve the role my late father would have been expected to do. German traditions are not as complicated as those of the Irish. I tried to suggest your happiness is more important than Old World traditions. I am glad I didn't make matters worse.

"Has Molly seen your new home?"

"No. Not until the wedding."

"She's arriving days before, can't she see it then?"

"If I can't see her dress, she can't see the house."

"Seamus, that's shameful," Axel protested.

"Who's side are you on?" Seamus pretended to be angry.

Just then, Axel noticed Rady at the doorway. He excused himself and went to him. Rady began to cry. He picked him up and brought him to the table.

Sobbing, Rady said, "Scared."

"Why?"

"Lady die."

"Indian lady?"

Nodding, he whispered, "Yes."

Hugging him, he held him in his lap. Axel lifted Rady's tears from his cheeks with his finger and put them in his shirt pocket. Rady noticed what he was doing. With his own finger, he wiped away a tear and put it in his father's pocket as well. Looking up into Axel's face he asked, "What do?"

"I'm saving your tears. Tucked here in my pocket, they will bring you happiness."

Chapter Forty Five

September 3, year of our Lord, eighteen hundred and thirty six. A day as fine as a day could be. The summer heat had eased. Rain the previous week had greened up the sagging plants and bushes and restored the prairies. The dust of the streets had settled. The muddy puddles had dried up. The air is fresh, rinsed of summer's oppression. Everywhere, strangers cheerfully greet one another. Petty feuds have been cleansed, friendships repaired for the moment. Surely there is not a person who does not feel a surge of optimism, a belief all is well.

Seamus paced back and forth in the bedroom he and Molly would soon share. He had not been this frightened since the night he hid behind a rocky ridge as his traveling companion had been killed on an island off the coast of Ireland. Seamus had been fleeing from the mud hut which was the only home he had known. He had traveled after dark, on foot, for nights, avoiding contact with anyone, afraid he would be turned over to the British. He had met Rohan Quinn along the way. The two were determined to escape Ireland and come to America.

Rifle shots had dropped Rohan. The British soldiers cursed the young Irishman, searched his pockets, confirmed he was dead and dragged his corpse away. Seamus shivered in fear. The cold and dampness penetrated his very soul. He felt panic.

Seamus pushed away the memory, straightened himself, for the umpteenth time combed his red thatch of hair and braced himself with confidence. It was not fair to compare what he was feeling now to back then. Smiling, he looked at the bed where tonight, he would finally become a man.

"Seamus, we will be late." Axel's voice was tinged with impatience. This was the fifth time he had called to him. Each time, louder and more insistent.

Axel, Seamus' closest friend, is a German Lutheran. Seamus had not told Father Timothy O'Meara that Axel was not Catholic, thinking, "How can it be wrong to have him stand up for me? To witness the happiest day of my life?"

Father St.Cyr, who had built St. Mary's Catholic Church at the southwest corner of Lake and State streets, had been reassigned and replaced by the English speaking O'Meara. Soon after his arrival, Father O'Meara moved the church building to Wabash Avenue and Madison Street. Seamus had gone to watch St. Mary's be lifted and moved five blocks.

"Seamus O'Shea, either you come out this minute or I shall drag you out." Captain Farrell O'Flaherty had also been pacing back and forth. The father of the bride was almost as nervous as Seamus, even though he had been through this before with his two older daughters. Molly, his youngest, was his favorite. He tried never to show she was closest to him.

Opening the bedroom door, Seamus stepped out, his cravat in place. He was uncomfortable in his new suit. New, nay, he thought, his first suit. The first he had ever owned. Axel had insisted he have a tailor make it. "You must look your best on your wedding day."

In front of Seamus' home, stood Axel's carriage and team of horses, with Anders Johansen, waiting to open the carriage door.

"This way Mr. O'Shea. May the Good Lord grant ye many little ones," Anders said with his distinct Swedish accent.

Seamus climbed up, followed by Captain O'Flaherty and then Axel. Grinning at Axel, Seamus asked, "Did you ask Anders to say that?"

Axel shrugged, his smile his answer.

"Anders is anything but Irish."

"Today, anyone who knows you, Seamus, is Irish," said his soon-to-be father-in-law.

The carriage began the journey to St. Mary's Catholic Church.

"We could have walked, Axel. It is only four blocks."

"Seamus, you can walk from now on. Not today."

Arriving at St. Mary's, the three men stepped down and entered the church. They were almost an hour early. No one else had arrived.

Anders took the carriage to the Greater Bank of Chicago. Upstairs, the women were in a flurry of activity. Lina was helping Rose Kathleen with her dress.

Her voice confirming her unease, Rose lamented, "I can't believe how nervous I am today."

"Rose, you are not nervous. You are excited with joy," Lina reassured Molly's mother.

Anna, who was expecting in a matter of weeks, had volunteered to stay with her children and Lina's.

When Lina objected, insisting Anna should come to the wedding, Anna, in no uncertain terms stated, "I am as big as a house and do not wish to attend!" That was it. Lina was relieved knowing Anna would take care of the children. Rikert was never far from Lina's thoughts.

Molly had been ready for almost an hour. She was lovely in her white dress. She wore Irish lace covering her hair and trailing down her back. She would pull it over her face before she entered the church.

Finally ready, the three women descended to the front door where Anders was waiting. He helped each into the carriage. Moments later he assisted them down and through the side door to St. Mary's. Guests were beginning to arrive.

When he entered St. Mary's, Axel was struck with the similarity to the Lutheran Church in Bodden, Germany. The interior was simple, the altar not much more than a heavy wooden plank on two large posts. The cross with the crucifixion was small. Only when he approached it was he surprised with the gruesome portrayal of a bloody Christ.

When he was fifteen, Axel had gone to Schwerin with his father. It was the farthest he had been from their home. One morning, while out for a walk, they passed a large Catholic cathedral. Parishioners were entering for, his father explained, the morning mass. Heinrich suggested they enter so Axel could see the contrast with their church back home and observe the differences in the service.

The ceiling soared high overhead resting on rows of pillars lining the two long side walls. Half way up each pillar, mounted on a gilded, ornate shelf, was a figure carved in white marble. His father concluded they were Catholic saints. The features of the faces were finely painted. Their crowns were gilded, as were their wide belts and the helms of their robes. Some sternly glared down at Axel. Others looked up toward Heaven with angelic expressions.

To either side of the main altar were side chapels with smaller altars. Over the one to the left was a statue of, they concluded, the Holy Mother, the Virgin Mary. To the right was a male statue. They were unable to identify who he represented. Before each side altar were many small, lighted candles.

It was the main altar which made the greatest impression. There was a vivid crucifixion of the Christ, rising high above them. The sorrow on Jesus' face was difficult for Axel to see. His body, twisted in pain, the bright red blood oozing from the nails in the feet and hands and the pierced side, caused Axel to look away, yet return over and over again to catch another glimpse.

Neither father nor son could understand a word spoken by the resplendently robed priest. He read from a large book held before him by a younger, robed man. The priest's strong voice was monotone, without any emotion or expression. Heinrich leaned over to whisper to Axel, "He is speaking in Latin."

They were seated in the back of the cathedral. Axel had struck his shin as he entered the pew. "That is for prayer," his father explained. "It is pulled down for prayer."

Axel responded, "I am ready to leave."

The two quietly departed, the service far from over.

Seamus and Axel met briefly with Father O'Meara in a tiny room off the sanctuary. He explained the order of service. Axel, feeling it was his responsibility to guide Seamus through the ritual, tried to remember all the priest said. Perhaps he read the look of concern on his face because he assured Axel, "I will guide the two of you during the service."

The small sanctuary was filling. Seamus tried not to stare at the congregation to see who had come. He did, however, take a quick glance. In that brief moment he saw Dominick Breen. He had not seen him since he gave most of his savings to the Irishman. Dominick had disappeared the next day. He wanted to go to him and ask what happened to his money. The quick dash of anger, followed by relief he had returned, had a calming effect on Seamus.

Axel spoke softly to his friend. "Seamus, this day will be one of the happiest in your life. Enjoy it, relish every minute. We are all here to tell you what you and Molly are about to do is God's plan for both of you."

Seamus had never heard Axel speak so before. Lina had often told Seamus her husband is deeply religious even though he never speaks of his faith.

The windows were open. Fresh air off the lake reached everywhere. A small choir in the back of the church began to sing. Seamus, Axel and Captain O'Flaherty stood facing the congregation. In came Briana and Nora O'Shea, Seamus' sisters, followed by Molly's sister, Amber. Next came Rose Kathleen followed by Molly.

Molly's gown glowed as the afternoon sun streaming through the windows lit the white fabric. The Irish lace tumbled over her face and down her back. She held a bouquet of late summer flowers tied with a piece of Irish lace.

Captain O'Flaherty softly exclaimed, "She is lovely!"

271

Seamus didn't move a muscle, apprehensive the vision would evaporate. As small as St. Mary's is, to Seamus the time it took Molly to reach him was an eternity. Axel stepped forward and guided Molly to her father who took her hand, kissed it and turned to give it to Seamus. Still frozen in adoration, Axel had to gently encourage his Irish friend to take her hand and step before the priest.

Lina, sitting in the first pew with Briana, Nora and Kathleen, followed their lead throughout the service. Standing, sitting, praying as they did. She did not understand the words spoken but sensed their meaning. The service was not that different than back home in their Lutheran church in Dobbersen, Germany. Fleetingly she promised herself to see if she could find a book which might compare the two faiths – Catholic and Lutheran.

At one point, Molly and Seamus walked to the side altar to pray to the Virgin Mary. Molly laid her flowers on the small altar. Seamus helped her up to make sure she did not step on the Irish lace which hung beyond the length of her dress.

Axel found his mind wandering. What was the priest saying? Why was it taking so long? The service when he and Lina married, would have been over some time ago. Did the Catholic service make Molly and Seamus more married than he and Lina?

Feeling ashamed of such thoughts, Axel began to study the congregation. John Wright, Sr. and his son John Stephan Wright, Jr. were near the front. Several of the I & M Canal Commissioners were present near the front. In the back, Axel concluded the men in clean, but informal clothing, were Irish laborers. Doc Wooten, Philo and Ann Carpenter and Lieutenant Grege represented those who came to Chicago with Axel and Seamus.

Axel was not the only male present whose mind began to wander. Captain O'Flaherty, Molly's father, having performed his brief ceremonial function, sat mulling over his wife's weeks of planning in spite of her daughter's insistence on her own plans. Rose Kathleen was determined to follow Irish wedding traditions. She had accepted it was not possible for her husband to meet with Seamus' parents. She was still somewhat distraught the wedding had not delayed until it could take place on Shrovetide. Her husband said, "You would have them wait until three days before the start of Lent next year?" She knew, from the tone of his voice, she had to give in.

Rose Kathleen was pleased Axel had insisted Seamus have a tailor make his suit.

"In Ireland, the groom must visit a tailor. Tailoring is the oldest craft in the world. After all, it was a tailor who sewed clothes of fig leaves for Adam and Eve."

Rose was also pleased it was a sunny day. Her mother had told her, "The sun shining on the bride, it is a lucky omen for rain foretells hardship in a marriage." She hoped this would offset Molly's refusal to delay the wedding. Rose had told her, "Those who marry at harvest time will spend all their lives gathering."

She was pleased Seamus had accepted her plea that a plate of oatmeal and salt be placed on the altar. She had insisted, "If you and Molly each take three mouthfuls it will protect you against the power of the evil eye."

The service ended with the priest commanding Seamus, "Give your wife a kiss of peace." This, he said, in English. Rose relaxed, another Irish tradition heeded.

The choir sang. The congregation stood. Looking at them, Axel wondered if their smiles were for Mr. and Mrs. Seamus O'Shea or relief the service was finally over. The O'Shea's walked down the aisle to the carriage waiting for them. The guests followed. Carsten and John Dean Caton handed each guest an envelope with a handwritten invitation to the Tremont Hotel to celebrate.

Johann Wellmacher had outdone himself with several large wedding cakes. His wife, who had come from Germany with their children, served each of the guests a piece. Those who knew the Irish custom, in exchange for the cake, placed a donation on the table for the priest.

When all were served both cake and champagne, Axel stood. In his booming voice, he offered the toast Rose Kathleen insisted he say.

> Health and long life to you,
> Land without rent to you,
> A child every year to you,
> And death in old Ireland.

A few days later, both the *Democrat* and the *American* published articles about, what they reported as, "the wedding of the year." Molly proudly gave her mother, just before she and her father and sister left on *Princess Rose*, copies of both newspapers. Once in her cabin and underway, Rose read the papers and cried. It was, indeed, a lovely wedding.

Chapter Forty Six

Rufus exclaimed, "Damn! This Ogden fellow jus' got here. We need Kinzie. His daddy was a pioneer. We needs someone knows this place, like John Kinzie. Besides, Ogden's a lawyer. I don't like fast talking lawyers. Cain't trust 'em. Ain't never met a lawyer who weren't out to make his self money from poor fools like me. Besides, this Ogden ain't got no stick-to-it-tism. Jumps from one thing to 'nother. Just got them Irish digging the canal and he's off building a rail train. You want some one like that for mayor?"

"Rufus, you're talking through your hat," Sonny responded angrily.

"At least I still got me hat," replied Rufus.

Getting heated up, Sonny angrily spit out, "John Kinzie no better'n his pa. Traitor, his pa backing the British until he saw they were going to lose. His boy's no better."

The two men continued arguing for some time. They hadn't seen Seamus enter Mark Beaubien's Sauganash. It was late in the afternoon. No one else was there. The evening crowd had not yet started to arrive. Seamus was sitting several tables over, taking notes. They continued to argue, taking no notice of the Irishman.

"You going to vote, Rufus?"

"Reckon I will. You?"

"Haven't decided," said Sonny. "I don't want more taxes."

"Since when do you pay taxes?" asked Rufus.

"Since men voted Chicago to become a city. Still can't believe it. Remember March 4, 1837? That's the day we will live to regret. Them politicians like to spend other people's money. Specially if we get a mayor. Next thing he'll be calling hisself King."

"Sonny, you're hopeless. You don't have no sense."

Sonny jumped up and grabbed Rufus by the collar. "Don't call me no dummy."

Rufus knocked his hands from his coat and pushed Sonny back down. He shoved him so hard Sonny fell backwards, knocking over the chair and cracking his head on the floor.

"That's enough!" shouted Mark as he stormed over and restrained Rufus, who was about to attack the downed Sonny. "Both of you get out of here and don't come back until you can behave."

Rufus shrugged his shoulders and walked out. Sonny, groggy, stumbled when he got himself up and teetered forward. Mark caught him and guided him out the door.

Turning to Seamus, Mark asked, "What you doing Seamus?"

"Taking notes."

"What the hell for?"

"I'm a reporter for the *Democrat.*"

"Canal fire you?" asked Mark.

"The Commissioners are running out of money. Because of that and the colder weather, they've shut down work. Molly and I are short of money. Reporting doesn't pay much. Every bit helps. I also have negotiated a reduced percentage of the profits from Wrights General Stores."

"The *Democrat* making enough money to pay you?"

"Not always. With competition from the *American,* both papers are having hard times."

"Is it true Calhoun sold the *Democrat?*"

"Yes and no. He sold the paper to Horatio Hill."

"Where'd he come from?"

"Concord, New Hampshire. Hill gave Calhoun a bank draft for $750 and promised to pay all of John's debts. When Calhoun took the draft to Axel he discovered it was worthless. By the time Calhoun found out, Hill had fled Chicago. John Wentworth's the editor now."

"So Calhoun still stuck with the paper?"

"He and Wentworth are negotiating. Wentworth has agreed to take over Hill's deal and buy the *Democrat.*"

"So who hired you, Seamus?"

"Wentworth. I get fifty cents for every article he publishes. Axel tells me the financial problems out east are headed our way. Says to save all I can."

"How come I haven't seen anything written by you?"

"You have, just don't recognize it. I sign my pieces 'Nosey Neighbor.' "

"Well I'll be damned. No wonder you were listening to Sonny and Rufus arguing about the election and taxes. You write that piece about the ponds on La Salle Street?"

"You mean the one called 'Frog Heaven'? I did."

"You have a wicked sense of humor. Particularly about the mother stomping into the pond, yelling at her son for getting muddy. Him covered with mud from head to toe. She sure changed her tune when she saw how many frogs he'd caught. Was about to swat her kid when he held up his bag of croaking frogs.

"What was it he said, 'Them's for dinner tonight.' That sure changed her tone. I could picture her laughing as she tugged the boy out of the mud and water.

" Her son sure resisted her, saying, 'Leave me alone.'

"Laughed till I cried. She got him home, dragging him all the way and insisted on washing his face only to discover he was not her son. Once she let him go, he ran out, but not before he grabbed his bag of frogs, leaving one in the middle of the floor. Guess that was one lucky frog as he hopped after the boy. He lived to croak another day."

"Glad you liked it. I've been working on a piece about the tele-graph. Samuel Morse, the artist, designed this tapping machine. Stretched ten miles of wire around a room in the U. S. Capitol and tapped this key to send a message. I can't figure it out. Guess it made quite an impression on the politicians. Even President Van Buren came to see it. Morse is convinced someday wires will stretch to Chicago and we'll get the news as it happens."

"That doesn't sound like something the Nosey Neighbor would write about, Seamus."

"Wentworth wants me to try my hand at serious writing. If he likes it, he wants me to write about the election. How you going to vote, Mark?"

"I voted for Chicago becoming a city. Glad it passed. Hell, we're over 3,700 now. Bigger than many eastern cities. Time we join their ranks. And a city needs a mayor. I agree with Rufus. I'm for Ogden. You know him. What do you think of him?"

"He's smart, honest and hard driving. He'll set a high standard. Wentworth is going to come out in support of him."

"Did you know Kinzie's father was born in Quebec City in Canada? His father was Scottish. Spelled his name McKenzie. John not only dropped the Mc but changed Kenzie to Kinzie. Never said why. His son, John Harris Kinzie, the one running for mayor, might have been born here, but I'm not impressed with him. Now Ogden, he's had real experience and seems to be a real go-getter."

276

"May I quote you, Mark?"

"Sure, why not. He's a Democrat. Kinzie's a Whig. I don't trust the Whigs.."

"Thank you Mark. I better get home for dinner. My sweet Molly has a temper if I am late."

Walking east, Seamus passed a number of crude signs posted here and there touting Kinzie, and many more for Ogden. There were still some signs up for and against making Chicago a city.

Coming toward Seamus was none other than John Harris Kinzie. Seamus had to admit, Kinzie cut a dignified figure. If it were only a matter of appearance, he'd be elected. Problem is he's overbearing.

Kinzie called out, "I'd like to talk to you, Seamus. You have time for a drink?"

"Thank you, John, but I neither drink nor have time right now."

"Well. You heading home?"

"I am, John. Perhaps tomorrow?"

"I'll walk with you." Striding alongside Seamus, John Kinzie made his case.

"You know, Seamus, Ogden has an advantage in this election. He wrote the City Charter. Doesn't seem fair to me. Our first mayor shouldn't win through a rigged election. He's new to Chicago."

Seamus' ire flared. With effort, he kept silent. John's voice became angry as he berated Ogden. Approaching the O'Shea home, Seamus was determined not to invite Kinzie inside. Normally Seamus found great joy in welcoming anyone into his home. He was determined to keep John out.

"John, I would invite you in to talk, but this is not a good time."

Without another word, Seamus opened the front door, quickly entered and shut the door immediately. He felt as if Kinzie's eyes were burning a hole in the door.

"Seamus, are you all right. Was someone chasing you?"

Kissing Molly lightly on the cheek, Seamus said, "You might say so. John Kinzie is politicking. He was bending my ear to get me to support him."

"You men and your politics. Someday women will be given the vote and things will change for the better. Wash up. Dinner's ready."

On May 3, 1837, Chicagoans voted again. This time to select a mayor. William Ogden won by an overwhelming margin, 469 to 237. There never was any doubt of the outcome, yet those who voted for Ogden uttered a sigh of relief.

Part Twelve

Going Back Home

Chapter Forty Seven

Gentlemen, I have three issues on the agenda today. First, I would like to introduce our new board members. Second, the actions I feel we need to take in light of the financial panic gripping New York banks. I will speak of the third item a bit later on."

Looking around the table in the conference room, I once again realized the magnitude of the change in membership. Only three directors were carried over from the previous Board: Philo Carpenter, John Dean Caton and Dr. Charles Wooten. I had met with the three ahead of time to ask them to each serve as mentors to two of the six new members.

"I have taken the unusual measure of placing name cards at each place. Since six of you are new to the bank board, I have arranged for new members to sit on either side of an existing board member. In the weeks ahead, to the extent you find it productive, I ask you to meet with your mentor to ask questions and gain a deeper understanding of your duties as a board member.

"With that, Philo, would you introduce yourself and the new members next to you?"

"Certainly. I am Philo Carpenter. I have been on the board since the bank was founded in 1833. Axel has asked me to work with John and Archibald. You will soon learn of Axel's precision and order in things. Notice, he has assigned us alphabetically."

Turning to the man to his right, Philo asked, "John, please introduce yourself. Then Archibald, if you will do so as well."

"I'm John Calhoun, former owner and publisher of the *Chicago Democrat*. I published a newspaper back in Watertown, New York, before packing up my press and coming to Chicago in the fall of 1833. I was successful until the *Chicago American* was founded. The competition coupled with some personal financial problems forced me to sell the *Democrat*. I was kept afloat for many months with loans from the Greater Bank of Chicago. I must admit it came as a surprise when Axel asked me to be on the board. Perhaps he needed a financial failure to counterbalance all you successful businessmen."

Philo interjected, "I should point out John has just conducted the assessments of property for Cook County as the County Treasurer."

I nodded to Archibald. "I am Archibald Clybourne. I was born in Virginia and came to Chicago in 1823. I was appointed Chicago's first constable at the age of twenty-three. I turned to buying cattle in central Illinois and built Chicago's first slaughterhouse. I have negotiated with the Army to supply fresh meat to Fort Dearborn and three other forts.

"Been a justice of the peace, trustee of the School Section, and Cook County's first treasurer." Turning to Calhoun, Archibald said, "Let me know if I can be of any help to you, John. I've dabbled in real estate. My real interest, however, is to establish Chicago as a major cattle trading center. We are in a perfect location to supply meat to the Midwest and the East Coast."

I called next on John Dean Caton. "I have been on the Board now for two years. As a director, each of you will need to make difficult decisions from time to time, need to keep what we discuss here confidential, get to know what is going on in Chicago and gain a deep respect for Axel and your fellow board members. I look forward to working with all of you.

"Gentlemen, I am pleased to introduce Silas."

"I'm Silas Bowman Cobb. My mother always insisted I make mention of the Bowman in my name. I was born in Montpelier, Vermont, in 1812. Came to Chicago by schooner in 1833 without a penny in my pocket. I got employment as a carpenter working on several buildings, including the Green Tree Tavern. Two years ago, with the benefit of a loan from Axel here, I began my Saddle and Harness Manufactory. It has turned profitable. Proud to say I paid off my loan ahead of time. I am a volunteer with the Pioneer hook and ladder company fire brigade. Made the leather buckets for the company."

"Augustus, would you please speak next?"

"I am Augustus Garrett. I arrived in 1834. Came from New York with my wife Eliza. We opened a store. The following year I invested my meager funds in Canal land. A year later, I auctioned off my holdings. I was startled with the huge profits I realized in a year.

"Currently I am branching out into spirits, beers, ales and, to please my wife, teas. My wife and I are still boarding at the Sauganash Hotel. She keeps after me to build a home. I would appreciate advice

282

after the meeting from any of you who have experience in building a home."

I called on Doc Wooten next.

Not waiting for him to be introduced, the next new board member spoke up. "I am Walter Newberry. I was born in East Windsor, Connecticut. I must admit, I can't spell well. Always had trouble with Connecticut and now with Illinois. Why wasn't I born in an easy state like Ohio?

"My older brother, Oliver, and I went into the shipping business in Buffalo, New York, in 1822. Four years later we moved to Detroit where we founded a dry goods company. I joined with several others investing in real estate in Chicago, Milwaukee and Green Bay. You might have heard of them, William Astor and Lewis Cass.

"I moved to Chicago four years ago. I have continued to invest in land and now, in banking. I am currently working with William Ogden to establish the Galena and Chicago Union Railroad."

John Caton asked, "Does your brother Oliver live here in Chicago?"

"No. He is still in Detroit. He has a fleet of his own boats. He ships goods and supplies to forts and trading ports throughout the northwest."

Doc turned to his left and nodded to the last new board member.

"I'm William Ogden. You might know me as Chicago's first mayor."

There were expressions of congratulations around the table. Holding up his hand in embarrassment, he continued.

"I'm sure you are tired of hearing men talk about me. Mr. Garrett, I have just completed building my home. Please come to dinner and bring your wife. I can show you my home and answer any questions you might have about building a home in Chicago."

"I don't know who would be more pleased to accept, me or my wife," Augustus replied.

Doc asked, "Mr. Mayor, you have been in office now for, what is it, six months? Will the financial crisis bring the growth of Chicago to a halt?"

Looking at Axel, Ogden said, "I believe that is the second topic on Axel's agenda."

I nodded yes.

Walter Newberry spoke up. "Before we move on, may I ask you a question, William?"

"Please ask," replied William Ogden.

"Isn't your role with the Canal Commissioners a conflict of interest with the proposed Galena and Chicago Union Railroad? Won't they be competing with one another?"

"Interesting you should ask, Walter," Ogden replied. "I presume you are asking since others have not. As you noted when you introduced yourself, you are working with me on the concept of bringing the railroad to Chicago. I realize many want to know why I am promoting both efforts.

"I believe the demand for cheap transportation of goods and people is great and will accelerate in growth in the years ahead. I believe both the canal and the railroad will profit. When we tap the grain and livestock on the farms in Illinois and eventually the neighboring states, the canal and railroad will assure Chicago becomes the center of the nation's agriculture output."

Augustus Garrett eagerly jumped in, "Thank you, William. I couldn't agree more. The panic just hitting us will eventually pass and we need to be ready to foster the growth of our city. The canal and railroad will do just that."

I took advantage of a lull to turn to the second item on my agenda.

"Gentlemen, I have asked Reinhold Schwoup to present the latest financial status on the bank's assets and liabilities. Reinhold."

Pulling back a pair of green drapes on the wall, Reinhold uncovered a large slate blackboard. Standing in front of it, with paper in his hand, he began to write down figures. As he did so, he spoke, explaining the numbers.

"Our assets currently exceed our liabilities (loans) by a ratio of four to one. Our reserves represent more than half of our assets. Eighty percent of the reserves are in gold. Mr. Konrad has been converting notes and papers to gold over the past eighteen months. To grow the reserves, he has been actively seeking further investments from both our East Coast supporters as well as a substantial deposit of funds from his family Germany.

"I believe we will be able to sustain even the loss of many of our loans as businesses collapse and fail. This places us in the position to extend deadlines for payment of interest due on most, if not all, of our outstanding loans."

"Thank you, Reinhold. I am sure the new board members will quickly learn to appreciate the soundness and accuracy of your reports. Gentlemen, are there any questions?"

Silas Cobb was the first to speak. "Would you please explain to me your statement about extending deadlines for payment of interest?"

"Reinhold, would you, please?"

"Yes. When we make loans, they are for a set period of time. Most often, five years. The usual terms of our loans are the borrower must pay interest on the loan every six months. It is more frequent for larger loans. At the end of the term of the loan, say five years, the borrower must repay the full amount of the loan. So if the loan is for one thousand dollars and the annual interest is five percent, he must pay the bank twenty-five dollars every six months. At the end of the loan period, he will have paid the bank two hundred dollars in interest plus the principal amount of one thousand dollars.

"Mr. Konrad is suggesting we allow the borrower to miss interest payments without foreclosing on the loan. Mr. Konrad wishes the Board to discuss this proposal."

"Thank you, Reinhold. Well put. Since we have ample reserves, I propose we establish a policy of leniency. Reinhold, please write down the options we might consider?"

Reinhold listed several examples of existing loans ranging from small to large amounts. For each, he showed the semiannual interest amounts and the flow of income they represented to the bank. Next he showed the impact were the bank to foreclose on each, explaining the resulting impact of the repossession of the properties.

"To repossess properties would mean the bank would be holding such properties as a stable, a partially constructed silo or even a church. In the current economic climate, either the bank would have to sell the properties, difficult to achieve at this time, or manage the property until the economy improves. Personally, I would rather not be responsible for running a stable or placing guards on a partially constructed silo and, certainly, I don't want to run a church."

Reactions around the table were interesting. Some laughed, some frowned and others were stunned. I once again thanked Reinhold and opened the discussion.

"Gentlemen, I would appreciate your questions and suggestions."

William Ogden began. "Both as a citizen and as Mayor, I fully support leniency on a case by case basis. I suspect there may be some loans which would be in default even in a good economy. Cases where the underlying basis of the original loans were either poorly conceived or the projected needs for the facilities were unrealistic and therefore unable to support the interest payments. In these instances, leniency may be wrong both for the bank and the borrower."

Doc Wooten became defensive. "Are you suggesting the board was wrong to have made some loans? I am sure once you sit through some of our discussions of loan requests, you will think differently."

"Sorry to offend anyone, Doc. Even the most thorough analysis can not always foresee the future. I am suggesting there may be some cases, albeit few, which won't warrant forbearance."

Reinhold responded. "Both of you are correct. I agree we should look at each outstanding loan before granting leniency."

Walter Newberry spoke next. "Should we also take into consideration the impact foreclosing would have on the city? By that I mean, how essential is the service being provided by the borrower to the well-being of our citizens?"

John Caton jumped in, "Excellent point, Walter. Foreclosures could hurt many of our citizens. Calling in a large loan could result in many workers being put out of work. The ripple impact would be to limit families in their ability to make purchases. This would harm still more businesses as they lose customers."

"I may not understand banking, but I know people. I run a small shop," joined in Cobb. "I have already noticed a significant drop-off in customers. Luckily, I have paid off my loan. I can cut back on expenses and should be able to make it. If I had interest payment to make, I don't know if I would be able to and also feed my family. If I had a loan and you foreclosed on me, I would have to shut down my business and move move back East.

"Delaying the interest payments would help. Let's say this happened a year ago when I was faced with the full repayment. It would have definitely been a death blow. I support the idea of forgiving the full amount of the loan when justified. If we do, many business will survive and revive as Chicago does."

Reinhold offered, "In instances where the borrower can afford the interest payments but is at the end of the loan term and can't repay the full amount of the loan, we could extend the loan for another term. Such cases, however, should be reviewed to assure they still are sound."

"Gentlemen, are there any other comments or questions?" No one spoke up. "You have offered some excellent suggestions. Reinhold, please draft a leniency policy taking into account all we have discussed. We can formally consider it at our next board meeting.

"The third item on the agenda is personal. For some time now Lina and I have been thinking of visiting my parents. They live in Germany. If all goes well over the next few months, I would like to make the trip early in the Spring of 1838.

"Should we make the trip, I would like to propose who will act in my absence. Further, in the unlikely event we encounter tragedy, the disposition of the bank upon my death."

My announcement caught everyone off guard.

"My brother-in-law, Carsten Baruth, is drafting documents to deal with all possible contingencies. With the Board's approval, I would like to appoint two of you as vice presidents of the bank. John Caton to serve as vice president and Reinhold Schwoup as executive vice president. Reinhold would act in my absence, consulting with John as appropriate. Reinhold will keep all of you fully informed by conducting regular Board meetings. In the event Reinhold is incapacitated, John would take over. I have talked with both and they are willing to accept these responsibilities, again, with the approval of the Board.

Philo was quick to speak. "Although taken by surprise, I heartily endorse your proposals, Axel. You could not have made better choices. May I ask for a vote by the Board in support of the nominations of Reinhold and John?"

Doc seconded the call. Philo asked for each member to voice their vote. Everyone said yes.

I closed the meeting thanking everyone and assuring them there would be three or four more Board meetings before Lina and I left for Germany.

Chapter Forty Eight

Climbing the stairs to our apartment, I could hear the cry of our fourth child, born a month ago on September 11, 1837. How our family has grown. We no longer call Henry, "Little." He is four months short of his fourth birthday. Adelina Wilhelmina is two. Rady has grown up. He's tall for a five year old. I look at him with a profound sense of pride. There are moments, however, when I feel a twinge of sadness knowing Rady came to us in the aftermath of baby Axel Heinrich's death a year ago.

I opened the door. Adelina was sitting next to her mother. When she saw me she climbed down and ran to greet me. "Augy crying," she said excitedly. I picked up my tiny daughter with her big eyes and wisps of blond hair tied with two ribbons. I kissed her cheeks. She is so much calmer than our sons. Adelina is much like her mother. To me she is my Little Lina.

Augy, our new son, August Heinrich Konrad, was born with no fuss. Anxious after the loss of our infant son a year ago, both Lina and I are relieved Augy is robust and always hungry. It is not uncommon for newborns to die, often in their first six months. Doc Wooten has assured us we should have no such concern about Augy.

Leaning down, I kissed Lina. Cradling Augy in her arms, Lina asked, "How did the Board meeting go?"

"Well. Where are Henry and Rady? It's so quiet."

"Molly insisted on having them come for the afternoon and dinner. She can't wait until she and Seamus have children. Until she does, she loves to have the boys visit her.

"How did the directors react to our plan to go see your parents?"

"They approved all of my proposals including us going to Germany."

"You don't sound pleased."

"I worry about going and leaving the children. What if the Pitchfork Murderer decides to harm them while we are gone?"

"Axel, he has not harmed any of us. If that is his intent, he could do it at any time. Spring is a long way off. Perhaps he will be caught before then."

As Lina spoke, she gently moved Augy to her breast, modestly covering herself as he suckled.

"Mother wrote. She would like to go with us. She says she wants to live the rest of her life in Germany. She misses my brother and sister and her own siblings. She is not comfortable speaking English.

"Axel, we could go with her to Dobbersen. I could show you my home. You could meet my family. Could we?"

"Of course. I shall write to my parents and tell them. They will love to meet Minnie."

"Thank you, dear."

"Lina, I wish Henry and Rady were older so we could take them with us. Perhaps we could go back when they are."

"Axel Konrad! You plan too far ahead. For now, going in the Spring is enough of a challenge."

I will never forget the events of the next day, October 27, 1837. I was at my desk in my office when Reinhold entered. "Seamus is here to see you. He is quite agitated."

I didn't even have a chance to get up to greet my friend. He pushed past Reinhold and entered.

"Axel! We need to talk."

Reinhold withdrew and closed the door.

"Axel, I have committed murder. I don't know what to do."

I have never seen Seamus so panicked. His face was wreathed in fear. There was blood on his pants. He began to pace back and forth across my office. When I suggested he take a seat, he snarled, "I can't."

"Calm down my friend." Walking to him, I forcibly pushed him into a chair.

"Take deep breaths." I stood behind him and held him down while slowly massaging his shoulders. My grip and quiet commands began to ease his resistance.

"I need to go confess. Do I need to go to the constable? What should I do?"

"Talk to me. Start at the beginning. You can trust me. I will do nothing unless you agree."

After a long pause, Seamus began. "This morning I met with John Wright and his father at their north side store. I had hitched Tin Bucket in back. He likes the dry grass.

"After our meeting, I had just mounted Tin Bucket when I noticed someone back in the tall grass and shrubs raising what appeared to be a pitchfork into the air and viciously plunging it down into the ground. I jammed my heels into Tin Bucket so hard he lurched forward. As we galloped toward the man, he raised the pitchfork again. Blood was dripping from the tines. Before he could force it downward again, I shouted for him to stop.

"Startled, he looked toward me. Tin Bucket shot forward, knocking him over. I lost control. Turning around, Tin Bucket stomped on the downed man. I pulled so hard on the reigns, I think I broke one of my fingers. When we came to a stop, I jumped down and rushed to the fallen man. There, in the grass, were two bodies. The head of the man with the pitchfork was a bloody mess. Tin Bucket's hoof must have crushed it. The would be murderer was dead, his face unrecognizable.

"The second man was moaning. He was on his stomach, his hands and feet bound. Three holes in his back were oozing blood. I turned him over. He was coughing up blood. I shall never forget the intense fear on his face. His eyes flickered as he tried to focus on me. I asked him his name. He did not respond. I felt I had met him before. I don't know when or where.

"I lifted his head and asked his name again. I did not recognize him.

"He tried to respond. He coughed up more blood. His body convulsed. His eyes opened wide. He stiffened, gasped and went limp. He was dead."

With this, Seamus slumped in the chair and began to shake. I knelt before my friend and took his hands in mine. He was cold. I stood, went to the door and called Reinhold, "Please go get Doc Wooten as quickly as you can."

Returning to Seamus, I poured a small glass of brandy, held it to his lips and insisted he take a sip. He did not resist. Color returned to his ashen face. He pushed the glass away. The brandy and his rising anger brought him back from the depths of despair.

"Damn you, Axel. I do not drink. You have started me down the path to drunkenness."

I put the glass aside, and talked to Seamus as calmly as I could."

"You did not murder anyone. It was an accident. Tin Bucket did not murder anyone. Both of you were trying to save the stranger.

"In fact, you may have saved the lives of others. You may have caught the Pitchfork Murderer. You are a hero, my Irish friend."

"I am no better than my father, Axel."

"Nonsense. You did not willfully kill. You tried to save someone. You will not become a drunk. Believe me, you will live a life of sobriety."

Taking my hands, Seamus pleaded, "What should I do?"

"When Doc arrives, I want him to check you out. Then the three of us will go to look at the bodies. Did anyone see you or them?"

"I don't think so. The area is quite isolated even though it is close to the back of the store. It is a marsh most of the year. Without any rain for some weeks, it has dried up."

"After we check everything out and Doc confirms both men are dead, we will contact the constable. Doc and I will assure no blame is ascribed to you. It is important to record the full story. We should impress upon the constable how important it is he begin a thorough investigation to determine if the Pitchfork Murderer has been found.

Doc arrived moments later. He listened to Seamus tell what happened. He checked him out, listening to his heart, checking his pulse and looking into his eyes.

"You are in good health, Seamus. When you totally relax, you will find yourself quite exhausted. This is a normal reaction to shock. I agree with Axel, we need to immediately verify what you have told us."

Doc had brought his horse. Tin Bucket was hitched in front of the bank. I went around back to saddle up Thor. After Smithy's murder, I could not bear to go to his stable. I had a small barn built behind the bank where I keep Thor and my carriage and team of horses.

It took only ten minutes to get to the prairie marsh behind Wrights General Store. Our approach on the scene caused several eagles to lift in flight. They had begun to peck away at the corpses. Doc examined first the victim. He confirmed he was dead, concluding he was around thirty years of age. He drew careful sketches of the pitchfork holes, as well as the over all body and the tied hands and feet. He even drew a sketch of his face.

He examined the murderer next. He drew several sketches of the man's smashed skull and what remained of his face. There was enough remaining for Doc to draw what the man's face once looked like. Opening his clothing, he concluded he, too, was around thirty. His muscular upper arms and chest suggested he had been used to hard labor. In sketching what his face must have looked like, he drew a bushy beard and shoulder length hair. He noted the hair was dark brown. The intact eye was also brown. His nose, as best as he could tell, was quite prominent.

291

There were several keys in his pocket. Also a small bag of gold pieces. A leather folder held several letters written to Clancy Grob. The most recent was dated August. All were from Frank Grob, apparently the man's father. We each took a letter to read. Frank encouraged his son to come back home for a fresh start. Best we could tell, home was somewhere in Kentucky.

We agreed Doc and Seamus would remain and I would ride to the constable's office and bring one or more of them back. I felt relief Oremus Morrison had moved on to become an alderman. In the elections of past May, besides selecting William Ogden as Chicago's first mayor, John Shrigley was elected high constable. John had strongly supported me when Oremus had accused me of murdering Smithy. Born in England, I found Shrigley fair and intelligent. His fine English language enhanced his inherent politeness.

John was in his office. He and his office clerk hitched up the coroner's wagon and followed me to where Doc and Seamus were waiting.

The next day John Wentworth came to interview me about the double murder for a lead article in the *Democrat*.

"I have never seen Seamus so shaken," he told me. "I found John Calhoun's background notes on the Pitchfork Murderer and will honor your wish. I will not connect them to the incident in Germany. Have you talked to anyone at the *American*?"

"No and I would rather not. I appreciate your pledge to keep my name out of the paper. While there is no proof of connection to the incident back in Germany, I am convinced my relative is behind these grizzly murders."

"Axel, have you or anyone else seen your cousin in Chicago?"

"I have not seen him here. Other than my wife and sister, I know of no one in Chicago who would know what he looks like. I can not figure out his motive, other than to torment me about the past. I worry about my wife, children and sister. I hope John Shrigley's investigation is successful. From what I read of Frank Grob's letters to his son, however, I doubt Clancy committed the Pitchfork Murders stretching back to 1833. I feel my cousin is involved in some way. I can't believe he would risk being caught in the act of murder. It is possible he has found some strange sick satisfaction jamming a pitchfork into the bodies after they are dead."

"If you learn of anything you would like me to publish, please let me know. If I think of anything, Axel, or hear of anything from my readers, I will let you know. I hope your long nightmare is now over.

After Wentworth left my office, I sat for a long time, once again wondering who the Pitchfork Murder is. How could so many be murdered without any witnesses. I got no further than I have before.

A thought came to me which brought a smile to my face. John Wentworth is an ally in my quest for answers. The same John Wentworth I met on his way to Chicago, pouring whiskey on his blistered feet.

Chapter Forty Nine

John Shrigley and his staff immediately began to conduct interviews. Their primary goal was to learn more about Clancy Grob. How long had he been living in Chicago? Where did he live? Did anyone know him? Could he be the Pitchfork Murderer? If he was, what was his motivation? Or was he hired by someone as an assassin? By Rikert? Constable Shrigley came each morning to tell me how the investigation was progressing. Five days after the murder, Dr. Wooten's sketches of the victim and the murderer appeared in both the *Democrat* and the *American* with an urgent request for information. Several days later, Constable Shrigley came to see me. I knew the minute he walked into my office he had something significant to tell me.

"Axel. So far, I have received several anonymous notes as well as visits by eight people. All have been in response to the published sketches. Two are more promising than others.

"Seamus O'Shea came to see me. He recognized both of Doc's pictures. The man with the pitchfork was Clancy Grob. He once worked at Wrights General Store. Seamus fired him for not showing up for work or when he did, not on time."

I asked, "You still believe the death of the murderer by Seamus' horse was an accident, don't you John?"

"I do, Axel. I'd like to keep all of this quiet for now to avoid vicious gossip."

"You said Seamus recognized both drawings. Who was the pitchfork victim?"

Rather than answer my question, Shrigley held up Doc's original sketch of the victim. "Does he look familiar to you Axel?"

I studied it carefully. "He does. I can't place him." I stared for some time. Shrigley sat patiently.

"My God, it's Charlie!"

"Who was Charlie?"

"It's been over four years. You said Seamus identified him?"

"Yes. Who was Charlie?"

"He rode shotgun on the stagecoach we took from Detroit when we first came to Chicago back in 1833. He couldn't speak. Indians had cut out his tongue. He couldn't write, so we didn't know his name. Someone along the way named him Charlie. He was a gentle, kind man.

"You said two came forth with the best leads. Who was the second person?"

John scratched his chin before answering. "A familiar drunk, Amos. I've never seen him sober before. When he came to see me, he had even cleaned himself up.

"Said he didn't know the man's name. I showed him Doc's sketches. He pointed to the murderer. Told me he lived in the old Koebbemann cabin in the woods. I asked him how I'd find the cabin. He said Robinson knew.

"I've talked to Alexander. He said he could show me the cabin."

"Chief and I are going out there now. Care to join us?"

I am not a person who shirks his responsibilities. When I plan to do something today, I do it. Yet I wanted to go with the Constable. My indecision gave way to my need to know.

"Yes, I would like to join you. If you can give me a few minutes, I will rearrange my schedule."

I went out to Reinhold's desk, quietly explained and asked him to handle my meetings. "Please don't alarm Lina, just tell her I have gone to visit several of the Board members.

I went around back, saddled Thor and joined Shrigley, two of his staff and Chief Alexander Robinson, who were mounted and ready to go.

I regretted I had not taken the time to get my coat. It was windy, overcast and cold, a reminder winter was not far off. The five of us crossed the river and followed the main road until Chief slowed down so he could find the faint trail which led west, away from the lake. We entered the woods. Eventually we had to dismount because of the low tree branches overhead.

"How do you know of this place?" one of Shrigley's men asked.

Alexander smiled slightly. Something I have rarely seen on his stoic face. All he said was, "The woods are good for hunting."

I sensed a faint smell of smoke. The Chief stopped, signaling us to be quiet. We tied our horses. The path was now so overgrown, I could not have followed it. Alexander gestured we were to wait. He stepped forward. The path turned north. We lost sight of the Chief.

Minutes passed. I became impatient. Shrigley must have been as well. He began to follow where Alexander had gone. The rest of us tagged along. We turned at the bend. The Chief was coming toward us.

He announced, "We are too late. The cabin has been burned to the ground."

He led us on. There was a slight rise ahead and a clearing. Embers and ashes embraced the stone fireplace and chimney, all that was left. A few tendrils of smoke lazily rose above the ruins. From a freestanding shed off to the right came the braying of a donkey.

I walked to the ruins hoping against hope I could find something, anything, to answer my questions. Perhaps a charred book or documents. Nothing. I walked into the coals, still emitting heat. My eagerness overwhelmed my usual caution. I grabbed a fire poker and tried to pry loose the stones of the fireplace. I ignored the heat on the soles of my feet from the still hot remains. I could not, however, withstand the intensity of the hot poker. It burned the flesh of my palms. I dropped it and hurried to the well I had seen near the shed. The bucket was full. I plunged my hands in the water. Tears filled my eyes.

The Chief and Shrigley had stood watching me in dismay. Neither had ever seen me lose my reserve and act so impulsively.

One of the constable's staff called from the shed. "Should I untie the ass?"

John called back, "Let me see it first. Might be something of interest."

Alexander moistened some dirt with water making a thick paste. He swathed my hands with the mud. The pain eased.

I sheepishly admitted, "Foolish behavior."

Alexander shrugged and walked to the shed. I followed. He walked to the edge of the woods. There was a mound with a wooden cross. Exquisitely carved lettering read, "Here lies April Blossom, mother of my child."

"Axel, I believe this is the grave of Radiant Sun's mother."

I looked at Alexander, wondering how he knew.

I knelt down to read the rest of the inscription. The lettering was quite small.

Born April 15, 1815
Died January 10, 1833

Getting up, I asked Chief Alexander, "Does this mean the murderer was Radiant Sun's father?"

"No," responded Alexander. "It explains Radiant Sun's blue eyes."

"How do you know?"

"There are some things one knows without knowing."

I found this unacceptable. I need facts. I abhor not knowing. Just then Constable Shrigley came over. "We might have found something."

Alexander and I followed John to the shed. Carved in one of the beams holding up the roof was the same exquisite lettering as on the cross. It was in German. I read it aloud, "Hartmann Koebbemann and April Blossom, husband and wife, this eighteenth day of June, year of our Lord, 1832."

Rady's father was a German! I asked, "Chief, do either of the names mean anything to you?"

"I knew April Blossom when she was only a girl."

John observed, "She was seventeen, almost eighteen, when she died. Could she have died giving birth to your son, Axel?"

"It is possible."

"Where is Hartmann?" I asked. No one responded.

Constable Shrigley asked, "Your cousin is German, is he not Axel?"

"Yes."

"Hartmann Koebbemann is or was German. Would there be some connection between the two of them?" Shrigley asked.

"Could a man who can carve so beautifully," asked Alexander, "be a murderer?" No one answered.

I observed, "Have you noticed how well built this shed is? Seems to me too sturdy to just stable an ass. Could it have been Hartmann's first log cabin? Big enough for a single man. Why would he have carved their names and marriage date in his shed?"

Nodding agreement, John said, "We need to go over every inch of this place."

For an hour, we poked and probed the walls, the floor, the beams overhead. We found nothing. It wasn't until I was ready to give up that I noticed the Chief was not inside. I found him at the well. He was holding a second bucket.

Alexander asked me, "When we entered the clearing, did you notice we had to step over a small creek? Why would they need to dig a well with a creek nearby?"

"Because the well is closer to the cabin?"

"Yes, but why go to all the work to dig a well?"

"I don't know. The bucket of water I plunged my hands into is right here." Pausing, I asked, "Where did you get the second bucket, Chief."

"Mr. Konrad, now you know I don't like to be called Chief."

"I know, but I consider it a title of respect, Alexander. Where did you get the second bucket?"

"From the bottom of the well. You need to be more observant, Axel. The rope is still hooked to the handle."

Reaching into the bucket, Alexander pulled out a packet and handed it to me. It was wrapped in deer skin and coated with wax. The others had joined us.

"Constable," I said, "I think you should have this."

Holding it as if it were the Holy Grail, John thought before speaking. "I would like to take this back to my office before I open it. There is nothing else to be found in the shed. Is there anything else in the clearing of interest?"

"Only probing the stonework of the fireplace and chimney when it has cooled down," I said.

"That might take several days."

We walked back to our horses. They were more than ready to leave the dark woods.

Chapter Fifty

Once back in Chicago, we went our separate ways. Constable Shrigley and his men went to his office. He wanted to study the packet without me or Chief Alexander present. I was relieved to back off. Alexander headed to his home. I stabled Thor and gave him an extra feed of oats and rubbed him down with some straw.

Two days later, John Shrigley sent one of his men to invite me to a meeting in his office. After the way Oremus Morrison had treated me over the death of Smithy, I had moments of panic, but calmed myself down knowing John was nothing like Oremus.

When I entered the Constable's office, I was pleased to see Seamus, Doc Wooten and Alexander were already present. Surely if John were going to accuse me of wrong doing, he would not have them in the meeting. No one else from the Constable's office was in attendance.

After we were all seated around the small table, John began.

"Thank you for coming. Today I would like to review what my investigation has uncovered since the unfortunate murder on October 27th. I have conducted a number of interviews. I have received a total of 23 notes, letters and visits in reaction to the sketches which appeared in the two newspapers.

"For the benefit of Doc and Seamus, I would like to begin with our investigation of the log cabin in the woods northwest of the city."

Only infrequently referring to his notes, John described all we had found, including the deerskin wrapped packet in well.

"When I opened the packet, I found a number of documents as well as money and a will. The will included instructions for the care of his son. He stated he was going to leave him with you, Alexander. All of this was written in German. I had it translated into English.

"He included two hundred-thirty-seven dollars which he directed be used for the education of his son.

"Also in the packet was a history of the events leading up to his anticipated death. I should have begun by stating that the packet and the documents within were written by Hartmann Koebbemann.

"Hartmann built the shed eleven years ago. He explained he had come to America fifteen years ago with his parents. They settled in Cleveland, Ohio. They never learned English. Being German Jews, they were treated badly. His parents died, first his father and then his mother. Hartmann headed west, settling in our area around 1825. He never learned English. Afraid he would also be treated badly, he hid in the woods, building first the small cabin, then the larger one.

"He was thirty years old when April Blossom found his cabin. She had been captured and taken to one of the brothels in the Sands. She escaped before she came to any harm. She didn't stop running until she happened upon Hartmann's cabin.

"They developed a language of their own. He set her up in the small cabin while he built the larger one. Each found peace with the other. When Hartmann made one of his rare visits to Chicago to sell his wood carvings and purchase critical supplies, he ran across an itinerant man of the cloth who agreed to marry the two of them. Hartmann was almost twice April Blossom's age.

"When his wife was with child, Hartmann panicked. He felt he was not worthy of being a father. He worried about his religious background. He worried he was too old for April Blossom. As the day of delivery approached, he struggled with the need to seek a midwife. He had no idea how to find one. The day came sooner than April Blossom anticipated. With no other choice, Hartmann delivered his son. The hemorrhaging was uncontrollable. Two days later, April died. Hartmann's grief was overwhelming. He nurtured the infant as best he could.

"Caring for his son became more and more challenging as Hartmann's health began to declined. From his description, Doc tells me he probably had a case of the wasting disease. When he became weak and was coughing up blood constantly, he took his son to your home, Alexander, and left him for you to raise. On the way there, he lost the note he had intended to leave for you.

"When he got back and entered his cabin, he discovered Clancy Grob had moved in. Hartmann was so exhausted, he dropped onto his bed and slept for many hours. When he woke, Grob was gone. Hartmann immediately began to gather the materials he put in his packet and started to write the history. When he heard Grob returning, he hid everything and struggled back to bed.

"Grob left each morning, returning after dark, drunk. Hartmann knew his days were few, the wasting disease ravaged his body. When he had completed his history, he wrapped everything in deerskin and dripped the tallow from a candle on the package until it was sealed. It must have been torture for him to crawl to the well and place the packet in the bucket and drop it down."

We had all sat motionless and silent as Constable Shrigley told the sad story.

Doc asked, "When Hartmann died, what came of his body?"

"I had my men return to the site to see where Grob might have disposed of it. We missed the obvious for the better part of a day. We looked for a mound indicating a grave site. We even looked in the surrounding woods. One of my men suggested April Blossom's grave. He was right. The mound was too high. It should have settled down more than it had. We found his body a foot below the surface."

Doc asked, "Was there any evidence of foul play?"

"No. Grob had wrapped him in a blanket and laid him respectfully on his back with his hands crossed on his chest. We found no wounds. His body just gave up the ghost."

Seamus, who had been silent, suggested, "Grob must have lived in the cabin since that time. Explains how the donkey was still alive. What caused the cabin to burn down?"

"I doubt we will ever know," replied Shrigley.

I asked, "Does any of this answer the question as to whether or not Clancy Grob was the Pitchfork Murderer?"

"I am afraid it doesn't, Axel."

Doc asked, "Who was the man Clancy killed? Anyone identify him?"

Shrigley answered, "Doc, I am surprised you did not recognize the face you sketched. Seamus and Axel did."

Doc, clearly miffed, said, "I'm confused. Who was he?"

I suggested, "Doc, look at your sketch again. Think back to when we all came across from Detroit."

Looking, Doc exclaimed, "Damn me! It's Charlie! I was so focused on sketching I was too close to see who it was. What a shame. He had more than his share of pain."

I pushed on. "So what do we know about Clancy Grob. Were you able to contact his father?"

"No. I have written to several locations suggested in Frank Grob's letters. No one has responded. It will take time. The mails are improving but are still not reliable. Since I don't have a precise address, or even know the state or town for sure, my inquiries are really shots in the dark."

Shrigley summarized what he knew for certain. "Did Clancy Grob kill Charlie? Yes. Did it match the pattern of the earlier Pitchfork Murders? Yes. Did he commit all of the previous murders? Possibly, but I doubt it."

Seamus had remained silent throughout Constable Shrigley's presentation. Turning to him, John asked,

"Seamus, you encountered Grob as an employee at Wrights. Do you believe he was capable of committing multiple murders?"

"Physically capable? Yes. Smart enough to avoid detection for four years? No. He didn't strike me as very smart. Besides, he would have been unable not to boast about the killings if he did them."

John asked Seamus, "When did you fire him from his job at Wrights?"

Seamus answered, "May, three years ago."

"That would have been May of 1834?"

"Yes."

"Have you had any contact with Clancy Grob since you fired him?"

"No. Wait. Yes! About a year later. He threatened Josie Durst."

Shrigley asked, "How?"

Taking a deep breath, Seamus explained. "He asked her for a thousand dollars not to reveal the name of the father of her son, Nicholas Durst. She told him it was no secret. He said he had other information about Nicholas' father. Miss Durst told him to go talk to him directly and not bother her again."

"How do you know this?"

"Josie told me. I suggested she send a note to her son's father requesting he protect her."

Shrigley observed, "I gather the father doesn't live with Josie?"

"That is correct."

"What happened next?"

Seamus continued, "The father came to Josie right away. Josie asked me to remain hidden so I could overhear their conversation. He promised to make sure Clancy Grob left Chicago forever."

Shrigley said, "That would have been three years ago, about the time Grob moved in with Hartmann. Seamus, you have been careful not to give the name of Nicholas Durst's father."

Seamus said, "I do not wish to."

Constable Shrigley paused, and said, "For now, I will not press you for his name."

None of us said anything for a while, absorbing all we had just heard. I finally spoke.

"John, I have to ask this. Lina and I are planning on going to Germany in early spring. We will leave our children in the care of my sister. If Clancy did not commit all of the previous Pitchfork Murders, could there still be someone out there behind the deaths?"

"Yes, I believe so."

" Will my children be safe in our absence? Will Anna be safe?"

"Axel, I don't know. Over the years these murders have occurred, neither you nor your family have been harmed or directly threatened. If it is indeed your cousin behind these horrendous acts, my guess is his objective is to torture you with fear not actual physical harm. If I am right, it may be safe for you to travel."

Seamus, bless his soul, angrily said, "That's not very comforting Constable. That's like predicting rain as it is falling."

Doc spoke up in a calm manner. "Axel, I do not believe in living in fear of what might happen. To do so is to shrink oneself until becoming a hollow shell. You and Lina should go. I pledge to help watch over Anna and your children. I am sure Seamus is willing to do the same thing. And, to the extent his official duties permit, I am sure John will use his men to the same end. Although Philo is not here, I know he will as well. You have many friends in Chicago, any one of whom will gladly take on some role to protect your family. Every day you give of yourself for others. It is time to allow them to give of themselves in return."

I was so taken by what Doc said, I could not speak, ashamed my voice would quiver with emotion.

Chapter Fifty One

October slipped into November, December into January. The shock of the most recent Pitchfork Murder once again receded from my conscious thought. Constable Shrigley's investigation was inconclusive. He no longer came to report to me on his progress, there being nothing new. He assured me he and his men would pursue any new lead.

I went to see him in early March, 1838.

"John, my wife and I will be leaving for Germany in several weeks. Is there anything new in your investigation?"

"No. I have been unsuccessful in learning anything further about Clancy Grob other than he held a few jobs now and then to earn enough to buy essentials. All of my attempts to find his father have failed. I have written to several more locations hinted at in Frank's letters with no luck. I am sorry.

"Was Grob the only Pitchfork Murderer? I don't know. Some days I am convinced he was. Most days, just the opposite. I'm afraid we may never know. My advice to you? Take your trip and trust all will be well."

Plans for our trip to Germany fell into place. Molly was thrilled her parents would arrange to take us to New York aboard the *Princess Rose.* Captain Mahler promised to be in New York in late March and have cabins ready for Lina, Minnie and me. Mamie would set aside her best rooms for us at the *Eagle.* James Dowling made plans for a dinner party at Morgan's home. Minnie and Lina wrote almost daily, their excitement and anticipation mounting with each letter.

Our children began to pick up our excitement the closer we got to our departure. Dear Anna and Carsten increasingly had one or more of the children spend the night with them, aiming to make them comfortable with their aunt and uncle in our absence.

Since our home is larger than theirs, we decided Anna and Carsten will move into our apartment while we were gone. This would minimize the disruption for the children.

I marveled with Lina's wisdom. She had each of the older children begin to work on small gifts they would send with us for their grandparents, aunts and uncles in Germany. When it was two weeks before our departure, she took turns having the older children help her pack our bags. There were moments when one or the other would grasp what was happening and cry, or beg we take them with us, or not go. Lina never lost patience. She hugged them and promised all would be well. She really got onto something when she told them they could come up with games to play with Anna and Carsten. The best inducement was their realization cousin Teddy would be living with them.

Aboard the *Princess Rose*, as we waved our final goodbyes, I felt sick with fear in the pit of my stomach. What if? I came close to ordering Captain O'Flaherty to turn around. Lina, knowing as only she can, my anxiety, took my hand and urged me to come below to our cabin.

The trip has become very familiar. We were in New York in no time. There, the days flew by. Minnie joined us at the Eagle with all of her luggage. We jammed much into our three days. What a joy to see Mamie and James every day.

Mamie's staff at the Eagle could not leave us alone. Our meals and our comings and goings were like celebrations to them. The *Deutschlund* arrived two days ahead of schedule. Horace Morgan hosted a dinner for Mamie, James, Minnie, Lina and me as well as Captain Mahler. Horace asked questions of each of us to encourage conversation. Minnie soon had us laughing, telling how Lina and I were smitten with one another, but afraid to show it on our crossing to America.

"Dear Gerhardt used to say to me, 'Don't the youth of today know how to court? If I were as reticent as Axel, we would never have married.'"

Horace asked Lina, "How is Mamie's son doing in Chicago? He have a practice yet?"

"Very well. He has gotten many clients through Axel's connections."

"Horace," I asked, "Why don't you come visit us in Chicago. You could travel with us when we get back from Germany."

"I don't know, don't know. What would I do? Hunt? I don't hunt, don't hunt."

James, never tiring of hearing about Seamus, asked, "Tell us about Molly and Seamus. When is my first great grandchild expected?"

Lina answered, "September."

Turning to Mamie, "You must come to see your grandson. Teddy is so cute."

Somewhat mournful, Mamie responded, "I wish I could. I would like to."

"Why not come to Chicago," I asked.

"Someday," Mamie said. "Someday."

I asked Horace about his sons. Smiling broadly, he told us how each of his sons has found a wife, career and place to settle down. One is living in Cincinnati, the other in Peoria.

"All the more reason for you to come visit us in Chicago. You could invite your sons and their wives to join us in Chicago," I suggested.

"I wish I could. Wish I could. But too much for me."

"Why don't you have Henry travel with you as a valet and companion. He could handle the arrangements along the way."

James surprised us all. "Horace, I'll go if you will."

When dinner ended and we were leaving, Horace said, "James, we need to talk about this further. Might be good for me, good for me."

Our crossing was unusually smooth for so early in the spring. When we arrived in Hamburg, I could not hold back my emotions. There on the dock were my mother and father. Lina and they embraced between their unabashedly emotional kisses and tears for me.

We spent our first night in the finest hotel in Hamburg. The next day we began our journey to Bodden and Schloss Hagenhoff. My father had bought a new carriage. The ride was smooth, the space inside roomy and comfortable. So many things along the way reminded me of my youth they threatened to reduce me to an emotional mess. Olaf Nelson, who had taken me to Hamburg seven years before, didn't know how to react to my hearty embrace of him. Emil, his son, who had been a stable boy when I left, had come along to handle the luggage. No longer a lad of twelve, he is tall and, as Lina said later on, quite handsome.

I noticed we were not heading directly east, but rather north. We came to the Village of Satrup and stopped for lunch in the inn. Father explained, "I would like to show you where I was born.

"Lina," he said, "my father, Eldric, managed the estate of Prince Frederich of Denmark. The Prince rarely visited, trusting my Father or, as Father used to say, didn't know any better."

Father fell silent as we approached the estate. The fields were idle. We saw no workers. The low stone walls along the side of the road were tumbled down in several places. The massive gates at the entrance were askew. The trees lining the road to the manor were untrimmed. The palace appeared abandoned. Several panes of glass in the large window over the entranceway were broken. Father had Olaf stop in front of the door. He stepped down, looked around, reentered and directed Olaf to leave the grounds immediately. Turning to us, he wistfully said, "This is not what it once looked like."

Once back on the main road, my father spoke. "Minnie, Lina, we are in the Principality of Schleswig which is nominally part of Denmark. The majority of Schleswig is of German rather than Danish descent. Over the centuries the Danes and Germans have battled for supremacy. Immediately to the south is the Principality of Holstein. In 1815 Holstein joined the German Confederation. The Danish crown has never given up their claims, however."

"Heinrich, I am sure neither Minnie nor Lina is interested in a history lesson," Margaretha gently chided her husband.

Minnie said, "Margaretha, I would like to hear more."

Smiling, my mother settled back, she had tried.

"I mention the history to explain the apparent abandonment of his estate by Prince Frederich. Unrest in this area has grown. At the time my parents sent me away to live with my aunt and uncle, I did not appreciate their wisdom. Had I remained, I, too, would have been killed by Napoleon's troops.

"It is likely the abandoned manor is being used by drifters. I am sure the furnishings and anything of value were stripped from the place years ago. We needed to get out of there to avoid an unpleasant incident."

Two days later we came to Tessin. "This," Father said, "will be better. My mother's sister, Meta Hagen Landzettel lives here. She is in her eighties."

"Go on through the village, Olaf. I will tap when we get to her cottage."

Moments later, Father used his cane to rap the side of the carriage. Olaf pulled off the road and stopped in front of a stone cottage with a thatched roof. A low hedge surrounded a garden in front. The brown branches of rose bushes were yet to sprout. Spring bulbs were up. The snow drops were in full bloom, just like back in Chicago. Other plants were bravely punching through the winter-hardened soil. We all stepped down. Father swung open the low gate, escorting my mother.

Lina and I followed, with a reluctant Minnie hovering behind, not wishing to intrude. Olaf and Emil took the carriage around back.

Father had hardly knocked on the door when it opened and my white-haired Great-Aunt Meta broke into laughter. "Heinrich, Margaretha, come in." With a shout of joy, she greeted me, "Axel! Is this Lina? Come in!"

Lina pulled her mother forward. "Aunt Meta, this is my mother Minnie."

We stayed only short time. Aunt Meta begged us to come visit when we could stay longer. "I will gather my children next time." Pausing, the smile leaving her face, Aunt Meta took my hands and said, "I lost your Great-Uncle Harold six years ago. I miss him. I...." stifling a sob, a strained smile returned to her face. For those brief moments, she looked haggard and much older.

Back on our way, Minnie broke the sad silence. "I felt a closeness to Meta. It is not easy to be a widow. To no longer have the love of your life. I feel more than ever it is right for me to come back home. It is where I belong. America is for the two of you, Lina and Axel. It is your home now. America is not Germany. I want to live the rest of my life where I was born."

No one spoke. Each thinking their own thoughts, remembering the past and anticipating the future. I studied my parents. Their faces have aged in the few years I have been gone. They both appear strong and healthy. Even so, they are entering their sunset years. Their children are grown, with secure futures. The years ahead for my parents will be, if there are no tragedies, a time of constancy, caring for one another, recalling memories more than promises to come. For a moment I caught a glimpse of myself decades from now also on the edge of my sunset years. I pray Lina is at my side to the end.

The countryside was just beginning to turn green. Workers were preparing the fields. As we passed, they doffed their hats. I told my Father, "How I wish they would not do that, Father. No one does that in America. We are all equal."

"I have given up trying to get our hands to stop the practice. For generations they have demonstrated obedience. I am afraid it is ingrained in their very existence."

Wherever we stopped for the night, Father had prearranged rooms in the finest lodgings available. At first, Olaf and Emil were reticent to accept a room, rather expecting to sleep in a common room or the stable. They finally acquiesced when Father insisted.

Turning south, we came to Grammow to visit my mother's sister, Frieda and her husband Herman. Aunt and Uncle Schultz had two children Martha and Horst.

"Lina, you will recall Horst died aboard the *Deutchlund* on our way to America. This will be my first time seeing them since his death."

We found Horst's parents unemotional and reserved. After they welcomed us and we were seated in the parlor, I spoke of how brave their son had been. How he asked me to kiss his mother when I saw her. She burst into tears and blessed me. Hardly what I deserved.

We stayed two days. Mother had brought gifts for Frieda. Lina gave Frieda and Herman pictures from our children.

Herman, normally very quiet, said, "I shall put these with Horst's drawings. He never spoke of it, but I think he dreamed of being an artist."

My mother and Frieda were inseparable. Lina fit right in. She was treated more like another sister than a daughter-in-law. At night I told Lina how my mother and sister had lived with Frieda and Herman for months during the aftermath of the Rikert incident.

"How awful those days must have been for all of you."

We finally arrived in Boddin. We stopped to see Rev. Steinhoff. Mother invited him to dine with us the next day.

At last we approached the entrance to Schloss Hagenhoff. Even before we arrived at the massive gates and long road to the manor, I recognized our fields. They were in fine order. Hands were plowing them for spring planting. The pastures were clean, the grazing cows healthy.

Lina gasped when we went through the gates and began our way between the trimmed linden trees, just bursting into green buds. We entered the perfectly straight lane of finely crushed stone. At first, far off, only a portion of the manor could be seen. As we drew closer, our view widened, revealing more and more of the manor.

"This is where you were born? How is it you didn't grow up spoiled and arrogant?"

"Father and Mother would not allow it. Father insisted I learn each of the trades and crafts on the estate. I cleaned stables, tilled fields, trimmed the linden trees, mended fences, cut firewood, worked with the blacksmith. I learned how to keep the books and pay the workers.

"Mother took me with her when she visited our ill and elderly hands, or take food to a new mother. Our workers are like family to us. We have never stood on ceremony."

Chapter Fifty Two

It has been years since so many have gathered around the dining table. Not since Rikert cast an evil pall on his parents and all of Schloss Hagenhoff. His cruel behavior so struck his mother, she never recovered. She passed away before her time. Her happy nature gone, her generosity squelched, her kind demeanor lost forever. With her death, Rikert's father sank into depression, living out his few remaining years in impenetrable loneliness.

Several months after his father's death, Rikert returned to destroy all civility and caused us to move to a cottage on the estate. We avoided contact with Rikert. The household staff left. Rikert had no desire to hold formal dinner parties. His rowdy friends from the past were his only guests.

Today, all has changed. The manor is once again as it had been for decades. The crystal chandeliers sparkle, the carpets are spotless, the floors glisten. The draperies are perfectly hung, the furniture has been repaired or replaced. Schloss Hagenhoff is as it was when I was a boy, a place of warmth and graciousness.

There were ten seated around the table in the formal dining room. I gazed from one to another, lingering on each, giving thanks for their presence. At the head of the table, my father, Heinrich Konrad, always able to look both distinguished and friendly. At the foot of the table, my mother, Margaretha Konrad. Her graying hair done up with a strand of pearls woven in it. She wore a soft pink gown with a frothy white lace collar. Everything about her, I thought, is delicate, yet underneath is a strong, determined woman.

To my father's left sat Wilhelm Anwalt, the family solicitor. He had waged legal war against Rikert's attempts to have the courts rule his father's will invalid so that he, Rikert, could inherit Schloss Hagenhoff rather than my Father.

To Wilhelm's left sat Olaf Nelson, now the overseer of the estate. To his left sat Olaf's wife, Anneken. Neither joined the conversation until my Mother drew them in.

I was next to Anneken. Across from me, to my mother's left, sat my mother-in-law, Minnie Albrecht. Next to Minnie was Lina. Sitting across from the two of them, I enjoyed comparing them. They are both beautiful and delicate. I could imagine Lina many years from now, as fetching as her mother is today.

To Lina's left was Rev. Steinhoff. And to his left, my father's right, sat young Emil Nelson. After we had retired for the evening, Lina commented, "Your father really practices what he believes."

"What do you mean?"

"By inviting Olaf, his wife and son to dine with us."

"And you wondered why I wasn't arrogant or spoiled," I said, teasing Lina.

"Parents can't always instill their beliefs into their children. From all you have told me, Rikert is an example of even a son of sweet parents can go astray," Lina countered.

"I have often wondered why? What caused his drunkenness and destructive nature? I pray none of our children are anything but a blessing to us."

Dinner began with a light split pea soup. A butler served and afterward a maid cleared off. I did not know either. When they were out of the room, I asked who they are.

Mother explained, "Two years ago I began to hire house staff again. Only, I should add, at your Father's insistence. He broached the subject with temerity, not wanting to suggest I was too old to carry on, but rather it would free me up to teach all the children of the estate to read and write."

Plates were placed to our left with warm rolls, fresh butter and a dollop of potato salad. I have not found anything as delicious in America. Tasting it, I was not disappointed. The wine served with dinner induced everyone to talk

I was so engrossed in the conversation I was unaware our dinner plates had been placed before us, with my favorite, 'pigs-in-the-blanket.' A slice of bacon rolled around a wedge of onion inside a thin slice of beef, all cooked in a thick gravy. Mother had selected a meal of my favorites including riced potatoes and early snow peas.

Before we began our feast, Rev. Steinhoff offered grace. "Our Heavenly Father, today you have fulfilled our prayers, bestowing safety and joy to this family. Bringing Axel home, vindicated as he so justly deserved. His reward, and ours as well, the blessing of Lina. What joy you have given us to welcome Minnie. It is no mystery where Lina gets her beauty and grace. We also thank you for the presence of the Nelson family. Your children, Heinrich and Margaretha, have never wavered from the path you wish all of us to follow. And finally, we thank you for our good friend, Wilhelm, who guides us as I know you wish him to do. May we always be nourished with this food and your continued love of us. Amen"

Sometime between the soup and the salad, Father brought up the subject we all had on our minds, Rikert.

"Axel, is there anything new about Rikert and the murders in Chicago?"

I could tell from the astonished look on Rev. Steinhoff's face, Father had not told him of our problems in Chicago. My mother commented before I could answer.

"Heinrich, this is neither the time nor place to ask that question."

"Perhaps not, Margaretha, but I insist. I do not believe only men should discuss such matters, while women are kept in the dark. I am sure Axel will respond with sensitivity."

I thought carefully before I began.

"Each of you knows all that Rikert did here and why I left to go to America and why Anna also has come to America. It is a sad and grizzly story which we thought we had escaped. For Lina, Anna and me, there is still no resolution. An incident, which occurred last October, may have brought an end to it all, although neither I nor the constable believe so.

"It took much thought before we left our home in America. Anna and Carsten are caring for our children. Our friends in Chicago are aware of the circumstances and are watching over them. Will they be safe? I wrestled with this very question long and hard before we left. We have made every possible arrangement for their safety. They are in God's hands."

The hushed silence was punctuated by Pastor Steinhoff's firm, "Amen."

"Father, I have a question for you. Is our homeland any closer to unification?"

Before he could respond, Mother again warned, "Now Heinrich, we don't need another history lesson."

Father nodded his head in acknowledgment then proceeded to answer.

"We are a strong and determined people, yet we are divided and suffer from the lust of other nations for our lands. My parents lost their lives at the hands of Napoleon's troops. Yet from his wars against so many nations, came the first real step of bringing the German speaking peoples together. It was through his edicts that over three-hundred German speaking independent states, cities and principalities were reduced to less than forty.

"The resulting Confederation of the Rhine, while weak, has many now thinking differently. Princes and kings do not wish to give up their power over the people. At this time, their power is greater than the desire of the people for freedom.

"To answer your question, Axel, we are getting closer each day to unification. Sadly, it is still decades off. The unrest which caused my parents to send me here to Mecklenburg has never been resolved."

"Are you and Mother safe?"

"I believe we are. Olaf, you are closer to our employees, how would you answer that question?"

It was as if he had not heard Father. He said nothing for several minutes. Knowing him well, Father waited.

"Safe? Yes, for now. Our men and women often come to me with rumors they hear when they go into the village or talk to laborers from other farms and estates. They come to me with stories of cruelty and abuse by overseers. Brutal whippings and punishments for minor infractions or for no reason at all. For most, their homes are abysmal, their food distributed at the mercy of the landlords. They cannot believe we pay our hands, provide for their medical care, assure they have adequate food and solid cottages. Some invite their friends to visit them here at Schloss Hagenhoff. Seeing what we have here, however, raises their ire and heightens their determination to resist when ordered by their overseers to do something unjust. They increasingly are making demands.

"I am proud of what you have accomplished here. I fear we will be accused by the other landlords for fomenting rebellion. I have tried to explain this to our hands. It is not something they can easily understand or accept.

"Seeds are being planted each day. Not just in the fields, but in minds. I fear there will be upheaval before change is achieved."

I was astonished with Olaf's wisdom. With how articulate he is. Not being able to read and his reluctance to speak as a carriage driver had masked his intelligence. Father has always been a good judge of character. He has always motivated others to think and act and speak.

Minnie joined in. "We experienced the same thing. Gerhardt and I were fortunate to own our farm and have children to help us.

"Axel, you mentioned how in America field hands are not expected to doff their hats to the landowners. This by no means suggests Americans don't also view themselves in separate classes. I have been working as a house maid. The Sauberts are kind to me and were to Lina as well, but we lived on the top floor of their mansion and had to use the back stairs. We were only allowed in their living quarters or the dining room when serving them. When I left or entered their home, I had to use the back door.

"I don't mean to complain. They were good to me. I suppose it will always be so. Wasn't it Jesus who said the poor will always be with us?"

Lina reached for her mother's hand and gently squeezed it.

Rev. Steinhoff spoke. "We all have heavy burdens. No matter our station, no matter our craft, we all must cope with illness, loss and grief. As a child, our burdens are light. As we grow into the world around us, we are laden with both the good and the bad. A schoolchild may have a teacher who mistreats him. A young girl may not be as pretty as her friends. A young adult raised in a wealthy family must learn who to embrace and who to hold at arms length. Even as a pastor, I have burdens. Only with prayer and faith can we see our burdens as gifts. The older I grow the more clearly I see. What was unbearable yesterday fades and what I learned from it stays with me forever.

"Forgive me for appearing ungrateful."

"Pastor, I understand," my Mother said.

Emil spoke for the first time, asking, "Herr Konrad, do they have railroads in America?"

"Yes, only a short run or two. We have someone in Chicago pushing to build one. Are there any here?"

Emil eagerly said, "Yes. Father and I saw one near Hamburg. They ride on tracks. The engine is noisy. It belches out a plume of smoke. They make horses get jittery, even run wild. I would like to know more about trains. I would ..." Emil blushed, embarrassed with his enthusiastic outburst.

Olaf, clearly proud of his son, spoke, "I must admit, I am also excited about this new invention. There is something so strong and confident about trains. There is order to the tracks. I believe this is just the beginning. I believe the next time you come to visit Germany, you will ride here on a train."

"Emil, I hope you will continue your studies," my mother opined. "You have learned all I can teach you. You are strong in mathematics. I believe you should go to the university to learn how to design better trains."

"If your parents agree," my father said, "I would like to send you to the University in Schwerin. I understand they have an excellent program in applied science."

It was evident this was something my parents had been thinking about for some time. Mother must have been waiting for the right time to bring it up.

Olaf did not react. Not so Anneken. She spoke up, "Emil, would you like to go to university?"

"I would."

"Olaf?" his wife asked.

Addressing my father, Olaf said, "I don't know what to say. Are you sure you wish to do this? You don't need to."

"I would consider it an investment. Germany needs educated, bright minds. Emil is our future. I consider it an obligation to my country."

"It's settled then," Anneken said confidently.

"Olaf, could you and Emil meet with me tomorrow morning? I would like to give you the information I requested from the University. We could work out the details together."

It was Emil who asked, "What time would be convenient for you sir?"

Smiling, Father replied, "Shall we say, nine?"

All Olaf could do was nod his agreement. This was a big step into the unknown for him.

Wilhelm Anwalt, who had been silent all through the dinner, changed the subject. "I have learned that the lawyer, who represented Rikert in the matter of the estate, has gone to America."

"Where? Why?" I asked.

"I have made inquiries. All I can learn is he was a failure in more than just our case. It is speculated he wants a fresh start. Where in America? No one seems to know."

Pastor Steinhoff asked, "Could Rikert have asked him to come work for him?"

Minnie angrily asked, "Will this never end?"

Lina again patted her mother's hand. "It may already be over and we just don't know it."

While we had been talking, the maid had cleared off the table and the butler had placed small plates in front of us. He and the maid brought in dessert. Mother had the cook bake a variety of my favorite sweets. The silver serving plates were passed around the table. As each came to me, I could not resist. I was determined to sample each. The room broke into laughter when Mother noticed my plate. I had filled it to overflowing with several pieces of marzipan in the shapes of flowers, three mozartkugel, a large pfannkuchen, two lebkuchen, a small schaumkuss and topped the mound with a slice of bienenstich.

When I looked at my smiling mother. She said, "Welcome home, Axel."

I was unable to eat it all. My eyes were greater than my appetite. When we retired, Lina teased, "More dinners like that and you won't be able to fit into your clothing."

Chapter Fifty Three

Lina, Minnie and my mother spent each day in conversation and laughter. Mother took them to visit many of our workers in their homes. Much to the consternation of the cook, the three insisted on baking and cooking some of the meals and sharing recipes. I remember as a child, watching my mother add ingredients from memory, rarely measuring anything. Lina and Minnie are more precise in their measurements. They cook from memory as well.

Several days after our arrival, Lina, Minnie and I took the carriage to Dobbersen. Olaf and Emil insisted on taking us even though the distance was short and I certainly knew how to drive a team of horses.

Minnie and Lina still can't believe they live so close to Schloss Hagenhoff. My wife and I grew up so near to one another. We didn't meet until we were in the hold of the *Dueschtlund* heading to America.

As we approached Dobbersen, Minnie stopped talking and turned to look out the carriage window. Excitedly, she announced, "I see the church steeple! There! Lina, There! Axel, can we stop here? My son lives here!"

Olaf heard Minnie.

"Down the lane. There, to our right."

We passed several small cottages before coming to a larger one. A woman was beating rugs hanging from a wooden device.

Olaf stopped. Emil helped Lina and Minnie step down from the carriage. Turning to the commotion, the woman dropped her switch, placed her hands on her hips and stood motionless.

Minnie walked to her, stopped, puzzled by her stone-cold face. "Clothilda, it is Minnie, Minnie Albrecht."

Clothilda, her lips opened narrowly, said, "I can see who you are. Why are you here?"

"To visit, dear. We have come from America."

317

There was no response.

Lina stepped forward. "It is good to see you, Clothilda. Where are the children?"

"Go inside if you wish to see them. I must finish what I am doing." Clothilda stooped, picked up the switch and resumed beating the rugs, sending forth a cloud of dust.

Lina looked back at her mother and me and said sweetly, "Let us go see the children." We passed through the cloud of dust and into the house.

Seven children we in the large room, quietly playing with bits of wood and cloth. The older children were caring for the younger ones. I have never seen children so docile, as if afraid. They looked up at us, expressionless. Lina spoke. "Children, I am your Aunt Lina. Most of you were born after Mother and I went to America."

There was absolutely no reaction, no response. Minnie went to the oldest and tried to kiss her. She turned her head away. "Marlis, I am your grandmother. You were two and a half when I last saw you. May I kiss you."

"Mother doesn't believe in kissing."

Sighing, Minnie gasped, "Oh child."

The youngest child, a boy who appeared to be three, stood up and walked over to Minnie, extended his hand and said, "I am Rudi."

Stooping down, Minnie took his hand, leaned forward, and kissed the top of his head. Rudi giggled.

We could hear Clothilda still hitting the rugs with mighty blows. Her pace quickened in anger.

I suggested we sit down and wait for Clothilda to finish and join us. We each talked to one or more of the seven children. The older the child, the less they spoke. They were clearly terrified.

"Do you think," I asked, "they are afraid of us?"

"No. They are afraid of their mother," Minnie whispered. "She has never been friendly, never this hostile."

Lina suggested, "Axel, Wilhelm must be in the barn or the fields. Why don't you go look for him. Mother and I will sit and wait."

I located Olaf and Emil and asked them to join me. I explained the situation. Together, we walked around the house to the barn and out-buildings. They were empty. We walked beyond and saw a man walking behind a horse, tilling the field. I shouted to catch his attention. He stopped and came toward us.

"You must be Axel! Axel Konrad! You have arrived."

Wilhelm is six years older than Lina. He looks so haggard one would think he was twice her age. Wiping his hands on his trousers, Wilhelm smiled enthusiastically.

"Where are Mother and Lina?"

"In the house with the children. Wilhelm, this is Olaf and his son Emil."

"Welcome to my home."

I brazenly asked, "Is Clothilda not herself? She seems surprised and angry to see us. Did you not get out letters?"

"Letters? I only got one. I told her you were coming from America. I didn't receive any other letters."

I could tell Wilhelm was pondering if he should say more.

"No, Clothilda is not well. Since the twins died in January she has been brittle. Anything I say makes her angry. The children are afraid of her. Clara says we must be patient."

"Is there anything we can do?" I asked.

"I was hoping your visit would lift her spirits. Why don't you go back to the house and I'll put the horse away."

"I could do that, sir," offered Emil.

Wilhelm looked confused. Olaf said, "My son and I will take care of the horse and plow. You and Axel go in."

We found Clothilda inside. She was apologizing for how she looked as she pulled off the cloth she had wrapped around her hair, letting her long curls tumble down onto her shoulders. She brushed the dust off of her apron. Her words were more welcoming. Her voice was colorless. She rapid fired directions at her older children. The house was spotless. She ordered them to clean and straighten up what needed neither.

Minnie offered to help. Clothilda's voice rose in anger. "That won't be necessary, Mother Albrecht. You never have thought I kept house to your standards."

She ordered her oldest daughter to begin making the noon meal. The daughter stared at her mother, afraid to ask whatever was on her mind.

Wilhelm, who had said nothing, since he had entered the house, stepped forward and greeted Minnie. "Mother! You arrived safely. I wasn't sure when to expect you." He leaned down and kissed her on each cheek.

"My Willie," was said with choked emotion. Standing back, she looked at him, saddened by his obvious exhaustion.

"Wilhelm! Go clean up. How dare you enter my home without washing up first."

We were stunned by Clothilda's harshness. Wilhelm bowed slightly and left the room.

I tried to relieve the tension. "Clothilda, we only stopped by to say we had arrived. We must leave to go see Clara and then return to my parents' home."

Minnie added, "I will be making arrangements with Clara to move in with her. I have decided to live my remaining days here, in Dobbersen."

"NO!" shouted Clothilda. "You and Gerhardt left the farm to me. You can not have it back! Now get out!"

The daughter, who Clothilda had ordered to begin making the noon meal, asked her mother, "What will we eat Mother?"

"You heard me. Now go." Before the girl could step back, Clothilda struck her in the face, leaving red imprint of her fingers on her pale cheek.

The girl bowed her head and walked from the room.

"Mother Albrecht, I hope you are not planning to spend time here. We are much too busy to have visitors." Clothilda's tone was only slightly moderated.

Minnie looked ready to confront Clothilda. I said, "Come, Lina, Minnie, we are late. Goodbye, Clothilda. Sorry we disrupted your routine."

I took Minnie's arm and guided her outside. Lina followed. I helped both into the carriage. "I will go find Olaf and Emil."

I headed around the house to the back and found they had set the horse free in the small pasture. The plow was standing in the barnyard.

"We must leave. Lina's sister-in-law is not well."

Minnie was furious. "That woman is evil. She lured Wilhelm into her bed so he would have to marry her. I have never said this before, hoping she would change. Did you see those poor children? They are terrified of their own mother. I came back to peacefully live out my remaining days, only to find this."

"Mother, please have patience," Lina urged. We are almost to Clara's."

Lina had given Olaf directions. Dobbersen is a small village surrounded by good farmland and pastures. The cobblestoned main street is not very long. On either side are buildings crowding the street. They are side-by-side with no space between them. Some are two-story with shops on the ground level and apartments overhead. There are several taverns and two bakeries, one being Clara's. There is no town square. The gathering place is at the end of the only crossroad which

320

leads to the church. There, on a grassy patch, are held all important events including the Saturday fair and market.

We rode down the crossroad to the lane running along the backs of the buildings, stopping behind Clara's bakery.

I helped Lina and Minnie down. We walked to the half-door, the top open. The marvelous scent of yeast greeted us. Minnie reached in, unlatched the lower half and swung it open. The clicking of the latch alerted Clara who was kneading tomorrow's bread dough.

"Praise the Lord! Mother! Lina! You must be Axel! Come in."

Clara wiped her hands on her apron. Tears of joy ran in rivulets through her flour-covered cheeks. I stood back and watched the happiness of the three. The contrast with Clothilda made her ill humor even more unexplainable.

"Please go into the parlor while I tell Gudrun you are here."

I followed Minnie and Lina into a small, beautifully furnished parlor. The puffy feather stuffed cushions on the sofa and chair sank as we sat. I had forgotten how much fun I had sitting on feathers and how my mother would fluff them up the minute anyone stood.

"Gudrun is so capable for one so young," Clara said as she joined us. In the few minutes she had been gone, Clara had cleaned up, taken off her apron and brushed the flour from her face. She was wearing a plain white blouse over a floor length pale-green skirt.

Clara is Minnie's middle child, three years Lina's senior. Clara is attractive. She is unmarried. She has the same demeanor as her mother and sister. Again I reflected on the contrast with the harshness of Wilhelm's wife.

"Did you stop to see Wilhelm and Clothilda first?" Clara asked. "Ah, from your expressions, I can tell you did."

"What is going on? Forgive me, but Clothilda treated us with disgust and destine. Is she always so unpleasant? So mean? She is abusive to her children and even poor Wilhelm. She..." Minnie paused, gasping for breath. "How long has she been this way? When we left seven years ago, she was not this bad.

"I receive no responses to my letters to Wilhelm and Clara. If it were not for your letters, I would not even know how many children they have."

Clara shook her head. "I know. I know." She paused before asking, "Have you eaten? I can't imagine Clothilda offered anything."

"We have not," Lina answered.

"Neither have I," Clara said. "I get so absorbed in baking, I often eat late. Let me put something together."

The three went to the kitchen. I looked around the room. Clara had her parents' cherished furnishings and pieces of china. Gerhardt's farm must have been profitable to earn enough for Minnie to purchase all of this.

Lina came in and invited me, "Join us Axel."

Off the bakery kitchen was a small room with a table and chairs. We had a plain meal. Clara waited until we had finished eating before she spoke of her brother and his wife.

"Forgive me for what I am about to say. It has been hell keeping all of this to myself. It has been nearly impossible for me to say nothing to Wilhelm other than to encourage him. I have dared to have some of their children visit me. When Clothilda hears of it, she explodes and the children shrink further into a place of fear and hopelessness. They are such dear children, smart, caring, but withdrawn from the world around them.

"Wilhelm is pathetic. I can't help but think the Lord is punishing him for his youthful indiscretion. I can't imagine how that hussy wooed him into making her pregnant so she could force him to marry her."

None of us responded. Our seething anger had yet to subside and change to pity or remorse.

"She is a baby machine. Axel, forgive me for being indelicate. You should have seen her as a bride. There was no disguising her wantonness. She was six months with child. She flaunted it as a victory. Poor Wilhelm, just sixteen. He was both ashamed and proud of himself. Father spoke to him. Wilhelm felt he had no choice. There were even rumors at the time how Clothilda had bedded more than just Wilhelm.

"Clothilda has had at least a child a year ever since – nine in nine years."

"Now, Clara, two of those were twins," Lina said.

"The twins. They were the final straw. She became worse than ever when she lost them. They were three months when they died."

"When was that?" I asked.

"Late this past October. A rumor persists that Clothilda killed the two. I have never asked Wilhelm if it is true. Oh, Mother, I have cried myself to sleep so many nights. I don't know what I can do."

"Why does Wilhelm continue to go to bed with her?" asked Minnie. "Surely he sees how badly his children are being treated. Does he not know he should not father more with this woman?"

"Mother, I agree. I don't know how to talk to him about it." Blushing, Clara said, "I have no knowledge of such things."

Lina asked, "Is it possible to see Wilhelm without her knowing?"

"He comes early every Saturday morning to bring products to the market. He has come to see me when he can if he sells enough before the end of the market. If you can come back this Saturday, I think he would make an effort to see you here. I will go visit on Friday and let him know you will be here."

Chapter Fifty Four

Many days during my time at home, Father and I rode throughout the fields and forests. I had a joyous reunion with the blacksmith. He had two apprentices, one from our estate and one from a neighboring estate. He made me blush when he claimed I was as good as he.

All the barns, stables and work buildings were in perfect condition. The workers' cottages looked better than ever. Father is reinvesting profits into upkeep and modernization. He had me go through his account books. He still keeps them in just as great detail as when he was working for Uncle Lorenz.

One day, while we were in his office, I asked, "Father, do you remember my tenth birthday. You gave me my first horse."

"I do."

"All was so happy then. Why did it have to change? I still find myself reliving the day in the barn when I had to save Anna from Rikert. I cannot forget his falling on the pitchfork. Father, I never told you, but I was angry he didn't die. I have been ashamed of myself ever since, to wish the death of another person."

"Son, you had cause to feel angry. You did no wrong. You did not act on your feelings. You must forgive yourself."

"I know, Father. I try. Each time there is another Pitchfork Murder, everything comes back – vivid memories of that day, followed by my feelings of guilt. Even now, after each new murder, I think of finding Rikert and killing him."

"Please go see Rev. Steinhoff and talk with him."

I went two days later. Rev. Steinhoff was in his cottage, reading the Bible. He greeted me warmly.

I hesitated to tell him why I had come. Sensing my discomfort, he engaged me in conversation, skillfully drawing me into my confession.

"Axel, have you told this to your father?"

"I have."

"What did he say to you?"

"He suggested I come to see you."

"Before that."

"He said I have done no wrong. That I have not acted on my dark thoughts. That I must forgive myself."

"I'm afraid I have the same counsel. You may well be inflicted with, as you put it, your dark thoughts the rest of your life. We all have weaknesses. We are, after all, human. None of us can live the pure and perfect life. Your thoughts may be God's way of reminding you of this. It may be important in driving you to be a good man, living with concern for others, remaining humble, striving to live the lessons of the Bible.

"At the end of each day, I used to list the things I had said or done during the day which were harmful or wrong. I went to sleep with the resolve to do better the next day. Alas, the next day, I rarely did any better. Some years ago I fell into a different pattern. Why? Was it God's will? I don't know. I now end each day enumerating all I did of which I could be proud. My perpetual guilt evolved into joyous celebration of my day.

"You may not be released from your dark thoughts until Rikert meets his demise. Even then, you may continue to be haunted. You must change this. Each time your guilt surfaces, stop to think. First, pray for strength to forgive yourself. Each evening think of all the good you have done during the day. You will be surprised with how much you accomplished and the joy it brought to you and others. Thank God in prayer and fall asleep with humble pride rather than falling into the sink hole of despair."

Two weeks later I had just stabled Atlas and was walking to the manor when Emil approached me.

"May I speak with you Herr Konrad?"

"Yes. Would you walk with me to the orchard?"

I turned to the east. We walked down a small lane, neither saying anything. The greening of the estate is greater than the day we arrived. As we walked in silence, I thought of Pastor Steinhoff's advice. I have tried it. I often forget. I now write down my accomplishments for the day. I do this first thing in the morning and reflect. It lifts my spirits at the start of each day.

Emil finally spoke. "Sir, after the university, I would like to build railroads. In America."

"Why not here in Germany?"

"America is a new nation. Germany may not become a nation for many years. I want to be part of something new, something exciting, not wait here for our time to finally arrive."

"If, after university, you still dream of America, come to Chicago. The future is there. I will welcome you, make introductions and help you in any way I can. In the meantime, write to me. I will be interested in your education and your plans."

"Thank you, sir."

"All of this is on the condition you talk with your mother and father. Seek their support and understanding. We will be leaving soon for America. Between now and then talk with your parents. After you do, I would like to talk with you and your parents about your plans.

"I left Germany seven years ago with my cousin Horst. I had long conversations with my parents before I left. Horst was afraid to talk to his parents about coming to America. He died after he left home. His parents still grieve. Had they had an open discussion, each would have had a chance to raise their concerns. Had Horst listened to them, perhaps the outcome would have been different.

"I believe your parents will accept your decision. Give them a chance to voice their thoughts and listen to them openly. They are wise. Carefully consider what they say. They will be giving up their only son. Not an easy thing for any parent to do."

"I will. I promise."

A week later, Emil and I spoke. He assured me his parents were in agreement with his desire to come to America. I thanked him and made him promise to write to me to tell me of his progress at university.

I did not tell him Olaf had talked to me the day after Emil talked to his parents. Olaf was proud of his son. He told me he would understand if Emil wished to come to Chicago.

I told Olaf, "If Emil does come, you will see him again. I am sure he will come back to see you or to stay. Also, if Emil does come, I hope you and Anneken will visit him in Chicago to visit. Each day more and more Germans are immigrating to America and settling in Chicago.

Chapter Fifty Five

This morning, Lina, Emil and I went back to Dobbersen to hopefully meet with Wilhelm. We took the smallest of Father's carriages. I sat up with Emil so we could talk. I look forward to the day when my sons are old enough for me to have adult conversations with them. The sky was overcast, a cold wind was whipping down from the Baltic, driving a light rain. We passed a group of laborers working on the road. They were meeting their monthly obligation to work for the government at no pay. The life of the peasant is never easy.

We turned onto the side road. It was a short distance to the market. Many of the farmers and vendors had already left. Clara had told us Wilhelm usually set up his wagon on the west side. Those with better locations had been coming to the market for thirty, even forty years.

We found him. The space next to his wagon was already empty so Emil pulled into it. I gave him some coins and suggested he do some shopping for himself. I got down and greeted Wilhelm.

"Lina is in the carriage. Why don't you join her and have a chat. I can stand here and guard your wares."

"Not much to guard. Sales were surprisingly good, although I didn't have much to sell. Clothilda said it was a waste of my time. How could I tell her just getting away from her made it worthwhile." Poor Wilhelm blushed. "Sorry, I shouldn't have said that."

Later, Lina told me she and Wilhelm had a good talk. "At first he asked me about you and our children and America. I finally broached the subject of Clothilda. He sighed deeply. He spoke slowly and carefully, as if she were present. When I prodded, he opened up.

"Seems he never loved her. He felt he had to marry her because he committed a sin being with her. I tried to suggest he should have no more children. He blushed and changed the subject. Suddenly he said he had better get back home.

"He said a hasty goodbye and jumped out of the carriage. I failed to openly talk about having no more children."

"When I saw Wilhelm leaving the carriage and walking toward me, he was so agitated I guessed you might not have had any success. I decided to be more direct. He and I are men. We can more openly talk about such things.

"I asked him if he realized how difficult his children's lives were. I said it was unfair to bring so many into a home so unable to provide love. I thought he was going to hit me. I said he was in control. I said without him there could be no more children. His face turned red. Not with anger, as I first feared, but embarrassment. He told me he knew what you and I were trying to tell him. He said he agreed with us. I was stunned by what he said next. He said when his wife enters their bed she turns into a different person. To put it delicately, she seduces him. He said he is a man with needs and cannot resist her. Each time, afterward, she cusses him, accuses him of violating her and makes him leave the bed until the next time she repeats the performance.

"Your brother is under her spell. He knows it and even thinks she does this to keep him from divorcing her. I told him that under the circumstances, his primary responsibility is to his children and their safety, no longer to his wife. I suggested she is unbalanced and someday could harm him, the children or herself.

"Lina, I told him he should talk to his minister. Also, now that Minnie will be living here, he should rely on her and Clara to help. I hope I have not made matters worse."

After our meeting with Wilhelm at the market, we stopped to talk to Clara. Lina and I told her what we had said to him. I said less than what I had told Lina.

"Clara, I hope we have not caused further anguish which could lead to harm," I said. "Do you think Minnie should stay with you or should we take her back to America?"

"Of course, she should stay with me. We are strong women. From what you have told me, Wilhelm listened. He did not argue. That tells me he was not only receptive to what you said, but hungry to hear your suggestions.

"When are you planning to go back to America?"

Lina said, "Within a week. We are both getting more and more anxious about our children."

"Can you bring Mother here tomorrow? Sunday is the only day I don't bake. I can help her unpack and make herself at home. Could you stop by the day you leave your parents?"

Both Lina and I said, "Yes," at the same time.

Our farewells were difficult with my parents. I urged them to come visit us in Chicago and meet their grandchildren.

Chapter Fifty Six

May twenty-third, 1838, will forever be etched in my memory. We left Schloss Hagenhoff an hour after sunrise. The top and back of the carriage were loaded with luggage including all Minnie had brought from her years in America. Olaf and Emil had helped the staff load the carriage. After a robust breakfast with my parents, we headed down the long lane. The linden trees were in full leaf. How quickly spring rushes toward summer.

Dobbersen was just coming alive, Clara's bakery already open. Aroma of fresh bread made me wish I had not eaten such a huge breakfast. Olaf drove around back, not wanting the luggage to tempt a light-fingered thief. Clara's assistant answered my knock on the door. She was shy, bowing and stepping back. Clara, again dusted with flour, was subdued.

Olaf and Emil unloaded Minnie's things and carried them to her room upstairs. Lina went with Minnie, insisting she help her unpack. I knew it was my wife's way of delaying our departure for Hamburg. I stayed in the kitchen. Clara stopped working, wiped her hands and asked me to come to the parlor.

"Axel, Wilhelm came to me this morning while it was still dark. I arise at four to begin my day's work. He had awakened around midnight. Clothilda was not in bed. He looked for her. She was not in the house. He went out to the privy. She was not there. He checked the barn and the other buildings. She was nowhere to be found. He went back to their bedroom with a candle, thinking she might be hiding. It would not be unusual for her to do so."

Seeing my expression, Clara said, "I know. I have not told you most of what has been going on. I didn't want to burden you and Lina. I believe Clothilda is insane. She refuses to see a doctor. You saw enough of her behavior to know she is unbalanced. What you have not witnessed are her extremes. Her meanness and mistreatment of the children one day can be followed by uncontrollable laughter and frivolous actions the next

"Wilhelm said her carpetbag and clothing are gone. He searched the bedroom further, hoping to find a note. He thought she might have decided to go to her mother's home. Their horses were in the stable. He tried to see if he could find her tracks. It was too dark. He inspected the kitchen for any signs of what she intended or where she might have gone. As best he could tell, there was no food missing.

"He woke the oldest child to tell her Clothilda was missing and watch over the younger children. As soon as he told me, he left me, intending to rally men from the neighboring farms to help him search once the sun was up. I have heard nothing further.

"Axel, what should I do?"

"You must tell Minnie and Lina all you have told me. I shall ask Olaf and Emil to go with me to the farm and join the search."

"Please send us word when you have any news."

Olaf, Emil and I found a group of farmers gathered in front of the house. Wilhelm rushed to me.

"Axel, I am worried. In the past few weeks Clothilda has tried to harm herself. I thought it was just another way to get my attention."

"Wilhelm, I will stay with you until we find her. Before everyone starts running in all directions and unintentionally disturbs any tracks, why don't you and I walk around back and see what we can find."

It took only minutes for me to find footprints in the dirt heading from the house, past the barn, into the pasture. I asked what is beyond.

"The creek. Oh my God. Could she have drowned herself?"

"Stay calm, Wilhelm. Who is taking care of the children?"

"No one. My oldest. They are asleep. I don't know what to do with them."

"Would one of the men out front have a wife who would be willing to come and help the children get dressed and have their breakfast?"

"Yes. Simon. He lives closest. They have no children. His wife would be good."

Simon fetched his wife. Wilhelm had the men come around back. I walked across the pasture following the direction Clothilda footprints suggested. The men fanned out to our left and right, about twenty feet apart from each other. We generally walked east. One of the men to our right called out, "I've found something."

I called to the other men to stay where they were in case it was nothing. Wilhelm and I walked to see what the man had discovered. It was Clothilda's empty carpetbag. She must have decided to carry her clothing in her arms. I called the other men to join us.

"This is Clothilda's bag. It is empty. Fan out again, we are heading in the right direction. Watch carefully for anything she may have dropped."

A few minutes later, I found a shoe, further on, a scarf. Wilhelm, rushing ahead, found a skirt. He turned to me, "Axel, we are near the creek."

"Is it deep enough to carry a boat?"

"Yes, with the spring rains. I keep a boat on the bank. I use it to carry goods to the next village. Why did she empty her bag?"

"I don't know. Men, head toward the creek."

When we reached the creek, we stretched along the bank. The water was rushing south. The boat was still on the bank. In it were more of Clothilda's clothes and the other shoe.

"Could she have drowned herself?" Wilhelm asked again?"

"Is there anyplace we can cross to the other side?" I asked.

One of the men pointed north. "There is a bridge a short distance that way."

I suggested half the men cross over with Wilhelm and me. "We can look for any signs. The rest of you begin to walk south along the creek. Call if you find anything."

Wilhelm ran to the bridge, we followed. Once on the other side, we looked for footprints or other clothing. We found nothing. I suggested four of the men spread out and walk north and call if they found anything.

Wilhelm and I, with two other men, walked south along the creek. The men on the other were further along than we. Suddenly they stopped and shouted. "There, on your side, in the fallen tree."

We rushed ahead. Our way was blocked by the uprooted tree. It had left a gaping hole in the ground some distance back from the creek, its mass of roots pulled from the soil. The top of the tree had fallen into the rushing water. Walking to the water's edge, we saw Clothilda caught in the branches, her head bobbing up and down in the surging flow. Wilhelm jumped in and tried to free her. She was tangled in the young leaves and twigs. I jumped in and pulled Wilhelm back to shore. Others took over, breaking off branches and, as carefully as possible, freeing the limp, battered, bloodied body. They laid her on the grassy slope. Her face was at peace.

Wilhelm knelt at her side, lifting her head. "Her neck is broken. My wife's neck is broken." One of the men urged him to let them take Clothilda to the village.

Pale, wet and cold, Wilhelm began to cry in heaving sobs. I lifted him in my arms and carried him back across the bridge on to the farm house.

Wilhelm offered no resistance. He had passed out. I felt relief. Wilhelm is free at last. The children are free. They will be safe. I had difficulty then and days afterward feeling any sympathy for Clothilda, only pity.

I sent one of the men to the village to summon the doctor, as well as Lina and Minnie. They soon arrived in the doctor's wagon. They knew Clothilda had been found dead, nothing else.

The doctor revived Wilhelm. He and I took off his wet clothing, put him to bed. The doctor pulled out a small bottle, removed the cork and lifted Wilhelm's head, told him to drink it all. My brother-in-law quickly fell into a deep sleep. I was thankful we were able to get him upstairs without the children seeing us.

Simon's wife came to us. "I saw you carry Wilhelm upstairs. Is he hurt? Where is Clothilda?" I explained everything. She agreed to help Lina and Minnie for as long as they need her.

The doctor advised, "Wilhelm will not wake for many hours. He should be watched for a few days." Minnie said she would not leave his side.

Our departure for Hamburg was delayed five days. My parents came to the funeral. When Wilhelm woke, he accepted his new life. The children slowly loosened up. The older ones had questions. They listened to the news of their mother's death with no visible reaction. They took longer to become free of their years of abuse than their younger siblings. Lina and I knew we could leave when laughter was no longer a rarity in the Albrecht home.

Olaf and Emil, who had returned to Schloss Hagenhoff, came to take us to Hamburg. Only when we packed our bags did Lina find our children's gifts for Clara, Wilhelm and his children. We gave them after the funeral. I thought we should wait. Lina felt they would lighten the atmosphere. She was right.

We arrived in Hamburg the day we had arranged with Captain Mahler. He was staying at our hotel. He was watching for us. He greeted us in the lobby. The hotel staff took our bags from the carriage. We bid Olaf and Emil farewell. I promised to write to them as soon as we landed. We joined Captain Mahler in the dining room for the noon meal.

"We should be ready to leave in three days. The crossing will be less than half the time it took to come here. I have a new ship with an engine to augment the sails. I will no longer be carrying emigrants in steerage, only regular passengers in individual cabins. I could no longer tolerate the deaths and illness of so many jammed in the hold. I have named my new ship *Hope*. I like the sound of hope in English better than in German."

Our fellow passengers, able to pay the fee for passage, were well dressed and generally pleasant. The crossing was so much more enjoyable, the food excellent, although for many of the days, few were able to eat. The Captain ate with us. The conversation was uplifting. We had several Americans who had been studying painting in Paris and wanted to experience the new ship. In four weeks we landed in New York. After a few days at the Eagle, we headed home, more eager than ever to see our children, praying they were well and safe.

Part Thirteen

At Last

Chapter Fifty Seven

Complete and utter joy. We arrived back in Chicago. Carsten was at the dock as the *Princess Rose* arrived. He was smiling and unabashedly waving at us. He had a young man at his side who helped us with our luggage. Captain O'Flaherty promised to come for dinner with us the following evening.

"Are the children well? Is Anna safe? Teddy? Anneliese? Everyone healthy?" Lina anxiously asked.

Carsten merely said, "Yes."

"Are you sure? Are you just not saying? Is something wrong?"

Carsten looked sternly at Lina and said, "I swear. Come see for yourself."

Lina walked to the carriage. I lingered behind. Carsten looked at me and muttered, "I have never seen her so anxious."

"She is with child. You know how that is. Say nothing until she announces it."

"Guess I don't need to ask how Germany was." Carsten had a knowing smile.

Our older children were overjoyed to see us. It bothered Lina that our youngest showed no recognition of us. Much has seemed to bother her. I hope now that we are home, she will regain her composure.

Anna insisted on staying to make dinner. Carsten, Teddy and Anneliese stayed as well. Anneliese was born the previous October and was now almost eight months old. Teddy, almost two, is beginning to say recognizable words. With our brood, Anna had been caring for six children. When the Baruths left to return to their own home, it was Rady who seemed most upset they were leaving. It took us several days to become reacquainted with our own children. Each day they told us more and more about the days we were gone. We waited two days before we began to give them the little gifts we had brought back.

The morning after we returned, Constable Shrigley came to see me at the bank.

"I know you just returned and probably have business to deal with, but this is important. I want you to hear it from me first."

I felt a cold sweat gather on my brow. I tried to calm myself. John saw my reaction and hurriedly said, "The Pitchfork Murders have been solved. It's a long story. I would like to give you all the details as they unfolded. Can you give me several hours."

Breathing deeply, I agreed, offered John coffee and asked him to join me at the easy chairs. I poured, offered cream and sugar and my favorite sugar cookies, sat back and forced myself to calm my pounding heart.

"Axel, some of what I have to tell you is upsetting. I assure you everyone is safe. I would rather pull no punches. Is it acceptable if I tell you everything?"

"It is."

"First, the hardest part. Shortly after you and Mrs. Konrad left, Rady disappeared. Anna came to me immediately. I mobilized my staff, the volunteer firemen, your friends and many strangers. We scoured the city for five days. No one had seen anything of your son. I lived in fear we would find the little guy skewered on a pitchfork.

"The evening of the fifth day, Rady was seen casually walking back home. Someone stopped in my office to tell me. I came to your apartment immediately. Rady was in his aunt's arms. Tears were streaming down her face. She gently quizzed him as I listened.

"Of all things, the little guy told us he went to his mother. Somehow he felt he could find her. Best I can tell, he walked to the woods northwest of the city. He described the ruins of the burned cabin where Hartmann and April Blossom had lived. When he saw it, he knew she had gone to be with the Great Spirit, turned around and came home."

"Poor Anna. She must have been in utter panic."

"Your sister is as strong as you, Axel. You can be proud of her." After pausing, John asked, "How was your trip?"

"Not now, John. I'd rather hear the rest of what you have to tell me."

"Anna asked Rady how he knew where to look? He said he was guided by a voice. One he could not hear. One in his head. The next day I told Alexander Robinson what Rady had said. The Chief explained many Indians have the ability to see into the past and be guided by the voice of the Great Spirit.

338

"Two weeks after Rady was safely home, Seamus got a message from Josie Durst. She lives south of the city in a large home. She wrote it was urgent. He went immediately. She told him her husband had been killed."

"Josie? The prostitute?" I asked. "She was married?"

"For someone with his hand on the pulse of the city, how could you not know about her?"

"I didn't."

"Josie never married."

"You said her husband had been murdered."

"I did. They never married. She's a grass widow.

"Miss Durst had received a note from Lotus who runs the Pleasure Palace in the Sands. Josie and Seamus came to see me, showing me the note. It was quite direct. 'Miss Josie, your husband was killed sometime last night. A maid found him in his apartment, his throat cut.' Even under such circumstances, Lotus wanted to protect Josie, calling him her husband.

"My men came with me. We followed Josie and Seamus to the Sands. The area has been the bane of my job as Constable. I can't believe Chicago allows it to exist. I have only been to the Pleasure Palace once before. It was when Morrison was Chief Constable. We were following a hunch we might find the Pitchfork Murderer there. It was quite an education for me to see a high class brothel.

"Lotus met us at the door and guided us through the place to a locked door. She had the key. It leads to an elegant, two-story apartment with original oil paintings and sculptures, thick carpets, opulent furniture, crystal lamps and chandeliers. Each room has a fireplace with marble hearth and mantle. It's all fit for royalty.

"The bedrooms are on the second floor. I asked Lotus if the apartment was for her special customers. She said the apartment belonged to Evert Unruh and was for his exclusive use. It has a separate entrance. The locked door we used was for emergencies only.

"She opened the door to his vast bedroom. You'd have to see the decorations to believe them. Everything is either red, gold or cut crystal. It was dark. Lotus lite some candles. Their beams were captured by the crystal sending rainbows everywhere.

"The bed is the largest I have ever seen. On the ceiling overhead is a mirror as large as the bed. In the center of the bed was a naked corpse. The bed coverings were a rich red. Only with inspection did I realize the covering was wet with a pool of blood. His neck had been cut from ear to ear. The blood gushed out until the body was drained.

"I inspected the body. I concluded the man was between forty-five and fifty. When I turned him over, I found scars which I instantly knew were made by a pitchfork. I would say the scars were five to ten years old.

"I wondered, of course, if this was your cousin. Lotus assured me his name was Evert Unruh. She never heard of anyone named Rikert Hagen. She knew little of his past. He came to Chicago early in 1833 from New York. She believes he was born in Germany.

"Lotus said Mr. Unruh had come to her first place of business in the log cabin. He was with her several times and was very rough. When Miss Josie came to live with her, he kept trying to get Lotus to allow him to bed her. She guarded Josie like she would her own daughter. He would not give up. Lotus said Miss Josie never was a prostitute. She protected her from any exposure to what she did.

"I learned all of this interviewing Lotus and Josie, some of Pleasure Palace girls, Josie's maids and Seamus O'Shea, who has watched out for Josie in recent years.

"Lotus was ambitious. She wanted to expand her business and upgrade it to induce only gentlemen to use her services. Lotus was getting tired and too old to continue. She wanted to attract young, pretty girls to work for her. She told this to Unruh. He had money and offered to go into partnership with her. He financed the Pleasure Palace and she ran it. They split the profits fifty-fifty. Lotus feels he did this, in part, to woo Josie.

"Mr. Unruh found Josie charming. I can't imagine Unruh ever thinking of anyone in terms of being charming. Josie proposed marriage. She was not much more than a frightened, lost girl with no means of support. She feared being penniless and sought security. He refused to marry her. He agreed, however, to support her financially.

"They had separate bedrooms. He would invite her into his when he needed her. She refused. After a few times, he threatened her. He even beat her on several occasions. She got so she locked her door at all times.

"Their relationship changed when she told him she was pregnant. Fearful of harming his future child, he left her alone, visiting only to be sure she had everything she needed.

"Josie told Seamus she was with child. She also told Seamus of Unruh's abuse. Seamus counseled her to use the pregnancy as leverage to get lasting security. He suggested she demand Unruh give her a home of her own. She was adamant with Unruh that her child not be born or live in the Sands. He agreed. At the time, a wealthy New Yorker was intending to move to Chicago. He had a large and

340

extravagant home built on the south side. He changed his mind, never came to Chicago and told his agent to sell it. Unruh bought it. That is where Miss Josie's son was born in 1834.

"When I interviewed Josie, she showed little emotion. She confirmed the man was the father of her child."

"Oh Merciful God! If Evert Unruh was, in fact, Rikert Hagen, then I am related to Josie's child!" I said incredulously. "You said you solved the mystery of the Pitchfork Murders. Who did it? How do you know they have ended?"

Constable John Shrigley paused, then continued. "After we removed the corpse, my men and I began to search the room. We were helped by Josie and Seamus. I focused on his desk, going through papers and documents which confirmed he was born in a place called Schloss Hagenhoff, the names of his parents and, interestingly, a file on his court case aiming to overturn his father's will. It confirmed all you have told me about the legal battle by your father to keep Rikert from inheriting the estate."

"If the corpse was Rikert Hagen, why was he known as Evert Unruh?"

"That troubled me. We searched the room for the remainder of the day and returned the next day to search his office. We found nothing to explain the name change and nothing to connect him to the Pitchfork Murders. I was convinced he was behind the murders, but I couldn't prove it.

"On the third day, I returned, alone, sure there had to be a hiding place somewhere in his apartment where he kept records. I had found no financial records. If he was so wealthy, there had to be evidence of it somewhere. I went back over and over again, two, three, four times. I looked behind paintings, behind and under furniture. I even cut open the bottoms of chairs to see if anything was inside the upholstery. Nothing.

"I had to stop looking for several days to handle other business. Something kept nagging at me. I couldn't put my finger on it. A week later I returned to search yet again. This time I stood back and studied the arrangement of rooms. I paced off their dimensions. I drew sketches of each room, side by side. That was when I found his hiding place. There is a hidden space between the bedroom and office. It's the depth of the rooms and three feet wide. The access is not from either room, but rather from the floor below. In the back of the larder off the kitchen is a large, floor to ceiling cabinet. It can easily be swung to the side. Behind it is a ladder up to a trapdoor in the ceiling which is the floor of the hidden space overhead.

"I pushed up the trapdoor and entered a world of evil. I found pitchforks mounted on both sides of the long, narrow space. Each has dried blood on the tines. Next to each pitchfork is a tag with a description of the victim, such as: 'vagrant, boatman or drunk.' A few have the victims' names. Most do not. The tags also describe the method of murder as well as the date when Unruh plunged the pitchfork into the dead body. There are a number of new, unused pitchforks on the walls. The used pitchforks disgusted me. The pitchforks hanging there, intended for further murders overwhelmed me. Who would have been next to be slain and skewered? I came close to being sick. I felt faint, crushed by both anger and anguish. Against one wall is a desk and chair. I made my way to the chair, sat, closed my eyes and hung my head into my hands. I must have sat there for many minutes, hoping that when I opened my eyes, the horror would have miraculously disappeared. It did not.

The collection contains eight used pitchforks. Our records indicate there were eight murders. Including the murder behind Wrights General Store.

"I began a careful search of the space. I opened the doors of a cabinet with trepidation. By this point I was apprehensive of what gruesome objects it might contain. It has shelves filled with bottles of brandies, whiskies and liquors from around the world. It is an amazing assortment.

"I went through a set of drawers at the end of space opposite the desk. Carefully laid out between square panes of glass were handkerchiefs with reddish brown stains. Each is identified by a piece of tape on the corner of the glass with a date. Only later on was I able to confirm they represented the dates the pitchforks were jabbed into the dead bodies.

"I felt I was getting closer, but still had no definitive evidence connecting it all to Unruh or his motives.

"I had to stop. I felt sick and filthy. I put everything back in place, climbed down the steps and pushed the cabinet in the larder back against the wall.

"I did not tell anyone of the room and its contents. If I were, who would I tell? What would become of the information? What purpose would be served? I had to continue my search, and do so alone. I had to put the mystery to rest."

"John, were you in some way trying to protect me? Or worried I was somehow involved?"

"I don't know, Axel. I was so thrown by it all I was unable to think clearly. I didn't want to besmirch Chicago. No, that is inadequate.

I never considered you as part of this. I need you to help me understand such evil. I intended to go no further and wait for your return.

"One, two, three weeks went by. I could wait no longer. I had to return and solve the puzzle once and for all."

Chapter Fifty Eight

Reinhold knocked on the door and entered. "I am sorry to interrupt. Doctor Wooten is here and would like to see you, Axel." I looked up, and assented. "By all means." I rose and walked to greet the good Doctor. For that brief moment, I felt I was freeing myself of all Constable Shrigley had told me.

"Good morning, Doc."

"Welcome home, Axel." Seeing John Shrigley, Doc apologized. "I'm sorry. I didn't know you were in a meeting."

"If you have time, Doc, please join us. John is reporting to me about the Pitchfork Murders. Please have a seat. John, I hope you have no objections to Doc joining us?"

"Not at all."

"Doc, may I offer you coffee and a sugar cookie?"

Sitting, Doc said, "Yes to coffee. I'll pass on the cookie."

"Before I continue reporting to Axel, I gather you have something important Doc?"

"Happily, I do. Axel, Lina is correct, you are to become a father again."

"Congratulations," John offered. "No wonder you put off telling me about your trip to Germany. Guess you did accomplish something there."

I must have blushed as both men laughed.

John said, "Doc, please fill in anything I miss. I was just telling about the hidden room with its gruesome collection. Perhaps you could tell of your examination of the corpse."

"I performed an autopsy of Unruh. Or rather, of Rikert. Having seen the devil's handiwork on so many victims, I was interested in the scars on Rikert's back. I dissected the area around each of the tine

344

scars. I was able to follow the path of each into his body. It is a miracle he survived the wounds.

"His spinal cord was missed. Surrounding muscles were injured and partially severed. In healing, they caused contraction which was the reason for his deformed posture. Both lungs were punctured. They healed. The tine headed toward his heart stopped half an inch short or he would have died instantly. His liver was nicked. It also healed.

"It is remarkable he was not fatally injured. Even more remarkable, he did not die of sepsis. Whoever administered to the wounds was very skilled.

"I believe science someday will advance to the point where the brain of a deceased will be studied and the cause of aberrant behavior such as Rikert's will be discovered. From all you have told me about your cousin, he was a drunkard. I believe it will also be proven, some day, that alcohol can damage the brain as well as the liver."

"Thank you, Doc.

"John," I asked, "did you find anything to explain his motives?"

"Ah, I was just going to get to that. After about an hour in the hidden room, I thought I would be sick if I remained. I left and went to see Doc. We discussed who should join me in further investigation. Doc suggested Carsten Baruth. We are both impressed with his legal mind and objectivity. He agreed and came with me the next day.

"Carsten found Rikert's journal. It was in the hidden room. One of the ends of the room has a false wall. He discovered how to access the space behind it. There we found a stash of gold and a hand-written journal.

"I should back-track. In his office we found several legal documents he had prepared in New York. Apparently he went there several times. His will left the Pleasure Palace to Lotus. His half of the profits would be given to Josie.

"Upon Lotus' death, the Pleasure Palace will be passed on to Josie's son with the caveat half of the profits earned from the Pleasure Palace would continue to go to Josie. He left his substantial stash of gold to Josie. Finally, he directed the contents of the hidden room with the exception of the gold, be given to you, Axel."

"You mean he wanted me to have the pitchforks?"

"Yes, and the journal as well."

"What is in the journal?"

"The journal Carsten found is an accounting of his income going back to when he was to have matriculated at the university. Apparently his father sent him funds for his education. He never entered the university. He invested half his father's allowance and spent the other half on daily expenses. His listing of these expenses describes a life of debauchery and bribes. Even as a young man, Rikert was evil.

"He was brilliant in his investment choices. For a mind dimmed by drinking, his investments grew year by year. At the time of his death he was a very wealthy man."

"Does the journal also speak of the murders and Rikert's motives?"

"It does not."

"Then how can you say there will be no further Pitchfork Murders?"

Constable John rubbed his chin. "I was haunted by that very question. I knew there had to be more. I returned repeatedly, day after day, but there was nothing further to be found. I had so neglected my other responsibilities I halted my search for many weeks. I knew something was missing. Something right in plain sight. I just was blind to it.

"It came to me one day at dinner. My mind drifted as my wife was talking to me. I half heard her complain about the scrape on our new dining table. How strange our minds work. I suddenly saw the clear image of scrape marks on the floor in front of Rikert's desk. It is opposite the wall where Carsten had found the hidden compartment. The next morning I rushed to the Pleasure Palace, entered the larder, pulled back the cabinet, climbed the ladder, pushed up the trapdoor and entered the hidden room.

"I approached the desk and held my lantern to the floor. There it was. The scrape mark on the floor by the right front foot of the desk. I tried to pull the desk from the wall. I had no luck. I pulled harder, it would not move. I sat in the desk chair. There had to be a trigger to release the desk from the wall. What was it? I got so desperate in my frustration, I lifted each item on the desktop, hoping one of them would unlatch the hold. Nothing magical happened. I laughed at my futile efforts. I had even lifted the inkwell as a possible release.

"Sitting back, I closed my eyes and thought. Nothing came to me. I got so mad I stood before the desk and lifted it. The feet on the right side of the desk were longer than those on the left. The longer feet fit perfectly into carefully cut indentations in the floor boards. Once I lifted them out of the sockets, I was able to easily swing the desk from the wall, the feet tracing the scape mark.

"I pulled the desk far enough from the wall to squeeze behind it. I moved the lantern closer and studied the wall. It was unremarkable. There had to be yet another hidden space. Rikert would not have devised such a complicated system if nothing was being concealed.

"I looked closely, studying the wall from side to side. Nothing. I ran my fingers over the wall, covering every inch of it. Nothing. I became inpatient. Damn Rikert. I slammed my fist against the wall. It sounded hollow. I repeatedly hit the wall, albeit with less force, to save my hand. The hollow sound was limited to only a portion of the wall. I shouted, "Oh no! Not another trigger?" Where was it? To my right was the nearest hanging pitchfork. Intent on using it to smash a hole in the wall, I pulled it down. With that, a section of the wall opened. The trigger was the peg on which the pitchfork was mounted. The opening was so well disguised, even after I knew it was there, I could neither see nor feel it.

"I lifted the lantern to look in. I found more bags of gold, a large velvet bag and a large leather bound book. My hands were shaking as I placed each item on the desktop. I decided not to open the velvet bag until either Doc or Carsten were present. I opened the journal.

"Axel, it is terrifying. If I were you, I would destroy it after Carsten says you are no longer legally bound to keep it. As constable, I won't need it for evidence once I have found the survivors of the victims. I doubt I will find many since the victim's identities are so vague. Once I have concluded my efforts and have cleared it with Carsten, I will release the book and bag to you."

"Is Lotus aware of the hidden room?"

"No."

"Is Josie?"

"No."

"Have you read the journal, Doc?"

"I have."

"Does it explain Rikert's motive?"

"It does. Every entry is dripping with his intense hatred of you and his plan for revenge."

I asked, "Does it speak of a scheme to physically harm me or my family?"

"It does not. His goal was to slowly drive you insane. He wrote in startling detail what you would look like and act like when locked up in an asylum for the insane. It is frightening to read. You should not."

I thought through his advice for several minutes. I am a decisive person and usually act quickly. For this, I needed to consider what I should do.

"I do not wish to read the journal or even see it for now. I may change my mind later on."

I was surprised with the clarity of my line of questions. I was calm and focused. I wondered if I would have a reaction later on.

"What has been reported in the newspapers?"

"Both papers have printed only what I have told them," John said.

Doc interjected, "John has been masterful in his handling of this situation. He has suggested that Evert Unruh was behind the killings, stating, in most instances, others committed the murders at his direction."

"Most instances?"

"He insisted on being the one to jam the pitchfork into each victim's back. Several times, the victim was still alive. In those instances, it is possible his action was the actual cause of death. He describes each case and seemed to delight when he realized he took a few of the lives himself."

"So he went to the location of each death to stab the pitchfork in the victim's back?"

"Yes. I told you the journal is sick."

"Did he fantasize I was each victim?"

John looked to Doc to answer. "Axel, I can only speculate. I have limited experience with insanity. I think he found revenge imagining, or even believing, each victim was you."

I sat stunned. My long suppressed hatred of Rikert erupted as I thought of all the innocent men he ordered slaughtered.

I don't know how long I sat there dwelling on all I had been told. Doc and John patiently waited for me to speak.

"Did Rikert record in the journal the names of who committed the murders and give the basis on which he selected them?"

"He did," John said. "Each murder was committed by a different man. In each instance they were men who owed him money from gambling losses. He selected the men carefully. He required they have no relatives in Chicago, were not very intelligent and were not well-known. They were often recent arrivals to Chicago.

"When each reported they had accomplished a murder, Rikert quizzed them on who, when and where. He would then go a night or two later to use his pitchfork.

"He ordered each of the men to immediately leave Chicago and never return. If they did, he warned he would report them to the law. He forgave their gambling debts and paid them a thousand dollars each."

Doc interjected, "One did not leave Chicago and was murdered days later."

"John, thank you. I agree with Doc. You have handled this masterfully. I shutter to think of what former Constable Morrison would have done in your place. Doc, thank you for all you have done over the years. Your support has kept sane."

After saying that out loud, I stopped. I thought of myself, Axel Konrad, being insane. I began to shake, sweating profusely. I know little of the insane. I have read of asylums described as filthy cages restraining wildly demented human animals. Images flashed before me. I saw myself, wearing dirty rags, my body covered with bugs. My bearded face distorted so it was unrecognizable.

Doc called to me. "Axel, are you ill?"

His voice snapped me out of my torturous trance.

"Sorry, gentlemen, I was caught in a whirlpool of dark thought."

Gathering myself back to the present, I asked, "By chance, do either of you have copies of the newspapers reporting on this?"

"I do," John responded.

"So do I," Doc said.

"I should like to read them. After I have, I would like to meet with both of you again. At that time I may reconsider my statement about not wishing to read Rikert's journal of murder. I definitely would like to read his journal of accounts."

Chapter Fifty Nine

The two men closed the door, leaving me alone. I sat for over an hour thinking through all they had told me. I understand myself and my need to put things in order before I act. I am methodical and yet intuitive.

I reached two conclusions as to my course of action. First, as I stated to John and Doc, I will read the newspapers. This will arm me to know how to respond to comments as I reintroduce myself to the Board of Directors, our friends and those I come in contact with in business. Once I have read the clippings, I will list my questions and meet with Doc and John. Based on their answers I will decide if I wish to read Rikert's other journal. I will immediately read and analyze the journal of accounts.

The second conclusion I made concerned Lina and Anna. For the time being, I will do all I can to shield them from what John found in the hidden room. Only when I know the full dimensions of Rikert's reign of terror will I be able to formulate what I should and shouldn't tell them. I know from the past it is important I tell both of them all I can. I must be mindful, however, of what will hurt rather than ease their anxiety over the Pitchfork Murders.

It took me a week to read the newspapers. I only read them in my office while resuming my full bank responsibilities. I took notes. When done, I arranged to meet with Doc and John.

When they arrived, I told Reinhold we were not to be disturbed.

"Gentlemen, I have a few questions.

"How did Rikert select the victims?"

"Best I can tell," John said, "Rikert used several criteria. Initially the victims were selected randomly. He directed his killers to murder anyone they could find out at night in isolated locations. After a while, he selected specific individuals who would send a clearer message to you. He became increasingly disturbed that you were not publicly reacting. He had hoped you would unravel and go mad.

"That is why he diabolically planned the incidents involving the Indian boy, Smithy, the victim found on the land you own in the prairie south of the city and the case of the mute stagecoach man."

"Does Rikert's journal list more victims than have been found over the years?"

"Yes."

"How many more?"

"Three."

"Does he record why they were never discovered?"

"He does. In one instance, the murderer disposed of the body so well we never found it and when Rikert asked where it was, the murderer told him he could not remember. Two weeks later, that man became a victim himself.

"In another case, the victim apparently survived and fled the city. Rikert's entry was uncharacteristically vague. The third victim we were able to find after we read the journal."

"How many Pitchfork Murders were there in total?"

Doc answered rather than John. "Axel, there were ten."

Shaking my head, I sadly said, "Had Rikert died when he fell on the pitchfork, all of these men would be alive today."

"As Constable, I deal with murders, drunken misadventures and wife beatings. After each case is resolved, I find it difficult not to delve into the same thoughts. I agonize over "What if I did more?" It gets me nowhere. I suppose Adam and Eve dealt with the same question."

"Finally, my last question. You said there was a velvet bag in the space behind Rikert's desk. What is in the bag?"

John said, "Doc, would you mind?"

"Axel, we don't know what Rikert's intent was. My guess is the bag represents things representing persons or events of importance to you. He began to assemble them in Germany. Each item is in a separate bag with strange notes taunting you about how they were taken. Their significance is meaningless to John or me. Some, you would recognize. Other items would be a mystery to you.

"Was the collection for Rikert's sadistic satisfaction?" Doc continued, "Or did he intend to someday present it to you to finally push you over the edge? We don't know. Whatever his intent, it was sick."

"Doc, should I have the bag? Is it worse than the journal he kept of the murders?"

"It is."

"Can you at least give me a general idea of what is in the bag?"

"Doc, let me answer that."

John spoke slowly, carefully selecting his words.

"Axel, best we can tell, Rikert obtained something from each member of your family. They did not give the items to him. Rather he, or someone at his command, stole them. As I read his notes, I was plunged into rage and then, putting myself into your place, racked with terror. I felt chills when I held some small, seemingly unimportant thing, until I knew its significance. They represent yet another invasion of privacy of those you love most dearly or consider important friends. It was, I suppose, his way of telling you "Look at what I did. I could have done much worse. I could have killed them.""

Taking a deep breath, pressing the palms of my hands onto my desk, I stood. Doc and John watched with apprehension. I began to pace back and forth in my office. They watched me, ready to stop me if I seemed ready to become violent. I stopped, looked at them and realized I was frightening them.

I walked back to my desk, sat and calmly spoke.

"I didn't mean to panic the two of you. I usually make decisions quickly. This whole thing has shaken me to the core. Not just the revelations you found in the hidden rooms, but all the way back to the start. Back in the barn in Germany. I have been holding myself together with faith in the Lord. My nature is to always keep myself under control. I rarely speak of my love of my family and my beliefs. I have suppressed my pain, my fears, my vengeful thoughts. I am strong. I have accepted this, both mentally and physically. These revelations are both a blessing and a curse.

"A blessing the long nightmare of Rikert has finally come to an end. A curse because the remnants linger on, haunting me to delve into them or ignore them. I guess what I am saying is I must no longer suppress this. I must face up to it and finally put it to rest. To do so, I must read the second journal and open the bag. Only then, as painful and sickening as they may be, will I finally know all. Even if understanding and forgiveness may never come, I will be able to know it is over."

Doc said, "The more I see of you, Axel, the more I am impressed with you."

John said, "I shall bring the journal and bag to you later today."

I thanked the two. After they left, I sat in one of the chairs by the fireplace, closed my eyes and fell asleep, a deep and healing sleep.

Part Fourteen

The Future

Chapter Sixty

ood evening. I am not sure why you selected me to address you on this, our last meeting in 1839. You asked me to give my perspective on the future of our city. There are others here who have been residents of Chicago more years than I have. Any one of you is better suited to speak of the future knowing more about the past than do I.

"Why, you may ask, do I mention the past when I am to talk about the future? As adults, we were shaped and formed by our childhood. Each of us has a unique past. We are who we are because of how we reached this point in our lives. The same is true of Chicago.

"When I arrived on May 8, 1832, Chicago was a collection of log cabins, a deserted Fort Dearborn, the threat of an Indian war and roughly 150 residents. With me that day were Philo Carpenter, Doc Wooten and my Irish friend, Seamus O'Shea. They were and still are the core of my most respected friends.

"The first person I met of importance was Mark Beaubien. He hired me as a waiter at the Sauganash. There I met others who are here tonight. I am especially pleased to acknowledge Judge Lockwood and my hunting partner, Alexander Robinson.

"When I arrived, I spoke broken English. I was seventeen. I didn't know what the future held for me. I knew whatever it was, I was determined to work toward the betterment of Chicago and its people.

"In May, 1833, I proudly brought my new bride to Chicago. Here we have celebrated the births of our children. Here I founded the Greater Bank of Chicago. Here I have watched the crude settlement grow into a city of over 4,000 residents. I have watched clapboard and brick buildings replace log cabins. I have welcomed the board walkways to lift us out of Chicago's eternal mud. I have seen the threats of Indian war fade as our government unceremoniously evicted the original Illinois natives from their ancestral homes. You may disagree with me. I feel the government treatment of the Indians continues to be unjust and brutal.

"We have grown as a city in both size and sophistication. We have two highly respected newspapers. We have a library. Artists and actors visit our city. Each day our port is exporting more farm products and receiving increased volumes of materials and manufactured goods from the East. I shall leave the evolution of our politics for others to discuss on another occasion.

"This is not, however, what I was asked to speak about this evening. Before I go further, I thank you, both members and guests of the Chicago Lyceum, for asking me to look into the future and tell you what I see. That is a tall order indeed. Ten years from now, what I say this evening may well be the subject of a good laugh. I hope, however, this evening simulates your minds and lifts your spirits. The economic downturn we are mired in will end. The future is bright.

"Many ask me if my bank and the city will recover from the financial panic. My simple answer is yes.

"I shall begin with the health of the Greater Bank of Chicago and the city. The bank's Board of Directors took important actions when we first learned of troubling signs which eventually led to the financial collapse in New York. We have built up large reserves. We continued to increase them. As a result, when the crisis hit, we were never threatened.

"I am proud of the many citizens and businesses we have saved from ruin by our liberal policy to defer the payment of interest on loans. In other instances we have forgiven interest entirely and in still others, we have forgiven of full loans. Chicago is a better place because we did not allow citizens and businesses to fail.

"Chicago stayed afloat largely because of former Mayor Ogden. He encouraged the City Council to issue unsecured script to pay bills. As a citizen, he himself pledged his personal funds. He was effective in getting his colleagues back in New York to provide the city with funds as well.

"Many other cities have collapsed financially forcing their residents into dire conditions. We have not. While many have been hurt, we are generally making it.

"Speaking of Mayor Ogden, I would like to quote from a statement he made about himself. It symbolizes, I believe, the spirit of Chicago which will guide us into the future. Mayor Ogden, writing about himself, put it this way.

I was born close to a sawmill, was cradled in a sugar trough, christened in a mill pond, early left an orphan, and graduated from a log schoolhouse, and at fourteen found I could do anything I turned my head to and that nothing was impossible, and ever since...I have been trying to prove it with some success.

"It is this spirit which will see our city to a bright future. Now, at last, to my prediction for tomorrow and beyond.

"Regretfully, I do not see an early return to a robust economy and growth. The Illinois and Michigan Canal is an example. It will be several years before work will resume. Nor will William Ogden's dream of a railroad connecting Chicago to the farms west of the city be started anytime soon. The entire nation is in the doldrums. The flow of new arrivals to Chicago is down to a trickle. The population has hardly grown at all for months.

"Will Chicago fade away?"

"To the contrary. It will become one of the major cities in America. The East needs food. Our farmers are becoming a major supplier of grain and beef. We are on the brink of an explosion of growth once the financial institutions sort out the mess caused by President Jackson's ill-guided attack on the National Bank.

"We have only to look to our past. The pace of growth of Chicago in the past few years has exceeded that of any other city in America. We are well positioned for the future. The canal will link the East coast through us to the Gulf of Mexico. Trains will connect Chicago to New York within a decade.

"Territories to the west will develop as more and more states are created. Both the canal and railroads will enable farmers throughout Illinois and these new states to ship their products through our city until Chicago becomes the nations' hub of commerce and industry.

"We already have a wide range of places of worship. As the population grows, this religious foundation will serve us well. All else will follow: libraries, universities, hospitals, cultural institutions and more.

"The future? I am confident it will be bright and prosperous. You in this room will make it happen."

I sat down to sustained applause. I felt drained. I silently prayed that my view of the future would come to pass.

Chapter Sixty One

The children were in bed, asleep at last. The boys had been excited about tomorrow being a new year and wanted to stay up. They dozed off long before midnight. Lina and I snuggled together on the settee in front of the fireplace. The logs were dwindling down to embers, no longer giving off much heat. The wind outside was driving the last snow of the year. Tomorrow would begin 1840. Actually, in just two hours. We had been talking softly about all that has happened since our return from Germany. We lapsed into silence, snuggling together in our own thoughts.

I was taking stock of our family. We have five children, not counting our son, Axel Heinrich, who died when he was only weeks old. Our grief was eased by Chief Robinson, when he asked if we would take in an Indian baby. We joyously welcomed Rady to our family.

Henry, our first, will be six in two months. Rady is actually our oldest. He will be seven in a week. Our first daughter, Adelina, is four. She will tell you she is four and a half. She is a beauty like her mother and has the same gentle disposition. August Henry, who was born on September 11, 1837, tries to keep up with his brothers and pouts when they won't include him in their games. Minna was born on December 18, 1838, the year we visited Germany.

As if she had read my mind, Lina asked "Axey, can you believe we have five children?"

"And a sixth on the way, dear."

"Yes, God willing." I know Lina faces each birth with trepidation the baby might not live.

"I am so thankful the Pitchfork Murders ended. It has taken me until now to accept we no longer have to fear for our lives."

"I agree," I said. "Rikert was such an evil man I felt no sympathy over his death. To be honest, I felt more than relief, I felt elated. Not a very Christian reaction."

"But understandable, my dear."

I was surprised when Lina said, "I wish Constable Shrigley was able to find out who killed Rikert."

"I, too, have been thinking about that, I said. "I have thought of two possibilities. The killer was one of the men he promised to forgive his debt if he would commit another murder for him. My theory is he invited the man up to his apartment to plan the next murder and for some reason, the man refused, Rikert pulled a knife to kill him and the man turned the knife on him instead. Because of the separate outside entrance to Rikert's apartment, no one would have seen the killer enter or leave.

"The other possibility is one of the prostitutes killed Rikert. This would explain his nakedness."

"Axel, is it possible Lotus killed Rikert?"

"Possible, I suppose. She had the access. She despised him. She could enter his apartment through the emergency entrance. He might have been expecting one of her girls to come and entertain him. She told Shrigley he was too rough with her girls. He might have been particularly brutal with one which was the final straw for Lotus.

"Its been a year and half since Rikert's death. We may never know. I can live with that, knowing you, our children and Anna are safe from the monster."

"Axel, what do you see ahead for the bank and the city. Will both recover from the financial panic?"

"As I told the Lyceum last night, the bank is in no danger and the city will survive. There are still months ahead of stagnation before the economy gets better. The longer term future is bright."

"I worry about Molly and Seamus. With the canal shut down, he is back working at Wrights General Store and writing for the *Democrat.* Are they going to make it? Seamus has four mouths to feed."

"Babies don't eat much. Molly is handling that, I'm sure."

"Axel! How can you say that?"

"Una is only 18 months, Molly Deirdre, four months. Would they not both still be breast feeding."

"Yes, but you made them sound like Molly is nothing more than an old porridge pot or something."

Attempting to change the subject, "Seamus told me he hopes their next will be a boy."

"Did he tell you Molly is carrying?"

"No, he didn't."

"She is due in six or seven months."

"Dear, you don't need to worry about them financially. Please keep this in confidence. Captain O'Flaherty has been giving them funds to supplement what Seamus earns. He is particularly proud of their support of the Irish causes back home."

"I shan't say a word. It was good Dominick Breen turned out to be honest. Molly was so worried, not about him, but about how Seamus would react if he was a charlatan."

I felt Lina shudder. I felt her nose. She was cold. "Should we go to bed. You are shivering with the cold."

"No. We so seldom get to talk."

I got up and found several lap robes. We wrapped ourselves, again mining our own thoughts.

I broke our silence. "Do you think Anna is happy?" I asked.

"What a strange question. Do you think she is not?"

"I just get a feeling. Ever since we returned from Germany, I have sensed she is lonesome for our parents. I have suggested she and Carsten go visit them. She says he is too busy and she doesn't want to leave the children."

"I will talk with her. She might still be grieving over the stillborn in March. You know Anna is like you, needing to do everything perfectly. She might feel she failed at something she can never correct."

"Another reason for them to go visit my parents. Paid dividends for us."

"Axel, you are terrible. Little Minna would have been whether we had gone to Germany or had not."

"Just suggesting a solution."

"I'll talk to her and see what happens."

We sat there until the clock chimed twelve times.

"Glückliches neues jahr, Lina"

"Alles gute zum neues jahr, Axel

1840 had arrived. We kissed and went to bed.

Thomas Reimer was born in Chicago. He graduated from Northwestern University's Technological Institute. He worked for the government. After his retirement, he delved into genealogy, tracing his ancestors back to Germany. His research culminated in three books. He also wrote his autobiography before entering the world of fiction. His first novel, *Death of the King,* is based on the real life of King Ludwig II of Bavaria.

Mr. Reimer's second novel, *Wild Onion,* introduced the reader to Seamus O'Shea and Axel Konrad, two immigrant lads, one Irish, the other German, who met in New York in 1831. They became friends, journeyed west, survived an Indian attack and settled in Chicago. *Wild Onion* tells of their adjustment to America, the primitive nature of the village of Chicago and challenges to their health and very existence.

In *Pitchfork Murders,* Mr. Reimer continues the story of Axel Konrad and Seamus O'Shea in Chicago, picking up where *Wild Onion* ended. Seamus becomes involved in the expulsion of the Indians from Illinois by the government and the construction of the I & M Canal by Irish laborers. Axel Konrad manages his bank through the Panic of 1837, helping many survive the depression. At the same time, Axel is haunted by the Pitchfork Murderer.

Mr. Reimer is currently writing the sequel to *Pitchfork Murders.* He anticipates continuing the *Wild Onion Saga* in a series of sequels following the lives of the immigrant lads and their descendants over the decades through to 1920.

CPSIA information can be obtained at www.ICGtesting.com
Printed in the USA
LVOW080017261212

313170LV00001B/179/P